UNTOLD HISTORY

CHRIS RIMELL

ISBN: 9781097137596

Untoldhistory.co.uk

From the heavens they fell,
by the light of the moon,
crying green tears for their dead.

For thirteen days they mourned,
in thirteen days they faded away.

Their green tears remained,
their glowing green tears made the world...

- Except from "Song of Creation"
Translated by Mark Besant

BETH & THE LETTER

CHAPTER 1

1st September 2021

"You're firing me?" I glared at Peter, then back to the unfolded letter clutched in my hands. "This can't be right." A fiery rage catapulted the bitterness of bile into the back of my throat. Restless feet shuffled beneath my seat.

I'd assumed Peter needed another report when he called for me, too work-shy to compile it himself, but now I understood. A smug smile played on his lips, it told me everything I needed to know; he was enjoying this.

For a moment he appeared devoid of life like the bare walls and dusty blinds of his office. His clasped hands rested on the edge of his precious mahogany desk, but he remained silent, my questions unanswered.

I looked at the typed stationary, my mouth open and dry. I'd flogged our company's software to forty clients in the last month including two existing customers, which is a difficult job when they already know the crap they are getting. Nonetheless, it put all my colleagues to shame. The licensing revenue was enough to pay my wages twice over, so where had this come from?

"What's going on?" I dropped the redundancy notice onto the desk.

"You've been here a long time Mark, you know how it works. The company isn't performing, our competitors are luring away our business. We need to adapt." At this my jaw clenched. "We've been forced into this situation."

To my annoyance, the corners of his mouth twitched with delight.

"Look." He stood, hands resting palms flat on the edge of the desk. "We want to make this as easy as we can for you."

"This *has* to be wrong." Shaking my head.

"I am sorry." No sympathy in his voice.

"After seven years, you're just going to let me go? I've put my life into this place."

"I'm sorry," he said, once again, turning his back to me and gliding over to the window as he employed his classic avoidance tactic. Whenever he wanted to escape a conversation he just stared out across the carpark. As he stood there, ignoring me for a moment, I realised I'd been taken for a fool. The last few weeks he'd been treating me with extra care, I should have known he was up to something. It was all part of his lead up to this day.

"I'm the best one in the team – you said it yourself, three weeks ago when the latest figures were released." He remained impassive at the window, it was as if he didn't care to hear me. I changed tact. "How did you get this past Bob?"

"This is *my* business, not my father's!" He snapped round to face me, his eyes appearing to bulge. Veins on his neck pulsed, his designer stubble hiding what I thought might be red cheeks. Everybody in the company knew it was Bob Malone's business, despite his son's denial.

"Don't bullshit me!" My angry bellow did nothing to move him. "What lies did you spin, I want to know? Did you show him fudged statistics, tell him I'd been stealing...what?" I watched the corners of his mouth turn up as an inane grin formed, his trademark. It sent the heat in my cheeks soaring in frustration.

"Like I said, the business isn't performing, you've seen the results..."

"You're a fucking weasel!" I was surprised by the strength of my anger and for just a moment there was a look of sheer panic in Peter's eyes. He was afraid of me, petrified of what I might do. Good! I grabbed the letter from his desk and stood, shaking my head in disgust.

"You're lucky I'm being so generous," Peter said as I yanked open his office door.

"Fuck you!"

When I got to my desk, I found my belongings packed into a cardboard box.

"Well thanks a bunch!" I roared. The office ground to a halt, a stunned silence filling the air, the foul stench of unease in my nostrils. I didn't want their sympathy.

I dropped my company mobile onto the desk with a clatter before I left the building, never to return.

2

Just like that, I was unemployed.

In the blink of an eye, my whole world changed and I struggled to comprehend it, my mind devoid of thought. Still fuming, I crossed the main Exeter Road and burst into Café Nevada.

Beth glanced up from behind the counter, startled, almost spilling the pot of tea she was setting out for another customer. I took my usual table, staring out of the window.

"What's the matter with you?" She asked, as she passed, tray in hand.

What's the matter? I yelled inside my head, wasn't it

obvious?

As soon as Beth finished serving, she came over and set herself down opposite me. Her warm smile welcomed me and part of my anger melted away.

"What's happened?" She said, "I thought you said today was going to be a good day?"

"It was meant to be," I let out a heavy breath. "But Peter..." I couldn't stop my lips curling into a sneer, my sentence remained unfinished.

"Oh." A knowing head-bob. "Shall I fix you up a cappuccino?" Beth read my mood, I didn't need to respond.

I watched Beth work, her hands glided in a seamless motion, her slender arms busy preparing the ground coffee. Underneath her white apron she wore dark trousers and a pale cream shirt, which suited her natural tan. She looked fantastic for her thirty-five years, not a single worry-line to show. Being a waitress didn't have the same toll on the body as the high-pressure of sales in my world. When I looked in the mirror these days, all I saw was the tortured face of hard labour.

"You ready to talk?" Beth set the foaming mug on the table. The fragrant aroma of the fresh drink brought me out of my daze with a snap.

"Peter screwed me over," I said with contempt. "He let me go."

"No!" Beth let out in a sharp puff of breath. Her legs dropped from under her as she pulled herself into a chair in a single movement, well practised I guessed. "Tell me what happened."

"I thought he was too lazy to be manipulative," I said through gritted teeth. "But just shows you can't trust what you see of people." Beth tensed. "I didn't mean..."

"Don't worry about it." Beth took my hand in hers. "Have you given any thought to what you're going to do?"

It hadn't even crossed my mind, and now it exploded into

full view and I felt a fresh wave of anger. Only earlier in the morning I'd been planning a few beers in the local with the lads from work, but that meant nothing now. I didn't have a job, and the bills still had to be paid.

Beth must have known what was going through my mind, she squeezed my hand, bringing me back.

"You don't need that place, right?" She said with optimistic cheer. "It was only a stop gap, now you have the chance to find something you really enjoy." Beth was right, it had been a temporary position, but after seven years I'd still not found my ideal job and had stopped looking. Knowing others were in a similar situation was of no comfort.

"I'd rather not think about it yet." I'd never been out of work, I didn't even know what I was meant to do. My head hurt and I shook it, clearing my thoughts.

"I know what'd make you feel better," Beth said. "I'll get you some of my special chocolate cake."

"Thanks Beth," I said. "You really know how to cheer a bloke up."

"Well, that's what my ex- used to say." She chuckled, swiping her long hazel brown hair out of her face. I returned her cheer but knew her laughter covered up for the emotional scars of her ex-husband's torment, always keen to fix other people's problems but never facing her own.

Beth sat with me as I gorged on the cake, there were few customers around. I felt calmer with Beth near, and it was obvious from the length of time she spent with me that she felt the same, even if we'd never said as much to each other.

I polished off the last of the cake, and downed the bitter dregs of the coffee before getting up to go, ready to tackle the world head on, but Beth grabbed my arm as I stood.

"You can't go yet." A gentle scolding, but she looked concerned. "You don't want to be alone right now do you?"

Her words were manipulative, but I understood the sentiment. "I'm off in half an hour."

"You're right." I sank back into my seat. "I could use the company right now, but I'm not up for much."

"Let me take you to a movie," she said with a smile. "My treat. You need to cheer up, things probably aren't as bad as they seem. You've got a real chance to change your life. Most people would love to be in your position." I didn't argue although I disagreed with her. In my experience, change was the biggest cause of stress.

"I knew Peter was devious, he always picked on Lee until he left, but I wasn't expecting him to start on me." I felt the injustice stirring, so changed the subject. "A movie would be good. It'll stop me thinking too much."

"I promise you, by the end of the night you won't care." Beth winked as she got up and went back to work. My mind wandered, replaying the events. I still didn't understand how I'd ended up unemployed.

"What d'ya know!" Joe's unmistakable gruff voice. He owned the café. "Shouldn't you be at work or something?" He glanced at his watch. I said nothing.

Beth shook her head as Joe took his position behind the counter. I heard her muted voice scolding him.

"Oops." Joe let out a short embarrassed laugh. "I hope you gave him a free drink. That's our best damned customer we've just lost." He tutted and shook his head.

"She's taking me to watch a movie," I said.

"You might as well head off now." He pulled on an apron, tightening the strings. "I don't mind the extra few minutes."

"Thanks," Beth said, patting his arm. Joe gave a wink.

A few minutes later, Beth hovered over me.

"We'd better get you home first." Her eyes cast over the junk from my desk.

"You sure?" I felt relieved. It gave me reason to get out of my work clothes and put the day behind me in more comfortable jeans and trainers.

"Of course, I don't mind the drive over. It's gotta be better than catching the bus." I relaxed, glad of the ride. My car, a dusty run-around, sat unused in the garage until the weekends. Keeping it running now was the least of my worries.

3

"Thanks again," I said, opening my front door. "And I don't just mean for taking me to the cinema."

"I'm glad to be of service." Beth rubbed my arm, it was reassuring.

I felt awkward, somehow my confidence had seeped away and I'd become a teenage version of myself. I steadied my nervous hand as I put the key into the lock with a click.

"Do you want to come in?" I clapped my hands together. "For a drink I mean?"

"Alcoholic beverages? In your state?" She laughed. "Sure."

An envelope waited on the doormat as I pushed open the door. It was an unusual occurrence to receive post these days, but I didn't bother investigating. It was probably a depressing final demand for a bill I'd forgotten to pay or something. I tossed it onto the table next to the sofa to be forgotten for a little longer.

I took Beth's coat, watching as she ran her hand through her hair, plumping it up. The television was on when I joined her in the lounge with a bottle of wine. She'd selected a film from my online collection. Beth took the bottle from me an examined it before she popped the cork.

"A fine choice," she said, sniffing the air before pouring two glasses. "Cheers." There was a clank as we toasted to nothing in particular.

"Cheers." I gulped a mouthful of wine. It was dry, but the quicker I drank it, the less I noticed. The background noise of the television drowned out my thoughts and I sank into its world.

"I'm glad you're here." I finished my glass, reaching to pour myself another from the second bottle we'd opened. I gazed into Beth's eyes and felt an invisible force, attraction perhaps, pulling me towards her. She looked hopeful and I knew she felt it too.

"Are you trying to seduce me?" Her eyes fluttered. "Because if you are, you've succeeded." She chuckled. I placed my glass on the table and stooped to kiss her.

"You know you want to." She used her best sexy voice and it made me giggle. I found her smile irresistible and I kissed her again, feeling the heat of her lips upon mine. I took her in my arms, her breasts grazing across my chest. At last our lips parted and I looked into her wide eyes, seeing her arousal.

In the early hours of the morning I stirred to find Beth creeping silently across the room. I rolled over and she froze. After a moment she lowered herself onto the edge of the bed, her head in her hands. I reached out, my hands brushing across her back. Beth jumped to her feet in an instant.

"Sorry," I yawned. Even in the dim light I saw her frantic eyes, darting back and forth. "Is something up?"

"I couldn't sleep," she shuffled her feet with unease. "I went downstairs for a drink."

I said nothing. There was something about the way she

spoke, so quickly. Maybe I'd startled her more than I first thought.

Beth shivered.

"You're cold," I peeled back the covers, motioning for her to get back in. Beth lay next to me, and I wrapped my arms around her. Her tremors continued for some time.

"I should get some rest," was all Beth said. I remained awake until I heard her soft, rasping breath.

4

In the darkness of my dreams, I opened my eyes.

I stood in the shadow of an ancient weathered ziggurat, its stepped majesty towered above the landscape, much like those found in Mesopotamia. The image had followed me throughout my life. Sometimes there were strangers; lost in the deserted world, remnants of life that had settled there perhaps. Most of the time I was alone with the tall platformed structure standing proud, built for an unknown purpose.

A small glowing river swept across the barren land, flowing strangely around the structure, as it eased up the gentle incline. Between the shoreline and the ziggurat was a small paved courtyard, central to this stood an obelisk projecting into the sky like a beacon. It too was stepped to a flat point. In the shadows beneath, traces of green light danced, a reflection from the waters.

It was a peaceful world, somewhere I could escape the mundane pace of life. Today, it was much welcomed. While I'd dreamt of this place for many years, as I aged the dreams grew more infrequent, but I was glad when they returned.

While I understood the dreams had no involvement in my life, I couldn't help associating them with my own reality. I'd grown to believe they acted as symbols to shore-up my own self-confidence and worth. Tonight, I was glad to frequent this dream world, more than ever.

Seated on the bank of the river, I watched the shimmering liquid flowing along its strange course, my anger and annoyance trickling away with it. Soon I felt the bliss of the dream.

In the quiet I heard movement, sand shifting under foot. It was unexpected, and I leapt up. Hovering above the shimmering river, coming towards me, was the partially shrouded figure of a woman, little of her face visible, but I saw her piercing blue eyes gazing at me, and a slender arm protruded from beneath, exposing a flash of her olive toned flesh. An echo of recognition flickered in my mind, but as I chased the memory, it faded. Defeated, I focused my attention. The haunting figure drew closer.

My voice caught in my throat as I tried to speak.

Why did I recognise her eyes? I'd never seen her before, I was sure of it.

Fear welled up. I felt like I'd insulted this figure by haunting her home all these years.

Wait, *her* home? Where did that come from? Who *was* she and why would this be *her* home?

"It's been a long time." The soft gentle lilt of her voice appeared to come from beyond her lips which never parted. "Do not be afraid." At this I dropped my nerves got the better of me and I dropped to me knees – I was unsettled, even though her words and voice was calming.

"Who are you?" I called out. "What do you want from me?"

"It is time," her voice almost whispered but I felt her words as a deep rumble in my gut. "You must remember your true purpose, little one. Your Magi awaits."

Without stopping, the figure walked through the river, past the obelisk and then something happened that I had never seen before. She began ascending the stairs. It was only as she reached the second storey that the gravity of the situation struck me. She was going to go beyond the final platform and leave me here alone.

"Wait!" I called after her. "Come back. Tell me who you are. Why have you come to me tonight, what is it you want me to see?"

But it was too late. The figure passed through into the building at the top of the structure with a brief green flash of light.

"Well, that was new." I settle back onto the shore. A sense of anticipation stole over me as I considered my unanswered questions in the depth of sleep.

When I woke in the morning, I could taste fermenting wine. A headache pulsed across my temples and my stomach felt raw. I yawned, throwing back the covers and hauling myself out of bed. As I stretched, I rubbed my forehead. The image of the woman from my dream flashed into my mind and the events of my vision flooded back.

Who was the woman in my dream? What did she mean I needed to remember my true purpose? And what was a Magi anyway?

A pile of notepads rested on the bedside cabinet. I took the top one, brand new I noticed, and went to remove the pen from the spine. I blinked. The pen was missing. Maybe I'd forgotten to replace it when I prepared the new pad. Whatever, I'd search for it later, for now any old thing would do. I found one, covered in dust, resting on the shelf opposite.

I jotted down the details of the dream, along with my

thoughts. It was a routine from childhood.

Aged twelve, my harmless dreams I'd had since birth became malevolent nightmares. It wasn't the garbled messages I'd scream in the dead of the night that freaked me out, it was the panic in my mother's eyes when she came to my aid. She pleaded with me, insisting I must see a child psychologist. Their advice was simple; record all my dreams and thrash them out in the daylight. They were the ones that pointed out to my mother that my doodles of the structures looked remarkably similar to the ziggurats found in Mesopotamia.

Even now, my dreams made no sense to me. They rarely changed. New faces had not appeared in a long time, and until now it was unheard of for anyone to speak to me. This was a major development, worthy of my time.

Is this the breakthrough I've been waiting for? She told me it was time. Time to understand? I scribbled on the pad. I wish I knew the answers, I want to know what you mean to me. I dropped the pen and frowned, hearing the steady stream of shower water.

It took a moment before quick disjointed images filled my mind; parts of the evening flooding back, like water cascading from the shower. Beth. I grinned with delight, but another part of me scolded myself for not remembering.

My mind replayed our kiss, feeling it all over again, her warm lips against mine.

I got up, beaming still, and went downstairs to grab some breakfast.

Beth glowed when she stepped into the kitchen, I took her in my arms and kissed her. "I'll pick you up after work and we can go out, get a drink or something." Beth said gathering herself together. "We can call it a date if you like?"

"That'd be good," I said as Beth left for work.

CHAPTER 2

The green figure flashed and I dawdled across the street, making my way home from the Job Centre. A car revved its engine, summing up my own mood. I'd wasted two and a half hours of my life. I could handle that, it was the clerk I had a problem with. He'd treated me like scum, glaring at me over his glasses and asking me questions in his superior tone. I wasn't just there to hold out a begging bowl, I'd never asked to lose my job and be unemployed.

The busy world passed me by as I considered my options. I needed to secure a job within a couple of months, if only to stave off my own boredom. It crossed my mind I could always ask my mother for help, but I dismissed it, I couldn't face speaking to her.

No, there was no question, I needed a job.

Maybe Beth could get me a part-time job at the café, just something to tide me over and lessen the decay of my redundancy package. While I knew I was a long way from finding a position, I felt it was only a matter of time before something came along. Beth was right. I could do anything

I wanted, I just needed to consider what that something might be.

Wafting on the breeze, as I approached my house, was the musty smell of cats. The next-door neighbour had two of them and they were always spraying up the front door. I opened the door quickly and went inside, shutting the stench outside.

With a steaming mug of tea to hand, I poured through my emails. They'd been piling up, mainly bills to be paid and promotions to purchase yet more stuff. It didn't take long for my patience to wear. I dropped my phone to the floor, littering it with my debt. One thing was certain, I'd need to economise. I couldn't waste the little money I had on things such as subscription television anymore, I'd have to find a better balance; Peter's pay-out was the minimum required by law which wasn't a lot.

The large sums I owed made for depressing reading. Desperate to escape, I stared at the corner of the room. I was about to switch the TV on when I remembered there had been some post from the previous day and I groaned. I needed to see how deep my troubles were and forced myself to reach over. The envelope was beneath a half-eaten pork pie with teeth marks. It left a grease stain on the front of the envelope. I was about to wipe it clean and stopped. Written on the front were the simple words, Mark Besant, hand written, no return address.

I ripped it open, unfolding the letter. A flyer fell to the floor. There were no distinguishing marks on the letter, not even a corporate logo or signature.

We would like to congratulate you, Mr Besant, on your acceptance into the SARA training programme. You are requested to attend at the address at your earliest convenience. Please read the enclosed literature carefully.

The address was in a small Devonshire village, Dunsford, nestled in the Dartmoor National Park. It was roughly an hour away from my door on the outskirts of Exeter.

"SARA?" I said, re-reading the letter. Who were they and what training programme had they enrolled me on? And most importantly, how had this happened without my knowledge? I placed the letter to one side and sat in silence, bemused by its bizarre contents.

Was it just a coincidence that I'd lost my job the same day this landed on my doorstep? *Nobody would go to that amount of trouble, would they?* I laughed it off, it was ludicrous, but still...

My attention turned to the leaflet, there was a logo, a blue outline of a man holding a rocket. Below it was the caption; *Welcome to SARA, delivering tomorrow's space technology today.*

For a moment my mind drifted, considering the infinite possibilities of our universe. Somewhere, there was a man with my name, the same dark hair and blue eyes, working on a top-secret component for a space probe. Maybe he was an astronaut destined for deep space. It was weird to think of him out there, waiting for this letter.

I shook the thought from my head. I wasn't an astronaut, any notion of that had come from my father's fantasies when I was a child, but they had died along with him. I continued reading.

As part of the SARA family you will be working in the new office development in Dunsford, specially built for the training and development of personnel for space exploration.

I laughed, unable to control myself. *Was this for real?* I looked over the pamphlet. There was an old RAF base in Dunsford which I knew was being renovated, but I'd heard it was a new aviation training facility. Of course, it could have been misreported by the media. But in Dunsford…what luxury!

Intrigued, I reached for my phone and typed 'SARA' into my search assistant and got millions of results, but nothing related to space. One last try, I entered "SARA Space Technology". The words 'no direct results' blinked back, but it offered me fifteen million alternative results. I gave up. My attention had been hooked by a hoax, a bad one at that.

I dropped my phone back to the floor, considering the contents of the strangest junk mail I'd seen in years. Maybe the same mailing had been sent to a group of suggestible people to experiment on them – who knew what was really going on at that old RAF base?

A moment later I broke into laughter at the stupidity of my own imagination.

2

Am I still dreaming? I thought as I looked out through my open eyes. The confusion passed as reality bit down, the cold air taking hold of me and I shivered. I took my dream journal from the side of the bed and recorded the afternoons events.

I stood at the ziggurat as usual, but I did not feel at peace. The river was stagnant, I could taste the decay. I reached down and touched the slimy film of the water. It shimmered like diamonds in the sand, but it felt so strange, tingling like it was producing a small electrical current. The feeling of raw power surged inside my body, my tongue prickled, flooded with the coppery taste of old coins.

It was like holding the energy of life itself. I felt like I could cast new stars into the sky, it was that powerful.

When I turned around there was a figure standing to the east side of the ziggurat. She had something in her hands, a disc shaped object. I watched her vanish through the mudbrick walls where there was no obvious opening in the structure. I am sure...

I blacked out the last few words. *I am not sure if the woman I saw was the same woman from last night, I saw nothing but the suggestion of her graceful movements.* I frowned as I reread my scrawling, things were getting a little strange.

The dreams were intense and with a frequency I'd not experienced since I started having them. I was beginning to see new details. Now the place was both familiar and unfamiliar at the same time, and I was no closer to understanding their meanings. My psychologist had told me that our sub-conscious mind can create dreamscapes to make us listen. If that was true, I really wasn't paying attention to my inner-voice.

A pounding knock made me jump.

Dazed and still sleepy I stretched before getting up and opening the door. Beth glared at me as I yawned.

"Do you always keep a lady waiting?" Her voice was tough, but I could see the corners of her lips twitching. "I've been standing here for the past fifteen minutes. I heard you snoring through the letterbox." She laughed. "You don't half make a racket."

After a shower my body felt a little more responsive, even if my head didn't.

Coming down the stairs I caught Beth thumbing through the SARA pamphlet. She dropped it to the table as I stepped into the room, but it was too late, I'd caught her snooping. I said nothing, letting it go. It was a bad omen to start a first official date with ill feeling I thought.

"Let's eat," she said, slipping off the sofa.

3

Dinner weighed heavy on my stomach, rendering me useless and my eyes heavy once more. The colourful images of the television did little but to rock me further towards sleep and I snuggled up to Beth.

Beth's grip tightened on the television remote, her hands almost white.

"Is something wrong?" I yawned, lifting myself upright.

"No." She had a smile stapled to her lips, the same fake smile she had around rude customers. "Honestly, it's nothing."

I knew *that* 'it's nothing'. I'd hated my teenage years, spending much of it cooped up, trying to deal with the death of my dad, but never finding an outlet for my emotions. It tortured me and ripped me and my mother apart. It was the same 'it's nothing' that kept us separated.

One day I was sure I'd grow up and open up.

"You don't mind do you?" Beth changed the channel, stopping on the news. I said nothing, blinking back another yawn. Beth tensed and I followed her gaze to the screen.

"We take you live to Washington DC where a specially convened press conference is expected to take place shortly, organised by NASA and the Russian space agency." The newsreader said. It hooked my attention – what could be so important that it'd taken over the usual looping feed of news. *"Our Washington correspondent Timothy Witting has all the latest."* The newsreader swivelled to face the video screen behind him. *"What can you tell us Timothy?"*

"I'm live in Washington DC where the NASA administration gathered earlier this afternoon in preparation for a statement this evening. Nobody has yet given any indication of what is about to be announced, but it is fair to say that this is an unusual move for NASA. There is immense anticipation here,

as we wait for what we think will be a significant conference to get underway, which we're expecting at any moment–"

"We have to stop you there, Timothy, as we go live to the conference." The newsreader's voice cut into the correspondent's piece to camera.

The picture changed and I saw a group of stiff-collared, and still mostly middle-aged men, sitting in front of microphones, cameras flashing in their eyes as photographers captured images for the morning papers. I was surprised to find the conference hadn't already begun as was often the case with these things.

"Good afternoon and welcome to NASA Headquarters, Washington. I am Roger Bates, the Administrator for NASA. Also joining me today I have Deputy Administrator of NASA, Charles Humber, along with the director of Flight Crew Operations, Sakib Khan and joining us by a video link from England is General Patrick Thacker, US Air Force Chief of staff. By satellite phone from Moscow we also have the General Director of the Russian space agency, the RKA, Gregori Sokolov."

"Thank you, Roger." According to the name at the bottom of the screen we were now looking at Charles Humber. *"After a number of years of negotiations which I am humbled to have been part of, there has been a meeting of minds to create a new opportunity in space exploration. Today, overseen by the President of the United States, the Administration has reached agreement with the General Director of the RKA and the President of Russia. Talks continue with our European partners, who are watching this development closely. Today, we are building a new united Space Agency for Russia and America, to be known as SARA..."*

Blood pumped in my ears, drowning out the conference as it continued. My heart pounded as I made the connection. I sat forward in my seat as the words sank in.

"Are you okay?" Beth asked as I stood up, one hand on my

hip.

"No," I shook my head still watching the screen. Mouths were moving but I'd stopped listening to what they were saying. As the camera flashes continued in the conference hall, I found myself drifting from reality.

In a flash I found myself with my phone in my hand, fingers fumbling as they typed 'SARA' into the search engine. The screen filled with results, but unlike my previous attempt the first link was to the NASA website and when I clicked it open, it displayed the same logo from the SARA brochure – the blue outline of a man, holding onto a rocket – along with a press statement which confirmed the news.

I remembered the letter, it suggested I possessed useful skills. Now that I knew SARA was real, I couldn't help question what these abilities were. I once dreamed of being an astronaut, but I'd known for years why that was. It had been my father's idea, he'd encouraged me, feeding me knowledge from his mountain of books. My father spent his free Sunday afternoons playing games with me; dressed as a Spaceman, wearing a tin-foil helmet I'd crudely fashioned and a red cape which was an old bed sheet. Remembering, it brought me a brief moment of joy before being replaced by confusion, once again.

The information I'd absorbed of space and exploration had long since gone. As far as I knew, I had nothing. As I hovered in front of the television, it became too overwhelming.

"I'm going out for some air," I said, leaving Beth alone and stepping out into the cool September evening breeze. I perched on the edge of the porch, the stench of cat piss filling my nostrils once again.

It was all too impossible, too incredible. My mind wrestled with the news, and I felt the meltdown rising as shadowy butterflies fluttered across my vision. Everything faded.

As the butterflies cleared I heard voices. They were talking to me.

I stared upwards at the blurred faces that were floating into view and then I felt a hand holding mine, pulling me upright. My eyes focused and I saw the figure standing over me. I'd expected to see Beth and blinked when I found myself in the strange dream world that usually occupied my sleep.

"Do not be afraid." I recognised the strange gentle accent of the voice, it was the same woman from the previous dreams. As before her lips did not move, the soft features of her face vaguely familiar.

"Who are you?"

"Don't you recognise your Magi?" She asked, but I said nothing, her expression betrayed her words, looking at me with the doting look of a mother. Her dark skin gave her a Mediterranean look, but her accent pattern didn't match. "My name is unimportant for now."

Slowly I felt my body ease and I struggled to get to my feet.

"Tell me what you want from me."

"We need you." The figure said simply. "You will remember, my child. Rediscover the memories of your past and it will begin to make sense."

"Sense?" I laughed. "None of this makes sense."

"Listen," she said, a soft note of concern, "You only have to look to the past to understand your future." With that she vanished, draining into the sand of the desert. I was alone, standing before the ziggurat in the strange world from which I now felt disconnected. Except deep in my heart, there was something...

My arm shook and I yelped in pain.

Then it came again and again and...

I screamed as another face shot in front of me. Out of fright I jumped up, pushing over something in the process. I looked back and saw Beth holding her face, tears in her eyes, a red mark clearly visible already from where I'd elbowed her.

I blinked, confused by the sudden intervention of the real world.

4

"I'm sorry." I apologised again, trying to end the uncomfortable silence. We sat at opposite ends of the sofa. "I hope it doesn't bruise." An image of Beth's swollen, purple face flashed before my eyes and I shuddered.

I'd never seen Beth look so troubled since she'd had all the problems with her ex-husband, maybe she was getting cold feet about our relationship, maybe it was too soon, after all his abuse went further than the healed dark welts I'd seen.

"You know my history." Beth spoke with venom. Her eyes remained fixed on the floor, avoiding my gaze. This annoyed me, why couldn't she share her feelings with me.

It was a vivid and disturbing memory, it was only the second month I'd known Beth. Even before I'd pushed my way through the lunchtime crowd to the counter, I'd seen the bruises extending from Beth's jaw to her hairline, a size ten boot matched the bill. There was sorrow in her eyes and all thoughts of my appetite vanished.

I'd waited until the busy rush was over before calling Beth to my table, pushing out the seat opposite. Without a word she'd sat and I just stared, mentally questioning her. It didn't take long for the tears to come, and I took her in my arms. I'd trusted her with my secrets – my dreams – it was her turn.

"He caught me packing my bags..." She'd told me, needing to say no more, the images of her ex-husband's blunt fists and kicking feet hanging in the air between us. I never wanted to see Beth in that state again, and that's why it hurt that she wasn't speaking to me now.

"I really am sorry," I said shaking my head, bringing myself back to the present. "I was in a daze." My apology fell on Beth's deaf ears. "It was an accident."

"Your words mean nothing," Beth snapped.

"What do you want me to say?" I attempted to keep cool, but my temper frayed. "I'm not your ex." She shot me a cool look and I felt I'd over stepped the mark, but I couldn't stop there. "What do I have to do to show you that? It was a real accident, I don't want to give you excuses."

"Don't!" She jerked away from me as I inched closer, attempting to put my arm around her. "Just get away from me." I felt shut-out, but I guessed she was questioning if she'd stumbled into another abusive relationship. I turned away, frustrated.

"We can talk some other time." I studied the silent television in the corner of the room, the images it had shown still fresh and haunting in my mind. When I turned around, Beth's fragility was clear, tears streaming down her face, the pain all too obvious.

"Maybe it was my fault," Beth said through her tears. "I try to be strong but..." Right then I understood how she'd stuck by her ex-husband, allowing herself to succumb to his barrage of insults for so long. Somehow Beth believed she deserved the pain I'd inflicted, regardless of how accidental it had been. It was all too easy for her to accept.

I approached her cautiously, taking her in my arms. Her eyes told me she was shouldering the blame and she responded to me, her guilt preventing her from seeing the truth; I'd struck her. Even in a blind panic, it was still indefensible.

I kissed the red patch below her cheek, feeling her pain as she tensed.

"Sit with me," she said. "I don't want to be alone." I felt

uncomfortable doing so, knowing that I was taking advantage of her vulnerability. "I shouldn't have punished you like that – you're not him." Her eyes caught mine and I looked away. "I'll make it up to you."

I wanted to tell her to stop, to think about what she was saying, but my words stumbled. I was only human, astonished by her performance.

We sat in silence.

A little while later Beth excused herself to use the bathroom. After ten or so minutes, I went upstairs to check she was okay, I didn't want to leave her alone too long in her fragile state.

As I padded up the stairs, I heard her elevated voice, "he's not as easy to handle as I first thought. He's unpredictable." Was she referring to me? I didn't think I was hard to handle or unpredictable. There was a pause and then a forced, "yes sir."

Sir, just who was she talking to?

"Truth," I heard a muffled groan. "Oh Beth, you don't even know the meaning of the word." A moment later the bathroom door burst open and I jumped.

"Are you okay?" I shifted my weight, leaning against the banister. "I heard you talking."

"It's nothing," she said. "It was one of my friends checking in."

"Sounded pretty heated to me." Beth brushed past me.

"You know how it can be." She dismissed my concern with a wave of her hand. "Some people just can't take no for an answer." As Beth disappeared down the stairs, I stood alone, considering. Beth's mood had jack-knifed all evening, and I felt exhausted and out of the loop. I'd definitely heard her shouting, she never spoke to friends that way and I was confused by what I thought I'd heard her say.

Not wanting to cause any further imbalance, I made a mental note to question her about it further, in the morning perhaps. I returned to the sofa without a word.

"What do you want to do?" Beth looked up.

I took a moment to think about this. So much had happened in a short few hours and I didn't feel like I'd had the room to stop still. Could I stop now? I guessed not, the decision made.

"Hand me that leaflet," I pointed to the table. "I'd better find out what's going on."

"What is this?" Beth's face brightened as she peered at the leaflet as if she'd never seen it before. I was annoyed at Beth's behaviour, she was lying to me. But I said nothing, dialling the number I'd been provided.

It was engaged.

I tried again, but the line remained busy.

"I guess they're probably inundated after tonight's news or something." I relaxed into the sofa and dropping the phone. It would have to wait after all.

CHAPTER 3

The sun shone through the open curtain revealing another cloudless September sky. I checked my phone, it was after eleven. I rolled out of bed and gazed out the window, catching sight of a blackbird swooping to the lawn where it bobbed back and forth for a moment.

I stretched out, basking in the warmth emanating through the glass. The weather was too pleasant to remain cooped up indoors so I gathered myself together and went out for a walk, following the trail to the park and then east along the path. It led down into a valley, shaded on all sides by the overhanging branches of tall oak trees. To my left, a brook burbled, full of overnight rain. There was a rustle of leaves in a tree above me and when I stopped I saw two squirrels chasing each other, jumping from branch to branch. I took a deep breath, inhaling the peaceful morning air.

The path continued for a while, and I relaxed, taking in the wildlife. In the distance I heard a car horn honking in frustration on a nearby road, but even this didn't break the peace. For the first time in years I felt I was enjoying nature without witnessing it through the second-floor window of an office block. Up ahead the track forked and I came to an abrupt halt. I took the path to the left, having never followed it before. It led me across the brook and into a tangle of overgrown brambles. I pushed through their thorns, moving them aside, I felt like an adventurer deep in the jungle, unknown dangers waiting for me in the bushy cover. I grinned with child-like ambition.

Fighting my way through the dense undergrowth of the forest floor I realised I never took risks, I didn't have adventures anymore. Before my dad died we'd go camping or trekking through forests and moorlands. I missed all that, I was still lost without him. Of course, there could be no replacing him, but I hadn't even tried to find someone to remind me of the great times we'd had together, and to continue to explore with. While I liked Beth, I didn't think she was the outdoors sort, and I couldn't put my finger on it but I couldn't help feeling she wouldn't be sticking around. No that was a lie, I was allowed to put voice to my feelings. She wasn't the woman I thought she was. She was withholding information, and she had covered up when she'd been caught. I couldn't trust her.

I stopped in a clearing, stunned by the force of the two deep realisations that had hit me in quick succession. Maybe SARA could bring some adventure my way. I sucked in a breath as this struck me, a new route in life had revealed itself to me.

My mind was settled and a stood tall. I'd try calling SARA again when I got home, but first I needed to find a way back to the main path. The explorer in me took over, and I could taste the sweetness of freedom.

I was still grinning to myself, pulling thorns from my clothes, as I rounded the corner of my street. I froze, recognising the back of my mother's head from her short grey hair, the same tuft always sticking out. Her posture had worsened since I'd last seen her, she stooped over with age.

"Mum." Unable to hide my surprise. "What are you doing here?"

"Is that how you greet all your friends?" A frown crossed her brow. Her fingers fidgeted at her sides in the awkward silence. I stood in the warm breeze for a moment longer, my eyes failing to meet my mother's. Seven years was a long time, I didn't know how to act around her anymore.

The deep ravine running between the two of us had its roots in my father's diagnosis. I was thirteen when cancer struck him. Maybe it would've been easier to handle if we hadn't been so close.

I let myself in, pushing past my mother and her handbag, leaving the door wide for my uninvited guest. I went straight into the kitchen and began organising a cup of tea for myself. When I heard the door close, I assumed my mother had left. Relief washed over me until I turned to see her standing in the kitchen doorway, watching me.

"I don't mean to be rude," I said, "but what are you doing here?" She stepped closer, took the kettle from my hands and placed it on the table before taking hold of me. Tears formed in the corner of her eyes.

2

My mother, Margaret, sat at the kitchen table, opposite me. She had hold of my hands, her silence reinforced my dread. Saying we weren't on the best of terms was an understatement, but even I couldn't be so heartless to turn my mother away. Something was wrong, that was clear.

The kettle boiled and clicked itself off, leaving us to our

awkwardness.

"I'm sorry," she said finally.

"For what?" I snapped. "Why are you here?"

"Can't a mother visit her child?"

"No mum," I said. "*You* can't." It was harsh, but I couldn't deny the truth; life had been better without her. There were fewer arguments for a start. I took a moment, letting my bitterness subside, and decided I needed to change tact. Treating her roughly would get us no place fast. "The floor is yours, I assume you came here for a reason." I knew she was too proud to break the silence of our arrangement on a whim.

"Oh let's stop this," she said, slamming her fist onto the table, her wrinkled face tightening in a flare of anger. "Why can't we just get along, like we used to?" Her fist unclenched and she let out a sigh. "When Leon was around you'd never have spoken to me like this. Your father wouldn't have allowed it."

She got up and made tea. When she sat back down I looked at her with concern. "It's been seven years." I shook my head. "I'll be civil. But you need to start talking. You can start by telling me what brings you here."

"I found something of yours I thought you'd want back." I was intrigued, it had to be important; she'd broken our arrangement for it. Besides, I'd taken all my stuff when I'd left home. Well, anything of value at any rate. She retrieved a plastic bag from her handbag and handed me an aged sheet of folded paper, the edges were frayed and dark.

"Where did you find this?" I asked opening it and staring at the ziggurat structure I'd painted when I was seven. A small glittery river ran around the structure and I traced it with my fingers feeling the tranquillity of the scene, old glitter falling from my hands. The peak of the towering obelisk sparkled silver and green before the steps leading upwards.

"I discovered them in a box, among your father's things," she said.

"What was it doing there?"

"He kept it for you." I frowned, sure she wasn't telling me the whole truth. She hadn't just found this, there was more to it than that. "I've thought about this for so many years, and I've never found a way to say it, so I'm just going to show you..." She pulled out a second sheet of paper, it was slightly torn and from the way the tear had aged it told me it was much older.

"What is this?" I took the page and unfurled it, revealing another image of the same ziggurat. I didn't recognise it as my own work, and it was incomplete. "Where did you get this?"

"It was your father's," she said.

I looked at the picture of the ziggurat, it wasn't as tall and the glittering specks of the river swept differently across the landscape. There was no obelisk standing as a beacon on the landscape. Even so, the form of the ziggurat and the way it was drawn was identical to my own picture. I shook my head and sucked in a deep breath, trying to keep my cool.

"Did he draw this?" I asked dangling the picture before my mother. "Did he have the same dreams?"

"Yes," she said, biting her lip. "And your grandfather."

"Okay." I took another deep breath, suppressing my rising anger as I remembered how she'd made me feel. She'd frightened me, her reaction to my dreams had me thinking I was possessed by an evil spirit in the way that young minds do. I felt it all over again. "Why were you so concerned about my dreams?" I needed to know. "You made me see a psychologist. You treated me like I had an illness. Why did you do that when both dad and grandpa had the same dreams?"

"I was scared." She pushed her cup around the table, the liquid slopping over the edges and onto the table. "Your father was involved in…things."

"Things?" I snapped, my temper fraying. "What *things*?"

"I…"

"I can't believe you!" My voice louder. "You can't just waltz in here and start talking riddles. Do you realise you put me through hell? I thought there was something wrong with me, that I wasn't normal. The other kids teased me, their names used to hurt. But not like this. Why are you doing this to me mum?"

"You're not normal." Tears streamed down the deep wrinkles of her cheeks to her chest, staining her blouse. "You are special."

"What the hell is wrong with you?" I flinched at the strength of my own voice. "What does that even mean?" I shook my head in disbelief as she avoided my gaze. "Why are you here? Why now? You've had all this time to tell me and now you expect me to listen to your half-truths. Am I just meant to guess what you're talking about? You really are unbelievable!" I slumped back in my chair with a huff, she was making this too difficult.

We sat in silence, tears still seeping from my mother's eyes. I didn't enjoy seeing her in this state, her face screwed up, her blouse spotted. I studied her, where had things gone wrong for us? A wave of sadness flooded my senses, why was everything so difficult and uncomfortable between us? I'd hoped time would heal the wounds, but it had only driven us further apart. *Well, no more running. It's time to face the truth.*

"Why do we do this to each other? Why can't we get past all the pain and hurt? Dad's gone. We should be able to move on from that, right?" I looked into my mother's eyes for just a moment and saw a glimmer of acknowledgement, I smiled back. "I wish you'd treat me like an adult." I spoke gently, leaning forwards and taking her hand into mine.

"I'm sorry," she said wiping her eyes and recomposing

herself. "You're right, we've spent far too long blaming each other for what happened. It was tough when your father died. You lost a dad, I lost a husband. Do you know how excruciating it was to look at you after that? I always saw his face; people always said you looked alike and I never saw it until he'd gone."

"You could've told me." I squeezed her hand, but she shook her head.

"I used to look at you and part of me wished it'd been you." For the first time, the raw truth was open to see, and I blinked. "I couldn't help it and I didn't mean it." She tried to limit the damage, but I wasn't hurt, I actually understood having thought the same thing about her, although I didn't think it would help to say so. "When we had arguments, I wished Leon was still alive, I convinced myself it would be better for me, that I could live without you."

"And?"

"It hurt," she said.

"But we've survived," I said. "Christ, we've gone seven years."

"I know." Her eyes dropped to her twiddling fingers. "I respected your space, giving you distance. Sometimes that's all people need. You are your own man, you didn't need me holding you back."

"And now?"

"I'm not deluded," she said. "I know we can't mend things overnight, but I want you back in my life. You're the only part of him I have left." I was touched by my mother's words, they'd taken a long time to arrive and now I felt disappointed by the years we'd missed. I realised I'd never once stopped to think how she was feeling or how she was coping; it'd always been about me.

"I should've been more supportive," I said. "I'm sorry for that."

"You were young."

I stood, taking her in my arms and hugging her tight. The sweet scent of her familiar perfume filled my nostrils, a bouquet of lavender and roses. Memories flooded back.

"So, the truth from now on?" I caught my mother's eyes. "You can start by telling me everything you know about these dreams."

3

"Your father was a good man." She blew into her fresh tea before taking a sip, a new cloud of vapour mushrooming out. "But his job dictated certain things. He signed agreements ensuring his silence, nobody could know the details of his work."

"I don't understand." I frowned. "What has that got to do with his dreams? Anyway, dad used to tell me about his job all the time, where he'd been and the equipment he'd used." I remembered his trips to the Antarctic, the Himalayas and other exotic places. He was always travelling. He'd spent almost three full months in Mexico the one year.

"I'm not proud of our lies," she said with a slow shake of her head. "But you have to understand we had to tell you something. At some point you were bound to question your father and it was better to create the lie before." Her eyes pleaded with mine. "We never meant for you to get hurt. If you believe only one thing, you have to believe that." There was truth in her voice, and I let this slide without protest. "Your father came up with the job in the oilfields, it gave him reason to tell you about the places he'd been, that's how much he wanted to involve you in his work."

"So, what did he do?"

"Some things I didn't even know until late into your father's illness," she said. "It took me a while to understand.

Both your father and grandfather worked for the same agency, a silent branch of government."

My eyes narrowed.

"His travels were real, he went all over the world, monitoring extra-terrestrial phenomena where it happened. The government were jumpy, anything unexplained, they wanted to know about it." For a moment I thought she was playing more games with me and I laughed, but her face remained serious. Slowly my smile faded as the impossibility of her words sank in. *Was she still lying to me now?* I studied her expression and demeanour, looking for clues of her deceit but finding none. In fact, she seemed pretty relaxed.

That didn't matter though, I felt a rising sense of unease. Could I trust her?

"I don't understand what any of that has to do with anything. Are you trying to ruin the precious few memories I have left of dad? Do you want to destroy everything of him in me?"

I'd never seen my mother hit anybody until her hand struck my cheek with a resounding snap. I reeled backwards, knocking the chair over. It stung, but it was the shock that hurt the most. I imagined this was how Beth had felt the first time her ex-husband laid his hands on her, and this was only a taster.

"I'm sorry." She stood and came to my side. My cheek burned. "I shouldn't have done that." She took me in her arms. "Please forgive me." I remained silent, stunned by her actions. "I'd better leave."

"Wait," I said, moved once again, reining in my anger and resentment. She turned back and looked into my eyes. "I shouldn't have spoken to you like that. I'm sorry for that, but please stay, I need to know the truth."

4

"Here," I said handing my mum a rosy glass of sherry, the only alcohol I had in the place. Its heavy aroma clung to the air, cloying at the back of my throat. It was strong, but sweet. "Why are you telling me all this now, after all these years?" I held up the picture of the ziggurat my father had drawn, comparing it against my own. I shuddered at the eerie likeness.

"There are some truths you need to hear before..." Her sorrowful eyes caught mine, my mind finishing her sentence, knowing she never would. My dreaded suspicions were right; there are only two unmistakable facts in life. I took her hand in mine and squeezed. She sniffed loudly.

"Oh mum." My voice tender.

"Don't worry about me," she said, taking her hand back and wiping her face. "I'm not here to talk about that. You wanted the truth and there it is." From the lack of discussion, I assumed some form of cancer. "Your father saw things even before I knew him. Dark images. He used to say I brought them to life, giving them colour." Her lip quivered for a second, but she recomposed as she continued. "I thought he was trying to charm me, but he believed it proved we were meant to be together and the moment you started drawing the same images I knew he'd been right. I never believed in fate until I saw it first-hand. Your dreams are sharper still, you're very special."

"You think this is a gift?" I pointed at both the images now on the table.

"I felt it was a curse." She shook her head. "But your father was right, it is a gift and it's *your* gift. You gave it to him." I considered her words in silence, but I could not stop a frown from creasing my brow; was she saying I was genetically inevitable? "I hope you can find it in your heart to forgive us for the lies we told."

I thought about everything I'd said to my mother minutes before. After asking for and then hearing her truth, I couldn't refuse to accept it.

"I can." Even though I felt a little resentment for the lies, I knew I couldn't fault her honesty now. "I wouldn't like to live without my dreams. They bring peace to my life."

"You sound just like him." She reminisced. "Leon was a good man."

"Yeah, he was." It was a shame he'd left us before his time. "So why did you come here today, besides your illness?" I asked, vocalising what she wouldn't.

"I..." Her words stumbled. "Your father was working with someone in America before he was diagnosed," she said. "When this man found your father he was very interested in his dreams. He had a theory about them. I don't recall the details, but I remember him saying they were connected to some ancient events."

"Do you know who he was?"

"I met him once."

"Maybe I could get in contact with him, see if I can make light of his theories."

"That's the thing," she said. "It's why I'm here. He's already tried to make contact with you." I looked at her, frowning.

"Who?"

"Pat Thacker." Her eyes met mine before dropping to her glass.

I didn't recognise the name, I couldn't place it. I'd not spoken to anyone really in days, except maybe Beth and the guy at the Job Centre. Was it recent perhaps? I cast my mind back, struggled to place the name, and then it clicked.

I'd heard the name on television at the press conference for SARA. It all fell into place. The anonymous SARA letter had been from him; General Patrick Thacker

"Did he ask you to come here?" The question lingered, her eyes avoiding mine. The silence told me everything I needed to know. My anger had a new direction.

5

After my mother left, I grabbed the SARA pamphlet and dialled the number. I was determined to get the truth out of Thacker, but I knew I needed to remain sceptical. He'd gone to a lot of trouble to get hold of me, that much was clear, but it was one thing to send me a letter, a totally unacceptable other to manipulate my sick mother. If he'd gone to that amount of effort, it was no more unbelievable to consider he'd arranged for the termination of my employment – and that thought fuelled my anger.

"Good afternoon, how may I direct your call," A female voice answered. I thought about launching into a tirade of abuse, but that would have been no help. Instead my words caught in my throat. "Hello, can I help you?"

"Yes." I finally got out. "My name is Mark Besant–"

The words barely left my lips before the woman interrupted. "I will connect you straight away, Mr Besant."

The phone rang.

"Ah, we finally get to speak." A gruff male voice spoke with a mid-western American accent. I suspected he'd smoked far too many cigarettes over the years. "I thought we'd never hear from you."

"Thacker." I said, swallowing my anger. I'd shoehorned the truth out of my mother and now I wanted the truth from him. "I know your work well." Venom in my voice.

"I take it you've spoken with your mother." I could hear his sneering smile.

"What do you want from me?" I asked, bringing an end to his psychological games. "What possible use am I to you? And another thing, who are you? I mean, what's your involvement with this SARA thing?"

"One question at a time," he chuckled. "I am, or was, the Chief of Staff for the US Air Force, but I've accepted the position of Administrator for SARA."

"Okay," I said. "So what do you want from me?"

"It would be best if we could discuss this in person."

"I'm not getting involved in anything until you answer some questions." I couldn't ignore his blatant attempt to skim over my concerns. "What is this about?"

"You may be younger, but you're the same man as your father; he couldn't walk away and I'm willing to bet you can't either." I felt insulted, who was he to tell me what I would do. "Tell me, don't you want to know about the dreams? Your father was very interested and we made progress on my theories."

"What theories?" He understood how to hook my attention.

"I believe it's in your blood and even stronger with you than it was in your father's case. I know, because I feel it too." He paused. "It is part of who we are. Part of our untold history and if you're the man I think you are, you will want to know why."

The line went silent.

"Will you at least meet with me?" Thacker paused. "You are a hard man to get hold of."

"What right have you got..." I stopped. Thacker had given me nothing so far, getting annoyed was not the right approach. If I really wanted to get to the bottom of things, I'd have to agree to his request – although it felt more like a demand. "I'll give you an hour to convince me," I said. "But I want assurances, my decision is final. No more games or messengers. Agreed?"

"I'll arrange everything, then we can discuss things properly and you can make your decision." He avoided answering my question. "No pressure."

Of course not, I thought.

6

I was aware of the weight of the duvet, pinning me in position.

My eyes opened and I glanced across at the empty space next to me, Beth's body absent, the covers peeled back and lumped on top of me. I hauled myself upright, rubbing my face with one hand while reaching for the lamp with the other.

I squinted in the light, noticing my dream journals were missing.

The bedroom door was ajar, a slither of light coming in from below. I got up and padded across the carpet in the relative darkness towards the open door. It was silent below as I stepped out onto the landing. Over the banister I found the source of the light, the kitchen. I went downstairs.

Beth glanced up from the kitchen table, her face flushed with rosy colour: I'd caught her in the act. I followed her gaze down to my dream journals sprawled out in front of her, some open at seemingly random pages, others closed, stacked neatly to one side.

"What are you *doing*?" I plucked one of the journals from the table to take a closer look. It was open at an entry from a few days before, the words caught my eyes *what is a Magi?*

"I..." Her words froze. I thought I heard her gulp.

This was akin to reading someone's personal diary, an invasion of my privacy. I opened my mouth to tell Beth how I felt when I realised she might consider we were in a relationship now. I'd told her about my dreams before, I'd trusted her then; wasn't this just an extension to that?

"You could've asked me first," I said, switching the kettle on. I might as well have a drink, it would be a while before I went back to sleep. Beth didn't say anything until I sat in front of her with my steaming mug.

"I'm sorry," she said. "I woke up..."

"Don't." I was too tired to argue. "Just ask in future." I relaxed into the back of the chair, stifling a yawn. It felt uncomfortable for a moment as I studied Beth, her eyes fixed on me, and then her guilty look faded. "Did you find anything of interest?"

"I don't have a theory, if that's what you're asking." She stretched with a yawn of her own. "I'm almost done anyway."

I took another sip of tea before I realised I wasn't in the mood for it after all.

"I won't be long," Beth smiled as I got to my feet. I went upstairs and crawled back into bed, curling up in the warmth. I remembered Thacker had mentioned something about a theory?

A theory, I thought as I drifted off to sleep.

SARA

CHAPTER 4

Beth's figure swam into view as I rolled over. She stood watching from the doorway, her eyes twinkling. I hauled myself upright, taking the covers with me and shivering. It was a cold start.

"Morning," I said, stretching. "Do you have to go to work?" Beth's bottom lip curled over the top as her saddened eyes gazed back at me.

"You know I have to." Although her eyes said she didn't want to leave. "Maybe you should get out of here today, it's not good to stay indoors for too long. Why don't you meet me at lunch? We can take a walk into town."

"I'm not sure I'll have the time." Beth frowned, curious. "I was so exhausted last night I forgot to tell you. I've agreed to meet someone from SARA; General Thacker."

"Oh?" Beth squirmed, perhaps unconsciously. She'd wanted me to call SARA, but it was obvious the news made her uncomfortable, her posture shifting by the second.

"I'll be down in Dunsford of all places." I chuckled, still unsure why the Americans and Russians were using England as a base. Maybe the British government trusted the unification of the old Cold War enemies, demonstrating it through the use of its lands for the SARA training and research facility.

"Whatever he wants from me, it's to do with my dreams. I got the feeling they are pretty important to him, although I don't really know why SARA would be interested in them." I scratched my head. Beth continued to wriggle with nervous unease. "He worked with my father. Can you believe that? Do you know, he even sent my mother around to grab my attention? I mean how unethical is that?"

"He's a creep." Her voice forceful.

"Is everything all right?"

"Yeah," she said, but she was shaking her head. "It's just..." She trailed off, looking at her feet. I joined her, lifting her chin so I could see her face, there was sadness in her eyes. "Just promise me you'll be careful. I don't want you to get hurt."

"Don't worry about me, I can handle myself."

She forced a smile.

"You best go," I said. "You'll be late for work." I gave her a final hug before she left.

2

I arrived at the SARA compound around midday, five miles outside of Dunsford.

The instructions were easy to follow, although I was unnerved when I turned off the main road onto an unmarked one, narrow and winding into the countryside, trees on either side of the road forming a dark foreboding tunnel.

A while later I came out from the cover of the trees, revealing a dull chain-link fence that surrounded the site.

Formidable hazard signs, vibrant yellow, warned of the high voltages passing through the reinforced cables.

I pulled up at the gate house.

"Hello," I said to the man in the booth. "My name is Mark Besant, here to see General Thacker." He looked down at me from his vantage point but said nothing. For good measure, I added, "he's expecting me."

Without a word he took hold of the phone in his booth. The breeze was still cool so I wound up the window as I waited. Ahead, I gazed through the fence at the rolling hills of the Devonshire landscape filling the view, not a building in sight. The sky was almost cloudless, except the odd wisp here and there.

"Go through sir," I heard the muffled voice of the security guard call. I watched as the heavy gate slid open and then I drove through. As the car crept over the brow of a hill, I finally saw the buildings, down in the valley.

I parked up, and stepped out, eyeing up the place for a moment, the sun warm on my back. Darkened glass windows ran along the lower floor, each pane had a blue outline of a man holding a rocket, the SARA logo perhaps, it had been on their literature.

I pushed the button at the entrance and waited as the intercom buzzed. A moment later the door clicked as the lock released.

Light poured into the modern foyer through the bank of windows. The sky appeared a dull shade of grey compared to the deep blue I'd seen outside.

"May I help you?" A buxom woman looked up from behind the reception desk.

"Mark Besant." I stepped towards her. She tapped on a tablet in front of her and then took out a visitor pass, pushing it onto the counter.

I took the plastic badge and attached it to my shirt pocket.

"Take a seat; I've notified General Thacker, he'll be with you in a moment." I walked to the window and gazed out. In the distance there were more wispy clouds gathering on the summit of the hills. I knew from experience it wouldn't be long until rain clouds formed.

I heard the door click to my side.

"Mark." It was Thacker's drawl.

3

"Can I offer you a drink?" Thacker asked showing me into his office.

"No," I said. "I'll be fine." Thacker poured himself a glass of water from the cooler at the back of his office.

"Help yourself," he said taking a seat at his desk.

"So tell me, what does SARA want with me?" My question cut straight to the point. "What kind of space agency is interested in dreams? What are you looking for?"

"You're just like your father." Thacker's smirk grew. "Did you know I had the honour of working with him, before his illness?"

"Yes," I said bitterly. "My mother mentioned that during her impromptu visit. You've got no right to use a dying woman like that." I didn't sound as offended as I'd intended, too rehearsed. While I'd fumed about Thacker's manipulation, I couldn't help feeling his meddling had brought my mother and I closer. We were talking, that was a start.

"I should apologise." His voice remained flat. "Maybe you'll forgive my being pushy when you've heard what I have to say." I didn't trust him, his intentions still unclear. "I guess it's best if I show you." He tapped a screen on his desk.

Two pillars of light appeared behind his desk, running from ceiling to floor. I pushed my chair back, startled. His fingers danced over the screen, tapping at different sections until the two beams of light turned black. Thacker stood and walked behind this, now completely hidden by what I assumed must be some kind of holographic video wall. It was like nothing I'd seen before.

Thacker stepped through the blackness, smiling. I shook my head.

"How does it work?"

"SARA is a combined venture between Russia and America, so we get to share each other's technology." His eyebrows raised. "Pretty great if you ask me. The RKA developed this years back. By modifying ionised particles, it projects microscopic images, like pixels on the old computer screens."

Thacker shoved his chair out the way and tapped the screen on his desk again. Bright pictures hovered in the air, projected onto the virtual screen. The footage consisted of images taken from many different satellite probes, I'd seen some of them before. The images stopped changing. We were now viewing some kind of moonscape.

"This is the most detailed picture NASA obtained from the lunar surface," Thacker said. I could just make out two blurred shaded areas; it wasn't clear what they were and the images were black and white, very poor quality at that. "Four years ago, NASA launched the *Mistral* probe."

My silence said everything. He'd need to explain.

"*Mistral* was scheduled to conduct an in-depth study of the ice on Europa, one of Jupiter's moons. During the first stage of the mission, debris struck the probe knocking it off course and into a spiral trajectory. Shortly after that, the probes diagnostics reported catastrophic systems failure. We lost contact and were unable to re-establish communications. *Mistral* was lost." I frowned, this wasn't answering my question. "Two years ago we learnt that the Russian RKA intercepted a transmission from the *Mistral* probe and that formed the basis of the SARA talks."

"What do you mean?" Puzzled by Thacker's massive leap. Had I missed something? "How?"

"NASA were in discussions with the RKA over the future of the International Space Station. It rumbled on for years. Everyone wanted the ISS to continue and expand, but the Russians wanted more control than NASA was willing to offer, that's why they used leverage against us. When we learnt they'd intercepted transmissions from *Mistral* the discussions took a different shape. They were willing to offer money in exchange for greater control. The rest is a matter of history."

"Why didn't NASA pick up its transmissions?"

"Nobody is sure," he said. "A technical fault, but nobody has provided a sufficient explanation that I'm happy with at any rate."

"Why did America care about the *Mistral* probe? That's not really leverage."

"The probe in itself was of little interest to them or us, it was the images they captured. See, they intercepted *Mistral* in a low lunar orbit. What they showed was of great interest to my work. These are just a few of the pictures RKA released to us."

He jabbed at the screen and the picture changed sharply. The difference in detail was startling. A large shaded area was visible in the colourful image, it was quite clearly a stepped structure and not a rock formation, although it was hard to say if it was natural or not. Thacker pinched the screen and the image zoomed in, increasing the level of detail. As he zeroed in on the structure, the texture of the mudbrick construction was clear, and then I saw the individual blocks.

I recognised the place instantly. It was from my dreams.

I took a sharp intake of breath.

"What do you know about this place?" My voice full of hope.

4

"Do you want to hear my theory?" Thacker finally asked. I had questions bursting out of my mind, each of them multiplying and conceiving others. The moment Thacker spoke, it all melted away. He watched me, a crooked smile on his face.

Thacker had hooked my interest, but I still felt uneasy around him. There was something unsaid lurking over him, and was I meant to just forget his behaviour?

"Tell me."

"For many years I have collected evidence pointing to a civilisation that once lived there, on our moon. Your father believed this to be true, that's why he said I should find you, when the time came. He said you'd understand."

He was wrong, I didn't.

"The data from *Mistral* proves my theories are correct. The ziggurat is the surviving remnants of these people, our ancestors." Thacker stopped short and I knew there was more.

"You're making no sense," I said. "The moon doesn't have an atmosphere. It's not capable of supporting life. If life existed, we'd have found a trace of it before now, so why has no one spotted *this* before?" I pointed at the incomplete images on the screen. There was no river, no obelisk, just an overbearing stepped structure. "I have seen this place in my dreams – that's where I saw *her*." Thacker raised an eyebrow but remained silent. "How is that possible?"

"Nobody noticed because nobody was looking for this."

"Except you?"

"Except me, yes." Thacker said. "NASA's early satellite images were too grainy, lacking detail and the orbit of the moon lander was too high. Later, when the Russian and Indian space agencies mounted their own missions, they used higher resolution imaging – but they saw what they wanted to see and nothing more."

I'd heard of these missions, but they'd been no mention of structures of any kind. Was I meant to believe that everyone, with their great minds and analytical skills, had somehow missed seeing this?

"This area of the moon is inside a crater, overshadowing the ziggurat. Even with a variety of terrain mapping methods, the structure remained invisible until now. As for your dreams..." Thacker leant forwards. "There are a few of us around the globe, we share more than just our dreams. We have common ancestry, and as impossible as it might sound to you, we have a direct connection with this civilisation." He pointed at the image. "We've been passed a gift through the ages. And answers about our existence lay within those walls. We want to send a mission to this area of the moon to investigate further; the *Constellation* programme."

I noted Thacker hadn't answered all my questions, including how the moon, a barren satellite with weak gravity had supported life, but now I had a new, more pressing one. I shook my head as I said, "I don't understand why that makes *me* of use to you."

"There is so much I want to share with you," Thacker said, his accent grated. "But you understand that much of our work is of a classified nature." His words were careful. "However, what I'm prepared to tell you without getting into a legal quandary is that I believe we're waking up. You have dreams of this place, but not only that you have memories in an advanced state of regression. We need you to help us understand what happened to our ancestors. I think they left us a message, and I believe you are the key to deciphering it. That makes you very valuable to us."

"My dreams?" I frowned. "Wait!" My palms flat out. "I haven't spoken with my mother in years, how do you know so much about my dreams?"

Thacker remained silent.

"Do you know what?" I said, my suspicions raised. "You had me interested, almost had me caught on your ideas, but I can't trust you. I mean you know things about me that you couldn't possibly know. How did you get access to my dream journals?" My question went unanswered.

I stood up to leave.

"It's like you're inside my life and I just want you out of it!" I was annoyed because Thacker's arrogance was losing me the chance to finally understand my dreams. "I'm not playing your games." I shook my head as I reached for the door.

"I have *all* the answers you're looking for."

I didn't respond and stormed out, leaving Thacker and his deceit behind.

CHAPTER 5

It was an awful drive back to Exeter. All I could think about was how Thacker had gotten into my life and manipulated things. His actions were beyond comprehension, leaving a bitter taste I couldn't ignore. The dark clouds above pelted the car as they relinquished their burden. The drumming made my head throb. By the time I pulled into my road, I felt drained.

I ran inside and dropped to the sofa, staring at the blank television screen. *Was Thacker watching me, even now?* It was a ridiculous thought, but somehow he'd found out things about me he couldn't possibly know. Besides, I didn't think it was Thacker's style, he'd shown no attempt to act tactfully and with grace. No, I got the feeling Thacker didn't go in for surveillance, he was manipulative, he used other people. Take my mother, she was as stubborn as me, yet he'd somehow convinced her into taking an unusual action and breaking our agreed silence. To break her obstinance required psychological warfare. Had he somehow convinced her it was right to go through my things while she was with me? I thought back, trying to remember if she'd gone to the bathroom at any stage. She hadn't.

Gazing into the darkness of the inanimate television, images of Thacker's smug grin began to fill the screen, causing my head to pound harder. I closed my eyes and saw pages of my journals fluttering into the murky depths below me. I could taste his deceit and a wave of gloom stole over me.

If he was prepared to stoop to the level of manipulation I was accusing him of, what else was he capable of? He probably treated his relationship in the same way, trapping his victim in a calculating power grab. There was a term for people like that; he was a gaslighter.

I recognised the traits. I'd seen them before…

My eyes sprang open at the thought.

It was Beth that had helped me understand gaslighting and the physiological games that occurred. Her ex- had been such a vile excuse of a man. Now my thoughts turned to Beth, remembering what she'd said about Thacker; he's a creep, she'd said. It wasn't what she said that had intrigued me but how she'd spoken. There was disdain in her voice, as if she'd dealt with him in the past. At the time I'd thought it an odd comment for someone she knew nothing about.

I couldn't believe Beth would violate my trust by handing over my dream logs to such a man. A faint image fluttered in my mind, Beth at the kitchen table, my journals spread out in front of her. I'd trusted her intentions, but now it jarred.

A second thought struck me. The pen had been missing from my notepads, I'd assumed Beth had borrowed it and not put it back. I bolted upstairs to check. I looked under the bed and felt around in all the dust traps but there was no pen. Unless someone had broken in, which was not impossible, but very improbable. There was only one other person who had been in my house, besides my mother, with opportunity to steal my dream journals. A new wave of raging anger flooded my body.

Beth had cheated me.

2

My feet wouldn't stay still, pacing back and forth as I contemplated how best to confront Beth. There was no doubt in my mind, she'd allowed Thacker to corrupt her. She'd befriended me and then used our relationship, feeding Thacker the information he needed. I couldn't be sure if anything had been for real or if it was all part of their game. I could hear them laughing at me, both with inane grins plastered to their faces.

I thought about the times we'd kissed and fucked, it stripped me bare thinking it was just a job to her. Did that make Thacker her pimp? I remembered the phone call I'd overheard a few days ago. Now I understood, she'd been speaking to Thacker.

I didn't have to wait much longer; a knock came at the door.

"You look dreadful." Beth looked concerned as she came inside. "Did you find out what they wanted?"

"It doesn't matter." I contained my anger. "I'm *not* going to join them. I can't trust that guy, Thacker. He's used my mother to do his dirty work. I can't work for a man like that." Beth looked relieved, a weight lifted.

"I'm glad you've made a decision." Beth took me in her arms, hugging me. I didn't hug back and bit my lip, it was now or never. I would give her one more chance to tell me the truth.

"I want to ask you something," I said, pulling away from her warm body, propping myself against the bay windowsill. "I need an honest answer."

"What's wrong babe?" Beth seemed concerned.

"I went to make a note of a dream last night but the pen was missing." I studied her eyes but they said nothing to me. "Did you borrow it?"

Beth tensed, and for just a fraction of a second her eyes glanced to her left. I was sure she was trying to decide what story to tell.

"I think I did." She blinked, a note of caution in her voice. I knew instantly Beth was lying to me, her eyes darted to the left once again and then back. "Yes, yes I remember now."

"Stop it," I said, raising my voice. "Let's stop the pretence. Did you give him my notebooks? Did he ask you to do it?" Anger seeped into my voice and there was a look of terror in Beth's eyes. Her lips began to tremble, and I knew where she was heading. It was another lie. "Don't think you can get out of this by crying, telling me he forced you into this situation. You're an intelligent woman, don't sink to his level. I want to know the truth."

All expressions on her face dissipated, I knew reality had landed.

"What do you want me to say?" She spoke with indifference. This made my world cloud up with an angry red mist, confirming that everything we'd felt together was fabricated, all that emotion meant nothing. I pictured us together and it made my stomach churn.

"How could *you*?" The light in the room seemed to flicker as my temper rose. Beth didn't move, her face stone cold, her eyes only darkness to me now. I felt so foolish and slammed my fist against the wood of the window frame, the room appeared to shake and Beth jumped. I couldn't control myself, but Beth no longer looked afraid. Had the story of her ex-husband been another lie, an excuse to get close to me? "I let you into my life. I trusted you. Don't you have anything to say?"

"It wasn't meant to be like this." Beth stepped forwards,

a blank robotic expression on her face. "You have to understand what I did was just a job, but I have always had feelings for you."

"You let me fall in love with you!" I yelled.

"I fell for you." She took another step towards me but there was nothing of our passion in her eyes, no pleading in her voice, not a tear on her cheek. It felt to me like she wanted some kind of punishment from me, but I wasn't going to play that game with her.

"I can't trust a word you've said!" I roared. "Don't you have anything more to say?" She said nothing, it was the last straw. I exploded. "*Get out*!" I studied her blank expression as it stared back at me. For a moment I thought she would do or say something to show me she was human, but Beth stood still and silent. "*Get the hell out of my life*!"

The front door slammed closed.

It was all over.

3

In the depths of sleep, I regarded the benign moonscape with envious eyes.

Things were much simpler believing that the dream world was of my own imagining, a sub-conscious process trying to tell me something I didn't want to acknowledge. Now, it actually meant something, wasn't that what I'd wanted? But I hadn't anticipated the truth, or the people it had used to get to me.

My anger burnt still as I stared up at the hauntingly silent lunar ziggurat. Right before my eyes it transformed, alive somehow, as if it had become a reality to me. Infused into the peace and tranquillity was a note of discord. The bitterness in my heart dissolved.

Fuck Beth, fuck them all, truth went beyond them.

In the distance I saw a cloaked figure coming towards me and when her warm, soft skin touched me I shivered. She led me to the shore of the backwards flowing river, and together we sat in its shimmering light.

"It's time to remember, Mark." Her voice gentle as before, and then she reached for the hood of her dark cloak, revealing her identity for the first time. I looked deep into her vibrant eyes, swirling orbs of wisdom and mystery. "Search the depths of your soul and find that place you've hidden so well. Dig it out, open the doorway and let the torrent of our ancestors' blood-soaked memories come to life. Don't be afraid, you are ready to glance into the mirrors of truth."

My eyes snapped shut as I listened to her words, now an echo in the darkness of my mind. And there, in the stillness of my dreams I began to remember.

The dazzling light of burning torches filled my eyes. I looked out into a shallow cavern. There were a dozen strangers crowded around, watching, waiting for me to do something.

"When I open the gate, you must hurry through." I was surprised when the voice of a boy came from my lips and I realised that I was watching the world through his eyes. No, it was a memory. My memory. "We don't have much time." The boy turned and from behind his eyes I was faced with a large stone structure that jutted from the wall. It was undecorated and traced the general shape of a human. It reminded me of ancient Egyptian sarcophagus, but this was plain by comparison to ones I'd seen in the British

Museum on a school visit.

The boy held something metallic in his hands, but before I registered what it was, it vanished into a small recess to one side of the sarcophagus. The room filled with a blinding flash of white, forcing my eyes closed. When I looked back, shimmering light emanated from the activated sarcophagus.

"Go, now." His voice was strong, but I felt his terror. He was afraid of what might happen if they were caught, but there was more. Beyond the light, he knew nothing of the daunting future waiting on the other side. He was blind, and leading his Master's people into the darkness.

The strangers began to pass through the light, each of them moving with panicked unease and disappearing from sight. Once everyone else has stepped into the light, the boy turned to face the cavern, taking me with him. The flickering torchlight faded.

You did well little Russia. I recognised the familiar feminine tones, it was our master's voice. Y*ou have made me a very proud Magi.* The boy turned back and without hesitation stepped through the light into the unknown, a new world his master had told him.

4

"Am I little Russia?" I asked into the silence of my empty room.

The light of the lamp flickered, reinforcing my dream as I scribbled the fresh details onto my pad. I couldn't go back to sleep now, too many questions buzzing in my mind. In my heart, I knew there was only one man who could help me and the anger started to rise. I was trapped.

I'd also learned something terrifying and exciting at the

same time. Our ancestors had some kind of teleportation device. That was crazy and impossible, yet there it was, as clear as day in my dreams. Except it wasn't just my dreams. It was a memory.

I'd have to forget being angry. Thacker's theories were too compelling to ignore. There he was, offering me everything I'd sought throughout my life, could I really resist the chance to understand? Maybe he knew who Russia was and why I was remembering him. Maybe he could explain why a boy was named after a country?

Thacker was searching for similar answers. Had his questions led him to my father? That raised other questions. Had Thacker been watching me since he'd met my father, waiting for the right time to make contact? It was a chilling thought, but nonetheless intriguing and a potential insight into Thacker's world. Turning the situation on its head, if I'd been in his shoes, wouldn't I be just as persistent?

Probably, I thought.

There was no doubt that Thacker had meddled in my life and I could see the chain of people he'd used, grooming me to get the results he needed. It was no coincidence I'd lost my job and Beth was there to pick up the pieces. It made sense that my invitation to join SARA had been hand delivered, Beth had seen to that herself. She had ample chance, already knowing where I lived. Beth had also given Thacker easy access to my dream journals, which in my mind was the most deceitful act of all. How would she have reacted if I'd woken up and caught her in the act?

Idiot, my mind screamed, *you did catch her, you just didn't care to question.*

Still, did Beth have no shame?

I realised it was all inconsequential now. I couldn't rectify the wrongs of the past or undo my thoughts and feelings, I could only look to the future and act as my conscious mind dictated.

I needed those answers, that was the truth I had to face. Thacker held the antidote to the destructive poison raging within me. Without it I might perish, or drown in the torment.

I closed my eyes, stripping my thoughts bare, it was an easy decision to make. Life or death. Blissful knowledge or torturous ignorance. I knew I'd come to the right conclusion, I'd inform Thacker in the morning.

CHAPTER 6

"You wanted me, now you've got me," I said taking a seat. "But I won't play your games anymore. Tell me what you know, I've got many questions."

"You're welcome." Thacker pushed a pen across his oak desk towards me. "But first I need you to sign this." He took a form from his drawer. I shook my head; I wasn't signing anything until I knew what it was. "Don't worry," Thacker smiled. "This isn't a contract."

"What is it then?" I relaxed a little, my fingers playing with the pen, feeling the engraved letters running along its side; SARA stationery.

"It's a non-disclosure agreement, for confidentiality." I glared at him, waiting for further explanation. "To save you calling your attorney I'll give you a brief summary. You will not discuss anything you hear, see or experience with anyone outside of SARA or without sufficient security clearance, up to and including the agreement itself." His voice was formal and methodical, how many times had he repeated this same speech? There was a pause and I digested. "Should you break this agreement, you can expect the swift and full penalty of the law." I shuddered, remembering what my mother had told me.

I scanned the document, making sure there weren't hidden clauses that Thacker had failed to mention. Although it was in legalese, it read as Thacker stated. The pen in my hand hesitated before scrawling my signature.

"By signing this agreement, I am also obligated to treat any information you give to me as confidential, up to and including your dream journals. As you are not employed or contracted by SARA, we cannot claim any knowledge of said information. If you do decide to work with SARA any further information you provide will belong to SARA." For the first time, I felt like Thacker was really levelling with me and I watched as he signed the agreement too. "I'll get my assistant to send you an electronic copy of the agreement for your records." Thacker relaxed back into his leather chair, adopting a more informal approach.

"Tell me what you know," I said.

Thacker pushed a black electronic gadget across the desk towards me. It was the size of my mobile phone, there were no identifiable buttons. Embossed at the top in silver was the SARA logo.

"I've loaded all the classified files you'll need onto that secure handset, you're free to read them at your leisure." Thacker paused. "I promise, you'll find far more questions in there than you've got for me right now."

I hesitated in taking the handset, for a moment unsure whether I was dreaming. Reality felt distorted, flipped into a new dimension.

"I have spent a great deal of time and effort over the years tracking down people like you. Every one of us has a different memory of a different person and collectively we make up part of a forgotten history."

"Why am I so important?" I asked, and then added "Why is little Russia so important?" Thacker's eyes lit up at the mention, a beaming smile filling his face. "And what is our connection with the moon civilisation?"

"I could tell you," he said and for a brief moment a flame ignited inside of me, I couldn't work with Thacker if he kept me in the dark. "But it's best if you see it for yourself..."

"Where?" I frowned, curious.

"An archaeological site in the Rora Habab plateau, Eritrea."

It meant nothing to me.

2

White hot flashes of lightning arced through the sky illuminating the darkness outside the window. Thick angry clouds released their awesome black fury on the world below.

The aircraft banked for a second time, shuddering in the unrest of the storm, taking my stomach with it. My fingernails gripped the armrest of my seat tighter as I struggled to maintain control over the mediocre dinner the airline served.

"Are you okay?" Thacker asked, leaning across from his seat. "I'm sure I heard that aeroplanes are built to withstand direct lightning strikes." I gulped back the rising acid of my stomach.

"I've never been a comfortable flier," I said trying not to focus on the flashing bolts searing through the sky outside, but it was no better inside, the red lights of the seatbelt signs blinked rapidly. "I don't much like thunder storms either."

"Whatever happened to the British stiff upper lip?" Thacker laughed shaking his head. Maybe he hadn't seen the memo – the British weren't stuffy prudes, we hadn't been for a long time now.

"If God had meant us to fly…"

Thacker cut in, "Let's leave God out of this." He had thunder in his eyes. "God has little to do with any of us." I studied Thacker and for a moment forgot we were flying inside a metal cage, 12,000 metres above the Mediterranean. It didn't last. Another bolt scorched through the bitter darkness, sending searing pain across my retinas and my stomach lurched.

"What does that mean?"

"Have you seen evidence that proves, conclusively, the existence of God?" I shook my head. "Show me one gram of godliness, or one atom of 'his' fury and I'll perhaps change my mind." Thacker smiled, pleased with himself. Put like that, it was the quickest argument in the world and I knew disagreeing with such a clear-cut fact would not lead to a resolution but frustration and anger.

The plane lurched, jolted by turbulence and my fingers sunk deeper into the armrests.

"Where do you fit into SARA?" I asked. "Aren't you a military man?"

"Yes, US Air Force, although I never flew in combat," Thacker's smile relaxed a little, his voice distant as if he was no longer beside me. "On a routine patrol mission in nineteen-eighty-eight, three of my unit drifted into a storm, about as dangerous as this one." I shuddered. It was one thing to be inside a passenger plane in this kind of weather, an altogether different experience in a fighter jet I imagined. "An unidentified object flashed on radar, flying directly towards our formation. It moved with incredible speed, far superior to anything in our inventory. That was the first time I came into contact with one of *them*."

"*Them*?" I asked confused.

"An alien spacecraft."

"Oh," I let out, surprised by the sudden change in direction and how nonchalantly Thacker spoke those crazy words. Although crazy was a relative term; only days ago I'd have considered being on a plane with him crazy. "You might want to back up there."

"The American government has long accepted the existence of unclassified life. I was twenty-two when I encountered my first UFO. After the event I started investigating some of the unexplained military files and later joined a section dedicated to extra-terrestrial phenomena. We've collected much evidence, charting the exact location and frequency of visitations." I studied Thacker's face, searching for signs he was withholding the truth. I saw none. "Both your father and grandfather worked for a similar division for the British government. In fact, it was your grandfather who captured the first alien spacecraft."

"Seriously?" I shifted in my seat, adjusting my seatbelt a little so that I could face Thacker head on. "Are you saying the British have an alien spacecraft?" I looked at him, amazed by this fact. My dad had never much talked about his father, Joseph, but hearing all this made me proud to be a Besant and I couldn't keep a smile from my face. "When?" I asked. "Where?"

"Roswell, July seventh, nineteen-forty-seven," he laughed. "Even then we couldn't keep up with the British, your Grandfather had an extra-ordinary ability for forecasting sightings. He had a good nose for the job, you could say he sensed them coming."

"Where is it now?" I felt compelled to ask, wanting to see

it.

"The British government lay claim to the craft because their agent charted its course from a prior visitation in England. Their attorneys – or lawyers, whatever you call them – claimed the object was not man-made and nobody could claim jurisdiction based upon territory alone." Thacker waved his hand dismissively. "In essence, Joseph saw it first, so it was his." Thacker shook his head. "It was a technicality."

"I don't understand," I said frowning. "If there was so much legal wrangling how did the British manage to transport the craft out of the country and how did they get it past the military? Why didn't they just refuse to allow it?"

"You Grandfather was a sneaky man," Thacker smirked, it was obvious he admired such qualities. "The military only realised what'd happened after the event. While everyone fought to own the damn craft, Joseph hired a bunch of Mexicans from across the border. You must know what law enforcement is like in the US, it quickly diverted resources, and created a big enough distraction. So much so that no asshole was left watching the gate. Your government managed to get through the checkpoints unchallenged, and then of course once it was off our soil the we'd lost the battle. Hell, they tried to reason, but the deal was done. In the reports I've given you, the military estimated that the window of opportunity was less than fifteen minutes. We eventually got wind it had made it to the United Kingdom, but by then nobody was listening anymore. I tell you, if we'd been first at the scene, we'd have done the same I guess."

I couldn't help laughing at the misfortune of the Americans. It was hard to imagine that something as large as an alien spacecraft could simply be picked up and shipped off. It crossed my mind that maybe they could've flown the thing out of there, but that was a big assumption.

"Can I see it?" I asked after a moment.

"Maybe one day, but we've yet to gain clearance." Thacker sniffed. "Even I've not been granted access. It's not like we'll steal it back."

"Would you?" Thacker grinned at my question.

"A challenge, for sure," he said. "But no, we've got to play fair, there is too much at stake, politically, for both SARA and America." I couldn't believe that something so vital to our understanding of our place in the universe and order of things was being blocked. Surely the UK Space Agency would share research information, it was a tragic loss if they were unwilling to do this. Maybe that was the reason SARA chose England for their facility, to get closer, build up trust.

Then it struck me, I *had* heard about the construction of the facility before. "SARA took what was meant to be the new home of the UK Space Agency."

"Of course, your government was compensated for the use of the facility. They were reluctant to join us though, although I'm optimistic that if all goes well with our mission, we might be able to form a greater alliance with all other international space agencies. I believe we are stronger together. And if my predictions are correct, we'll need all the help we can get." Thacker didn't expand on that point, and before I had chance to question him further a turbulent jolt made me push back into my seat and look through the window.

We'd flown through the worst of the storm, much of the flashing came from behind the wings of the aircraft, lighting up the sky. My stomach eased and finally I relaxed my grip.

3

There was a milder heat in Eritrea than I'd expected for mid-September, maybe pushing towards thirty degrees, but as the helicopter climbed the temperature plummeted and I shivered. It was a long ride from the airport at Asmara to the Rora Habab mountains and plateau, so I whiled away the time watching the rugged verdant landscapes turn from wild plains to the harsh desolation of desert and back again. A herd of gazelles roamed across the wilderness, grazing where they could.

The helicopter descended into dense mountainous forest, dropping into a saddle between two peaks, tall leafy Acacia trees sprung up around us.

"I didn't think Eritrea was renowned for its forestry?" I panicked, checking each side of the craft to make sure we had clearance, knowing that helicopters didn't respond well to treacherous landscapes.

Thacker chuckled, "it's an unusual terrain for Africa."

We hit the ground with a bounce. By the time I'd gathered myself together the pilot had already switched the engine off and slowly the whooping of the rotor blades died away.

"So why exactly are we here?" I asked as Thacker opened the door and jumped out. As I got out I peered over the sheer drop off to one side, way too close for my liking. "You didn't need to go to all this trouble and expense, just to bring me out to the middle of nowhere."

Thacker's lips twitched with a curious smile, his eyes electric and full of renewed energy which flowed into his voice as he spoke, "We're home, don't you smell it?"

I sniffed the arid air. I could taste the sweetness of the lush green surroundings, and yet there was a familiar scent to it that reminded me of ancient dwellings, dank and musty in equal measure. I saw what he meant, I felt somehow this *was* my home.

"This place is more sacred than the birthplace of Jesus."

"What am I meant to see?" I asked looking around into the dense woods, confused.

"Dozens of ancient archaeological sites have been found all across this region, some documented as the earliest human activity." Thacker explained, already on the move along a small dirt path barely big enough for one man let alone two. I hesitated for a moment, unsure of my surroundings, and then I darted after him. If there were snakes out here, I didn't want to be left alone to fend them off. "There is a network of cave systems carved out below our feet, we believe they were inhabited by the *first* humans."

"And you think this site is somehow connected to our dreams?"

"No," Thacker stopped and turned to me. "We *know* it is."

"How?" I asked but Thacker was on the move again and I had to jog to catch him and his long strides up.

The ground beneath us began a sharp descent into a deep ravine. I heard the unmistakable thundering of water cascading from a great height and as we dropped down I gasped to catch my breath as I chased Thacker. The waterfall plummeted from an overhang, dropping thirty metres into the valley below, and even from our distance I could feel the spray saturating the air.

"We're close to the source of the Barka river," Thacker explained from a few paces below. "It's rained here in the last few days so the cave entrance might be trickier than usual."

"That's a lot of rain," I said admiring the torrent roaring into the depths, out of my sight. I stood a moment longer before shivering in the chilled air and then made my way down to Thacker. The path ended abruptly at a cliff edge. I felt dizzy looking down into the abyss of the sheer drop off.

"Do you see that darkness over there?" Thacker yelled over the deafening roar. I followed his finger, tracing it across the wet jagged rocks until I saw the dark shadow. If I'd been on my own I'd have easily mistaken it for another rock formation. "The first chamber is slightly flooded so we'll need to wade through."

"Are you crazy? It doesn't look safe down there."

Thacker's laugh was lost to the water.

4

The track down made gentle work compared to the vertical drop at the top of the cliff face. At first it wound tightly away from the raging torrent of fresh rainwater, but as we drew to the bottom it burst out at the shore of the river, seven metres from the cave entrance. From here I could see it clearly.

"Is there much of this?" I jerked my thumb towards the water. I didn't fancy being wet, already clammy from the cool spray.

"No," Thacker said. "Once we push through the antechamber we'll be moving up into the hills. The site is roughly twenty minutes' walk back the way we came."

"This better be worth it," I said before pulling my shoes and socks off, rolling my trouser leg up to the knee and wading into the water; it wasn't as cold as it looked. Thacker followed. Soon I stood in the entrance of the darkened cave, peering into the abyss.

"Here," Thacker handed me a small pocket torch. "There is more equipment inside the next chamber." I shone the light around the cavern, illuminating mineral deposits on the low ceiling. Cloudy droplets ran along the stalactites, plopping to the fresh water beneath. There was just enough room to crawl. Straight ahead I saw a clear end to the antechamber, distinguishable by a set of carvings in the bedrock, the torch light bringing them to life, three haunting human faces stared back at me and I jumped.

"What is this place?"

"The birthplace of humanity," Thacker said nudging me forwards, the water was getting colder against my legs. We waded towards the faces, their eyes watching us. I reached out, touching the smooth rock. "They're Egyptian."

"Egyptian?" I frowned. "What were the Egyptians doing out here?"

A voice whispered in the darkness, "they were searching for the land of their Gods'." Another face floated into the beam of the torchlight and I stumbled backwards, dropping into the lukewarm water. I heard insane uncontrollable laughter.

"I told you last time, stop doing that," Thacker growled, the chuckling continued. The torch was lost somewhere in the water, dimly casting aspersions on the muddy rocks beneath. Thacker's hand appeared in front of my face, helping me to my feet. "You'll have to excuse him."

"Aren't you going to introduce us?" The other voice asked as I flapped away some of the excess water.

"Mark, this is Charlie McKenzie," Thacker said. "He's the linguist that decoded this site."

"And Anthropologist," Charlie threw in.

"He's a prick," I said pushing past Charlie's outstretched hand and moved into the darkness of the chamber beyond.

5

A faint musty smell filled the air, stale urine from sheltering animals perhaps. In the pitch-black I stumbled, dragging my damp shoes over a loose rock; I tripped and scrabbled to maintain balance.

"You won't get far without more light," Charlie spoke from behind, his voice rising in the darkness – it was his thinly veiled Welsh accent that gave him away – before a brilliant beam flashed in my direction, catching my eyes and I stopped, blinded. Charlie grinned at me.

I ripped the torch from his hand and started the climb along the steep tunnel, rising fast.

"So…what's he told you about this place?" Charlie remained chipper despite Thacker's scolding, it seemed like he was used to it. I stopped and turned to face him, scowling. "Not much? He was the same when he approached me. I've been working down here for close to six years now."

"You need to get out more," I said. "And will you stop shining that bloody thing in my face," I snapped, shielding my eyes from the intense beam of his flash light. As Charlie lowered it I caught sight of the paintings on the rock. I studied them, recognisable creatures depicted in action. A man seeming to ride on the back of a horned animal while other men chased a calf with their bow and arrows drawn. I had seen pictures like this before, but they were nothing compared to the bright contrast of the red ochre paint against the soft hue of the terracotta mudbrick. "They're untouched."

"Rainwater is channelled off through a network of underground rivers running for kilometres beneath the plateau," Charlie said. "These here are the latest paintings in these systems, they run all the way through this place. The deeper inside we go, the earlier they get."

I mulled this over for a moment. I'd seen Cave Art before. They were pretty old, an art form lost in ancient ancestry. If these were the last things painted in here, what lay further ahead?

"How old?" I asked reaching out to touch them but stopping short.

"These ones are around two thousand years old." Charlie watched me, smiling all the while. "As we get closer to the central chamber you'll see that some of the paintings have been overpainted. It gives us a chronology of the people that occupied the site, and those that have come back here before us. The rock art on the outer wall of the temple has been dated perhaps as old as one-to-two million years, dependent upon which dating technique you use."

"Two million years?" I let out a puff of air, winded. "That's incredible."

"It makes them the earliest known cave paintings ever discovered, without a shadow of a doubt." Thacker's voice came from behind. "It's an unpredicted development in our understanding of human history; this really is the cradle of our civilisation." I looked back at the depiction of the man riding the horned animal, overwhelmed by the seemingly incredulous facts being dished out like chocolates at Halloween. I shook my head, dumbstruck, before continuing deeper into the web of tunnels.

"This one is a perfect example of what I was talking about," Charlie said shining his torch against the wall, lighting up etchings on the cave. After our crude introduction I was starting to warm to Charlie. I got the feeling he was a joker, harmless and a little annoying at times. “You can still see a trace of the painting underneath.” His finger followed a faded line across the wall, drawing a man with a spear, sparse colour still visible. “The original painting is harder to date but given the phased order of this system we’re roughly at around two and a half thousand years.”

“It’s Egyptian again.” I recognised the styles.

“Anubis,” Charlie said. “The God of the underworld, you can clearly see the head of a jackal here and his human legs here,” he pointed at the faded paint as I squinted, trying to make out the figures. “He’s preparing the body to take it into the afterlife with him. Look here,” he pointed to the wall opposite.

I looked at the image, it was clearly a bearded man and a distinct feathered pattern behind him. I immediately knew it wasn’t Egyptian, the style was different even if the crude colourings were the same. “Who is that? This is a different style.”

“You’re right,” Charlie said. “This is Anu in Akkadian, although I prefer the Sumerian translation of An. It is said that when time began, the heavens became separated from the Earth and An took up residence there. He became the overlord of the other God’s, bestowing power upon them. It some texts he is credited with creating the universe, although there are different accounts of this of course.”

“Why is this here?” I asked, perplexed by the juxtaposition of the different periods of history.

“From historical records the Egyptians kept, we know they traded with the Land of Punt or *Ta Netjer*, meaning ‘the land of the Gods’. Their records tell us much about the trade deals themselves but it’s always been a mystery where Punt was. The first mention of Punt lands date to around two-thousand-five-hundred BCE – Before Common Era – let’s leave religion out of this, right?” He turned to Thacker, grinning. "From piecing history together, we know that Punt lies in this region, somewhere between modern-day Eritrea and Ethiopia, but no clear archaeological evidence has ever been found."

"That was before we found this place," Thacker added.

"We still don't know that for certain," Charlie shook his head and then turned to me. "In the east of Punt we would expect to find a temple in honour of the Egyptian Sun God, Ra, ours is the only Puntite site that has this vital place of worship and makes this the most likely candidate. This site links different peoples from different regions – the Egyptians, the Sumerian's, the Akkadian's and the Babylonians. They are all here, together."

"This place is unique. It's our history encapsulated in these very walls," Thacker said.

"And then of course there are the scriptures..." Charlie trailed off.

"Scriptures?" I asked.

"You haven't told him about the texts?" Charlie turned to Thacker. "How the hell did you get him out here without mentioning them? They are the most important piece of the puzzle." Charlie shook his head in disgust as he walked on into the darkness of the cave, for a moment I glared at Thacker before following after Charlie.

6

Warm lucent sunlight filled the temple chamber, pouring in through a series of small holes running in concentric circles in the roof of the rock, ten metres above. It was a stark contrast to the darkened tunnels and I blinked.

I peered at the bright walls, stucco white, plastered across this were fresh vibrant cave paintings. I followed the outside wall of the chamber, studying the depicted scenes.

“They look…new,” I said with disbelief. I looked across at Charlie, seeing him for the first time in proper light, he was about my age. He scratched his head before brushing his unkempt blond hair out of his face, and a small fragment of rock dropped to the floor.

“The archaeological team suspected that these images were painted later because of their pristine condition,” he said with a shake of his head. “But they were wrong, as ever – the radioactive dating confirms it. Most of their rule book got torn up while they were working here.” Charlie moved to me and pointed at the image I was studying. “We think this is what *they* might have looked like.”

“Who?” I examined the painting closer. A bald man stood with his arms open to the sky, before him there were many others, it looked like they were listening to him. As my eyes focused on the image, I felt I could see the people swaying before this one man, a leader perhaps.

“The very first humans,” Charlie said. “Come,” he motioned, leading me to the entrance of the temple. The faint flicker of a burning torch inside lit my way as I stepped through. The overpowering and unmistakeable odour of burning incense filled my nostrils, but before I could say anything it had gone as had the fire.

It was a single sprawling room inside, the ceiling low. A chimney towered in the centre of the room, the burning fire lighting the heavy rock construction. I peered at the walls, they were filled with wedge shaped symbols.

“This is the scripture,” Charlie said, a proud smile sitting on his lips.

I admired the ancient writing imprinted into the solid walls of the temple. Who had done this? An image sparked into my mind, a boy lost in the darkness. I reached out, my fingers tracing the characters of a panel through the air. I felt like I knew this, like I’d seen these texts before.

I fingered a character gently, feeling the coolness of the stone and a spark bolted through my mind pulsing through my body, the name Russia thundered all around me. The image of the boy appeared before me, but he was no longer in the dark. He stood with the flames of the fire bouncing off his skinhead, a cloak wrapped around his shoulders, his face blackened with dirt.

My mouth dropped open.

"I know who wrote this," I said glancing back at Charlie and then at Thacker. Neither seemed moved by this, which struck me as odd, but I was too agitated to worry about that. "I wrote this...I mean Russia did."

Thacker allowed a wry smile to develop and it became clear he'd known that all along.

"Thank you, Charlie, we've found our man." Thacker said, his hands coming together, his smile dancing in the flickering light. An excited grin spread across Charlie's face as Thacker turned to me. "I can help you remember so much more."

7

"Can you feel it?" Thacker asked.

Looking at the vivid coloured images painted on the chamber walls, knowing they were by the hands of my ancestors. I could feel them all around me, living in me, whispering quietly.

"Deep in the hidden recesses of our DNA, we store memories of our ancestors, telling us who they were, what they were like and so on," Thacker explained, his hand waving in the air. "As we reproduce, passing on our genetic code to the next generation, these memories become forgotten, diluted by the other parent's own memories." I frowned, retracing his logical steps. “Eventually these memories are so obscured by a genetic sludge that they can no longer be accessed. But are they still there?”

“Of course,” I said. “If I bury a penny in the sand somewhere it will still be there in the morning.”

“Unless someone sweeps the beach,” Charlie chuckled, Thacker shook his head. “But you’d still remember putting it there.”

“So you accept that it’s plausible?” Thacker checked. “We could recover these memories somehow.”

“I didn’t say that,” I said. “I forget stuff on a daily basis.”

“True.” Thacker sniffed. “But the stuff I am talking about can’t be forgotten. It’s not just a memory, it’s a genetic imprint of the person you used to be. If you could access that you could recreate the essence of that person.”

“Is that what is happening to me?” I asked. “Is that why I am remembering Russia?”

“Exactly.”

“So why did I... Russia write all this?” I peered at the symbols on the wall.

“It’s the original Bible,” Charlie said. “It’s a permanent record of events, something that would remind humanity of its humble beginnings. Stories that could be passed on to future generations. This is our untold history.”

“But I can’t understand it.” I frowned at the wedges that made up each individual character. “I wouldn’t even know where to begin. If the genetic memory of Russia is in my DNA, why can’t I understand this?”

“You simply don’t remember.”

“And that’s where my expertise comes in,” Charlie said triumphant. “I’ve devoted my life to bringing ancient languages back from the dead so that we can understand our past, but I don’t just study any kind of texts. I’m specifically interested in the ones we’d class as religious. I translated a script in Egypt which mentioned a temple in this region and that's how I ended up down here. There were local tales of found artefacts – bones, hand axes, the usual sort of things – but I never expected to find something as ancient as this."

"How old?" I asked.

"Just over two-and-a-half million years." He said in a matter of fact voice. Even though I'd already been informed about some of the stages of development of the site, it was still hard to digest and I sucked in my breath. "That's the Lower Palaeolithic era if you're interested, around the time of *Homo habilis* according to our fossil records."

"But what about the apes?" I asked. "We evolved from them, didn't we?"

"We evolved, yes. But to understand our path through life, you must separate it from the evolution of Earth and the creatures that lived here." I frowned. "These scriptures give us that power, that vital point of view to split the two." My brow creased further, confused by the contradiction in my mind. Everyone knew we descended from apes or at least shared a common ancestor, didn't they? "The fossil records on Earth are incomplete, so paleoanthropologists have tried to bridge this gap by making assumptions, which in context makes sense. But if you throw in what we now know, it is clear that apes were evolving, just not into the hominid form."

I struggled to understand and filed the thought for later.

"How is this connected to my dreams?" I looked to Thacker. "You showed me pictures of a ziggurat on the lunar surface. What has that got to do with any of this?"

"The scriptures tell us that human life *arrived* here," Charlie said. "They tell us that human life here on Earth did not happen because of evolution. We were sent here from another world, the civilisation you have dreamt, they came from our own moon."

I remembered the image of a large stone sarcophagus,

shimmering with light, "we travelled through some kind of portal." The words fell from my mouth before I had chance to understand what I was saying.

"Our best understanding is that through the ages we've tried to keep these memories alive. Take the Egyptians for instance, knowing what we now know we can cast a new interpretation on the pyramids of Giza. What if they were trying to recreate the past so that we never forgot our humble beginnings."

"You've translated the scriptures?" I asked, Charlie's eye lit up, enthused. "Do we know how the moon was capable of supporting life?" Charlie rapped his fingers gently on the rock, a knowing smile illuminating his face. "Okay," I groaned, the mountain of information creaking above me. Understanding what the scriptures said would have to wait for a while. "I've seen and heard enough."

"Time's up anyway, we'd better head back," Thacker spoke from behind. "Our flight will be waiting and it gets chilly out here at night."

Sitting in the comfort of the leather seat, the plane journey home gave me plenty of time to reflect on everything I'd seen and heard. I had come in search of some answers, but now I only had more questions, just as Thacker had promised.

What happened to the moon people, and why had they travelled here to Earth? Why did Thacker want me and my memories of Russia? Surely, he didn't need my memories for his Constellation mission as he'd suggested?

Charlie was snoring gently in the seat next to me, I leaned across him towards Thacker.

"The images of the moon you showed me were incomplete," I said. "What happened to the obelisk?" I caught his gaze and saw green fires raging behind his eyes. I saw the tumbling mudbrick blocks in my mind and as the last one fell, I understood. "That was our life support wasn't it?"

"Alien technology," Thacker said. "That's all we ever were up there..."

I couldn't help wondering, "Are you suggesting we were created?" The hairs on the back of my neck prickled.

"Precisely," Thacker said.

I didn't understand. Even if I accepted the notion that human life was created by some alien creators, why would they have gone to the trouble of creating a sanctuary on the moon for us, transforming an uninhabitable satellite and sustaining our lives – only to then rip it away from us – and all in the shadow of a perfect and inhabitable planet right next door? Nothing made sense anymore.

"I'm sure I'll come to regret this," I said. "I've made my decision, I'm in."

"Good," Thacker said. "Now get some rest." A triumphant look upon his face before adding, "You're going to need it."

CHAPTER 7

"Say that again." I leaned forwards, causing my seatbelt to tighten across my shoulder. Charlie turned in his seat to face me head on, there was frustration in his eyes.

"Okay, okay," he said with a wave of his hand. "Cuneiform is not a language itself, it's a writing system. The characters written inside the temple use cuneiform."

"So what language *are* they written in?"

"Ah, now *that* is interesting." Charlie's frustration evaporated, replaced by a crooked smile; this was *his* territory. Thacker was silent, his legs crossed, arms folded, body facing the door, the world flying past his window as our chauffeur driven car sped along the motorway. I guessed he'd heard it all before.

"The earliest evidence for written language is dated to around three-thousand-one-hundred BCE," Charlie said. "That language is Sumerian and it utilises the cuneiform writing system. What makes Sumerian special is that it's *not* related to any other known language. It either materialised in isolation, or its linguistic relatives died out before they were written down."

"So that's what I saw in the temple?" I remembered the wedge-shaped characters sprawled across every inch of the brightly painted stuccoed walls. The scent of ancient ash filled my nostrils and I coughed.

"Our site proves that modern thinking is, once again, wrong." Charlie's animated hands pointed at me, a silent accusation. It wasn't my fault, I barely even knew what he was talking about. "The scriptures are written in an form of Sumerian Cuneiform, perhaps the original form." He grinned at me.

"And they are two-and-a-half million years old?"

"Yes." Charlie's head bobbed back and forth. "Just like the Egyptians recording their trade in the Land of Punt, the Sumerians documented a place called Dilmun – the place where the sun rises. Although we can't prove it, we have clear evidence to assume that both Dilmun and Punt are in fact the same place, the same trading partners."

"You think they passed on language?" I understood the implications of what he was saying. If the Sumerians were in contact with the temple occupation, they may have traded in more than just physical goods.

"It's so much more than that." Charlie shook his head. "Most cultures – and yes I include religion as a culture – have borrowed from their predecessors. It's historically inaccurate to take, for example, the Bible at face value if you consider that any number of those stories have appeared in other religions – other cultures – around the world."

"How do you mean?" It was all new to me.

"We've spent the last twenty years ramming it home to people to recycle," Charlie explained. "But that's not a new concept. Throughout history, stories have been recycled. For instance, Noah and the Great Flood, it's a universal myth not just a story in the Old Testament. Then there are the creationist tales, you know God created the world, and everything within it, in 7 days..."

Thacker muttered something to himself, his breath misting up the window for a second, but Charlie was relentless.

"The Seminole, a Native American tribe from Florida, have a similar story, the Grandfather of the world created all the animals and sealed them inside a shell telling them to come out when the time was right. The Bakuba people of Africa believed a Mbombo snake-god ruled the Earth. One day he vomited the sun, moon and stars. When the sun had evaporated the seas and created dry land the snake-God threw up the first people." Thacker shook his head, flaming red cheeks indicated it was time to stop, but Charlie didn't notice or simply didn't care. "There is also Ishtar or Inanna, from my studies they have the same source, the mythical first woman. Guess what, she's in our scriptures too. My point is this: reading the myths and stories side by side, stripping all the extraneous details, they all boil down to the same things. By some divine act, life began. I'd stake my life that these stories all came from the same source."

"The scriptures," I said, more than guessing.

"Exactly." Charlie was grinning again. "Not just the first written language, but the language of the first people, a primordial text."

"But why would we do that?" I frowned. "Why go to the trouble of building the temple and filling it with these words. What was the purpose?"

"They act as a constant reminder of our heritage, but it's more than that." Charlie leaned closer, a dangerous look in his eyes, his face stern in front of mine. "The scriptures act as a warning, they tell us of our Creator's destructive force and that one day the world will end, if we let it..."

"The scriptures are incomplete," Thacker stiffened as he turned in his seat. "There are details missing, things that may have seemed unimportant at the time, but now could be vital."

"Is that what you are hoping to find? Is that the purpose of the *Constellation* programme?" My head filled in the missing link. "I need to know what I'm getting myself into, so I just have one final question...why now?"

"Don't you feel its stifling presence?" Thacker asked leaning forwards in his seat. "There is a blanket of darkness smothering the very air we breathe and it's getting closer." As I sat listening to the dull background roar of the moving vehicle, I thought I could feel it, whatever *it* was. "*They* are coming back for us."

"Who?" I shuddered. "What the hell are you talking about, *they* are coming back for us?"

"The alien race that brought us to life." Thacker's voice black. "They are coming back to destroy us."

"I don't understand? Why would they come back to destroy us?" I still found it difficult to swallow the theory that we were created by some mythical alien creatures, but there seemed no reason to believe they would destroy us.

"As I said, the scriptures are incomplete." Thacker flashed a smile. "But you can see it for yourself if you want to, just as I did."

2

"What is this?" I ran my fingers over the intricate design, feelings small dimples across its smooth surface, imperfections perhaps. The silvery-blue hunk of metal clung to the corridor wall inside the SARA building, there were more of them farther along. "Is it meant to be art?" That made Thacker chuckle.

"Our boys recovered them from downed alien craft," Thacker said, still amused by my ignorance. "They don't appear to do anything." I studied his expression for a moment, a question looming on my lips.

"Did the military shoot *them* down?" Thacker didn't answer, but he didn't need to, I saw the answer pressed upon his lips. I shuddered, it was clichéd I thought, but maybe the movies were true.

Thacker led me away from the strange alien objects and into the secure basement area. There were hundreds of metal cabinets set out in rows, back to back, each one numbered.

He stopped half way along, slid open a drawer and pulled out a small gleaming metal box which he placed onto a steel work surface. Thacker fumbled with the keys until he found the right one and unlocked it. The lid released.

The rock inside glistened in the light, the smooth surface reflecting brilliant green rays that created an eerie glow inside its container. It looked like jade, but it somehow seemed alive, glowing almost.

"Your father gave it to me," Thacker said. "Your grandfather recovered it from the Roswell crash site. Leon told me your grandfather was afraid of the rock, he thought it was a divine force that humankind shouldn't toy with." He looked at me as if he expected me to be scared. I wasn't. "Thanks to the scriptures we know what this is, and Joseph was right to keep it hidden. This rock is a source of power, but it is much more than that."

"What kind of power?" I asked. "Destructive?"

"Could be," Thacker said. "There is a passage in the scriptures which mentions the flowing rivers of the sacred, from which all life came. There is another section which mentions the same waters reclaiming life, reabsorbing it."

"I've seen the river in my dreams." I looked to Thacker and then back to the green lump sparkling under the strip lighting. "But this is just a rock."

"It's more than a lump of shiny green stone," Thacker

said. "It's a living, breathing entity in its own right. It's alive now, brimming with energy. This rock *is* the same as the river you've seen. Because of its strange and unique properties, the geologists created a new classification called Jeometamorphic – as jade is a kind of metamorphic rock they thought it would be somehow amusing. Some of the lab technicians have taken to calling it J-Power which I think is a bit too immature."

"Where did it come from? I mean how did it get up there." I pointed upwards, referring to the moon. "I mean..." I trailed off.

"Like I said, the scriptures are incomplete. But we do know that the lunar civilisation drank from the river and therefore the power of the Creator – the divine or whatever you wish to call it – was within them all, part of their blood, their DNA."

I could see where Thacker was going, my eyes were drawn to the rock, fixated by the luminescent green glow. Something about it felt familiar and called out to me. I noticed my hand twitch as I reached out to it – a tingling feeling grew in my belly as my hand approached and then withdrew.

"I can feel it." My heart fluttered, like thousands of tiny fingers prodding at me. My mouth was dry, a heavy sweetness lingered on my tongue.

"I did too," Thacker smiled. "The energy is so strong that even just this small piece of rock was enough to haul a large chunk of my genetic memory out of the sludge; it reconnected me to my past. This is how I know some of the other details that the scriptures cannot tell us. Even so, it is only my perspective, my former genetic self." My eyes remained fixed, my hands wanting to take hold of the Jeometamorphic rock. "I believe our bodies remember the flowing energy of the rock and it is this power that can help you remember so much more."

Lurking inside of me, I knew there was a genetic memory of a little boy who had a country for his name; Russia. I felt him restless, wriggling and squirming, wanting to be connected back to the life-force of the mysterious green rock. Who was I to deny him that?

"I've seen a woman in my dreams," I said. "I called her master, I feel I should know her...I wish to remember her." Without thinking I reached out and took hold of the sparkling rock, lifting it from its foam padding.

My breath caught in my throat as my body surged with tingling energy, the rock burnt in my bare hands but I did not let it go – no, I couldn't let it go. A brilliant green light filled my vision and I had the strangest sensation that my eyes had rolled into the back of my head.

3

The air throbbed with pulsing energy, alive. Sparkling flecks of white light hummed and whistling as they zipped and zoomed across my vision. I could smell stale air as the rock released forgotten memories.

An image flashed before me.

There she was, a pale woman hanging from a grimy chamber wall.

The rock dropped from my hands and my eyes opened. Thacker was smiling at me.

"What did you see?"

I couldn't answer, my body still under the influence of the rock, commanding me to take hold of it once again. I grabbed it, squeezing it tight. It felt glorious, but violent as it shattered through generations of burial, digging down into the hidden depths of my genetic code.

Sorrow. The woman I'd previously seen in my dreams

was hanging by glowing green restraints around her wrists, arms outstretched, body pinned to the sweat-soaked chamber wall. There was a dark angry gash on her side, piercing through her rib cage. Dried blood clung to her wounds, soaking the linen loincloth tied around her waist. There was a deep pain in her eyes, a thundercloud of unrealised rage and fury, undesirable emotions for a Magi.

I felt her pain. The foul stench of rotting flesh cloyed at my nostrils, but I fought the urge to leave and breathe fresh air once again.

I peered through the bars of her cell, angry, the dark purple welts across her face and chest summarising my mood. This was *our* Magi, the mother of our people, she did not deserve this barbaric cruelty. She had lived her life in the tradition of the Magi, she had never once broken their rules unlike so many that came before her. She never succumbed to the forbidden emotions. Most of all, she took care of me, nurturing me as only mothers can, bringing me up as her own even though we were not related. Magi did not have children of their own, she had told me, they must remain celibate, committed to their duty.

I remembered the stories she'd told me sitting in the comfort of her bosom. Magi must be strong but gentle, courageous and just. They must rid themselves of anger, bask themselves in love, and harmony and be at one with nature. Magi were peacekeepers and had a duty to appreciate what the Gods had given them and show others the way. These were the teachings of the Magi.

The dried bitter tears I'd wept stained my cheeks. My hands reached out, helpless, I could do nothing to assist her. She'd warned me this was how it would end, but I hadn't accepted it. Seeing her hanging before me, I felt ashamed. I should have listened, she'd never let me down before. It was too late to change things now.

The woman I called my mother shouted something, the

usual calm tone replaced with bitterness. I did not understand, but Russia did and for the first time I followed what was happening. I was seeing everything through his eyes, hearing his thoughts and feeling what he felt.

"You traitor!" For a moment I thought she was talking to Russia, but the shuffling feet behind us suggested otherwise. I felt hatred for the approaching man, he'd imprisoned our mother. "Not only have you betrayed me, but you are destroying my people. My son, I promise you, your treachery shall haunt you, in this life and the next. My people will never let you forget."

"Come now mother." A voice hissed from behind. "We both know you brought this shame upon yourself. You abused your power as our Magi. If it had not been me, it would have been another. There is nothing but compassion in my heart for you, my actions are born out of my love for you. Is it not better this way?" For a moment I felt sympathy in his voice, but Russia told me it was a lie, none of his words were to be trusted, but I didn't fully understand why.

"I give you three days!" Our mother boomed. "That is all I give you. You have chosen to destroy me, and I promise you, your world will be crushed into the sands, removing from you what you have stolen from me and teaching you the lessons you have refused to learn. Three days and the balance shall be restored." A shrill laugh erupted behind me and I shivered, but I could not turn, didn't want to see his foul, vengeful face.

The laughter died as the door behind slammed closed, rattling the bars of the cell. I peered up at my mother, her head limp, the ferocity of her voice gone, her body filthy from the dust of her mistreatment.

Her name finally came to me.

"Magi Eritrea," I whispered. She looked down at me and even through her obvious anguish, she afforded me a smile. "What have we done to you, mother." There was heavy sadness in her eyes and I wished there was some way I could help share her burden. There wasn't.

"My son, I will *always* be with you," she said. "No matter what happens you must keep the name of your Magi alive. Tell the others my story, never stop. Do this to remember me."

I promised myself I would never let my mother down. Her name would be remembered, I would make sure of it.

4

Even with the jade green rock secured in its box, I still felt the throbbing of its unique power loose in my body, pulsating inside of me. Sweat dropped from my forehead, running down the end of my nose and onto my shirt.

I felt breathless but alive, adrenaline still rushing through my veins.

Thacker remained silent, studying me with questioning eyes, a slight grin fixed upon his face. I could tell he was waiting for an explanation and I wondered if I had said something in the rock induced trance.

I finally caught my breath.

"I remember her," I said.

"Good." Thacker grinned at me. "What did you see?"

"I'm not sure." I lied. A sudden overpowering sense of mistrust washed over me. Perhaps it was the impossibility of what I'd seen or heard. "I saw Magi Eritrea, chained. Why does everyone seem to be named after countries?"

"It's the other way around," Thacker laughed. "What are the chances we found the temple in Eritrea? It wasn't even called Eritrea until twenty-seven years ago, isn't that brilliant, like somehow we always knew what we should call that country?"

It was, I thought. Russia had kept his promise to remember his mother.

"Is that all you saw?" Thacker asked, curious. I shook my head. My vision had felt so real, but now doubt and reason set in. "I'm sure in time you will learn to trust your memories." I frowned. Did he know what I was feeling? Was it that obvious?

"What makes you so sure I can help you?" I changed the subject. It was the same question I'd asked over an over since meeting Thacker: why me?

"Everything we know, *everything* we have seen. All of it, absolutely every speck of it came from your hands," Thacker said. "Whatever happened to our ancestors on this lunar world, you are inextricably linked to it. If we want to understand who we are and what happened up there, you are the best place to start."

"You want me to go to the moon, don't you?" I asked bluntly. Thacker flashed his teeth as he sneered. "But I'm not qualified and besides it could take years to train me. Why don't you send an accomplished astronaut? I could help from the ground..."

"No," Thacker interrupted, his voice firm. "It has to be this way. *You* must go."

"Why?" I asked.

"There is something in the scriptures," he said. "Before the final day, we shall return to the beginning." Thacker spoke with power, his voice full of determined strength. "*You* wrote that."

I shuddered at my ancestor's haunting prophecy.

CHAPTER 8

Satisfied, I drove home through the pelting rain to collect my things.

After years of unanswered questions, I finally had something to explain my dreams, however far-fetched it seemed, each part more impossible to believe than the next. There was the temple dating back millions of years; the existence of humankind on another world; the fact that we didn't share a common ancestor with apes; that we *were* created, although not by divine intervention as religion would have us believe.

My body was exhausted, my mind frazzled by the daunting task ahead. Even with the power of the rock still tingling inside of me, I couldn't keep my eyes open. If it hadn't been for my mobile phone sparking to life, I'm sure I'd have fallen asleep.

"Hello?" I yawned, answering it on hands free.

"Thank God!" It was my mother, she sounded relieved. "I've been trying to get hold of you for the last two days."

"Is something wrong?" I yawned again before blasting the fan, cold on my face.

"I wanted to check you were okay. You are okay, aren't you?"

"Yes mum," I said. It was nice to know she cared. The wounds of the past were healing. "I'm fine. How are you?"

"Coping," was all she said, but the flicker of pain in her voice told me more than she ever would. I respected her wishes, but that didn't stop this hurting.

We said our goodbyes before she hung up.

The instant I arrived home, I collapsed onto the sofa and closed my eyes. Brilliant sparkling green replaced the darkness behind my eyelids. Thacker had told me the rock was now working at a molecular level within my body, tracing my genetic memory, connecting the dots. Because the rock had once lived within me, it was now re-imprinting into my DNA, becoming part of me once again.

The glowing light didn't fade, even as I drifted to sleep.

My eyes opened into the dream world.

Magi Eritrea sat on the bank of the backward flowing river, the dark cloak I'd seen her wearing before replaced with a purple one. There was no hood, her face swathed in light for the first time, revealing her beauty. It was a stark contrast, I realised, picturing her chained to the wall of her cell, the matted tangle of hair now replaced with her warm flowing locks, the dried blood and brutal swellings replaced by her smooth olive skin. This was the real woman, before her mistreatment. She watched me, a mothering smile etched upon her face.

I took a seat next to her, staring across at the obelisk on the far side of the river.

We did not speak, but I felt there was no need for words.

I relaxed into the bliss of the tranquil world, watching the river ease along its strange course. The ziggurat offered little shade from the midday sun and as I peered up at it, I saw a fluttering butterfly drifting towards me. It hovered above my feet, its small wings stirring the sands with its effort.

With every beat, the ebbing sands revealed swathes of green, glowing beneath me. I leant forward. With a heavy flutter of its wings, the butterfly drifted towards Magi Eritrea, settling upon her shoulder as if they were equals.

I felt an ache in my chest, and I knew it was the jade green rock beneath me, urging me to hold it, to be one with it. My fingers reached out, tracing its outline beneath me, before pushing further sand aside to uncover it. Its shimmering surface glowed in the sunlight and I took it in my hands, gripping it tightly, feeling the surging force of its power as it rushed through my body. Lightning flashed before my eyes, blinding rays emanating from inside my cupped hands.

Magi Eritrea had a knowing look in her eyes, and gave an understanding nod of her head. It was time to allow the power of the rock to penetrate my soul. Thunder flowed through my temples like a headache but without the pain. My eyes slammed shut and I felt myself floating upwards. When my eyes finally opened I found myself soaring high above the world, spiralling into the darkness of space.

And then I saw it, a glimmer of light in the distance. Some kind of metallic giant zipped across the sky, an alien spacecraft hurtling towards me. Looking down at the planet I realised everything had gone, the ziggurat, the river, Magi Eritrea and the butterfly. I was alone in the midst of time. This was the beginning, the birth of a new world. The spinning craft dropped from the sky, plummeting to the depths of the sandy world below in a ball of fire.

Flames of green spat out in all directions, soaking into the ground of the fresh, untouched celestial body. The stench of death filled my nostrils, I saw no movement from the craft. A deep sense of sorrow stole across the surface of the world, and I felt like I'd witnessed the passing of a great spirit.

Bolts of hot molten earth rocketing into the sky, narrowly missing me as it whizzed past my face. I looked down at the deep gash that had erupted in the land, a flowing green river poured from the wound, snaking across the sands to form its new bed.

And as I watched on, I saw flashes of electric blue as the butterfly floated back down from the darkening sky. It drifted to the bank of the newly formed river and settled upon the sand. Another piece of hot earth zipped into the sky at full force, and as it hurtled back to the ground, I noticed an egg nestled inside it. Right before the rock hit the ground, smashing the egg, a bird escaping, flapping its wings for the first time.

I smiled, thankful I could witness these events. More explosions rang out, seeds falling from the sky for every kind of plant, eggs hatching for every kind of animal – even the mammals, to my surprise.

My eyes closed as an intense flash of white hot light engulfed everything. When my eyes sprang open I stared up at the dancing blue wings of the butterfly on Magi Eritrea's shoulder. The rock dropped from my hands.

I knew what I'd seen was as incomplete as the scriptures, but there was no doubt in my mind that in some form, I'd been a spectator at the birth of our civilisation – our creation if you will – but this was Russia's memory and that meant it was flawed. I reasoned that Russia hadn't been around at the beginning of time and therefore I'd remembered the myth handed down the generations to him. As ever, there is some truth to be found within a myth, but I didn't know how much I could believe. It was all too perfect, precisely told, a story passed on from mother to son, master to servant.

With an objective mind, I knew I'd have to view the myth with a certain amount of scepticism, but by no means would I disregard it. There was truth yet for me to find.

2

Thacker stood in the morning sun, a cigarette pushed between his fingers. As soon as he saw me, he gave a short wave before dropping the fag end to the gravel and stubbing it out with his foot. I pulled up next to him, and gathered myself together. Thacker helped carry my things inside and showed me to my living quarters.

"We'll be waiting for you in my office," Thacker said from the door. "Get yourself settled, take your time." He left without a further word.

It was a simple room, as clinical as most hotels – an ample bed, a basic bathroom and a static phone, which looked ancient, resting by the bedside. I dropped to the bed, I'd have to get used to the austere lifestyle, I'd be spending the next year staring at these four blank walls.

I set down the suitcase I'd packed in haste earlier that morning, I had no intention of unpacking it now. Instead I rolled over and relaxed into the bed, allowing my eyes to close.

My head bobbed and I realised I was in danger of snoozing. I sat up with a sharp intake of breath and pushed myself off the bed. I retraced my steps, steering myself to Thacker's office. The door was slightly ajar.

I raised my knuckles and paused. I heard the irate voice of a Texan – which I thought I recognised. "He may be here now, but you'll need more than luck on your side to pull this one off." I presumed he was referring to me. "We have a pool of better qualified astronauts at our disposal. It's ridiculous." I felt I should be insulted, but then this was not news to me, reflecting my precise feelings and some of my actual words.

"I'm telling you Roger, he's the one. I know it." Thacker's voice.

The jigsaw pieces clicked into place, and I saw the image of Roger Bates as I'd seen him at the televised press conference. I remembered he was – or used to be – the Administrator for NASA. The way Thacker dominated the conversation, I gathered Bates had been demoted and he sounded pretty pissed off about it.

"So you keep saying, but you *don't* know that!" Bates's frustration was clear. I was about to knock again when I stopped myself, the tension was seeping from the room. I'd never get a better chance to see Thacker in his true colours – behind the shield of his door. "I've seen your work, I know what you're about. You have a total lack of self-control and a complete disregard for the law."

"I get things done." Thacker snorted in anger. "You've seen the pages from his notebooks?" A wave of anger washed over me, but I held my ground, even if they were talking about me, it wasn't about my ego.

"That's something else, how did you get them?" Bates snapped. "If he didn't consent..." I caught my laughter before it escaped my throat. *Consent*, I doubted Thacker understood the meaning of the word.

"Don't worry about it, Beth took care of everything."

"Beth?" Bates's voice rose an octave. "Is there anything else I should know?"

"Trust me, everything's in hand."

"I don't," Bates said with a growl. "That's a problem. I don't care what kind of business you ran in the Air Force, but here we do things by the book."

"Of course you do." Thacker's voice was playful. "Indulge me. Tell me about *your* kind of business?" Bates said nothing. "Go on; tell me what *really* happened on the Apollo programme."

"That information is classified." I felt the full force of Bates's voice as his anger overflowed, a resounding thump as clenched fists hit wood. "I won't let you draw me into another of your games about the rights and wrong of the past."

I'd heard enough. My hand rapped against the door, interrupting the conversation.

Thacker stood when I stepped inside. Bates looked up, his cheeks flushed with ruddy colour, a pen top twiddling with unease in his fingers. After a moment he too got to his feet.

"This is..." Thacker began

"Roger Bates," I said, offering my hand. "I saw you on television." He took my hand with a firm grip, his hands clammy. When he released his grip, I felt like wiping my hand down my trousers to rid it of his sweat, but I thought better of it. I didn't want to create a bad impression. Instead I maintained a polite smile. "Nice to meet you."

"Likewise," Bates said, taking to his seat, the pen top once again bobbing nervously between his fingers. I remained standing even after Thacker sidled back into his leather chair. "Has Thacker given you enough information about our mission?" I remembered the device I'd been provided with, he'd said it contained all the data files I'd need. I'd not even looked at it yet. "I like to think all our personnel have everything they need, so please do tell me if there is something."

"Okay," I smiled, uncomfortable in the aftermath of their argument.

"Do you want to meet the team?" Thacker asked, leaning forwards across his desk, making to stand up.

“I’ll show you around,” Bates said, quick off the mark, the pen lid dropping to the desk. They really didn’t see eye to eye, that much was obvious. Turning to Thacker he said, “I’d like to get to know Mark a little better, besides, you’ve got enough to be getting on with.”

“Yes,” Thacker said, shuffling back in his seat. “There is always plenty to do.”

Bates couldn’t get out of Thacker’s office fast enough. The moment we were alone, I felt him relax, his frown vanished and a natural smile appeared on his lips.

“Don’t let him push you around,” Bates said as we moved through the corridor, passing a handful of the strange silvery-metallic objects which hung like art along the walls. “There used to be an old RAF base here, you know.”

“I thought it looked like a prison,” I said. He chuckled.

We turned a corridor and came to a set of double doors, he swiped us through.

“This is TICC –Terrestrial Inter-communications Control Centre,” he said, holding the door open, a prideful smile resting upon his face. “This will be the nerve centre of the operation.” I peered across at the banks of desks arranged in a semi-circle. Everything faced the central screens of which there were three. The equipment looked new and expensive.

I stepped inside, it was almost empty.

At one end of the room I saw a few people busy, one was reading from a print-out while another sat tapping away at a computer terminal, all wore casual clothing. So far, I hadn’t seen anyone in anything that resembled a uniform. As I looked to the next person my eyes caught those of someone I knew, it was Beth.

My heart jumped, seeing her face and then it sank. I let out a sigh.

“Ah,” Bates shook his head, following my gaze. “I must apologise for my colleague’s bullish tactics.” He sounded sincere. "I hope you won't find things too uncomfortable."

"No," I said. "Not at all," I lied. What Beth had done was unforgivable and there was no excuse for that. I'd do my best to keep out of her way, if only for the sake of sparing everyone else angry scenes and obscenities.

Bates led me down the steps and onto the control centre floor.

"This is Sakib Khan," Bates introduced me to the man sitting at the first computer terminal. "Khan is the director of flight crew operations. He is responsible for the day-to-day running of our missions on the ground as well as the crew's overall safety and wellbeing."

"I've been with the ESA – European Space Agency – for years," he said turning to face us, with a nasal French accent. "It's a pleasure to meet you." Khan offered his hand. He had a limp shake compared to Bates's but at least it was dry – which brought a smile to my face. "I hope you settle in quickly, it's always daunting being the new kid." I returned his polite smile. "Don't worry, we're all pretty friendly around here, you'll blend in before you know it."

"Thanks," I said. "So, you work for the ESA?"

"I did, until Thacker found me."

"You have the dreams too?" I sounded surprised.

"We all do," Khan said. "Most of us have been in these kinds of jobs for years like me." I detected a note of disdain, almost a scowl on his face, as if there was something wrong with me or how I had been chosen. It evaporated. "Well I look forward to working with you."

We moved on.

"Beth is our Capsule Communicator – CAPCOM – all communications to and from our mission goes through her." I avoided direct eye contact with Beth and was thankful when Bates didn't take me to her workstation. I guessed he saw through my lies, sensing the tension.

"This is Andrew Johnson," he said, introducing me to a

short fat man. He had a thick bushy beard falling from his chin, but not a single hair on his head. His hands were large and crushing as we shook. "He is our Flight Dynamics Officer, responsible for the flight profile, path and trajectory of the mission."

"Just don't call me FIDO and we'll get on," he smiled. I laughed, but didn't understand. It was obviously an in-joke.

"Last, we have Josef Kittler, our Integrated Communications Officer." I took his hand. "This is Mark Besant."

"I'm responsible for keeping communications channels open and the technology working," Josef said. I'd expected him to have a German accent with a name like Kittler, but he sounded Portuguese like one of my ex-colleagues who was born in Porto. "If the satellites stop working, I'm in big trouble."

"That's good to know," I smiled, feeling dizzy with all the introductions.

"Come on," Bates said. "I'll show you our technicians." I was grateful we weren't staying around to chat.

3

Equipment piled in mountains to one side, scientific instruments lay abandoned on large workbenches and a monster refrigeration unit hummed at the back of the room. It was a laboratory alright.

"Mark?" a familiar voice came from my left and as I turned, I saw a tall figure standing in the doorway to an office. I didn't recognise him at first glance. "It's been a long time. You look just as I remember you... although I think your hair is thinning a little." He chuckled.

"Randall!" I said grinning from cheek to cheek. I took my

old friend in my arms, patting his back. "You look so well." I stepped back. "It must've been ten years or more." Randall was a techie guy, we'd taken the same engineering class at college, we'd have been twenty I guess. "I didn't expect to see you here."

"I thought I'd heard your name bandied about." He had a childish grin etched upon his face. He just couldn't shake the geeky look. "It's nice to see you again. Have you kept up with your sciences?"

I was only one of a handful of people that knew his real name, Ronald Anderson, I could understand why. I never took engineering seriously, so when it came to projects I'd seen the benefit of the class geek. I never expected we'd get on, so when Randall started drawing me into his world, showing me gadgets he'd created, I was shocked and found myself in awe of him.

"No," I said, remembering the tapping device he'd fitted on the principal's telephone. It had provided us endless amusement until it was discovered and nearly cost him his place on the course. "I don't really keep up with things anymore."

"That's a shame."

I guessed it didn't matter so much to Randall, he looked like a propeller-head, his gaunt physique accentuating it, so it was natural he acted like one. Me on the other hand, I'd known technology didn't really pull the girls in, although that wasn't really the sort of man I was either – and it didn't stop me collecting gadgets.

"This must be techie heaven for you?"

"Hell yeah!" he chuckled. "I've had to give up hacking into government files though." I remembered with fondness the pointless hours we'd wasting in front of a computer screen trying to break through government firewalls to access classified information.

"About time," I said. "What changed your tune?"

“I was never a malicious hacker,” his voice reminiscent. “When I broke US encryption I let them know what I’d done and how to secure their systems. Eventually, after the third breach, they asked me to join their security team.” A beaming smile and a flash of teeth. “That’s right, I worked for them.”

“What brings you here?” I asked, trying to make the connection.

“They told me they wanted the best of the best, so they came to me. That’s right, *they* came to *me*!” His voice ecstatic. “Do you remember at college I’d been working on a new generation of communication device?” I blinked, trying to recall, but I couldn’t picture it. “It was like a mobile telephone for outer space, that’s how I would have described it to you at the time anyway.”

He’d said the right keyword and a light clicked on in my head, “Oh yeah, I remember.”

“Well anyway, in my spare time I was still working on those designs, trying to get some funding to do some proper research. I needed to develop a new power cell to make the technology work, something that could produce the right strength signal to transmit into the far reaches, without zapping the national grid. I approached NASA, but they practically laughed me all the way home. A few days later I get this strange call from a military man…”

“Thacker.” I shook my head, wasn’t it always?

“Long story short, he set me up with a lab-office and enough funding to get my idea off the ground. Unfortunately, the funding was pulled, but Thacker promised me it wouldn’t be the end, and he was right.” A triumphant look in his eyes. “This place is my baby now, my very own research and development laboratory.” He chuckled, he hadn’t changed at all, still way too excitable. “Hey, do you wanna see something neat? For old time’s sake?”

★ ★ ★

"This is an ordinary DVD." Randall said holding the disc up for me to see. It looked normal enough, although who used DVDs anymore? He placed the DVD on an elevated spindle inside a glass enclosure and locked the hatch. At the computer terminal he pushed a button and the disc started spinning, before a red laser light shone onto its surface. "This is how close the laser has to be to read the information," he said pointing at the moving disc. Then, turning to his screen he tapped on an app that brought up a series of streaming numbers – logically I recognised this was the data pouring from the disc in binary.

"Shouldn't we be worried about radiation?" I asked.

"It's nothing to worry about." Randall waved his hand dismissively. "I've modified the wavelength, it can't do any damage. Besides who am I kidding, I'm never having kids, right?" I chuckled, I'd missed being around people who didn't take everything seriously, and for whom work was an extension of playtime. He nudged another button and the laser whirred along the spindle drawing away from the disc. The stream of data fragmented and then stopped altogether. "Now watch as I pass the laser through a J-Power filter," he said, striking the return key.

The light of the laser turned brilliant green as soon as the fragment of rock passed across the lens. I noted the screen went crazy as the data whizzed from the disc, faster than before. After a few seconds, smoke came from the surface of the plastic disc as it melted, shards splattered against the glass enclosure and I jumped backwards from the sheer shock of the unanticipated explosion.

Randall didn't blink as he stopped the experiment.

"I haven't perfected the J-laser yet," his voice deflated.

"My equations are right, but that's the big problem with theoretical science, everything should just work. I'm not sure if I need thinner slices of the rock, pico-segments, possibly even smaller than that, but the technology we've got just isn't helping. If I can get it working, I've estimated that we could store up to four trillion times the amount of data as an ordinary DVD. I have also proved that we can use J-Power to store information on mundane objects like this," he said picking up his stapler. "This one has a movie on it." I could see from the creases around his eyes he was lying about the stapler, although probably not about the overall concept.

"How does it work?" I asked, intrigued.

"I'm still trying to understand it and tame its power." I detected a note of frustration in his voice. "We're talking about alien technology here, millions of years ahead of our own, just like understanding an ancient language we need to know what it is meant to say before there's any chance of decoding it."

"You've been talking to Charlie, right?" I chuckled.

"I heard he got you good," he shook his head. "He's a fool."

"Don't worry about it," I said. "He was interesting once we got past that."

"He's got plenty more of that," Bates interrupted from behind, "but maybe we should press on."

4

"I just need a signature from you," Bates said, clicking a pen in one hand while sliding the contract across his desk with the other. He had an understated, practical office compared to Thacker's, the walls bare, his desk in pristine order. I bit down on my lip as my eyes scanned the document. I took a black pen from the neat arrangement at the head of the desk, glancing over the ample offering.

I signed and immediately Bates relaxed, the pen dropped from his hand to the desk.

"Welcome to SARA," he said. "The training programme begins tomorrow, we're just waiting for one of our astronauts, Maggie Kelly, to fly in from Washington following an unexpected delay returning from the International Space Station. The whole crew will assemble in the conference hall at 9 a.m. sharp."

Bates had already told me about the training programme. I had a physical exam scheduled for the afternoon to determine my fitness level. As an astronaut I needed to be at my peak and maintain it. I hadn't been too kind to myself over recent years and my stomach was pushing over my belt. It wasn't much yet, but I'd have to address that quickly. I expected a harsh regime of early morning jogging and cold showers. I'd just have to buckle up and get on with the challenges as life presented them. I was determined to make this work.

The launch date for the *Constellation* mission was just over a year away, and I was only just realising how clueless I really was. I felt like someone had pushed me into the abyss and I was plummeting down, but still I hadn't reached the bottom. All I had to hold on to were my dreams and my memories.

It would be hard work, and I knew I had a whole lot of catching up to do.

"Tell me, what's the deal with you and Thacker?"

"It's complicated," Bates said with a wave of his hand. I studied him, imagining what secrets lurked beneath his dismissal. I'd overheard a conversation as we passed the break room, two of the technicians chatting. Even though Bates had talked all over them as we toured, I'd caught the odd word here or there.

Three words had caught my attention more than any other; illegal human testing. Bates had been flustered too, as if he knew what they'd been talking about. It was clear he knew more about Thacker than he wanted to let on.

"I guess he did what he thought was needed to get me here."

"He believes you're central to understanding what happened to our ancestors," Bates said, his voice gave nothing away.

"And you?"

"I believe that Thacker trusts you." There was a knock at his door and before Bates responded a young army officer pushed inside. "Yes?"

"I've got the sighting reports you asked for." He said stepping forwards and pushing a file across his desk. It was marked Sighting and Abductions. "Do you need anything else?"

"No," Bates waved at him. "That will do."

"Visitations are on the increase," Bates told me as he opened the file and glanced at its contents. "The media are starting to pick up on the unusual level of activity and it's only a matter of time before we're forced to go public, and trust me...they will demand action."

"Don't we need to understand the threat first?" I said.

"Of course." Bates was quick to respond. "That's why we can't afford to go public."

"There will be a media frenzy, especially in this country. I don't know what the journalists are like in America, but ours have teeth and they're not afraid to get caught using them."

"As far as they need know, we're on track to launch the scheduled *Constellation* project." I'd read up on that in Thacker's file. *Constellation* was the programme conceived under the Bush administration to deflect from his inadequacies, cancelled by President Obama in 2010 only to be reinstated five years later. "I guess we won't stray too far from the truth."

I let out a groan, resigned to the lie. "I guess it's only the nature of our mission that's different."

As I stood to leave, I peered out of the window into the autumn rain. Sodden leaves cascaded in a waterfall of browns and reds as the wind flung them from hibernating branches. It was time for us all to hunker down for the long haul.

5

Jets pulsed from the shower head, the room filled with rising steam. I stepped into the scolding torrent, washing away the confirmation of my fears. I was out of shape. I'd known that, but I hadn't understood how unfit I was until I'd been put through my paces.

I'd have liked nothing better than a beer or even a whisky to lift my spirits, but the physician had organised a dietary plan and alcohol was on the forbidden list. I guess the hardest part of my new diet was the fact that I could no longer eat after 6 p.m. I loved my late evening snacks, but from today that had to stop.

My target weight meant I needed to shed seven pounds over the next month and a further twenty over the next four. I'd never attempted to drop weight before so I didn't know how achievable it would be.

Eating apples and oranges every day wouldn't kill me, but I had a feeling the celery salad for lunch might.

The steam from the shower now engulfed the bathroom, misting the mirror and saturating the air with droplets of water which caught in my throat as I took a deep breath. I stood on the edge of a monumental switch in my life. For years I'd dabbled, unable to make a serious decision about my career and from today, in my mind, I was an astronaut. This thought triggered a smile to erupt across my lips. In a short years' time, I'd be up there, in space.

There were few things that brought me out into spontaneous laughter, but this was one of them, the ludicrous image of me inside a space suit, floating in zero-gravity, filled my head.

When the laughter died, I knew I'd be okay, I'd do whatever necessary to make my image a reality.

CHAPTER 9

All conversations died the moment I stepped inside the oversized lecture hall. Faces turned to eye up the newcomer. I tensed in the doorway, until I saw Charlie making his way over and I relaxed.

"How you doing?" A grin spread across his face. "Come meet the rest of the mission crew. I'll introduce you."

"I wasn't expecting to see you." Immediately I felt foolish. Why wouldn't he be part of the *Constellation* crew? The mission would of course call for someone with linguistic skills and an ability to document and decipher anything we might come into contact with. Charlie had decoded the scriptures, he was the man for the job. "Ignore me," I said, catching a glimpse of myself in a mirror window – I looked both startled and nervous. I shook my head and attempted a smile to hide the nerves, first impressions were important.

Charlie led me to the group waiting at the front of the hall.

"You must be Mark." A rake thin woman stood as we joined the others and offered her aged hand. "You look a little overwhelmed," she said. "Come, take a seat." She had a thick accent, from the drawl I thought it might be Texan. "I'm Maggie by the way."

"Hello," I said finally giving her hand a firm shake.

"Maggie's our mission commander, she'll be cracking the whip, keeping us in check." Charlie told me.

Feeling left out, I said, "Do you all know each other?"

"No," Maggie said. "We met over breakfast this morning, except Charlie, I knew him before, for better or worse. You have to watch him you know, he thinks he's funny, a real prankster." She didn't sound amused.

"A prick," Charlie said reminiscing, and I smiled uneasily. "And I resent that, I am funny!" I could tell from the smile twitching in the corner of his mouth that he was fooling around, acting like he was hurt. Maggie rolled her eyes at him.

"I didn't mean...." I began, my harsh words to Charlie coming back to haunt me.

"I'm just joshing." He nudged my shoulder. "No hard feelings."

"No." I smiled back.

"Charlie is our payload commander," Maggie said, resuming control. "He's there to manage our scientific mission and make sure we have all the tools to understand anything we find up there."

"Absolutely," Charlie's head bobbed. "If we find what we hope to find then we need someone to interpret."

I turned my attention to the giant man who had appeared to my side, now towering over me.

"Call me Tom," he said in an unmistakeable Irish accent. His hand was cold when he shook mine. "I've heard you're untrained." I didn't say anything, feeling uneasy again, being judged. "Do you have any fly time?" I stared blankly, unsure what he meant. "I cling to the hope that you're at least not afraid of flight?" He was shaking his head, seemingly alarmed by the prospect.

"That I can do," I lied, smiling to hide my terror. It worked. His apprehension vanishing.

"That's a start." He seemed brash, but I could understand why. These people were all professionals and throwing a civilian like me into the mix tipped the balance. I needed training and mentoring, back to school basics. "I've been a pilot for many years, I'll get you up to speed." I guessed from this, he was the mission pilot.

"This is Craig," Charlie said pointing to the older man to his left. Craig seemed annoyed, deep furrows etched into his brow, I got the impression he didn't approve of a lot of things. If he was that kind of person, I knew we wouldn't get on too well. I'd never liked people who were objectionable for no good reason, it would hammer my nerves. "Craig will be our mission specialist. This is Linda, our command module-pilot." Maggie stepped to her right and I saw a short, blonde woman smiling at me.

A smaller man with a moustache stepped from behind Linda, "I am Sergei," he said with a Russian accent. "But please, call me Serge. I've been a flight engineer for a long time. I was on-board the last Russian flight to the ISS before its completion." I shook his hand. What struck me as odd was that Serge was the first Russian I'd met since I'd arrived in the building. Wasn't SARA meant to be a joint venture?

"You all seem to have a title, some purpose on the mission. What does that make me?" I looked to Charlie. He turned to Maggie for the answer and I followed his gaze. Although Maggie was the commander of the mission, I guessed there was no harm getting into the habit now.

"I was told you were our payload specialist," Maggie said.

"Payload?" I frowned. "What payload?"

"Well..." she trailed off

"I suppose...." Charlie started. "You and me."

"Oh," I said. "I guess that makes sense."

Serge and Craig took their own conversation to one side, swapping engineering and flight stories. If we were all meant to work as a team up there *in space* I guess we all needed to get to know each other a bit better.

"So…how do you two know each other?" I was intrigued. Maggie seemed comfortable with Charlie, standing right in front of him, suggesting that they were more than just passing acquaintances.

"Thacker introduced us." Maggie smiled for a moment, her eyes glazed over and she went silent. A few seconds later, perhaps her realisation she'd drifted off, her eyes shot back to mine and her cheeks flushed with rosy red colour. I noticed that both Charlie and Maggie were around the same height, five-foot-eight perhaps – I felt slightly shorter than them both – I could imagine them together as a couple, they'd take the perfect picture.

"I was studying the scriptures," Charlie said. "Maggie was doing detailed studies of the *Mistral* data – Thacker told you about that right? – and our paths happened upon each other."

"We were married for a brief time," Maggie added, confirming my hunch. "But it turned out he was already in wedlock." I blinked, letting out a puff of air through my nose in shock. Charlie smirked. "He just couldn't commit to both; it was either me or those damn rocks."

"Ah," I let out. "I guess it would've been difficult with your jobs."

"We'll never know will we."

"No." Charlie turned to Maggie. "You always came second."

A smile flourished, hiding any remnants of my nerves. Spoken differently, the words could have been misconstrued, but there was compassion, understanding and not a hint of bitterness between them. It was refreshing to see a divorced couple acting in this way, reminiscing with each other, accepting their faults but without attaching blame.

"What's it like up there?" I asked, finally changing the subject.

"Beautiful." I detected a sense of loss in Maggie's dreamy voice as she summed up her feelings in a single word. It was clear she'd rather be in space, orbiting Earth, than stuck on solid ground.

The door to the side of the hall burst open, interrupting my thoughts. Bates thundered in followed by a stern older man wearing a tweed jacket with matching trousers, the only thing missing to complete his ensemble were the leather elbow patches. But still he looked like a teacher. The white spindly hair covering his balding head bounced as he marched in.

"Alright, that's enough chit-chat," Bates' voice roared over the top of the conversation Serge was having with Craig. Silence fell. "This is Professor Frost, he'll be assessing your mathematical, geological, meteorological and physics skills along with other basic sciences."

"I will personally mentor anyone who falls below *my* standards." Frost's voice was just as stern as his look and I shivered. I'd seriously neglected my sciences since college, the skills redundant. I knew I didn't have any option, I'd be Frost's student. I watched him reach into his jacket pocket, pulling out a pair of glasses before perching them on his nose.

"Try not to worry," Maggie said. "These things put the frighteners on us all."

I felt a slight sense of reassurance, but it wasn't enough to prevent all semblance of calm from disintegrating from my face. This was turning into my worst nightmare.

Bates left as we took our seats and Professor Frost began his examination.

2

At some point I knew I'd have to do it; I couldn't keep avoiding Beth. It was a matter of choosing the right moment.

For the whole week I'd been with SARA I'd successfully managed to keep my distance, but it was hard work. It was impossible to keep checking before I entered a room, and effectively sneaking around the place I had to call home for the foreseeable future. At some point we'd have to be in the same room at the same time, and the longer I put things off the more awkward it felt.

And so, as I passed the communal lounge – fresh from a mind-numbing session with Professor Frost where we'd discussed the uses of Quantum Mechanics in space travel and technology – and spotted Beth alone, I took a deep breath and vowed to be courageous.

I stopped in the doorway, but she didn't look. Her attention was grabbed by whatever magazine article she was reading. I was about to bottle it, when she finally looked up and across at me. She forced a smile.

Butterflies filled my stomach; at the same moment my bowels cramped and I winced. A thought passed through my mind, I could make up an excuse and leave. But the words didn't pass my lips. Finally, the words rolled from my tongue, "Do you mind if we talk?"

I sensed her awkwardness and she kept hold of the magazine as if she was torn between continuing the article or facing up to what had happened. A pained look crossed her face and her eyes filled with sadness. I knew we were making progress when her hands eased their grip on the magazine and it brushed closed.

"We should go somewhere a little more private." I agreed,

even though there was no one else around. While I was starting to get to know my new colleagues, I didn't want to share this with them. Charlie and Maggie might still be close, but I didn't feel the same way about Beth, and besides, their split was amicable. Neither one had cheated or lied to the other.

Beth led me out of the building and into the courtyard. The early evening sun was shining, its warmth gone now that autumn was taking hold. I took a deep breath of the fresh air; the smell of mulching leaves filled my nostrils.

When we sat down on a bench, I didn't look at her. The silence extended.

"I'm really sorry, for everything that happened." Beth finally spoke. "I never meant to hurt you, really I didn't." I kept silent, giving Beth the opportunity to explain. There was no point being childish about it, that time had passed. "It was meant to be a simple assignment." I wriggled on the cold wooden slats to warm myself. "I knew what I had to do, but I never anticipated *you*." She reached out and touched my hand. I felt compelled to look at her and saw tears forming in her eyes. "I never intended to get so close to you."

I looked into her damp eyes in silence, there was truth behind them, I could see it. There was compassion in her voice and I realised this was physically hurting her. In my anger, I'd failed to consider how she felt, but at the time why would I? She'd hurt me, right? I didn't think it was possible to repair the damage. As my father told me when he'd caught me lying about being inside his study, messing with his papers and books, trust was the cornerstone of a good relationship.

"I do understand," I said. "It wasn't your fault." The power of these few, forgiving words was instant; relief washed over her and the tears rolled down to her chin. "I know now Thacker was in the driving seat. For that, I can't blame you…" I trailed off, thinking of my dying mother. "But you betrayed my trust, you didn't have to do that."

"I know." Her voice taking strength from my forgiveness.

"We can't rebuild what is broken, but we can agree to forget. I'm willing to do this – we can't afford to ignore each other any longer. Our hearts will heal in time." I squeezed her hand tighter.

"I'm sorry." Her cheeks flushed red, "and thank you. I kissed her forehead and wiped a tear from my own eye. "Friends?" She asked, wiping her cheek with the back of her arm, smearing her make-up.

"Yeah, I'd like that," I agreed with a smile. I silenced my inner voice which told me this was a bad decision. It was trying to protect me but I could handle things on my own. Considering everything that Beth had done, I still saw us as friends. Maybe it was because we'd been close before we'd gotten involved, but I just didn't have it in me to *hate* her. I was angry and disappointed, but still, it was Beth, we'd shared a lot of time together and besides, I missed her company. "It will take some getting used to, I guess."

"I wish things could've been different."

The strangest thought filled me, I was actually glad things had turned out as they had. I had answers, and that was a massive achievement. *Sometimes knowledge really is worth the cost*, I thought.

3

"Mathematics are the building blocks of modern science." Frost roared, dropping a thick textbook in front of me which slapped onto my desk. He was an old-school professor. "You are not even close to mastering the simple principles of trigonometry."

I said nothing, watching the balding professor blow his steam. In three days I'd already learnt this was the quickest and relatively pain-free way.

"Up there you will not be able to understand the relationships between objects and their distance, or danger. In an emergency situation you will die if you cannot perform a vital spacewalk." I looked at the textbook, I could see where this lecture was heading. He took a piece of chalk and drew on the blackboard a perfect circle, quartering it with horizontal and vertical lines which crossed in the centre of the circle. From this point he drew a line pointing outwards in a north-eastern direction. "Read chapters ten through to twenty and then I want you to find the coterminal angle for this." A fine cloud of chalk dust filled the air as he wrote out his equation and I coughed:

Find coterminal angle A_c *to angle* $A = - 17 \pi / 3$ *such that* A_c *is* $>= 0$ *and* $< 2 \pi$.

As Frost left I turned to Charlie, who'd also failed Frost's basic mathematical criteria – of course all the others had passed – and shook my head. He peered back at me with the same concerned look upon his face. We were clueless.

"Sometimes I get the feeling I'm in way over my head," he said as he scribbled out the equation in his notepad before standing, taking his textbook and pad under his arm. "I signed up to understand the primordial language and the roots of human civilisation, not this." Defeat in his voice. "I need some air." With that he left.

I chuckled to myself as I jotted the details from the board. I just didn't believe life should be simple, sometimes to get what you wanted you had to climb mountains. I closed my eyes and I saw the deserted ziggurat of the moon and I knew that if I could survive my training I'd get more than just the simple answers I'd been longing for. It would be worth the struggle and I was prepared for that. Charlie clearly didn't see the world the same way. At least not yet.

I wondered what the others – Linda, Serge, Tom, Craig and Maggie – were getting up to while Charlie and I studied. I guessed they were working on the flight plans and other strategic mission programmes as well as maintaining their fitness levels. I didn't know who had the better deal, them or us.

Beth was waiting for me in the canteen when I arrived. She had a plate of lasagne with a broccoli side in front of her. I took a seat, dumping my books heavily on the table, rattling the empty tray beside Beth.

"It's going that well huh?" She caught my eye. It suddenly felt like my life had flashed back in time. Things were on their way back to how they'd started, except Beth was no longer serving me like she did at the café. "Is everything okay?" I realised I'd been silently staring at her.

"Yes," I said taking her tray. "I was just lost in my thoughts." I helped myself to a bowl of salad from the counter, drizzling it with olive oil before returning to the table where Beth sat.

"Looks like quite a problem," she said, flicking her head towards my notepad. "If you need any help, don't forget where I am."

"You can do trigonometry?" It was a redundant question, of course she could and I shook my hand, signalling to ignore me. All personnel had to pass basic mathematics and physics exams. My mind turned to her offer, could I ask for her help? Sure, we were 'friends', but a thought crossed my mind; what if she was spying on me still.

I dismissed my doubts, shovelling a forkful of salad leaves into my mouth. That kind of attitude would get me nowhere fast. And besides, there was no point spying on me now, I was already enrolled.

"Maybe," I said with my mouth half full. "But I guess I have to at least try and fathom it on my own. Frost will know if I've cheated, he seems to have a sixth sense with stuff like that."

"You're probably right." Beth sounded deflated. "You don't want to get on the wrong side of Frost. I've heard he threw a chair at a student. That's why he's no longer allowed to lecture at universities."

"He does scare me sometimes," I said. Frost was an old-fashioned kind of man, despised technology and refused to use it. As a teacher he demanded respect and discipline from his pupils and it wasn't difficult to picture him grabbing a chair from the conference hall and throwing it at me. It was a chilling thought and I shuddered. "Does he have the connection too?" I asked, referring to the dreams. Beth's smile confirmed my hunch.

We finished our lunches in silence.

4

"Just remember to breathe normally," The instructor said, before putting his own oxygen mask on and rolling backwards into the deep water of the pool. A hand appeared from beneath the surface; giving me the okay sign.

It's just like swimming, I told myself, trying not to panic at the thought, claustrophobic with the wetsuit tight against me, the mask stapled to my face and the weight of the tank clutching at my back. My breakfast lay heavy on my stomach, my heart pounding with anticipation as I slid my backside closer to the edge of the floating pontoon in the centre of the pool, staring at the shadowy figure shimmering below. I took a final breath, filling my lungs with the fresh tasting oxygen mix and pushed backwards. The world swam by in a blur of colour as I tumbled head-first into the still water with a crash, my neck feeling the strain. Bubbles fluttered past my face and as they settled I realised I had done it. I'd taken my first underwater breath, proud of my achievement.

I signalled to the instructor that I was okay, he confirmed and then we plunged deeper. This was only my first dive and I just needed to adjust to the breathing and the changing pressures of the water. The water was murky and as I pushed downward my goggles began to steam with the heat of my breath.

We sat on the floor of the pool, and I stared up to see the flickering light beyond the surface. The pool was adapted to accommodate an underwater simulation vehicle, and was deeper than I had expected. While I'd be nervous to take the plunge, I found myself eager to get inside the simulator. It would be a good few months before we got to that though, for now I had to concentrate on diving and my technique.

When I was ready, I pushed off from the bottom of the pool. I felt the throbbing pressure of the water in my ears and I closed my eyes as I kicked harder. My head burst through the surface and I spat out my mouthpiece and ripped my mask off, filling my lungs and coughing as I inhaled the heavily chlorinated air. I felt disorientated. It took a moment to adjust and as I looked out, I caught sight of Bates watching down from one of the observation windows above, perhaps checking on my progress.

"You did well." The instructor's voice appeared from my side and I turned to see him, I hadn't noticed him surface. "Next I want you to follow my lead, we'll do a couple of laps of the pool and then resurface, okay?" I glanced back to the window. Bates had gone. He seemed to be following me everywhere, a shadow I couldn't shake off.

I was exhausted by the time we climbed from the pool, but my day was not over yet.

"My answer is $A_c = -17\pi / 3 + 6\pi = \pi / 3$," I said, Frost's stern face in my own, his sickly-sweet breath fuming beneath my nose.

"Well, well!" Frost's expression did not match the elated surprise in his voice. "It looks like you are beginning to grasp the basics." He turned to Charlie beside me. "And what about you?" His voice returning to a normal growl.

I heard Charlie gulp and I felt him tense as Frost leant in closer.

"I got the same answer," Charlie said, but even I didn't believe him.

"Stand up!" Frost roared, his eyes blood-shot. Slowly Charlie stood, nose to nose with the fuming professor. "Do you believe I am a fool?" His voice growled. "Do you think I would accept your petty lies?"

"Stop," I said standing, Frost's angry gaze turning to me. I couldn't stand his pompous attitude. "We worked together." I explained. "We have the same answer."

The room fell silent and I could see Frost considering his options, but I didn't expect him to back down, and when I saw a flicker of uncertainty surface behind his eyes it surprised me. Frost turned away and began to scrawl a new problem on the blackboard, his chalk creaking under the pressure of his fingers.

Charlie looked towards me and mouthed the words, *thank you.*

No problem, I mouthed back.

5

It was late, darkness shrouding the outside world. I knew I should be in bed, resting for the morning, but I couldn't sleep. A cool breeze rustled past me, stirring a drifted pile of leaves to the side of the bench, blowing them across my feet.

The stars were playing their games across the sky, twinkling and shining as only they could. As I watched I saw a satellite whizzing on an orbital trajectory. Soon I'd be there, witnessing the world from above. I couldn't wait for that day.

There was a crunching of gravel, the unmistakable sound of someone coming my way.

"It's brisk." Charlie's voice. A moment later he stepped out of the shadows of the building and came to join me, taking a seat. "It's a nice night." He rubbed his hands.

"Yeah," I said. "I couldn't sleep."

"Me neither." His breath fogged in the light. "It's funny, we've been here for what? A few weeks? But I've not dreamt once since arriving." A darkened image flickered into my mind, my haunting, empty house, it was nothing without my company, just a hollow shell, just like my life back there. Back home I was nobody, but here I was somebody, and not just anybody, but an important and crucial man. I'd never felt like part of a family back at the office, not like this. "Do you fear your dreams?"

"I used to."

"But not now, right?" I caught a sparkle in the darkness as his eyes reflected the starlight. "Don't you want things to go back to how they used to be?"

"Why?" I frowned. "I don't want to wake up terrified. I want to understand them, and for that, I don't think there is room for fear…" My voice trailed off. "Tell me, don't you know everything those rocks can tell you? Don't you want to put all that knowledge into some kind of context? Wouldn't you like to see it for yourself and understand?"

"Of course," Charlie said, leaning back into the bench and stretching his arms along the back rest. "I just miss them is all." He sounded forlorn, and I couldn't hold back my laughter.

"You miss the rocks?" I asked, latching onto his train of thought. "Maggie was right, you really are married to them." Although part of me understood his passion for his work, I didn't know how he could let it rule his life, ruining everything else. Some things just aren't meant to be known. "Tell me about them."

"It took me a long time to understand them," Charlie said, his voice filling with the enthusiasm I'd come to expect from him. "Cuneiform is a major challenge to decipher. Over time, characters change and there are so many different versions. I used Sumerian as my base because it was the earliest known form." He looked at me, and although it was dark, I could see him smiling. "Cuneiform doesn't just represent phonetic sounds – the same characters can be used to express a word too. We call that logographic."

"How do you even begin to understand that?"

"With a great deal of trial and error." He chuckled. "I mean once you understand what a character is used for, what sounds it represents and what words it can be used to form, you can quickly decipher a text."

"But this one was different," I said, remembering everything he had told me inside the cave temple. "You said this was a form of cuneiform, how could you understand it?"

"Ah, now that was all me. I studied the differences between all the known versions of cuneiform to find out how the language changed over time. From that it was more guesswork trying to understand how the Sumerians had adapted the language for themselves."

"But how did they understand it?"

"The Sumerians had something that the tribe of Dilmun needed and they traded, passing along the knowledge." It was a guess, I could tell. "Of course, there is always Divine inspiration." He chuckled and I couldn't stop myself giggling along with him. "But seriously, we don't know for sure. There are no records available yet that can answer that question."

"Wouldn't you want to trade that kind of thing first?" I asked, maybe naively. "It doesn't make sense to sit on an ancient language like that and not share it with the rest of the world."

"But if the Dilmun tribe had forgotten some of the history themselves, and now revered the knowledge, they would want to keep it safe and out of other people's hands." He glanced across at me before looking up into the sky. "It's kinda funny when you think about it. There are *real* aliens out there and they took an interest in our kind. Isn't that just the irony of the century, all those volumes of science-fiction were actually correct."

"I guess it is." I said, having never given it much thought. "Why are they interested in us?"

"World domination is the usual favourite." Charlie was laughing. "Colonisation of the universe."

"A colony," I said, frowning. My words fell into the silence of the cool breeze of the autumnal night. I felt a throbbing at the back of my head, a pain burning, forcing its way to the front of my mind. I closed my eyes, taking a deep breath, trying to head it off but it was not to be, it was coming.

A blistering heat scorched at my temples, green glowing blinding me behind my closed eyes. I tried to scream, to call for help, but I didn't hear my voice, just the silence of the green light.

"We are not alone," I heard a voice, and then I felt a gentle hand rest upon my shoulder, bringing me out of my prayers. I opened my eyes, raising my head and looked up towards Magi Eritrea.

After a quick scan of the room I found myself perplexed. There was no one else around.

"We are on our own Magi?" I spoke the voice of Russia.

"No." Magi Eritrea shook her head. "Look." She pointed upwards to the skylight in the roof of her quarters. It was dark outside and even with the glowing embers of the fire I could see the brilliance of the shining stars. "That is another world up there, some are closer than you may think."

"Is that where *they* come from?"

"No." Magi Eritrea shook her head again. I was referring to the Creators of our world. "They do not live on a world like our own. They are roamers, wanderers of the sky."

"Like shooting stars," I said. Magi Eritrea looked at me for a moment with surprise and then she began to chuckle.

"Yes," her voice soothed. "Like shooting stars, *they* glide across the night sky. But I don't mean *them*. There are more, just like us, out there. We are the first of many." I frowned at my Magi, she was making no sense. Surely there couldn't be another one just like me out there. That was an insane idea. "You don't believe me."

"It's not that..." I trailed off.

"My little Russia," Magi Eritrea's voice was full of compassion. "I have seen them. My own eyes watched them going about their business, like we might go about ours.

They were just like us, in every way." There was concern in her voice. I'd never seen my master afraid before, but she was only human after all. She couldn't deny *all* her emotions.

"How have you seen them?"

"They watch me in my dreams." There it was again, cold, blatant fear.

"Why?" I asked.

"I..." a knock came at the door. The conversation was over.

CHAPTER 10

"What do you think it means?" Beth asked, studying me. I didn't answer, too afraid to voice the truth I already knew. "Do you suppose there *are* more...creatures, just like us?" She leant forwards, taking my hands into hers. I was suddenly aware that we were alone, the television quiet in the corner of the common room. "Tell me what's going on inside your head."

"I think I'm being shown that human life didn't just happen by pure chance." I said. "Maybe religion got it right... maybe some divine power or entity created us – just not the same *something* they all worship."

"Do you *believe* that?" Her words carried weight.

"You tell me what I should believe!" I said throwing my hands into the air. Her hands fell to her lap. "If there are more worlds like ours out there, filled with people just like us, you tell me what's true. Scientists have told us for a long time that the chances of complex lifeforms emerging elsewhere were slim, but this changes everything. Don't you see that? What if we were bred into colonies? I mean why would there be more like us?"

"It changes nothing," Beth said. "You're sounding like a conspiracy theorist – you've watched too many apocalyptic films. Have you seen one of these other worlds? Has anybody?" She glared at me. Slowly I shook my head. "Well there you go then." I refused to accept Beth's simplistic view; absence of evidence wasn't evidence of absence. I almost laughed, wasn't that the same argument religious leaders used? And wasn't it the same view of the physicists attempting to explain the laws and mechanics of the world we experience?

For life like ours to happen and survive on a planet, so many conditions needed achieving. One theory would be to say that due to the complexity of the requirements, if there were other green worlds out there with people just like us, they were probably placed there for a reason. Although it was only a single interpretation, it was nonetheless a worrying thought. If life across the universe had a reason for being, so too it was plausible that our own lives had reason. We *could* be part of that same larger purpose. It was logical reasoning, even if it required a leap of faith. It was however, full of many unknowns.

"I have to speak to Thacker or Bates about this," I said, standing. "It's the way Magi Eritrea spoke to Russia…" My voice gave a tiny tremble as I broke off. My eyes darted, and a thick furrow creased across my forehead.

"I can see you're unsettled," Beth said. "Even if I don't agree with your assumptions, you're right to talk to them about this."

"Magi Eritrea seemed fearful of the discovery, as if she knew there was a design to those worlds and believed our destiny was intertwined with theirs." I shook my head. "What if she was right? What if we are part of a network of worlds? She said we were the first of many and that means trouble."

Beth said nothing further, but she didn't need to, a slight

twitch in her head – the beginning of a shake – told me everything. She didn't believe, or wouldn't.

Was blind faith enough? I felt it might be given the circumstances.

I found Thacker in his office. I didn't wait to be invited in.

"I have to ask you something," I said from his doorway. "Do the scriptures mention anything about others? Other worlds and people?"

"No," he said, concern in his voice. "What makes you ask? Have you seen something?" It was clear from the way his eyes studied me, concern mixed with intrigue, he knew I had.

"What if there are others?" I asked, bypassing the obvious questions. "What if we were just the first of many; colonies, spread across the universe. What if we were created for a purpose?"

"Then our mission would become more important than ever," Thacker said. "The scriptures do warn us that our Creators will return, and our planet will crumble just as our ancestors' world did." I looked at him with disbelief, all this from a man who despised religion. "If we were created for a purpose..."

"Is there anything we can do?"

"Leave it with me," Thacker said. "But be prepared. We may need to launch early – the more we discover, the more I fear we're in danger."

2

Sitting in the narrow beam of light projecting from the bedside lamp, I crouched over the electronic reading device Thacker had given me before I joined SARA. Those days felt like a distant dream now.

One by one I scanned through the documents contained on the device. They weren't in any particular order. The first batch were eyewitness accounts taken by Thacker, abduction stories. While this piqued my interest, it was short lived. After reading a handful, they all ran into one another because they were so generic; lights in the skies, grey figures, probing fingers and glowing implements. While I made no judgement about the mental stability of the 'abductees', I didn't subscribe to the validity of the stories. I was sure there *must* be harder facts, something concrete.

The next batch of files studied the formation and structure of the moon with years of detailed research into the lunar-rock samples returned by the Apollo missions. They described how the Earth's satellite was created; how the strength of its gravitational field rendered it unable to retain any water which may otherwise have been locked into the bedrock when its magma solidified. Another report showed readings from India's *Chandrayaan-1* lunar spacecraft which found water-ice deposits, but all the conclusions were clear; the moon was incapable of supporting life.

I pondered for a moment what the authors would have made of Thacker's wild theory; third-party intervention, alien life-forms and technology beyond our science. It brought a smile to my face.

The next section on the device drew my interest. Attached was a memo from Charlie at the archaeological site at Rora Habab:

Evolutionary Theory: Evolution cannot begin to explain what I have seen, but if my thinking is correct (and I believe it is), then we have completely misinterpreted our understanding of humankind. Previous data is woefully inaccurate and major gaps in the lineage of time have been based on assumptions (at worst, best guesses). This report will not only change the thinking of ourselves but the world around us.

It was a bold claim. I couldn't resist its allure and read the file.

"I still don't understand," I said holding the small device up for Charlie to see. The moment his eyes caught sight of the title of the file, a glimmer of pride flourish across his cheeks.

"Which bit don't you understand?"

"If we didn't evolve from apes..."

"It's always the apes!" Charlie raised his voice throwing his hands in the air. "What is it with you people, why does everyone always get hung up on apes? It's like you actually *want* to be related to them."

I could understand his exasperation, although exaggerated as it was for show. We'd already partially had this conversation before, but I was so much in awe about what was happening that I'd not really understood or taken in what Charlie was telling me. But there was also something that puzzled me, and it was worth starting at the beginning again.

He took a deep breath. "Okay, forget everything you've ever been taught or heard about human evolution, it's irrelevant, we need to deal with things separately."

Tom was sitting across the room, a book in his hands, but he'd not turned a page since I'd arrived and it was clear he was doing very little reading. He closed his book and came across to join us. Serge had been playing a game of pool at the far side of the room, now he upended his cue and hung it back in the frame before drifting towards us.

Charlie let out a groan.

"Fossilised remains dating to roughly two-point-five million years ago were discovered in Africa – the first known humanoid form, *Homo habilis*. Anthropologists at the time were eager to uncover an evolutionary path from pre-homo to *habilis*, so they began to consider what that path could have been. That of course led them to the apes everyone seems so eager to accept as distant cousins." Tom chuckled at this.

"In 1974, fossil remains were found dating to three-point-two million years." Charlie was on a roll, his hands working overtime animating his point. "*Australopithecus afarensis* – or 'Lucy' as we called her – was almost hominid in form, and until now was thought to be ancestral. Thinking has changed very little since, but instead of believing we evolved from apes, anthropologists believe we both evolved from a common ancestor and that is what they are searching for."

I saw the obvious hole in this thinking, if I was to believe human life was introduced to Earth rather than evolving on Earth.

"Much more recently," Charlie continued. "Fossilised remains for *Ardipithecus ramidus* were uncovered in Ethiopia, dated to around four-point-four million years old. My point is this; everything anthropologists are finding supports current theories, but it is not *our* evolution they have been charting."

"Because the temple scriptures tell us that we, as a human form, arrived on Earth," Tom said, his head rocking. I frowned, still puzzled.

"But we look more like our lunar ancestors now than, say, Neanderthal man. How is that?" Everyone knew Neanderthals were primitive people, but our moon ancestors weren't like that. I stared at Charlie, disbelieving. "Why do all the people in my dreams look like we do now?"

"You don't seem to grasp the gravity of this." Charlie was shaking his head, agitated once again. "The theory of evolution is sound, we evolved. It's always a constant battle in nature for animals to adapt to their surroundings, to find solutions to keep themselves alive and we are not exempt from that."

"You're saying we evolved into more primitive people?" Tom asked with incredulity. It was clear he understood better than me or was just able to follow Charlie's logic.

"Precisely," Charlie said. "But there is more to it. The scriptures tell us that we fled our world before our enemies could destroy us. I've interpreted the scriptures both literally and figuratively, and I believe we *chose* to forget – a conscious decision to that forced evolution's hand and caused our bodies to degenerate and adapt to our new environment; to develop in a different way. Our brains shrank due to inactivity, and our skills vanished in a matter of a few generations. Of course, we can't know this for sure because the scriptures are not living documents, they were written at a single point in time. Archaeological finds are limited too, but that doesn't detract from the truth."

"So apes did evolve into what we call *Homo habilis*?" Tom asked and I frowned as I continued to be behind in this conversation.

"*Yes!*" Charlie's elation was clear and his head rocked with vigour. "There is no doubt that fossil records are correct, we've been mapping evolution through time, but it was not ours. In all probability, we, as a race, killed off *habilis* as we spread across the planet. Maybe our primitive form, our true ancestor, *Homo erectus*, hunted them to extinction. I've not been able to publish my findings yet. Thacker promised we could once we've produced a more complete picture."

Tom said, "I guess that explains why *Homo erectus* had larger brains then; because our ancestors did. Science has got a lot of catching up to do."

"But you're saying we've reverted back or re-evolved now?" I knew full well that in the history of Earth, modern man could be compressed into the blink of an eye.

"Not exactly," Charlie said with glee, his hands becoming animated. "Evolution doesn't work in that way, the challenges here on Earth are different to those our ancestors would have experienced. We've not reverted back. We've remembered our roots."

"Why?" Tom asked the question I had been leading to and the reason why I'd originally come to talk to Charlie. It just didn't make sense to me. In evolutionary terms, why did we need to remember our ancestors? It didn't make evolutionary sense to me.

"We don't know," Charlie said. "We can guess. Maybe there is something that we once knew, and we need to know it again now. Maybe we hid from the threat of our enemies, and that's why we regressed, but now that we're not under threat..."

"But we *are* in danger," I said. "Isn't that exactly why we're all here now? What you're saying – your theory – is that some of our ancestors rediscovered the temple, and since then we've been remembering our past, right?" Charlie gave a smile of agreement. "The temple itself is knowledge and the power from that may have triggered something inside us. Doesn't that make the scriptures self-fulfilling prophecies? In our archaic form we were safe, but because we're evolving, we're now endangered once again?"

"Yes, except –" Charlie paused. "Except we're very different to our ancestors. We have evolved independently – we are not them. Culturally we're different. We've developed into enlightened industrialists, we've split the atom, theorised quantum mechanics, and for our shame mastered nuclear fission. We had none of this in the safe bubble of our lunar world…or at least I have found no evidence of it in the scriptures and other artefacts."

"I've never seen anything like machinery in my dreams," Tom confirmed.

"All our technology was *their* technology."

"So, the question remains." I said. "Why now? Unless…What if the purpose of all of this was to buy us time. To allow our ancestors' genetics to live long enough to become a real challenge to *them*."

All eyes focused their attention on me. Thoughts exploded in my mind, quick succinct green flashes which revealed truth. When I finally spoke, my words came slow and in an eerie hushed tone. "We came to Earth to bide our time, we learnt skills that we couldn't develop in our controlled lunar existence. We became fighters."

3

My head was in my hands, my eyes burning into the textbook open on the desk in front of me. I felt saturated, information overload. An explosive force ripped through the room, the door rattling in its frame. I looked up, the noise had come from next door: Thacker's office.

Next, I heard Bates's thunderous rage. "You've got some *fucking* nerve!"

I jumped to my feet at his bellow and darted out into the corridor. There was already a crowd of technicians gathering.

"Get back to work." I waved them away, but naturally that didn't apply to myself – I was a superior in their eyes. This was where I could see the true dynamics of Thacker and Bates in action, the volatile friction finally at a head. Today's performance was due to Thacker's decision to cut short the mission training, bringing forwards the target launch date.

"Calm down," Thacker's voice remained the perfect picture of tranquillity, he didn't seem phased by Bates's outburst.

"Don't tell me what to do!" Bates barked. "Who the fuck do you think you are? You've put the mission in jeopardy. Are you trying to set us up to fail? It's not your fucking decision to make."

I was left wondering if Bates was right. Did Thacker have the authority to make that call, or had he spoken with the President of the USA? I couldn't believe he was working alone in this regard.

"No." Thacker tone remained composed. It was clear he'd anticipated this debate. "We cannot fail." Standing out in the corridor, I could visualise the red cloth dangling before Bates, he charged without thinking.

"You really don't have a clue, do you?!" He growled. "We're sending God-damned untrained civilians into space and asking them to do the same job we'd expect from experienced astronauts – no, we're asking them to do *more*. And you're telling me we cannot fail? Our mission is in danger because of your thoughtless actions."

I agreed with Bates. It was irresponsible to send inexperienced astronauts into space, especially given the difficulty of the mission. This wasn't the same as sending another cosmonaut up to join the already overcrowded ISS, some of us were just ordinary folk plucked from the world. True, we'd all joined up to SARA, but we had differing levels of experience and expertise. In my eyes, I was still unqualified.

"We will succeed," Thacker said once again.

"And how can you be so sure?"

"Because there is no room for failure." Thacker's argument was flawed logic, it was an endless circle of stupidity, I couldn't believe he was touting it. "We *will* succeed because there is *no* other option."

Bates was so annoyed he stormed from Thacker's office, slamming the door. It reverberated along the corridor, causing the glass in the picture frame opposite to rattle. He said nothing as he pushed past me.

4

I'd been inside a fairground simulator before, and when the time came to step inside the underwater tank that housed the flight simulator, I was surprised to see similar technology in use. As Maggie explained to me, it was ten metres under water to assist simulating environmental conditions. It was claustrophobic. The screens displayed realistic imagery, of course, but this didn't distract me.

It was as cramped inside the replica of the *Orion* crew module as the real thing we'd be taking to the skies in. The main difference now was that we weren't strapped to the back of the *Ares* rocket. The blue and red of the *Constellation* and SARA emblems branded every part of the interior and was matched by embroidered logos on our uniforms.

"You feeling it yet?" Charlie caught my gaze. "Esprit de corp."

"Are you trying to kill us?" Craig snapped as Tom piloted the craft. Since Thacker broke the news that the mission was being brought forward, the training had intensified and Craig especially was losing patience.

Tom grunted, but he didn't take the bait.

Strapped to my seat, I felt more like I was being driven on a day trip than training for a space launch. It even came with complimentary squabbling kids. Tom answered simply, "No."

As the mission payload, I sat to the back of the others which gave me a clear view of how they were working. Even though I was part of the team, I felt very much out of the action, although I was beginning to think that was a good thing.

My ears buzzed with the pressure of the gallons of water bearing down on the simulator, it made the movement fluid and atmospheric, creating realistic conditions to train in. At first, I found it difficult to concentrate because my mind remained focused on the facts; I was inside the dimly lit belly of a mechanical beast, breathing the stale regurgitated air of the underwater simulator.

"*Orion,* gently does it," Beth's voice came through the speakers inside the capsule, as CAPCOM it was her role to communicate with the lander. "You've got drag, you need to adjust your positioning."

The simulator lurched to the left and I felt unease in my stomach, Charlie also looked uncomfortable. We'd run through the programme so many times I'd lost count and each time I felt less confident of success, more convinced of failure.

"What the fuck was that!" Craig barked. "You're a fucking maniac."

The simulator jolted, pulling a sharp right. A siren blared and a red light flashed on the control panel in front of me. Linda shook her head in annoyance. I knew it was bad enough when things went wrong without some dick pointing it out and rubbing it in your face. Serge looked to me, amused, he was of little use for this part of the mission.

"Abort, thresholds have been breached. *Orion* crew in imminent danger." An automated voice cried through my headset. The lights returned to full brightness inside the simulator and the vehicle righted itself into the correct orientation, the entire cockpit revolving into position.

"We're getting nowhere," Maggie said. "Maybe we should

take a break."

"The hell we will!" Craig said. "This clown needs all the practice he can get."

"Keep talking like that and you won't make it to launch!" Tom glared back. I gulped, there was going to be a fight, I could feel it.

"Listen to me you two!" Beth said from TICC control, anger in her voice. "You better stop this bullshit right now or I *will* be forced to find replacements for both of you. Understood?"

Muffled replies came from both.

"I want to give it one more try before we call it a day," Tom said. "I can do this." He looked across to Linda. "We can do this, right?"

"Of course," her voice as weary as she looked.

"Take your time," Maggie said pushing buttons on her control panel. The simulator started up once again, revolving us back into our almost vertical assent position.

The simulated *Orion* module shook as we took off, accelerating into the virtual sky. Tom kept CAPCOM updated and Maggie fed a constant stream of data to both pilots, passing them instructions.

"Throttling up," she said as we reached the right point in the launch sequence.

"Roger, go for throttle up." Tom confirmed. Linda punched in some codes on her control panel.

The simulator shook again, as our mission took off after the slow down for Max Q, the region of maximum dynamic pressure. I smiled; I was starting to pick things up.

I was an astronaut now, I had to speak their language.

5

The buzzing 5a.m. alarm pulled me from my sleep. I forced my eyes open and waited for them to stop rolling in their sockets. I took a deep breath, before getting up and wedging myself into the pile of waiting training gear. I was enjoying the strict morning exercise regime; first up, a brisk jog in the fresh morning air for thirty minutes to build up my cardiovascular system, followed by thirty minutes of push-ups, stomach crunches and weights.

I didn't mind the jogging, it gave me plenty of time to think about things and it was getting easier with each passing day. Today, I turned my jog into a racing pace, pushing my body with every crunching footfall on the morning frost. My breathing didn't falter, I could feel the difference in my fitness. Only months ago, I'd struggled to run for a bus, a ludicrous thought that now brought a smile to my face.

As I ran around the perimeter of the grounds, my mind wandered. I considered everything I'd learnt, all the new information I'd gathered and helped uncover. *We are one of many*, I heard Magi Eritrea's voice, *we were the first*. I wondered if the people of the so-called colonies looked like us, maybe they had different genetics, or maybe we were relations. It didn't matter either way, it was still a scary thought. And then there was our own evolutionary path...

Did we really impose a massive change on our physiology, was that even possible? It was certainly Charlie's considered opinion, and I guessed he was right. He'd spent his life studying ancient humans, their civilizations and languages.

I passed the front gate for the last time and took the last leg of my journey back to my quarters, passing Linda who was just starting her daily exercise regime. I felt invigorated when I finished and found it easy to carry on with my other exercises.

After a well-deserved shower I poured myself a bowl of muesli and crunched my way through.

At ten to nine I left my room, a smile plastered to my face. It was my first go at g-force training, and I was looking forward to it. I'd seen videos as a kid, astronauts and pilots zipping around in the giant centrifuge. I'd always wanted to have a try of it. Now was my chance.

The room was cold. There were no windows. Rows of fluorescent tubes ran along the ceiling stretching to the edges of the circular walls. In the centre of the room there was a vast platform with large pressure gauges and wheels attached, and above this was a gigantic metallic tube which stretched from the centre of the room to one side.

"Welcome to the human centrifuge," Tom said stepping into view.

"It looks..." I trailed off. "Complicated."

"Not really," Tom said. "You'll be in the pod at that end." He pointed to the bit extending to the outer wall. There was a small, single pane of glass, a window. "The technicians will spin you around, varying the g-forces in order to assess how your body handles it."

"Is that all." My eyes wide.

"Don't worry about it." Tom smiled. "Almost everyone passes out on their first go, and don't fret if you feel sick, there are bags for that inside the pod." As an experienced pilot, I guessed he was used to the g-forces his aircraft produced and he somehow seemed to make it sound overly simple. “You’ll have a commander talking to you all the time, you just have to do what she tells you.”

“We’re ready for you,” a voice called from above. I looked up and saw a woman wearing a dark suit waving from the observation window above. It was no surprise to see the lurking shadow of Bates in the background.

“Good luck.” Tom shook my hand.

With a deep breath, I made my way up to the observation room.

“I’m Samantha and I’ll be coordinating your training.” The middle-aged woman smiled, flashing her white teeth. “First I need you to put on this g-suit, it will help keep your blood flowing.”

“I was kinda hoping my heart would do that for me,” I said before looking to Bates. He said nothing.

“Trust me, it won’t.” She sounded ominous and I said nothing more and pulled on the g-suit. It was tight and I felt claustrophobic, like I couldn’t breathe. The smell of rubber was overpowering. “Don’t worry about it,” she smirked, I guessed she could see my discomfort. “As soon as you’re in there, the last thing on your mind will be this suit. Take a seat.”

I struggled to bend my knees, the trousers of the suit restricting my movement.

“There are some simple techniques to keep yourself conscious inside the pod,” Samantha said. “Put your feet firmly on the floor, as close together as possible and squeeze all your muscles, trying to pull them in to you as much as you can.”

I did as she said, tensing my legs.

“Right, the next is to practise sucking in your sphincter muscle, like you’re trying to hold in gas.”

I smiled as I attempted the exercise. I felt a flush of blood to my face.

“Good,” she soothed. “You look like you’re getting the

hang of this. The last thing you need to remember is to listen to my every word. I will be with you the whole time, talking you through. Just do exactly as I say and you'll be right."

"What do I do if I want to vomit?"

"Allow your body to do what it must," Samantha said. "You may notice a loss of vision as we move you through different g-forces, just stay calm, listen to my voice and let me know what is happening, okay?"

"I could lose my sight?" I gasped, unaware of the danger.

"It's temporary," she said. "You may stop seeing colours, or you might feel like you're looking through a tunnel – everything on the periphery will disappear – just remember to keep calm. As soon as blood returns to your eyes, your vision will return to normal." I gulped, the thought of losing my sight, even for just a few moments was terrifying. "Okay, I think we're all set."

Samantha escorted me to the pod, helping me inside and strapping me up.

"Enjoy," she said finally as she sealed the door and bolted me in.

"You're doing good," Samantha's voice came across the speakers in the pod. "Take a deep breath and relax, your heart rate is elevated, I want you to try and bring that down before we begin. Just focus on your breathing."

I took a deep breath, held it for a moment and then exhaled. A moment later I repeated the process. I felt my heart slowing in my chest, the pounding eased in my ears.

"That's good," she said. "In a moment you will feel a slight jolt as the centrifuge starts spinning, it's nothing to get worked up about, perfectly normal." I felt a thud below me, a clamp releasing perhaps, and then I felt the jolt and I rocked back into the seat. "Okay, we're moving."

If it wasn't for the constant flickering of the strip lighting above the glass window, I wouldn't have known I was moving. As the speed increased, the strobe effect of the lights became a blur of white.

"You should start feeling like you're moving upward rapidly in a speeding elevator," Samantha's voice soothed. "Take a deep breathe again, relax. In a moment we're going to increase the speed gradually up to around three g's. You'll feel like you're on a great roller-coaster, just allow your body to feel the force."

The screen in front of me reported the g-force, it began to increase in steady notches. My stomach rose in my chest, it was like being on a never-ending elevator ride, constantly accelerating. The figures on the display stopped rising when they hit three-point-zero.

"You're doing perfect," Samantha reported. "In a couple of seconds, we'll increase to six g's. I want you to tense your legs for me like we practised. You might find it difficult to breathe so I'll instruct you to breathe every four seconds, okay?" I blinked into the camera in front of me.

The numbers on the display began to rise once again. At five-point-three g's I started feeling short of breath. Samantha's voice instructed me to breathe after counting to four, it was difficult to do while clenching my leg muscles and I felt my pain pulling across my stomach, the waistband of the g-suit digging in.

At six-point-zero, the numbers locked.

"Okay, now I want you to clench...breathe...as hard as you can, pull in...breathe...your sphincter, hold in that gas...breathe. We're moving up to nine g's."

I felt the mounting pressure threatening to snap my head back and it became more difficult to breathe. I focused my attention, concentrating and clenching, one eye remained watching the numbers on the screen. The blue neon colours of the digital display drained to grey.

"Eyes..." I forced out. "Colour." It was all I could manage in between breaths.

"You're doing great...breathe," Samantha said, her voice encouraging. "Your body is starting to draw blood from your head. Just keep breathing and clenching. You're now at...breathe...nine-point-two. We're just going to edge up a little to see how you handle...breathe."

My vision darkened and I felt a buzzing in my ears.

"Nine-point-nine, ten, ten-point-three, ten-point-five, ten-point-nine, eleven...." I was aware of Samantha's voice, calling the numbers but I was in almost complete darkness now, fading fast.

Butterflies were flapping their wings in my ears, muffling Samantha's voice and then drowning it out altogether. I fought to remain conscious, tensing my muscles as hard as I could. In the darkness, I knew it was futile, I couldn't stop the inevitable.

A sudden jolt in the pod made me jump. I thought the centrifuge might be slowing, but it was difficult to tell. One by one the butterflies fluttered away, and my ears buzzed with the electric whine of the mechanism beneath me.

"Excellent," Samantha's voice said, louder now, closer in the darkness. "You're slowing back down to two-g's. We're going to do a rapid onset exercise, increasing the speed rapidly and then slowing back down. Just remember to concentrate, listen to my voice and do what I tell you."

Blurred colours filtered through my eyes as my vision started returning. At first it felt like I was watching a computer-generated image being created, pixel by pixel, and then in a hurry, the image rendered. I focused on the blue haze of the display, I was still at two g's.

"Five seconds," Samantha said. "Okay, clench your legs

and buttocks...breathe..."

I saw the numbers rapidly increasing and felt the g-force thrusting me down and back into my seat. I squeezed as hard as I could and drew in a quick sharp breath.

"Lift your head up." I was aware of Samantha's voice.

"It is up," I said.

"Lift your head," she repeated. "Are you with me? Raise your head."

Yellow light filtered into my eyes and I realised I was staring up at the ceiling of the pod. I hauled myself upright and looked down at the display. The centrifuge had stopped, I was stationary.

"Do you know what happened?"

"Did I pass out?" Burning pain throbbed across the back of my head.

"Yes," she said. "It's called g-LOC – a g-force induced Loss of Consciousness. It's common, especially during the rapid onset exercises. You passed out on a rapid ascent to seven g's, which isn't bad for a first-timer. By using the exercises, you should be able to hold out to around nine g's or more. Over the next few months you'll get to practise this over with me."

6

A week later it was time to face my fear. Tom took me to an RAF airfield for my first flight in a fighter jet, Bates drove us. On the journey Tom told me he'd been stationed at RAF

Linton-on-Ouse as an experienced Wing Commander.

"This is a second-generation Typhoon Eurofighter," Tom explained as we walked out across the tarmac and into the open hangar. There was little wind, but there was a bitter chill in the air, I could taste winter. "It's the best fighter in its class, far better than the Raptors the American's *still* use."

He sniffed as he reached up inside the cockpit of the jet and pulled out a helmet for each of us. "It's a clear day so I hope to get us up to high altitude where we should be able to crank up over Mach 2. This jet will have us in the air in less than seven seconds." I understood the relationship between the speed of sound and an object moving through air. I'd covered it – at great length – with Professor Frost, I even remembered the calculation.

"I'm ready," I said, securing my helmet, the tight g-suit trousers still restricting my movement, but I was used to it. We climbed into the cockpit of the craft and Tom sealed us in.

"Enjoy the ride." Tom strapped himself in and pulled on his face mask. I did the same. From now on, we would only talk to each other through these masks, the speakers inside our helmets. Tom fired up the engines and rolled the craft onto the runway. "Hang tight," Tom's voice filled my ears.

The engines roared, the acceleration awesome, hurtling us across the airfield. I was forced back into my seat. I counted in my head, and as I reached six I felt the front wheel of the jet lift from the ground. On the count of seven the runway was already a distant memory. By nine seconds we were turning sharply to the left, my stomach lurched and I squeezed my legs as I'd been taught.

I watched Tom handling the controls, his hand controlling the joystick like a kid playing a video game.

"I'll do a few demonstration manoeuvres," Tom said into my ear, I could hear him smiling, proud of his abilities.

With a flick of his wrist on the controls, the jet accelerated further, banked sharply and I felt my body moving in an arched climb until we hung upside down. We flew like this on a vertical path for a minute or so before Tom flicked his wrist once again and we rolled over, flying in a straight line, the correct way up.

The jet bolted forwards, its nose now pointing towards the ground and I could see what I knew were rolling hills, but now appeared as patches of lighter and darker shades of green. We plummeted towards them.

At the last second Tom pulled the craft out, banked sharply to the right, round what felt like a full one-eighty-degrees and then flipped up so we were flying along the wing tips.

"How you doing back there?"

"Good," I forced out.

"Do you want to take over?" For a moment I felt like I was in a dream. At any moment the jet would crash into a hill or mountain and I would jolt awake. It didn't happen. "I'll bring her up onto a level." The jet corrected itself, now flying on a horizontal path once again. "Take the stick in your hand and just ease it forwards."

I did as instructed and felt the craft accelerate.

"Good, now pull back, gently." The craft jerked. "Don't worry, just remember to be slow and soft, if your movements are jerky then that's how she will respond." I waited for his command. "You have control."

"Okay," I said, edging the joystick forwards once again. The engines fired up once again, thrusting us forwards. "I have control."

"We want to make a right turn here." Tom didn't tell me how to do it, so I nudged the joystick to the right, as gentle as my hands could afford. The Typhoon responded, its wings dipping to the right, and slowly we mounted a curve. "Pull back a little," Tom spoke in my ear. "You're getting the hang of this." And I felt I was.

We flew for twenty minutes before Tom brought the jet in to land.

7

It was so sudden, I'd barely managed to peel my eyes from the textbook Professor Frost had given me to study. I looked up, just in time to see Craig's fist smash into the side of Charlie's head.

I jumped to my feet as Charlie cried out in pain and dropped to the floor, his hands clutching at his face.

"You're a fucking loser!" Craig spat before putting his boot in, kicking Charlie, catching his chest. Charlie let out a muffled moan before gasping for breath. I ran to his side, pushing Craig away.

"What the fuck are you doing?" I bellowed at Craig before turning my attention to Charlie. Beneath his fingers, I could already see the beginnings of an angry purple welt forming on the side of his face. "Are you okay?" It was a dumb question, I knew. Charlie said nothing, his eyes scrunched shut. "What the hell's going on with you?" I turned to Craig, fuming. "Maggie has already warned you."

"He started it!" Craig yelled back, still agitated.

"What? Are you like eleven?" I snapped, anger filtering into my voice. I'd come to think of Charlie as a good friend over the months, he was a good guy, very knowledgeable. Yes, he could act like a childish fool, but don't we all sometimes? Wasn't it just a little bit of freedom from society's rules and conventions, something to keep sanity in a manic world? "Sit the fuck down!"

Craig's face flushed with sudden shame, his head drooped, his arms dangling like a knuckle dragging teenager.

"Let's sit you up over here," I said helping Charlie to his feet and escorted him into a seat. "I'll fetch the doctor and if I can find her, Maggie." I shot Craig a quick look, a warning that he'd better not try anything further while I was gone. His eyes met mine for a second before his head sunk once again.

"Well!" Maggie's voice demanded, it scared me and I was innocent.

Craig scowled at Charlie, tight-lipped.

"You're such a baby." Charlie's hand reached for the purple swelling extending from his bottom jaw into the recess of his eye. It looked painful. "Grow some fucking balls!"

"No excuses you two," Maggie said. "We're not children here, you should have more self-control. If something is getting to you, see me." Maggie's gaze turned to Charlie. "I expect more from you."

"I went too far. I know I shouldn't have drawn those moustaches on your photographs. I'm sorry." Charlie sounded sincere.

Craig's expression didn't falter, he continued glowering at Charlie. It was clear no apology would pass his lips.

"Okay, now before you both go I want you to think a little more respectfully in future. This is your *last* warning, Craig. Do I make myself clear?" Silence. "I didn't hear you." She said, and I smiled, understanding her tactics. She was responding to childish behaviour by treating them like children, just like parents do.

"Yes." They echoed in unison.

"Off you go."

I watched as they both left the room. Maggie came over to join me on the sofa, she looked drained and stressed, her cheeks red with exertion.

"You handled that well," I said. She sounded just like a mother, but I didn't say it because I had a feeling it might be a sore point for Maggie. She'd mentioned about the lack of children in her life before, and well I didn't want to remind her of the fact. Especially as she had no significant other, and the spark was still obvious between her and Charlie. It couldn't be easy to deal with, knowing that the man you loved couldn't commit to you.

"I just don't get men sometimes," she groaned, throwing her head back into the sofa. "It'd be so much easier if they could just grow up."

"Can't do it, I'm afraid." I smiled at her. "It's just not in our nature."

8

It was mid-afternoon, two days before launch. The sun was beating down on me through the thick glass window, shining onto my bed, scorching my soul. It was unseasonably warm, one of the hottest beginnings to autumn on record, the temperature soaring to mid-thirties on occasion.

My eyes closed, an open book resting on my stomach, rising and falling with my every breath. Slowly, my mind powered down and I drifted off into a heat-induced sleep.

In the darkness I heard rasping, a creature speaking – I say a creature because it didn't sound human, the way the voice clicked in and out of words. I think they were words, but I didn't know for sure, for one thing they were too hushed to hear.

As I focused my attention, straining my ears to listen, I felt my body sinking, being dragged towards shadows lurking in the depths.

My eyes fluttered open, the brilliant light of another sunny day, but looking into the sky I saw a second planetary object and recognised the partial view as that of the Earth. It was a lunar morning.

I sat up inside Russia's body and listened to the strange noises once again, only this time they were closer. They were words, alien words and Russia understood. He climbed out of his bunk – a small down-stuffed mattress on top of a stone slab, it was luxury so Russia believed – and ran to the window, pushing the wooden slats open. In a rush of hot dusty air, he saw them.

There were three aliens, their skin darkly tanned. As they moved, flexing their muscles, silvery-green flecks sparkled across their scaled skin. One looked up at Russia in acknowledgement before continuing to speak with the others.

Russia knew from their clothing, the red loin cloth draped to their knees and their green robes that these were the Ambassador's guards, they appeared often, and on occasion helped Magi Eritrea to resolve disputes among her people.

"Does anyone attend your needs?" Russia asked into the air, he would be in trouble if the Ambassador's guards were not shown their people's hospitality. A series of clicks and short rasps escaped the holes in their faces; they did not have lips, or visible tongues.

"We do not wish for anything," they responded. "But you are tardy, your master will not be pleased."

"Accept my humble apologies," Russia held his hands together and bowed to the aliens, to me it seemed over the top, too gracious, but that was how things were done, there were protocols to follow.

Russia dropped his bed clothes – a single sheet of cloth placed over the head and tied at the waist – and prepared himself in a hurry before leaving for Magi Eritrea's chamber.

Inside he heard the hushed rasping of the alien Ambassador.

"We require three more of your people."

"You can't keep coming here and taking my people like this," Magi Eritrea's voice remained calm and gentle. "You may take two, a couple and offer them your better life, but I can allow no more."

"You are in no place to bargain with me!" The rasp of the alien sounded angry and Russia shuddered. He had seen their rage before in his dreams. The burning green flames escaping their craft and scorching the earth. He'd never witnessed it himself, but there were stories that spoke of fury beyond his imagination. It scared him.

"I am sorry," Magi Eritrea was gracious in her defeat. "I have no right to tell you."

"No, you don't." The alien spat. "Send me three of your strongest men, arrange for them to meet us outside our craft. I will return them by sundown." There was the unmistakeable sound of the alien Ambassador's padding footfalls coming our way. Just in time, Russia slipped into the dark shadows.

The Ambassador stormed past and out into the open air.

The bright light of the morning sun blinded me and I closed my eyes to shield myself.

When my eyes opened again, I looked up at the ceiling of my room in the SARA facility. I sat upright and considered what I'd seen. Where were the aliens taking our people? The files Thacker had given me were filled with alien abduction stories, I'd never believed them, but maybe I was wrong and maybe there was truth behind the stories.

A few minutes later I left my room to reported my dream to Thacker and Bates.

CONSTELLATION

CHAPTER 11

5th November 2022

It was an anxious moment as I stepped across the gantry between the airport terminal and the plane. The interior was plush, unlike the commercial flights I'd previously boarded. I felt a pang of fear as reality struck, training was over, this was for real – all the training hadn't prepared me for this moment. The rest of the *Constellation* crew were already settling themselves into their reclined seats. I felt like I'd known them forever.

I took a final deep breath of my native air and then I moved inside. The recirculated air smelled clinical.

The eyes of my fellow crew were full of anticipation as they glanced up at me, and Maggie stepped aside to let me get to my seat, but I noted she was watching me closely. It made me shudder, feeling suddenly claustrophobic, like I'd done the day I'd met them all.

"Are you okay?" Charlie looked over from the opposite seat, his brow furrowed with concern. "You don't look like you got much sleep."

"I'll be fine," I said, lying. "It was a long night just staring up at the ceiling." I turned my attention to the world outside the window. It didn't take long for our journey to begin.

My stomach rolled as the plane took to the sky on its journey to the *Centre Spatial Guyanais* in French Guiana. Moments into the journey I began to relax, my eyes closed although I didn't drift off, my mind was still full with the same thoughts from my sleepless night.

It was almost 1 a.m.

My room was still, the air stuffy. I lay on top of the covers of the bed, staring with wide eyes, my brain buzzing. In just under four hours my alarm would cry out and I would have to prepare myself for launch and I had yet to fall asleep. Insomnia was excruciating and inescapable.

Questions trickled through my mind, keeping me awake. Would we find the answers we were looking for? What if the aliens came while we were up on the moon? Would they attack? Did we have evidence to suggest they were hostile? Were they watching us, and how would they react?

I couldn't think of any reason to suspect they *were* peaceful. Colonising empty worlds didn't seem aggressive, but did we know or understand their intent? Here on Earth, colonial times were aggressive, bloody, and led to years of misery for the subjugated – most colonies had been created by violent force, claiming land and people as if they were entitled to do this. It was horrific inhumanity, targeting the weak, indiscriminately – friend or foe. For all we knew, we were born into slavery, it would explain why mankind had acted in this way throughout history. But that would be an easy answer in order to absolve ourselves of our indiscretions, a wholly unacceptable answer in my view.

In any case, that made no sense. I'd never once seen

Russia in my dreams as a slave to anyone other than Magi Eritrea – and even then, the term slave did not fit for he had freedom. All I knew for certain was that Magi Eritrea had concerns and it had something to do with the other colonies. There was nothing in the scriptures about this, I'd checked Charlie's translations in the little spare time I had had between my training and studying for my final exam with Professor Frost. I'd passed with exceptional ease.

It was Magi Eritrea's fear that remained with me, because my memory of Russia told me that this was so unusual for her. It *meant* something.

The plane surged upwards and I opened my eyes.

I looked out the window, tips of trees waved wildly beneath us as the ground approached. We banked sharply before turning a sharp right. A moment later the engines roared as we touched down, and I felt a sudden deceleration. I sucked in a breath, I still felt discomfort during landings. The plane taxied along the runway.

The changing pressure of the cabin throbbed in my ears.

Charlie looked over and I forced a smile.

2

Three hours were left on the launch clock, or L minus three hours, as we said in our vernacular.

It was time to get moving. We left the astronaut's quarters and made our way through the mass of media, each journalist shouting to make sure their question was heard above the others. We didn't answer any of them as we were chaperoned to the waiting transport vehicle.

The air was sharp with frost and my nose stung as I breathed in.

I found my movements stiff inside the restrictive space suit, that along with the super tight g-suit squeezing my legs, it was amazing any of us could walk. The first time we'd suited up Maggie told me how fantastic it was to be inside such a free moving suit. She recalled how heavy and bulky NASA's old suits were, which retired along with the space shuttles. I didn't fully appreciate her comments because I didn't have the luxury of her comparison, and even though I'd bulked out during training, the suits were still damn heavy.

We were driven to the launch site, I watched out the window the whole time. It was the first time I'd seen a real space vehicle up close, and it felt good to see the new *Orion* craft we'd be travelling inside.

Years ago, I'd watched the final voyage of the *Endeavour* space shuttle live on television and I'd seen the designs of the *Orion* and *Ares* rocket many years before its maiden launch. The inaugural voyage of *Orion* took to the skies three years later than the original plans. The systems had flown many times since, so I was at ease with the safety of the craft. Now SARA owned the craft and our mission marked the start of a new era, manned space exploration. It was the first time since Apollo 17 in 1972 that mankind would step on another world.

The rocket was surrounded by towers – mainly lightning arresters – but we would climb the larger one called the umbilical tower. I looked up, the elevator stretched all the way up; long and daunting. I was amazed by the sheer scale of everything. It was a scary thought that a single spark could set about a cascade of explosions beyond anything I'd witnessed before, unleashing the awesome fury of the fuel laden boosters.

The door to the elevator opened and I looked across the gantry towards the cockpit of the crew control module. It was much cooler up here. I hesitated before stepping onto the bridge, affording a single glance down to convince myself I wasn't dreaming.

Before I climbed aboard, I took one last breath of earthly air, knowing that it could be my last – 'prepare for all eventualities,' Maggie had told me early into my training. 'You never know where your last breath may come from'. I hadn't felt reassured, but now I felt more at peace. I looked back to see Charlie behind me. He had a look of awe in his eyes, and a giant exhilarated smile dancing across his lips.

Everything will be okay, I told myself, remembering my mother's words from our final telephone conversation the night before. 'Travel safe' she'd said to me, as if I were only trekking up the motorway to Edinburgh for the weekend.

I let out a sigh, *goodbye world.* I took my seat and strapped myself in. The others were already busy, checking the configuration of the equipment. Charlie sat down and looked across at me, raising his eyebrows.

A moment later, the hatch door closed and locked, and I felt a sudden panic. I was really doing this, I was going into space.

I closed my eyes, remembering my training. Everything would be okay. All I had to do was breathe normally. I kept my eyes closed and took one deep breath, expelled the air and then inhaled to the depths of my being, holding it for a moment before releasing, visualising the expelling of my anxiety with it.

3

Steam condensed inside my visor as I exhaled, the heat was uncomfortable. The countdown continued, L minus 20 minutes.

Tom and Linda ran through check-lists and confirmations, just as they had done in the simulator and then Tom relayed this to CAPCOM situated at the TICC. It felt relaxed inside the crew module, more so than in the training simulator. Maybe it was because inside the simulator errors could be made, but we all knew things were different there was no room for screw-ups. I found myself idling away my time, waiting for the launch. Charlie appeared nervous, fidgeting in his seat. I guessed he'd never been in any immediate danger before in his line of work. Neither had I, but I'd adjusted.

In my mind I had the end target in sight; the ziggurat. Whenever I closed my eyes or blinked, I saw the deep terracotta of the rough mudbrick structure etched into my lids. They felt closer than they ever had, knowing I would soon be able to see and touch it... It was the stuff of my dreams, literally.

Of course, there was an inherent danger with our mission, as Thacker had explained in our mission brief.

"Our presence on the lunar surface may trigger an Armageddon unlike anything we have experienced before." Thacker explained in dramatic fashion. I remember being shocked by his pessimism. By now, I understood life as we know it, didn't just happen by chance on Earth. It was brought here, led by my ancestor, Russia. But there was more to it than that. Life on the moon was not as natural as it had once appeared either. This too came from the outside, created by an alien race, for a purpose still unknown to us.

"Our activities on Earth have been monitored by *them* for as long as we have records. The *Constellation* mission could be seen by *them* as hostile and *they* may respond."

"If we truly have a purpose in all this," I said. "Why would they wait until now?"

"Mark is right," Serge said. "We've got nuclear weapons, what have they got?" I shivered. The way he spoke suggested we were about to enter a battle, a war beyond any scale known to mankind.

"Our weapons are powerful, yes," Thacker said. "But imagine *their* weapons. Earth's most powerful artillery could, put simply, be pea-shooters compared to *theirs*. We don't know enough about their technology, and what we do know is millions of years out-of-date. How far have we advanced in just a handful of decades?"

I shivered at the thought then and I did so again now. Thacker was right, his logic sound. We were expendable, they had demonstrated that to us once before, even if a few of us had survived the catastrophe that destroyed our home world. There was nothing to say they wouldn't do it again.

It meant our mission was short and precise, carefully planned. Our brief was simple, locate the ziggurat and search for ancient texts. If during our time on the lunar surface alien visitations on Earth increased or a massive invasion appeared on the horizon we'd abort, finished or not.

While I understood Thacker's logic, I simply didn't see what we'd gain by returning to Earth empty handed. All of this was based on best guesses, we didn't really know much about our alien creators, we didn't understand why they had created us in the first place. All we knew is that we had escaped once, and we were now different people, fighters. I didn't believe we could fight our way out of a mass invasion, our strengths lay in understanding their weaknesses.

4

L minus 9 minutes.

I caught Maggie's gaze for a second and she rolled her eyes. Charlie was talking solidly without stopping for breath. I yawned, realising I hadn't been listening and focused on his voice coming through the speakers inside my helmet.

"Just think, if there are others out there..."

"Anthropologists will be pleased," Maggie cut in. It took a moment for me to understand what she meant. If the 'human' form existed elsewhere in the universe and in other shifts of time, then what was known by anthropologists was only in its infancy. There was plenty left to argue over and I knew Maggie well enough to understand this was her ultimate point. "Cut the chatter, we've entering mission critical time." Charlie stopped talking without argument. Maggie had control over him, and not just as the commander of our mission. Maggie caught me smiling and I think I blushed, but it may just have been the heat inside my suit.

As silence stole over the crew module of the *Orion* craft, I questioned my own mortality. Would our journey be safe, and what of our return? I didn't suppose anyone cared if I returned or not, and then my thoughts turn to my terminal mother. Her illness had progressed and she was refusing further treatment, which would have been palliative at any rate. There was nothing I could do now but wait for the inevitable. I didn't look forward to that day, and what if it was during the mission? Would SARA even tell me? No, my fate hardly mattered if there was nobody waiting for my return.

The promise of a safe return was not mine to make.

Failure was always an option, although none of use preferred to consider this, but we could not predict the future. We were reliant on the past safety records of the craft and the experience of Maggie and the other experienced astronauts and the TICC team.

As for my knowledge of the lunar civilisation, my visions had stalled just like my sleep. Apparently dreaming and insomnia don't go together. I of course couldn't help but see the haunting image of Magi Eritrea hanging from her cell wall and that made me feel cold. I was sure though that our presence on the moon would trigger something inside of each of us and we'd have a cascade of memories flooding back to us. That was the hope anyway.

At L minus 6 minutes, Maggie reached over, took my gloved hand in hers and squeezed.

"Keep tight," she said. A moment later she released my hand and turned back to her console.

The sound of my breath echoed loudly inside my helmet.

5

Charlie broke the silence, saying, "I bet I will see the moon first." Maggie shook her head, and I couldn't stop myself from laughing.

"You wouldn't know what you were looking at," Craig said, jumping in on Charlie's childish game. I wasn't surprised. They were both quite similar in that respect. "You'll be lucky to spot the sun at twenty paces. I'll see the moon way before you know which way to look."

"Oh really?" Charlie sounded enthused, he'd hooked his target. "Let's bet on it."

"How much can you afford to lose? Twenty?" Craig said, Charlie instantly laughed. "Okay, fifty?"

Charlie snapped back with, “one hundred.”

“Will you two shut-up,” Linda’s voice croaked from Craig’s side. She was busy coordinating figures on her console.

“Deal,” Craig said turning around in his seat so he could shake Charlie’s hand.

“We just hit two minutes,” Maggie said. The pod went silent.

“The L-OX just undocked.” Craig was watching out of the small observation window to his side. I knew from all the simulations that meant the liquid oxygen arm had retracted from *Orion*. We were now running entirely on *Orion*’s systems. I took a deep breath expecting that the air would taste somehow staler, but it was imagination only. The air was fresh, recycling through the scrubbers.

The wait was almost over.

I could see images of people crowded around screens of all kinds, etched on the back of my eyelids when I blinked. They watched us, live, waiting to see the craft take to the skies. I wondered if anyone suspected the true nature of our mission, I didn’t know how SARA – even NASA for that matter – had managed to keep their discovery secret for so long. Surely everyone needed to know what was happening?

A sudden burst of excitement pummelled at my chest, but I shook my head, locking the feeling away, grounding myself. This was no time to lose my composure; everyone expected me to maintain my professionalism. I took another deep breath and remembered the simulations; I knew the order of running and I braced.

“Sixty seconds to launch,” Maggie confirmed.

Charlie blew me a playful kiss, smiling all the while. We’d become good friends, our time with Professor Frost had brought us together, allied against him. I enjoyed Charlie’s stories, even when they became tiresome and he wouldn’t take the hint to stop talking.

I returned a wave to him, before pretending to catch his kiss.

"Here we go," Maggie said as the pod jolted. The metal frame shook and rattled beneath my feet and I knew the main rocket engines had ignited. All the simulations had done little to prepare me for the battering vibration. "Hang tight."

I forced myself into the seat, squeezing my legs together and down against the floor preparing myself for the thrust. The last few seconds extended as I counted down in my head.

"All three at 100," Maggie confirmed as the rocket boosters ignited at L minus 4 seconds.

"There she blows!" Charlie shouted over the rising engine noise as we hit L minus 0. Extra weight bore down on my legs. The craft rocked wildly, everything seemed blurred. I forced my eyes closed, waiting for an explosion to rip through the craft and exterminate us. It never came.

When I opened my eyes again, I could see the vibration had eased because my vision was clear. In fact, there were very few visual cues that suggested we were moving. I glanced down at the screen in front of me, we were pulling a mild one-point-five g's. A new wave of tranquillity washed over me, even though I knew this was one of the most dangerous stages of the launch sequence.

The calm didn't stop my stomach lurching as the craft jolted me forwards.

"TICC, *Orion* roll program." We were eight seconds into the launch, our rotation program began. As the craft rolled, turning upside, my throat tightened and my breathing became laboured. I jammed my eyes closed and remembered being inside the fighter jet, trying to convince myself this was no different. In the darkness of my eyelids I saw the Typhoon jet, and remembered the powerful roar of the engines, picturing the ground as seen from inside. My breathing began to ease, under my control.

I attempted a smile, the g-force restricting my muscles.

At T plus 20 seconds we reached Mach 1.

"Throttling down," Maggie reported, we were reaching Max Q. I kept my body tight, my legs firm, my buttocks clenched. The craft began to bounce like we were driving over speed bumps at eighty or ninety kilometres an hour. It hurt, the waistband of the g-suit trousers pinched with every jolt.

"Throttling up," Maggie said. We were past the Max Q region.

"Thirty-five thousand, going through one point five." Tom reported our height and the Mach speed we'd reached.

"That's what I got," Maggie said. A few moments later she added, "Go at throttle up."

Two minutes into the launch, a sudden blast rocked me in my seat. Without needing to look, I knew the solid rocket boosters of the *Ares* launch vehicle had ejected. The g-forces began to rise steeply, but it was all under control. My eyes burst open with the force and I smiled inside. This was way better than any of the simulations, it was awesome.

I knew in another five minutes we'd technically be in space, but to me I was already there.

6

"*Orion* – things look good from here." It was Beth.

"Roger that CAPCOM." Tom answered. "Comms are a little foggy."

"Copy that," Beth said. "I'll get someone onto it."

"We're ready to take up our low Earth orbit." Maggie tapped the screen in front of her and ran her finger around the virtual dial to adjust trajectory. "Everything look good to you?" She was checking with Tom. The console in front of me flashed numbers, reporting our altitude, velocity, g's as well as atmospheric conditions according to the hundreds of sensors on the outside of the craft.

"Uh-huh," Tom said. "We're good to go."

The darkness of space stared back at me through the small glass porthole to Craig's side. I wanted to get out of my seat and take a closer look, see the stars for what they truly were, but I couldn't, at least not until we had reached a stable orbital trajectory.

"Do the stars always look that bright?" Charlie asked. I turned and saw he was glancing over my shoulder, peering at the reinforced window. He had an excited look in his eyes, the child in him awed.

"Always," Maggie said simply.

We still had a long journey ahead of us and I was living on adrenaline. I felt like I might crash any time now, my body exhausted. I shut my eyes, but I knew I couldn't keep them closed, there was a massive universe outside that window and it called my name.

"Later we can dim the lights so you don't get so much glare," Tom said.

It was almost time for the second part of the launch. The *Altair* Lunar lander sat on the back of another *Ares V* rocket, waiting for authorisation to blast into orbit. Once it reached the same low orbit our engines would fire up and the telemetry and automatic guidance systems would talk to one another to line us up so we could dock. This would give us all the time we needed to prepare the *Altair* module for the lunar surface.

I couldn't wait.

"*Orion* – initiating orbital sequence one," Tom reported to CAPCOM.

"Good to know." I heard Beth's voice, she sounded

pleased, relieved almost, as if she'd been expecting something to go wrong. It didn't inspire me with confidence.

I looked back to the window, longing to take a closer look. *It won't be long*, I told myself. I drifted into the darkness. Deeper down, sparks of green illuminated the way and as I moved towards them, a spark shot up towards me, striking me. The same tingling energy I'd felt when I'd held the green rock. It pulsed inside of me.

My eyes snapped open and I shook my head. That was weird.

When I blinked, Thacker's face swam into view. I could hear him, distant, but I recognised his drawl. It faded, but my frown remained.

CHAPTER 12

The ICC was a hive of activity, but Thacker preferred to observe from the office above, to him it was like watching ants working in co-ordination to achieve their goal.

Thacker topped up his glass of whisky and offered the bottle to Bates. Was it too early to be celebrating? He didn't care. Bates shook his head; he did care, apparently.

"Sir, I think we have a problem," Khan stepped onto the metal promontory, catching Bates's eye first. "We've received an error report on the comms link, one of the transmitters may have sustained damage during launch."

"Damn it!" Bates said, as if he'd been expecting it and stepped out to go make himself useful in the control centre. Thacker was slower to react, a nagging suspicion at the back of his mind. Maybe this was cause for alarm, but he didn't get up. Thacker stroked his chin for a moment.

"Is that all?" He asked.

"Yes, sir". With that Khan left the room. Thacker remained with his hand on his chin. Before he stood, he downed his glass. The smooth taste of the oak aged whiskey would remain for some time, just as he liked it.

He moved to the doorway and leaned out to see what was happening below. Bates was red-faced, hardly news of course since he seemed to bluster more than the stormy season. His hands were wild, gesticulating this way and that, before one reached for the balding patch at the back of his head and stroked it for a moment.

Thacker shouted over the railings to Khan, "Do me a favour. See what data you can pull from *Mistral.*"

"We need to keep our resources focused on the mission," Bates croaked, craning his neck to look up at Thacker.

"*Mistral* is still in close lunar orbit," Thacker reasoned. "I want to know if there is a wider issue with communications." He said nothing more, stepping back into the office and took up his seat.

He rested his feet on the desk, another glass of whisky clasped in his hand. He reached for his tablet device and tapped the file manager application and logged into the secured data storage and loaded a document. It was a large document, but Thacker scanned through it with ease, looking for a specific reference. His finger stopped in the centre of the screen.

"What's your theory?" Bates's voice demanded as he came into the office. Thacker looked up from his tablet and shook his head.

"It could be nothing," Thacker said.

"Even I don't believe that you believe that," Bates said flatly, resting his hands on the edge of the desk, leaving sticky sweat marks when he moved away. "I want to know what you're thinking."

"No," Thacker said, his eyes reverting to the document. Thacker highlighted the section of the page that concerned him. It was an extract from the scriptures; *they will know when the time comes.*

"You don't think *they* are here already?" Bates seemed

surprised to Thacker. When he looked across, there was panic in his eyes. Thacker knew that was the reason Bates lost out on the position as Administrator for SARA, he lacked backbone, at the first sign of trouble, there was always a sense of terror about him.

"Hell no," Thacker said. Bates eased. "I don't think Charlie's explanations go far enough. He suggests the scriptures were left as a warning for us, that we would know when the time came, but that just doesn't make sense. Why would we need a warning? A warning about what?"

"Or about whom," Bates offered. "Do you think *they* know?"

"Maybe," Thacker said, his hand now caressing his chin. Drastic times called for a cool head with plenty of thought. If there was something untoward happening he already knew of a possible solution, but it was risky. "We may need to reinstate *Project Serenity*."

"*Serenity*?" Bates blinked. Thacker almost let his eyes roll, it was clear Bates hadn't done his research. There were terabytes of data dedicated to the project Thacker initiated, and Bates had sufficient clearance.

"*Project Serenity* sought to build an interstellar communicational device, to develop an early warning system to spy on our alien friends, but the funding was diverted elsewhere and the project closed."

"If it's not live, we can't use it." Bates shook his head, stuck to protocol and rules.

"We could invoke *Serenity* now," Thacker said. "We have government backing, something I didn't have before." But Bates was still shaking his head and Thacker's eyes narrowed, frustrated. Bates just couldn't see straight in a crisis. Thacker couldn't understand how the man coped at NASA, it was beyond his comprehension that they'd let an unsteady hand take the top position. But Thacker's opinion didn't matter, it was all about appearance, and from an outward position Bates made the right impressions.

"It might be nothing," Bates said.

"Are you really prepared to wait this one out?" Thacker demanded to know, his feet flying to the floor and his body edging forwards in his seat. "There are lives at stake here, civilian lives." Just as he expected, Bates's face flushed with new vigour.

"We have to give it time," Bates replied. "Let's see what develops in the next forty-eight hours before we jump to false conclusions. We still have comms, maybe there was a problem with one of the sensors." Thacker felt he was missing the point, but Bates didn't hang around long enough for him to say so. Bates left and Thacker thumped the desk with both fists after him.

Bates was infuriating, his attitude unconscionable to Thacker. They were his decisions to make, Bates was simply there to help inform him, but how could someone with less objectivity than a mouse come to such immense conclusions – there were ramifications for both action and inaction, and if he was right, then they could be vast.

Something had to be done, waiting wasn't an option.

Thacker lifted the phone and dialled. It was time to get direction from a higher power.

2

The Earth looked glorious, a stunning beauty I'd never imagined seeing in this way.

I stood by the observation window and was the first to see back to Earth as our module rotated into position. It was perfect, vast swathes of white swirling around deep blues with crisp greens interspersed. For a moment it's no exaggeration to say it took my breath away, surpassing every experience of my life so far. If this was what being a cosmonaut was about then I wanted to be stationed up here. Seeing Earth in all its splendour, I began to understand why Maggie kept coming back. It certainly puts problems into perspective.

"Isn't she wonderful," Maggie's voice came through clear inside my helmet and I turned to find her right behind me. She'd been busy ever since we'd docked with the *Altair* module a few hours ago. We'd reached our higher orbit around Earth and soon we'd be in position for our slingshot to the moon, the precise details carefully programmed into the flight computer and painstakingly triple checked.

It would still be a full day's journey before we set down on the lunar surface and already I felt this was too long for me to wait. My chest burned with excitement.

"It's fantastic." Full of wonder.

"I never get tired of seeing her," Maggie reminisced. "I think I'm addicted to it up here." She looked into my eyes. "Do you think that's possible?"

"Sure," I said. A thought entered my mind, what if I never had the opportunity to see this view again. I shuddered.

"Sometimes I think Charlie wasn't the only one already committed." She shook her head, instantly changing the subject. "When I've been on the ISS, I find it so relaxing to sit and watch her on the observation deck. It's so hypnotic." Her voice drifted off.

"Yeah." I turned back to the window. "I can see that already."

As I closed my eyes to blink, I saw the Earth in my mind, it was more distant, but not too unlike what I was witnessing from the observation window. I realised I was seeing it from the Lunar surface and I was looking through the eyes of a child, Russia. A thought came to me, but it was not mine. Russia was sad for the woman he called his mother, Magi Eritrea. She would be executed soon. He knew he had to leave his home behind. He had to act fast; there were people to save before it was too late.

My eyes opened and the image faded but the unmistakeable gentle whisper of Magi Eritrea rang in my ears.

"It is time," she said. *"You must go now, hurry."*

3

It was early in the morning in Europe when we reached our optimum orbit around the moon, echoes of the sun's rays poking over the horizon.

It was eerie being so close to the moon. Charlie saw it first, winning the bet with Craig much to his disgust. I watched out of the windows, seeing the dead, lifeless planet. It looked empty, devoid of the life Russia's memories expected to see. Once it had been a vibrant place, filled with birds and animals of all kinds, much as Earth is today. There had been a green river glittering in the sun, vibrant grasses and dense jungles. Looking out of the craft, all I saw was a small and dusty, crater-ridden lump of rock. The atmosphere that once supported life, gone.

I felt the sadness of Russia inside me, his former home no longer visible.

"Mark," Maggie's voice. I took a moment before turning. "We're ready." I stepped away and followed her for briefing.

"We've lost part of our comms link," Maggie said. "We're still receiving a video feed but all audio feeds are down." She turned to Serge. "Do you see anything on the cameras?"

"Nothing," Serge said. "I don't see any impact trauma, everything is intact and good for go. I'd say we'd lost an antenna but I can see all four of them. It's likely to be an issue on the ground."

"Are we getting anything on the emergency frequencies?" Linda asked.

"All the same." Tom reported.

"Right," Maggie said. "Our nearest neighbour is ISS, try and raise them, maybe they can act as a relay until the link can be re-established with TICC."

Tom flipped a few switches and tapped on the screen in front of him.

"This is *Orion*, do you copy." There was silence. "This is *Orion*, ISS, do you copy?"

"We copy you." A voice came over loud and clear.

"We seem to be experiencing a comms blackout with TICC," Tom said. "Are you able to act as relay."

"Negative," the voice responded. "We're in the blind." I watched as the faces of the other crew moved from concern, to relief and back again. It was reassuring that the comms link was working, but we were still cut off from Earth. At least we weren't alone, figuratively speaking.

"Roger that."

Maggie smiled, "We'll just have to ride out the radio silence. Keep the comms open."

4

Thacker sat in his office, contemplating the issues at hand. Things had gotten worse, quickly. Bates was in the control room biting the heads off the workers. The swarm was in disarray, and that's why Thacker had closed the door.

The communications link was now out between Earth and the *Orion* module. But worse than that, it seemed all Earth-to-orbit communications were down. Pasadena were first to report radio silence on all missions including the ISS, then the old RKA monitoring centre informed of being in the blind. The Chinese media were reporting a loss of connectivity to the CSS, their own space station. The ESA – European Space Agency – were last to confirm a loss of satellite data.

But the mission had become the least of his worries. All mobile telecommunication networks were down and all cordless devices had jammed signals.

Earth had been disconnected.

The lead comms engineers had suggested to Thacker that they were experiencing a satellite loss or, somehow, *Orion* had scrambled their signals. Thacker dismissed him outright. He was wrong. Thacker knew this wasn't a man-made problem.

The word *trap* sprang to mind.

The President of the United States of America had definitely interpreted the data in the same way. His science advisers agreed, and the military saw the communication's blackout as a direct threat to the continuance of life on Earth.

Acting on the advice of the United States Armed Forces – USAF – the president agreed to a DEFCON 4 status, the first step down the line to a state of emergency. Even so, he had not authorised the reinstatement of the *Serenity* project.

Thacker knew they were dealing with a major unknown, and the President's response was not enough. This was a global problem and it required a multi-national response, but he'd have to deal with that issue later, there were more pressing matters.

He reached into his desk drawer, pulling out a small metal box. His hands worked quick, unlatching the lid before lifting it to expose the jade green rock. It glistened as it reflected the lights overhead, shimmering them back at Thacker.

Thacker took the rock in his hands; the instant his flesh

cupped the surface it began glowing and he felt it surging within him.

His eyes snapped shut as he connected to the power, letting it flow deep inside, a bolt of electricity pulsing through every cell of his body. He felt it writhing.

There were whispering voices in the silence of the office, they were talking to him. Thacker drifted towards them, moving deeper into the darkness behind his eyelids.

The voices grew louder and their hushed tones filled with depth.

There was a woman's voice, and she was talking to...yes, it was one of *them*. Rays of sunlight shattered through the darkness, sheering it in two. Thacker looked out, disorientated. It took a moment to understand he was inside the mind of his ancestor. He stood outside Magi Eritrea's chamber, the door ajar by a mere fraction, but it was enough.

He'd recognise the alien creature's harsh intonation, the way their words almost spat from their oral orifice even when calm and friendly. Thacker shuddered.

"...you will deliver Indonesia to us." The alien spat, speaking in the language of the rock, the power flowing within him translated.

"We have no use in our society for men like him," Magi Eritrea's voice and Thacker jolted, a wave of anger washing over him that was not his own. Thacker had long known he was Indonesia, one of the Magi's eldest servants. He had done her no wrong, and now this...

"We will see to it," the alien's voice growled. "He has proved himself disloyal and shall meet his ultimate punishment as will his followers."

There was movement inside the room and Indonesia fled to the relative safety of the courtyard, all the while fuming that his master was plotting against him. Thacker felt a hatred brimming inside, in previous visions he'd seen little

Russia whispering to his Magi and now he was starting to see they were all against him.

Their voices echoed in his mind as the power of the rock continued to sift through the genetic silt concealing the memories, cementing his new vision firm in its place.

A knock came at his door, bringing him back to the real world.

Thacker dropped the rock into the box and shuffled it out of sight before inviting his guest inside.

It was Randall.

"We've made contact," he spoke fast. "We're getting some data and video but no audio. It's very patchy."

"Any idea what's causing the failure?"

"No," Randall said. "But if I were to offer a theory..." Thacker waved his hand dismissively. He still felt Indonesia's anger, he was in no mood to hear wild and speculative theories, he only cared for the hard facts. "Two minutes ago, we received a relayed broadcast from the ISS. They made direct contact with *Orion* a number of hours ago so the issues appear to be ground to air only and are less severe than we first thought."

"You personally checked our equipment, right?" Thacker asked. "I presume we have no issues."

"None," Randall confirmed. "As you feared, it seems there is something blocking our signals."

"Any idea what?"

Randall shook his head before leaving, his duty done.

Thacker crossed his arms across and leant back in his seat, this felt all wrong to him but it was beyond his control. At least they were getting some feeds and he felt data was the most important thing right now.

5

Magi Eritrea came to me in my sleep, stirring me into a dream.

She took me on a journey into the world a part of me had lived in before. The land was lush, full of life, glistening as the sunlight caught it. Everything was covered with a sparkling green substance. It took me a moment to understand it was the Jeometamorphic rock, the life-force of the land. It was peaceful and as I watched a heard of gazelle-like animals grazing, I realised everything was in harmony, living in accord in the wilderness. Russia's memory used the words 'in resonance' to describe it to me.

Birds filled the skies, varieties I didn't recognise. As I watched, one landed on a palm frond beside me. It tilted its head, padding closer to observe. It examined me for a moment and then with one beat of its wings it took flight, its bright blue tail feathers catching the rays of the sun, a glittering green sheen rippled across its small body.

Everything lived because of the rock.

"We Magi are sworn to protect the sacred river," Magi Eritrea said. "We are guardians, protectors of balance and order; life and death; of hope and peace. The Magi has a duty to keep the natural order of the land." I caught her eyes for a moment and realised I'd never understood what a Magi was until now.

Symbolically, I recognised this was what the Magi were in the story of the birth of Christ. I knew that according to the Bible, the Magi were Jesus's guardians, protecting him from King Herod who'd wanted to harm the child. Now I understood what Charlie had said about recycling stories. It was a story recounted for the age of man, the truth lurking a little deeper as was true with so many myths.

The rock was a powerful force, something that changed your understanding of the world around you. I felt that Magi Eritrea understood its potency. I saw the green flames burning in her eyes.

"Come, let me show you," Magi Eritrea said leading me into the dense forest. After a couple of minutes walking, we burst into a clearing and as the ziggurat came into view my breath caught in my throat. They too sparkled in the sunlight, they too were alive.

We stood before the ziggurat I knew well from my dreams, the greenery of the jungle a vibrant contrast, accentuating the deep terracotta of the sun-baked mudbrick blocks. The river glistened with a green hue, running past us and then upwards around the giant structure.

I was speechless.

Magi Eritrea sat at the edge of the river. She reached down, putting her slender hands into the shimmering green and cupped, catching the running liquid. She drank it. This reinforced what I already knew; the rock lived as one with them in its liquid form, coupling to their DNA. She held out her hands, offering me a drink from the rock-based river.

I accepted, taking a seat close to Magi Eritrea, smelling her rich sweet scent – lotus blooms. My hands reached into the shallow water and as I did my eyes jammed closed. I felt the power of the life-force living within me, the water of everlasting life.

With a deep breath I cupped my hands and drank. It tasted fresher than anything I'd tasted before. My tongue tingled with every drop and as it trickled down my throat, I felt crystals of the rock forming and my mouth dried up. A moment later my breath caught in my throat and I coughed at the sharp stabbing sensation which spread into a burning fire, raging throughout my body.

I struggled, attempting to move, but I couldn't. And as the pain intensified, images flashed before my eyes as I entered a dream within a dream. I saw Russia standing in the chamber with his master, words whispered between one another.

My head shook.

Another image pushed in, a dark figure, hiding in the shadows outside my master's chamber. I felt a deep sense of distrust, and a cloudy red tint hung over them, rage perhaps.

I took another short rasp of breath. For just a moment part of the figure's face caught into a stream of light, a man, with eyes I felt I knew. There was a growl about his lips, hatred in his eyes, but he said nothing before skulking back into the shadows. I felt something was wrong, he shouldn't be there, lurking outside Magi Eritrea's chamber.

The image faded from my eyes, but not from my mind. There was so much anger clouding the vision, and while I couldn't be sure, I felt it was directed at me. What had I done?

"Is something wrong?" Magi Eritrea's soft voice brought me back to reality and I opened my eyes to Russia's world. I found myself sitting on the floor of her chamber, my legs folded before me, and yes...tears in my eyes. "My son, what brings tears to your bright eyes?"

"What you said to me earlier," Russia voice whined from my mouth. "You fear them, these others you see in your dreams?" Magi Eritrea looked at me with concern, but she did not flinch. "Why? Are we in some kind of danger?"

Magi Eritrea took a seat next to me, but said nothing.

"You are afraid."

"Yes," her voice was calm and soothing, devoid of fearful emotions. She took my hands into hers, and I felt her soft velvet flesh which stole part of the fear I'd experienced. "These people call my name, screaming for my mercy. I think they want me to help them?"

"Your help?" I asked. "What help can you give your dreams?"

"Oh, these are real dreams." Magi Eritrea's eyes danced truth. She leant forward and kissed my forehead with her warm lips. "You must promise never to speak of what I tell you." Her voice now stern and serious. "Can you promise me that?"

"Of course," I said. "It is my duty to serve only you master."

"Good," she said. "You must not let on, even to the others." She referred to the other servants. "If you were to learn your life was not your own, you'd want to do something about that, right?" I understood what she meant, but Russia didn't and frowned at the impossibility. How could someone not be their own? "These people have no control over their destiny and they wish to break free...and so do I."

"Whatever do you mean?"

"We were the first people; our fate is the same and so too is our plight."

"What are you saying?" I asked. "You know *they* will never allow..." I referred to our alien masters.

"Don't you see?" Magi Eritrea interrupted Russia. "That is exactly what is wrong with our world. We have no say, our voices unheard, our feelings unserviced. We are controlled by *them* always. Even I have little authority, they are not *my* decisions to make."

"But *they* look after us."

"Do *they*?" Her eyes wide, full of the same fear I'd seen earlier, but now mixed with rage. "*They* do not care for us," her anger grew. "*They* are only interested in our final destination. We are... *expendable*."

"But you can't bargain with *them*." I said squeezing her hand, begging for some sanity in our conversation. "*They* will remove you like all the others and if there are other worlds as you say, *they* will destroy them too."

"Then I must tread tactfully." Her voice filled with wisdom. "You have been a great help to me, please take the afternoon to amuse yourself."

I stood saying, "As you wish." At the door I turned back. "I beg of you, be careful." Magi Eritrea said nothing, giving only a gentle nod. Russia knew then, like I know now, that Magi Eritrea's fate was already sealed.

As the dream world drifted away, the images of the dark figure flooded my memory before I returned into a deeper state of sleep.

I woke. Maggie hung over me, it was time to get up, my sleep shift over.

My dreams were still fresh in my mind as I climbed from the crib. I coughed. My throat was hoarse and I felt a little dizzy.

It had been a dream, I knew, but it was ground in the reality of my past. Yes, a dream.

I reached out expecting to take my notebook from the bedside and realised I no longer had it. For a moment I felt lost, my routine broken.

CHAPTER 13

"I have made my decision," Maggie said, as she looked from face to face. Her eyes met mine, but I couldn't read them. The pause extended in my mind. "Our mission has not changed, regardless of our comms blackout. We'll proceed as planned."

"It's suicide." Craig was shaking his head.

"I've fully assessed our situation, being in the blind is no reason to deviate from our schedule." Maggie was calm and focused, her voice firm. "If nobody has anything further, please take your positions ready for separation."

Craig was still shaking his head as he climbed into his seat and buckled up. I strapped myself in and waited. Tom was checking the separation programme, simulations of our trajectory flooded his screen.

"Flight data check," he said, confirming to Maggie that the programme was ready.

"Take care," Linda said before sealing the hatch. As the pilot of the command module, Linda remained on-board *Orion*, staying in orbit above the moon. She didn't seem fazed by this, and of course she had no right to complain. It was the mission design and she'd known that all along. In fact, she seemed to enjoy her gig. For a moment I was envious, at least she got a break away from Craig. She'd get to watch our live video feeds, and hopefully hear everything that happened too. "See you in a few days." Her voice now coming through the internal comms link.

"You too," Maggie said. "Standby." Maggie pulled up equipment readings, they flashed in front of me. They appeared normal.

"Standing by." Tom confirmed.

"Initiating the undocking sequence." Linda's voice was tinny.

A blue glow filled the flight deck, confirming the activation of the control separation command.

"Enjoy the show," Linda said. The module shook momentarily as the *Altair* lunar module burst away from *Orion*. "Say hello for me." I knew this was the last time she'd speak to us until we'd reached the surface.

After the initial separation, we drifted, moving only by the burst of pressurised air released as we parted from *Orion*. It provided us with enough clearance to allow us to make a safe departure.

Once we'd reached fifty metres it was time to fire up the engines.

"Thrusters to twenty-five percent," Maggie barked her instructions. I watched Tom double check his screen to confirm the distance before completing the command. He flicked the cover, and the pressed the red button beneath. A deep vibration rocked me in my seat, the metal frame rattled and blurred. It was worse than lift-off, *Altair* was much smaller, a pressurised tin-can waiting to be crushed. I gulped back a breath and closed my eyes, it was enough to maintain my cool.

We flew out of our high moon orbit, heading downwards on our trajectory to a height of 15,000 metres. It only took a few moments for us to reach our first target altitude and then we continued at a lower lunar orbit. Charlie was watching out of the porthole hatch to his side, as was Serge, I caught only dark and light glimpses as their helmets eclipsed the glass.

After four further passes over the moon, we began the descent routine we'd practised over and over, knowing each of the stages inside out.

"Let's get her down there," Maggie said finally.

"We're go in ten," Tom reported. I counted down in my head and as I reached zero, I felt the sudden surge. The *Altair* pod rolled a little, pushing me deeper into my seat. "We're coming down a little short of our drop site."

"Correcting course," Maggie said, her fingertips tapping on her console screen.

When the first reverse thrusters fired, seven minutes later, I felt the pod slow. Maggie reported a success as we plummeted. Further bursts from the thrusters brought our speed under control but sent deep vibrations running through my chest. The low rumble grew as the lander dropped closer and closer.

In my mind I pictured us moving towards the ground, the ziggurat in the background. Seeing the landscape, I felt a sense of arrival; time began to slow as our journey reached its conclusion. I felt Russia's cautious elation within me, he was almost home.

A warning alarm buzzed. We were sixty seconds from touchdown.

I held my breath, counting the seconds in my head.

"Thirty," Tom reported. "We're steady." It felt like hours passing, and not seconds. "Ten." I braced myself for impact.

A second alarm went off as we approached the lunar surface. A final burst of thrusters brought us gently to a padded landing.

"TICC in the blind, we have touchdown," Maggie

reported.

The lander shuddered as the engines fell silent, and all vibrations ceased.

2

The *Altair* lander of the *Constellation* mission touched down in the Ptolemaeus region at 9:05 a.m. (UTC) on the 9th November 2022. We were the first humans to visit this region of the moon since the demise of the civilization that once thrived there, two-point-five million years ago.

I unbuckled, stretching my legs and nudged my way to the window, hoping to see the same pictures I'd seen in my mind, but I couldn't see the ziggurat. Perhaps they were to the rear of the lander. Instead, I witnessed the harsh reality of the barren lunar surface. There was no movement. Shadows overhung to the right where the mountainous rim of the crater reached ground level.

"We have a slight problem." Craig was hunched over his screen. "We've lost comms with *Orion*. We're on our own."

"Damaged?" Maggie wanted to know.

"No, I don't think so," he said, checking the feed from the outboard sensors. I looked across at his screen, everything reported a healthy status. "I'm simply not getting a feed from *Orion,* it's like it's vanished. I'd have said something was wrong with *Orion* but I'm not picking up the ISS or CSS. Whatever was blocking the *Orion's* signal is still with us."

"Okay," Maggie said, her voice thoughtful. "So, you're saying we're completely in the blind now."

"Yes."

Without missing a beat Maggie said, "Serge I want you to see if there is anything that can be done from inside." He stood to attention. "Charlie you take Mark and start the necessary preparations for our scheduled ascent."

I looked to Charlie. He was biting his lip which did nothing to reassure any of us, but he was watching Maggie and after a moment he seemed to relax. I found Maggie's strength and leadership direction reassuring, and maybe that was what had caused him to feel a little more at ease too. I smiled, they complimented each other so well.

3

A roar erupted as the screens went dead. Thacker slammed his antiquated and yellowing phone onto the desk, terminating his call mid-conversation. The cord shrivelled, retreating to the dark recess of its unkempt post.

"Speak to me," Khan's voice rose above the raucous, Thacker cringed, the man could shout when he needed, an admirable quality he thought. The control room fell back into its relative busy silence.

"Visuals and telemetry down," Josef reported.

"No change on voice," Beth said. "Still down from the earlier outage."

"Trajectory was spot on," Andrew added, bringing the flight descent onto the main screen. Thacker frowned at it.

"Okay, so tell me what's happening?"

An alarm blared, a blue light flashed above the top of the three central viewing screens.

"Incoming message," Josef pushed back to his terminal. "It's *Orion*."

"Pull it up."

For a moment Thacker thought balance had been restored and TICC returned to its calm working status.

A grainy image of Linda appeared on the central screen. It was badly pixelated and the picture kept distorting and cutting in the way that digital feeds do when there is only a partial data stream. Linda seemed to be speaking, her lips were moving.

"I still don't hear anything," Khan snapped.

"I've got something on audio," Beth reported. "But it's not related and it's on the *Altair* transponder." A moment later a deep rumble filled the TICC control room. Every few seconds a blip rang out, a beacon.

"Get me co-ordinates," Khan ordered. "I want to be sure it's *Altair*. Did they set down as expected?" Thacker recognised the sound, it was the emergency broadcast signal from the *Altair* lander, but he wasn't nervous. He had a nagging suspicion the *Constellation* crew had arrived safely. He could sense it. The video feed on the central screen faded, Linda vanished. "What the fuck is happening?"

"Lost all comms," Josef said.

"Anyone got me those co-ordinates?"

A second later a radar image flicked up onto the right screen, tracking the signal. As the red dot blipped, it closed in on the Ptolemaeus landing site.

"Okay, so we know the lander is intact, where are we on comms?"

"It's the same as before," Thacker shouted down. "Some major commercial satellites remain inoperable." This of course was a headache and Thacker had been on the phone to the President of one of the global conglomerates whose satellite had lost feed. "Let me know if anything changes."

He stepped back into the office and locked the door. He needed peace, no interruptions, it was time to rethink their strategy.

Thacker stared at the green rock facing him on his desk. The light fell on it in a strange way and it appeared to glow, pulsing. *It's time to see what other memories you can bring back,* he thought, his hands tapping at his knees. *Show me what I need to know.*

He placed his hands on the smooth surfaces of the jade green rock. His eyes rolled as the power flowed, and a green pulsing light filled the shadows behind his eyelids. He let out a short rasp before allowing his body to drift deeper into the darkness of his inner self.

Voices whispered.

He moved closer, floating towards the mumbling hushed tones. The green pulsing eased and slowly light sheared through and the dream world flooded into view. He edged closer, stopping in the shadows of a doorway.

He recognised the scene from his earlier experience. He caught the words of Magi Eritrea and the harsh rasp of the alien. Anger began to mount in his mind, remembering the words Magi Eritrea would say.

"We don't need men like him in our society." Thacker felt a deep pain in his chest, a stabbing through his heart at the deception of his once Magi. How could she do this to him?

Footsteps came towards him and he darted out into the courtyard.

The sunlight dazzled and he shielded himself with his arm and squinted. Thacker felt an explosion inside of him, a deep burning as more memories returned.

The intense light receded and he found himself standing before the portal inside the sacred ziggurat, a little boy reflected in the shimmering light of the mirrored surface; Russia. The boy turned, fear in his eyes. He did not speak, nor did he wait, Russia stepped through the glowing pool.

Thacker watched as the brilliant light of the portal faded and the room fell into darkness, silent and still. Inside the memory of Indonesia, Thacker left the portal chamber, stepping out into the courtyard once again.

His eyes took a moment to adjust. When Thacker could see again, he found himself standing in the central area of the moon colony, a stepped column with a flat point stood behind him, crowds gathered before him, watching and waiting. The crowd parted to reveal two men striding towards him, one carrying a sceptre in his upturned palms – it was the Magi's sceptre.

They reached the front and bowed before Indonesia, Thacker was confused. He'd never seen this before. Indonesia reached out and took the sceptre in his hands, raising it above his head.

"Behold!" The two men before him saluted. "Magi Indonesia."

Magi? Thacker gulped. He never knew he'd become a Magi, what had happened to Magi Eritrea? Indonesia's memory told him that there could only be one, true Magi and that meant Eritrea was...she was dead.

The gathered crowd dropped to their knees and bowed before him.

It was at this moment that the world began to shake, a deep rumble emanating all around. One by one the gathered crowd tilted their heads towards the skies, and soon screams filled the air. Some people dropped to their knees, others fled for cover. Indonesia looked up and Thacker saw *them*.

A series of alien craft hurtled towards his position at startling speed.

Indonesia had a thought, and now Thacker intercepted it.

They are coming for me.

Thacker squinted as a powerful flash fire swept through his mind.

Flames leapt up all around, engulfing everything in sight. He was surrounded. One of the alien creatures stood to his side, towering over him, his face drawn in what Thacker thought might be an angry scowl. Sharp white teeth showed over the edge of his oratory hole.

"You and your people will pay for your treachery," it barked at him.

Thacker yelled out as his legs shot out from under him. In the last moments of light, he saw two of the aliens carrying a silvery-blue orb, metallic perhaps. They set the object at the foot of the obelisk before taking it inside what must have been a hidden opening – Thacker had never seen an opening in his dreams before. When the two creatures returned from inside, they carried a larger object. Moments later the column began shaking as the earth trembled.

The first mudbrick block dropped to the ground with a thud. Burning pain ripped through Thacker's body as the world crumbled.

The rock dropped from his hand as he clutched at his chest. Thacker keeled over onto his desk. His final memory as he dropped out of consciousness was the knowledge of the column and its purpose.

He now knew with certainty that it was no accident they'd lost contact with the *Constellation* crew. But how could *they* know that one day we'd return to our homeland?

4

Maggie watched her crew busying themselves while she contemplated their predicament. At first, she'd been fine with the loss of communications, but now her mind was starting to wonder. What if the aliens were on their way? Would *they* travel to the lunar world and if *they* did would *they* come with hostile intentions? These were the questions mulling in her mind, a decision had to be made.

But this was the stumbling block. She had two voices in her head, the first an unintelligent one which told her *communications suck, they just slow you down*; the second and the better informed of the two said *we don't know the dangers, abort.*

As she looked around her crew, she felt she knew what their responses would be. Charlie, Mark, Craig and Serge would want to continue, any speak of leaving would be pointless and a waste of natural resources in their eyes. Tom was overly cautious – often triple-checking information when it only needed a second glance – he would fall on the other side of the argument, wanting to retreat because there was now an even greater number of unknowns to contend with.

That just left herself undecided – and it was her vote that counted, it wasn't a democracy after all. As Commander, Maggie knew her word was final and the others had to follow protocol and fall into line, of course they didn't have to like it, as long as they complied.

Maggie shook her head, slumping into her seat. Her pulse throbbed across her temples, a headache on the horizon. She took a deep breath to relax, her eyes closed for a second. Already she felt more composed.

When Maggie opened her eyes, she found herself standing in the darkness of the night, the ziggurat in the distance, the light of the distant stars shimmering across its surface. There was a voice, it sounded near and echoed across the land. She turned full circle, but there was no one in sight. Her eyes settled back to the ziggurat, now much closer, and then she saw it, flickering at the base of the structure, a flame, dancing.

“Come to me.” The voice called to her, and when she saw him standing in the warming light of the torch, a stooped stranger shrouded in a dark robe, she recognised him. It was Russia, his face concealed, only the tips of his sandals and hands visible. But it was unmistakably him. “Don’t worry, I am here to guide you.” His voice calm and soothing.

At this, Maggie relaxed, allowing herself to shuffle towards him, making her way across the dark lands. She trusted him. When she arrived at the entrance, the figure was gone, but his footfalls echoed inside, the light of his blazing torch illuminating the way.

“You must remember, do not fight it.” The voice echoed.

Maggie blinked. She hesitated before ducking inside, following the distant glow of the flaming torch. The air was alive with the warming odour of burning incense. As she drifted deeper she heard other voices up ahead. The light faded and Maggie found herself cast into darkness. Her ears began to buzz as they focused on the distant voices. She followed them.

Flames burst into life around Maggie and she gasped. Soon she was surrounded by the orange glow of burning torches. She was so focused on the flames, she hadn’t noticed the woman standing before her, around the same age as herself – maybe a little younger. Her hazel eyes bore into her own.

Maggie frowned, she recognised this woman.

There was something about her that struck Maggie as odd. The way her hair curled when it reached her shoulders, the way her head leaned to one side, the elegant way her legs shifted under her weight as she moved.

Maggie’s breath caught in her throat.

It was like looking into a mirror, but the woman wasn’t a reflection. Maggie felt like they were sisters.

Paraguay, the voice of Russia spoke to her. *It’s time.*

As if the woman had heard this too, she looked away and

drifted into the bright light of the next room. Maggie felt herself being dragged towards the light which emanated all around now, enveloping her. The woman disappeared into the light and then...

Darkness returned.

Maggie realised her eyes were closed and as she opened them she found herself sitting at her console, her body numb. *Was I asleep*? She blinked, the vision returning fresh to her mind. As she replayed it over she began to understand.

She had once been Paraguay.

Russia had led her away from the lunar world and now she was leading him back to it. A thought occurred to her, maybe it was in fact Mark that was leading her back.

Maggie knew which side of the line she fell upon. There was no way she could leave now, she'd had a taste and wanted more. For the first time in years, she actually felt excited by this new information.

"I've made my decision," Maggie said breaking the silence and making me jump. Her voice was filled with youthful excitement and was so loud it echoed in my helmet, making my ears throb.

I stopped mid-motion, still carrying the crate of supplies I'd been checking. Maggie turned to me, and as her eyes passed over mine, I felt a change. She'd seen something, I could tell. Maybe the life-force of the rock was changing me more than we all knew.

Whatever, I saw through Maggie's excitement. I perched the box on another as she stepped forwards.

"We are here to do a job, and we will finish it, regardless."

She looked to each of us in turn. I followed her eyes, a heavy frown creasing Tom's brow. "Serge, I want you to perform a thorough check of the outside of *Altair*, I want human eyes to confirm the non-existence of physical damage to our antenna. I want to be certain that this failure is not our own, strip it and rewire it if you have to."

"Understood." Serge saluted.

"Tom." Maggie turned and stared. "You remain with him. The rest of you, we will do a site survey, scope out our perimeter. We will spend a maximum of one hour outside and then we will reconvene."

5

The change in Maggie's mood was significant, a smile on her face and excitement in her eyes. She looked at me with the same intense passion as Charlie when explaining his life-long obsession of writing and writing systems.

I watched Charlie and Craig rotating the wheel on the hatch. While the locking mechanism was electrical, it required a manual override to unlatch, that way power failures couldn't prevent escape from the vessel.

"Standby for depressurisation," Tom said from behind. A loud hissing burst out all around, it took almost two minutes for the pressure to reach the correct level, all the while my ears popped, as if I was making my way down a steep hill. "Okay, you're good to go." He confirmed a few minutes later.

Charlie dropped the lever to the side of the hatch into the unlocked position, then took hold of the handle and pushed.

The door opened outwards.

"This is one small step for a man…" Charlie began as he

climbed outside and padded carefully down the ladder.

"Quit it," Maggie admonished. "Save it for when we have an audience."

"Yeah, someone has to film it from the outside," I said.

"Maybe later." Serge joined in. He'd told me once that seeing the footage of Neil Armstrong striding across the moon's surface and fluffing up his lines – even though it was by then archive footage – had inspired him to become an astronaut in the first place. Seeing Charlie disappear down the ladder and hearing his footfalls vanish, I understood the attraction.

Craig ducked through the hatch and began his descent.

I went last. When I maneuverer my helmet out, I looked into the darkness of space and the shimmering stars that surrounded us. It took my breath away.

"Wow!" I let out, before starting down the ladders.

I was four when my mum first took me to a fairground. It was an old rickety place by the sea. I had run to the front gate and stopped, amazed by what I could see inside. There were rides everywhere. Swirling giant teacups spinning to my left, the big wheel towering above everything. Standing there, at the bottom of the ladder, I felt like that child again. I was brimming with enthusiasm and excitement. Which ride to choose, which way to turn?

"It feels creepy out here," Serge said. I wondered if all of us felt it as we looked at the changed landscape, unlike anything any of our ancestors remembered. "I don't feel comfortable..."

"You've got Tom." Maggie reminded him. "Let us know what you find, if anything."

We broke into our groups.

During training we'd been prepared for the moon's gravity – one-sixth of Earth's – but wading in the swimming pool was nothing compared to this. Back in the time of Russia, I knew gravity had been much the same as Earth today (although Russia didn't understand the term). I guessed when the fires destroyed the world, they also destroyed everything that made it an inhabitable planet, draining all its resources.

Why is the ziggurat still here? Now that was a puzzle.

We moved round the *Altair* lander, the ziggurat structures slowly came into view.

My heart jumped, my dream realised.

Like the pictures Thacker had shown from the *Mistral* probe, the ziggurat appeared cold and empty, the landscape around it flat and barren, devoid of all the lush life that should have surrounded it. A little way off, on the rise of a hill, I caught sight of a small pile of rubble. I didn't recognise this area from my dreams. Russia's memory did, although it had not looked the same then. I looked away, but my eyes were dragged back to it.

"We have to go there." I pointed, listening to my inner voice.

"Not now," Maggie said, taking a step towards the ziggurat.

"There is something there." I insisted. "I *feel* it." Maggie squared up to me and looked into my eyes. For a moment I thought she was about to challenge me, to assert her will, but then I saw the flicker behind her eyes and I knew she'd changed her mind.

"Okay…yes. Prepare the rover," She instructed before breaking eye contact and turning away.

6

The lunar 'rover' vehicle was a small buggy, docked in the cargo hold of the *Altair* lander. I watched Craig and Serge unlock the mechanism holding the chassis in place and then rolling it out. Serge spent a couple of minutes looking for damage to the parts, but it wasn't a big vehicle and there wasn't much to check.

With a thumbs up from Serge, Craig started the electric engine and thumbed through the on-board systems. A few minutes later, we boarded the rover. Craig took the driver's seat, Maggie took the navigator's seat next to him, the rest of us stood on the back. We rolled away from *Altair*, heading straight for the rise where I had seen the rubble pile.

We pulled in close to the site and I jumped off, my feet falling into the dusty ground, moon rock covering the tips of my boots. I was sure I saw small beads of green in the dust, twinkling. I stepped forwards, moving in among the ruined pile of smashed rocks. They were baked mudbrick too, like the ziggurat, ancient and weathered.

"What was this?" Maggie joined me.

An image flashed into my mind, a tall mudbrick column reaching into the sky on the far shore of the river. "Of course," I said. "The obelisk."

Maggie stared at me blankly.

"Has anyone else seen an obelisk in their dreams?" The same image flashed into my mind and I shook it out of my head once again. As the image faded this time I felt my head buzzing and swirling. I stumbled back, dizzy, almost tripping over Maggie. She caught me and groaned under the strain.

"What's wrong?" She peered at me, curious. "Are you okay?"

"No," I said, grappling with my helmet as the ear-splitting buzzing rose. My eyes flickered shut and a moment later I felt myself falling, I tried to fight it, but my hands were useless, dead weights against it. I tried to scream, but nothing came out.

I descended into the darkness, falling deeper. With a

thud, I reached the ground, silencing the persistent buzzing. I passed out.

See it. The voice of Magi Eritrea.

My eyes sprang open and I gazed at rubble piled around me.

Stand up, her voice commanded.

I realised I was sitting among the jaded rocks, but I didn't remember taking a seat. I shoved the dirt hard with my hands, attempting to stand, but sank back, my body half-numb. Tiny bells chimed in my ears, and I could no longer hear my breath inside my helmet.

See it, the voice said.

The world flickered, pixelating, stretching and skewing like a computer-generated image. As it did, the rubble rebuilt itself, forming a giant column before me. The sunlight glowed bright on the baked mudbrick blocks, magnifying their intense terracotta, turning them deep rouge. The missing obelisk stood proud before me, complete.

At the base of the structure, there was a dark opening.

Go inside, the voice instructed.

I moved towards the obelisk, stepping across the threshold. A dancing green glow in the corner lit my way as I inched forwards. My hands reached out and traced the surface of the device, smooth and spherical. It felt metallic, alien. Energy pulsed in my hands, the heartbeat of the planet. This was the life support holding the atmosphere in place where none should be. Thacker had confirmed my thoughts about this before – the moon was not capable of holding an atmosphere. Alien technology sustained life.

Listen to it.

Without thinking, my head bowed until my ear touched the glowing device. A piercing squeal filled my ears and I jumped back. The deafening noise continued. It was inside me now, screeching. I clapped my hands over my ears, but that did nothing.

Through the agony, my eyes focused on the device. The little boy, Russia, recognised it. He told me this was a transmission, used by the alien race to keep in touch with the people of the lunar world.

I was sure this was the root of our current communication problems.

But could an alien device power itself for two-point-five million years? I shook my head, staggered by the scale of the alien technology, amazed that anything that old could *still* work.

My eyes jammed shut and darkness descended. I felt a searing heat against the side of my head, and then the high pitch squeal died, silence returned.

7

The harsh terrain of the lunar landscape flooded my mind, filling my reality.

I opened my eyes. Maggie's face hovered above mine, distorted through the reinforced glass layers of our helmets, but I could see her concern. A burning pain pulsed through my left side, and ringing filled my ears.

"Glad you could join us," Maggie said. I tried to speak but my throat was dry and I coughed, managing only a nod of acknowledgement. "Help me get him up onto the rover." Charlie was hovering on the edge of my vision.

"Let me stand," I croaked. "Help me up." I felt a sharp tug

and I swung my legs into position. Soon I stood, swaying.

"You look pale," Charlie said before checking the communicator on my wrist. "He's bradycardic, I'm getting a pulse of forty-five."

"How's his blood pressure? Is he hypotensive?" Maggie was studying me.

"Yes, I'm getting a reading of ninety-over-fifty."

"We'd better get him back and out of that suit in case of seizures." Maggie took hold of my right arm, Charlie touched my left side and I winced, the pain igniting across my body. I was sure I could feel a swelling on the side of my face, my cheek was thick and heavy. When I swallowed, I detected the familiar metallic taste of blood, maybe I'd bit my tongue when I'd collapsed.

"I'll be okay," I said turning my head back to the pile of rubble. "Did you guys see that?" They stopped moving. "It was there."

"What was?" When Maggie looked through the visor of my helmet I saw deep wrinkles furrowed across her brow. "What did you see?" She looked to the ancient destruction and then back at me.

"There was a device in there," I said. "I saw it."

"Device?" Charlie let go of my arm. "What kind of device?" Maggie shook her head. "We didn't see anything, so you're going to need to fill in the blanks for us."

"Thacker told me the obelisk housed alien technology. There was a device in there that somehow gave the moon a magnetic field, intensified gravity and generated a life-supporting atmosphere. But it was more than that." I maintained hold of Maggie for stability but pointed with my other hand to the unrecognisable rubble. "It also acted as a transmitter."

"Is it live?" Craig asked, it caught me off guard. He was off to one side of the rubble, kneeling in the dirt, surrounded by the fallen mudbricks. He had a small fragment of rock in his hand which he flipped over and over.

"Yes," I said. "I think so."

"What does that mean?" Maggie wanted to know. "Are you saying the moon could maintain an atmosphere again?"

"No," I said. "Or at least I don't think so."

"It means we're not alone." Craig's insight made me wonder what else he knew about the site. He'd said nothing about it before. Had he seen something at the same time I had? "We're guests here, and they've been expecting us."

"Let's get back to the lander," Maggie said as she helped me onto the rover. I dropped into a seat and turned to see Charlie staring out at the pile of unidentifiable rocks that had once been the obelisk. Craig continued turning the rock over in his hands, still kneeling. "Come on you two."

"Wait," Charlie said.

"What is it now?" Maggie sounded frustrated. Things weren't going according to plan, and we weren't helping her deal with her stress well, just adding to it.

"The question is, do *they* know we are here?" Charlie's voice was a whisper in my ear. "A cry at night is always heard, a beacon of light always seen. *They* know where to find us."

"The scriptures?" I guessed.

"I never understood," he shook his head. I caught Maggie's reflection in the glass of my visor, a brief fear in her eyes. Then it was gone.

"We need to get back to the others, we've been gone longer than planned already." A low rumble of dread in Maggie's voice. I shivered. Charlie must have detected it too as he bounced over to the rover and hopped on-board. Craig wasn't far behind.

8

The hatch door to the *Altair* lander sealed with a shudder, locking us inside. A powerful blast of air filled the chamber. Maggie wasted no time, as soon as the air pressure and oxygen mix reached sustainable levels she helped me with my suit, releasing the latches and catches that held it together before taking her own off.

I instantly felt better, able to breathe with ease.

"What's going on?" Serge flapped his arms, a circuit board from the comms system clutched in hand. He'd been working on it when we arrived, but Maggie hadn't explained, rushing him inside without time to replace the board.

"You saw something didn't you?" Tom asked gingerly, his voice distant.

"We found something all right," Charlie said, almost delighted. "A transmitter." By this point everyone had taken off their helmets, and Charlie was shaking his hands free of his gloves.

"What? Where?" Serge asked. "How do you know?" He looked from Charlie to Maggie. "Was it working?"

Maggie looked to me. "Mark saw it."

"The obelisk," I said. "I think it's still operational, but don't ask me how."

"I found no evidence of damage or systems failures with the comms units." He waved the circuit board. "So that could make sense. Did you get a close look at it? Can we stop it somehow?" I shook my head. I hadn't actually seen the device in the rubble, I'd seen it in my vision. I knew where it should be, not where it was.

"You're starting to colour." Maggie was taking my pulse with a digital reader which she pressed against my wrist. I felt the pounding of my heart throbbing where her hand squeezed. "Your heart-rate has returned to normal rhythm."

"Is everything okay?" Tom looked concerned. All crew had to know basic first-aid – 'spaceaid' as Charlie called it, to me that sounded more like a drug infused drink – but while I'd been learning mathematical formulae, Tom underwent rigorous medical training.

"I fainted," I said.

"He had hypotension and bradycardia," Charlie reported.

"We'd better keep him under close observation." Tom took the digital reader from Maggie.

"What about this transmitter?" Serge demanded to know. "What do we do about that?" He tossed the comms board onto his console, I guessed it was little use now anyway. "It's interfering with our equipment."

"Even if that thing *was* a transmitter, I doubt it's capable of much, there isn't anything on Earth that could power something for that long, I mean we're talking millions of years here." Maggie caught my eye and I knew she wanted me to back her up, a bid to calm our fears. "Am I right?"

"Millions of years." But that was all I could agree to. "Did you see the green fragments of rock?" I looked to Craig, he'd been kneeling among it, surely, he'd seen it. "Jeometamorphic rock is powerful stuff."

"So…" Maggie frowned. "Are you saying a lump of rock is keeping it juiced up? For millions of years?"

"Yes," I said, Maggie shook her head. "You have to remember that it's more than just a rock, it's a form of life. It's possible it lay dormant, in some kind of power saving mode, that would explain why the blackout only occurred after we left Earth. It would mean they've been listening to us this whole time."

Maggie's brow creased further; she didn't believe me.

"I guess anything is possible," Charlie said. "We're on the

moon for fuck's sake, how insane is that?"

"If we think of the rock as an animating life-force," Craig said, "then maybe it can recognise the remnants within our DNA."

"Are you saying the rock is intelligent?" Maggie's lip curled as a snort escaped her throat.

"Don't doubt it," Charlie said before I had chance to conjure an answer. "The scriptures say that this life-force gave birth to our civilisation, it gave us our wisdom. Think Adam and Eve, the rock is our apple."

"Mark's right," Serge said. I turned to find him staring at the flight screen. "I've got an unknown transmission on a sub-optimal frequency and it's coming from over there." He pointed towards the back end of *Altair*.

"What further proof do we need," I said. "They knew we were coming."

"This was something we prepared for," Maggie said, although she looked vexed. Of course, she was right. We'd considered a number of eventualities as part of our training and mission profile. We knew there could be challenges, and some of them could even be life threatening. But I knew Maggie wasn't afraid of the challenge, she was frustrated because it meant that we'd completed our objective; we'd proved the moon civilization existed *and* we'd demonstrated that alien technology was monitoring our activity. Unfortunately, everything else – all the good stuff that would help us understand our existence – was classed as none essential.

"Our assignment is over, prepare *Altair* for departure."

"No!" Craig yelled.

"Take your positions," Maggie responded, resolute, her voice calm and unwavering. "We'll launch in five."

"No." Craig spoke again, this time eerily calm. "I can't let you do that." I turned to catch a crazed look in his eyes and in that moment, I saw his intention, but it happened too fast for me to respond. He leapt across the lander to the hatch and clutched hold of the emergency override. His wrist tensed as Charlie stepped forwards. "Don't make me do anything rash." Charlie eased back.

"Don't be foolish," Maggie snapped. "You'll depressurise the lander and kill us all."

"Maybe we should take a vote," Serge said placing his gloved hand on Maggie's shoulder. She turned to him, fury in her eyes.

"I'm the Commander of this mission!" Hairs along the back of my neck stood on edge with her shrill voice. "It is *my* decision. Understand this, *all of you*, we are not in a democracy here. Any dereliction of duty is mutiny!" Maggie was right, I knew, but that didn't stop me agreeing with both Craig and Charlie. We couldn't leave, not now, we were only just starting to understand, it wasn't right to fall at the first hurdle.

Craig snapped, "Don't push me. I'll do it!"

"You don't have a say in this." Tom threw his weight behind Maggie, for what it was worth, always on the cautious side. "Our mission states that if we are in danger..."

"Fuck you," Craig hissed. "Crawl back up the hole you dropped from."

"The way I see it," I said to Maggie, "we have to take that vote." Her furious eyes bore into mine, scorching. "He has the highest ground, he could wipe us all out, you have no choice. You must comply with his demands." It was a rational argument, pitched to Maggie's logical side and as soon as I saw her shoulders sag, I knew I'd gotten through.

"Okay," her voice still angry. "Since I don't have a choice in the matter, I will allow you all to influence my decision." Craig's wrist went limp, his muscles relaxed. I glanced across at Charlie and winked. "As Commander, I have to weigh up the risks and it would be my decision, right now, to abort the mission and leave this place. We have no understanding of the real danger, and these are avoidable risks." I shuddered. She no longer referred to it as the moon anymore, it was *this place*. "We've lost communications with Earth due to what we suspect is alien technology, an alien ambush which detected our activity. We were expected." Her shoulders slumped further. "Anyone else who has a differing opinion should speak now." She shot Craig an angry look.

"I say we stay." Craig's hand dropped from the lever. I caught Charlie's eye once again and he edged forwards. "There is something out there that we don't understand fully, but we shouldn't just leave without exploring it first. It would be an incredible waste of time and money to leave now." While I agreed with him, I couldn't condone his threatening actions.

I saw our chance and yelled, "Now!"

Craig didn't seem to register what happened as Charlie plunged in, thrusting his elbow into Craig's chest, throwing him off balance. Craig toppled to the floor, and then Serge dropped on top of him, pinning him in place.

I looked to Maggie for guidance, but it was clear she was stunned by our actions. She'd not anticipated our move.

I took control of the situation. "Get something to restrain him."

"Here," Tom said rummaging through a box and handing me some plastic cable ties, just long enough for the job. With Serge's help we managed to flip Craig onto his front, wrenching his wrists behind his back and bound them together.

"What the hell just happened?" A slight quiver in Maggie's voice.

"You're the Commander of this mission for a reason," I said. "You didn't think we'd let him overrule you?" I could see Maggie was losing control, her usual decisive manner vanished. "Can we fly this thing without him?"

"Of course," Tom said taking his seat. "Everybody in your positions."

"What about him?" I tossed my head towards Craig.

"Leave him," Maggie said. "We can deal with the fallout later."

"What are you doing?" Craig yelled, nobody answered him. "Get away from there! I'm warning you." His words were empty of course, I knew he was no harm to us back there now.

Tom punched up the launch sequence on his console and checked the commands, but that was as far as he got. His screen died.

"What the..." His fist thumped the console, but it was dead.

"Mine's out too." Maggie reported and then turned to Craig. "What the fuck did you do?"

I looked over to see Craig's bound body sprawled across the floor. He stared back with a blank expression. He appeared bemused by the apparent failure of our equipment. It might have been a trick of the light, but I caught a sparkle in his eye, as if he understood the problem.

CHAPTER 14

Bates struggled to balance the two mugs of coffee he was carrying and open the door to the office above the TICC command centre. The handle wouldn't budge. He set the cups down and tried again. The door appeared locked. He wasn't aware of a lock on the door and when he searched, he found no keyhole.

"Thacker." He hammered on the door. "Are you in there?"

"I didn't see him leave." Bates jumped, Beth appeared behind him.

"When did you last see him?"

"About two hours ago," she said, "he went in and closed the door."

Bates frowned. Maybe Thacker had gone in to take a nap, or more likely had drunk himself to sleep. He pounded on the door once again, but there was no response. Bates leant his ear against the door, he heard nothing, not even a faint snore.

"I'll call security," Beth said disappearing.

"I'm coming in, one way or another, so you'd better open this door now!" Bates thumped one last time. He listened carefully, hoping he'd hear a snorted reply, but silence greeted him. "That's it!" He threw his weight against the door. It didn't budge.

Bates barged the door with his shoulder for a second time, and the door burst open with a piercing crack, the lock shearing off as the wood around it splintered.

He'd half expected to find Thacker sitting at the desk, smoking a cigar with a half-empty bottle of whisky perched in his hand, but he wasn't prepared for this. Thacker was slumped across the desk, unconscious.

"Get the on-call doctor!" Bates yelled. A few moments later Beth burst into the room behind him and gasped. "Help me get him to the floor."

Together they lifted Thacker and eased him to the floor. Bates worked quickly, pulling his limp body this way and that until they had him in the recovery position. Then he waited for a medic to arrive.

After Thacker was stretchered down to the medical bay, Bates stood in the office, viewing the scene. There was little on the desk to suggest what had happened, but as he ambled around he spotted a lump of green rock on the floor and stooped to pick it up. He thought he saw a spark of static as he lifted it into the light and then he frowned, his fingers tingling.

What was the rock doing on the floor?

He held it up to his security pass. The radiation dosimeter remained static, and then he dropped it into his pocket.

2

"I'm afraid there is nothing I can do." Serge turned away from his console, revealing the results of the diagnostics check. "Like the comms systems, we're reporting no damage."

"What are you saying?" Maggie voice filled with apprehension. It was clear to me she understood Serge, but didn't want to accept. "Are we stranded here?" Her words forced.

"*Altair*'s immobilised," Serge confirmed. "And since we have no means of communication, we can't call for help." Maggie shook her head in disbelief. Tom slumped into one of the seats, his head in his hands.

"I have a horrible suspicion we weren't meant to leave." A shudder shot down my spine as I spoke.

"What do we do now?" Charlie asked.

I stared into the corner of the room, I felt claustrophobic, our options rapidly closing. I could feel the panic hanging in the air, waiting to be expressed. What were we going to do? We had nobody to call and no way out. And then it struck me.

"Wait..." I said turning to Charlie. "You told me before that we travelled to Earth through some form of teleportation system. I've seen it before in my dreams."

"Yes," Charlie said.

"Well if the transmitter is still working, is it possible that the portal may also be working?" I looked to Maggie for approval. "I believe it's inside the ziggurat."

"That might work." Charlie's shoulder heaved. "The scriptures don't say what the portal was used for, but I guess it could still be configured from Russia's escape."

"Maybe that's how Magi Eritrea knew about the others," I said. "It makes sense if it's a connection to the other alien colonies, but why would the aliens install them and how come there was one on Earth?" The thought occurred to me that maybe Earth was waiting to be colonised before the exodus.

"Then we need to be careful," Serge chipped in. "We're

working on a lot of assumptions, but if the system still works..."

"You're all fools," Craig snapped. still sprawled across the floor and unmoving. He'd accepted his bound fate. It was a shame we hadn't gagged him too. "You're going to trust a whim?"

"What else do we have?" I shot back. "We're a long way from home, we can't just sit here and wait for our supplies to run out."

"We're no safer out there!"

"Who said anything about safety?" Craig said with a chuckle. "Didn't we lose that luxury when we started this mission?"

"Wait," Maggie said, eying the room. I could see she was working out where each of us stood. Although Tom hadn't said anything, I knew he was on the same side as Craig. Maggie appeared undecided though.

"This isn't some stupid game," Maggie said taking a step backwards and dropping into the commanding seat. "There's a difference between being in danger and putting ourselves in danger."

"Permission to offer you a thought," I said. Maggie looked to me. "As we all agreed when we joined this mission, our lives are expendable when it comes to the assignment. Although protocol dictates that our primary objectives are complete, we're stuck here in this predicament regardless of whether we stay in here or choose to explore. However, all is not lost. We may yet be able to achieve our secondary objectives."

Tom placed a hand on Maggie's shoulder and said "It's a convincing argument." I was stunned by this sudden shift, and when I scanned the lander, I realised I wasn't the only one.

"What about Craig?" Charlie asked. "What do we do about him?"

"Untie him," Maggie said. "We can't leave him here, we're not barbarians."

"Released early for good behaviour." Craig's smug smile angered me, but I kept control, I wasn't biting.

"You better watch it," I said, stern and serious. "One false move and we'll leave you here." It was an empty threat, I knew, but Craig seemed to take it as intended and fell silent, the devious grin vanishing.

Maggie tapped me on my shoulder and indicated she wanted a word. I followed her into the crew quarters, away from the others.

"What's up?" I asked

"I wanted to thank you for what you did back there," Maggie said, her voice soft, but a deeper emotion brewing. "You handled the situation with Craig well."

"Thanks," I said.

"You'll make a find Commander, *one day*." The words were a complement, yet the way she spoke was barbed. It came across as a warning. I was not Commander yet. And until that day, it was her job to lead.

Without another word she dismissed me. I thought about talking things though, explaining that I understood my position but I didn't and let her message remain unchallenged. I left her to her thoughts.

It took us five minutes to suit up and abandon the *Altair* lander. Although my training had prepared me for the low gravity of the lunar surface, I still found it hard work to keep control inside the restricted spacesuit. Maggie joined us outside but said nothing. We boarded the rover with a few hopping steps, and aimed towards the towering ziggurat structure that dominated the otherwise barren landscape. It was impossible to miss, but in the shadow of other geographical features it seemed obvious now why we'd never seen it before.

When I closed my eyes to blink, I saw the same gigantic

mudbrick construction in its full colourful glory. The lush terracotta contrasted against the green hue of the dense jungle surrounding it.

"Oh my," I said, taking a deep breath. My eyes opened and I saw we were there, moments later the rover came to a halt. Charlie jumped off and hopped as quickly as he could towards the structure, his gloved hand reaching out and touching its grainy texture.

"It's magnificent," Charlie whispered, peering up towards their peak.

My eyes cast across the dilapidated and crumbling structure, sadness washed over me. In a number of places vast parts of the mudbrick blocks had sheared off and large lumps lay half-covered by the moon dust. It was a far cry from the tranquil and beautiful structures I'd seen in my dreams.

There was no lush greenery, no vibrant terracotta. I looked around and found where the river had once been. Now all that remained was the same fine dust that covered everything. I felt disappointed. As I turned away, I caught a green sparkle out of the corner of my eye and I glanced back hoping for another glimpse. As I studied the ground, circling the area, I noticed the green sparkles moving around me.

"It's alive," I said, as if I hadn't actually believed it before. "It's really alive." I bent down and picked up a slice of shimmering Jeometamorphic rock from the dust. Even through my gloves I felt its power moving inside me, my fingers tingled inside my gloves, and a warming sensation filled my body. "It recognises me." I couldn't hide the surprise in my voice.

The rock hummed to me in my hand and as my eyes closed I found myself sitting on the bank of the river with Magi Eritrea. Her sweet smile intoxicated me.

3

It was like a dream.

Memories came, swift flashes in even quicker succession. They did not feel like images from Russia's life.

I saw people dressed in red and black robes, heads bowed as they flowed by. I caught a glimpse of something glinting in the light – the living river as it weaved its way up the slight incline around the ziggurat. It snaked round the back of the structure.

In the vision, my eyes adjusted and I found myself standing at the east side of the ziggurat. My foot shifted the dirt to one side, before I bent down and placed something I couldn't quite see into the hole. I covered it back over.

I felt my weight drop to the floor in slow motion and the vision melted away.

"Are you okay?" I was surprised when I saw Charlie's face hovering above me.

"I don't know," I said. "Something is happening to me. I'm seeing things." I tried to stand, but even in the low gravity environment the weight of my suit dragged me back. Tom grabbed my hand and hauled me up.

"What did you see?"

"I..." I shook my head. "I saw myself burying something in the dirt, except I know it wasn't Russia's memory. I think it might have been Magi Eritrea." I turned to Charlie. "Do the scriptures mention anything like this?" Charlie blew out a long breath, but he didn't answer. "I think something was left here for me to find."

"Where was it?" Craig wanted to know.

"This is absurd." Maggie sounded riled, maybe it was just her Texan accent, but I got the feeling she was on the verge of calling us back to the *Altair*.

"We're looking for a grain of sand in a sandstorm," Tom agreed. "You'll have to be more specific." He looked at me, his face suddenly dropped, a look of dread. "Is it me, or do his eyes seem to be glowing?"

Both Serge and Charlie crowded around me, peering at me with caution.

"I'm fine," I said. "We need to start looking."

I turned away before they could voice any further concerns and bounded towards the east side of the ziggurat. I stopped a few paces from the corner.

"I think it's around here somewhere," I said. "I'm sure of it." I turned back to see the others catching up. I'd found myself in control of the crew again, tackling the situation while Maggie was side-lined. I could see why she'd derided me earlier, I was stealing her duty.

We dug a small hole with the spade from the rover's tool kit, but found nothing. I stood, adjusted my senses, closing my eyes and feeling the shifting direction and then led the team to a new site, only a few paces away.

"I'm sure this is it," I said again, after a number of failures.

"You keep saying that." Craig whined. We'd been doing this for a while now and the repetition was starting to grate.

"I'm one hundred percent certain this time."

"What are you looking for?" Maggie's frustration was clear. It was her mission.

"I don't know," I said. "But it's important."

I stooped to the floor and drew a large circle around me, marking a small symbolic x in the centre and then moved outside my scribblings.

"Hand me the shovel," Charlie once again passed me the spade.

In the second load, I spotted a metallic object and grabbed it.

"What is that?" Maggie wanted to know, snatching the

disc-like object from my gloved hand before I'd had chance to study it myself. It wasn't subtle, I knew what she was doing, trying to wrestle me for supremacy. I didn't bite.

I peered at the disc, it was roughly five centimetres in diameter.

"That's weird." Charlie pointed. I followed his extended gloved finger. At the tip of which I saw a small carved picture, a man holding a rocket. It was the SARA logo. "What does *that* mean?"

"And what is it for?" Serge wanted to know.

The questions went unanswered. I felt out of my depth and I'd led the others along with me.

"There has to be an entrance around here some place," I said shaking my head. "I can't think why else this would have been left exactly here." I pointed to the dusty hole we'd created.

"Maybe it got destroyed," Charlie offered.

"No," I couldn't believe that. "We were meant to come here and I'll bet we were meant to use the portal."

"You think this is some kind of trap?" Tom reignited our old argument. It was clear he wanted to go back to the *Altair* where it was safe – relatively speaking of course. "I feel like we're caught up in a maze."

"That's it!" I exclaimed. "This whole thing is some sort of giant test."

"Why?" Craig wanted to know.

"The scriptures mention judgement day," Charlie confirmed. "Think of the Old Testament, God's fury, fire and might. I took the destruction to mean that which took place on the lunar surface, but that was just my interpretation. Another explanation could be the destruction yet to come..."

"What about consequences?" I hesitated before adding, "Of failure? Any mention of that?" Charlie shook his head. "Do you really want to find out?" Through the dark shadows of his visor I could see his wide eyes. We had no choice now but to locate the portal and successfully operate it to travel home, to Earth.

Maggie couldn't listen to the others anymore, she was frustrated and fucked off. Mark had hijacked her crew and was leading them on an unplanned and unknown assignment. And she'd taken the step of warning Mark against getting ahead of himself.

The sudden loss of control was a shock to her system and she needed to vent her anger. She broke away from the group, sitting in the dirt with her back against the rough sun-baked mud block of the ziggurat's lower construction. *I don't lose control*, she thought.

"But I have," she whispered to herself, closing her eyes. Maggie took a deep breath, allowing herself just a moment to think of home, picturing her little nieces staying for the weekend, bringing their little cat along for the journey. Maggie had spent so much time away from home, she never thought it possible to miss being there, but now she regretted not spending more time with her nieces, watching them grow into young women.

Opening her eyes, Maggie vowed that this was her last mission, assuming that Mark could lead them home, and they actually made it. She shuddered at the thought.

Taking another deep breath, she turned to look at the others, they were hanging on Mark's every word, they were under his command. She had seen the leadership potential in him when he arrived into the mix, but she hadn't anticipated that he'd effectively be taking control on this mission. Maggie wondered if it was his destiny, after all his ancestor had led humankind to Earth. Was it possible he was leading them back again? She'd never believed in fate, but now she wasn't quite so sure.

She had to admit, she hadn't handled the situation very well and a wave of regret washed over her. She felt so stupid and realised she needed to make her apologies.

As she hauled herself up, using the mudbrick wall of the ziggurat to balance her weight, her eyes began to trace a small black line moving upwards along one of the mudbrick blocks. It didn't take her long to follow this to its conclusion.

"Err, I think you'd better take a look at this," Maggie said with enough force to break our conversation. Maggie crouched alongside the ziggurat, her gloved fingers running along a small ridge in the mudbricks. "Is this what we're looking for?"

We all joined Maggie to see what she'd found. I saw the ridge she was tracing. Maggie had found a concealed entrance.

"It looks like it's been blocked up," I said. "Look, we finally found this." I showed her the metallic disc and turned it over in my hands. As I held it up an image flashed into my mind, Russia standing before the ziggurat, the same metallic disc spinning in his hands, a crowd of people gathered behind him.

The image was so powerful I stumbled backwards.

"Russia had something like this the day he escaped," the words dropped from my mouth. "I've seen this before." In other dreams I'd seen Russia in the portal chamber, holding a similar disc, only I hadn't known what it was then. He'd used it to activate the portal. “It’s a key, it unlocks the portal.”

“This is seriously fucked up!” Tom pleaded, but nobody reacted to him. “Don’t you see how fucking insane this is?” He turned to Maggie, looking for support.

“Fall into line,” she said. “That’s an order.” Even Tom was stunned by her apparent change of heart and he immediately stopped whining. If Maggie had accepted our fate, then so could he. I caught her eye as she turned back to the crack in the mudbrick blocks, and she smiled, but she didn’t explain.

“Let’s get this thing open,” I said, taking command of the crew.

4

The heavy reinforced steel crowbar from the rover’s toolbox was my first implement of choice, but it was of no use. It took three of us and a whole lot of grunting to snap a small fragment of mudbrick from the main block. The strength of the stone was surprising, given its ancient battered and beleaguered appearance. It was clear we needed more than sheer might to break our way inside.

I shuddered, feeling like a common grave robber. We needed to try a different approach.

“Here,” I said grabbing a small box of brushes, handing Charlie the fattest. “We should check there isn’t actually some sort of locking mechanism holding it closed. These blocks are heavy and I don’t think we’ve got the tools to smash our way in.” It was corny, I knew, but in all the films I’d watched there was always some kind of trigger or release. You just had to find it.

Charlie swizzled his brush in the practiced fashion of an

archaeologist uncovering a new find. He traced the fault line, moving sand and grit, revealing a much smoother line. He stopped for a moment before running his gloved finger along the gap, moving the residual dust out the way before continuing. It was clear from the speed of his work, this wasn't the first time his anthropological skills had merged into archaeology. It wasn't long before he revealed the dark gash running along and down, but there was nothing obviously lock-like.

"This could take a while," Charlie said reaching to the top right and beginning the process once again, but this time he focused on the stone inside the black rim. As his brush worked its way across and then down in a systematic fashion, I turned my attention to Maggie. She was watching Charlie with an intense look. The moment she noticed me staring, she blinked rapidly, as if embarrassed.

"The temperature is starting to drop off," she said to me. "You'll want to start thinking about calling it a day and returning to *Altair*. We've got an hour or maybe two before the cold sets in."

"Thanks." I understood her subtext. "I guess we need to take a break anyhow."

"There is definitely something here," Charlie sounded excited and when I looked back I found him kneeling, his helmet practically touching the rough rock at waist height. "Look." He ducked out the way, revealing the two vertical ridges. "It might be a character of some kind."

"Cuneiform?"

"It's hard to say," Charlie said. "Either it's really badly worn or someone smashed off the other part of the character. It could be a cuneiform character, but I'd need a lot longer to decipher even that."

"We don't have that kind of time tonight," I said.

"Wait!" He ran his gloved fingers across the ridges. "It feels warm." As he did this, a fragment of rock chipped off, revealing part of what looked like a circle. "It's changing." He glanced across his shoulder at me. "The rock is changing density, like it's alive."

"Maybe it is." I smiled.

Of its own accord another small fragment of mudbrick dropped away, revealing another part of the circle. Maybe I just imagined it, but I thought I saw a faint green line flowing across one of the blocks, arching like lightning across a murky sky.

"It's about the same size as that disc." Even Maggie sounded excited.

Charlie moved quickly to prize the rest of the crumbling debris, uncovering the perfectly round hole.

"What do you think?" Charlie looked to me.

"Let's do it," I said, placing the disc into the space. It was a snug fit.

The ground jolted as the disc locked into place and began to spin turning into a green ball of light.

"That was pretty and all," Maggie said, "but it didn't do anything."

"Maybe the power's drained," Tom said.

"Give it a chance." Serge hovered next to me. "If you were over two million years old, you'd take a long time to work too."

What if it doesn't work? I thought. We'd be left stranded.

A deep rumbling shook the ground beneath us and a loud grating noise echoed through our suits. Maggie reached out to steady herself, grabbing hold of Charlie, taking cover in case this world ended. It didn't.

The mudbrick blocks glided inward, retracting and revealed an opening into a dark passage. Tom grabbed a torch and shone it inside, but it was too deep to see anything.

I stepped forward and stopped.

"What is that?" I was afraid of the answer.

My vision distorted slightly and when I looked back, I saw a different moonscape; that of our ancestors. From inside the ziggurat, I heard a hiss and then a click. Flames erupted all around, lighting the corridor into the underbelly of the ziggurat.

5

The reality was a stark difference to my vision. The magical corridor of light was replaced by the dark abyss, dimly lit by the beam of my torch. Foreboding.

I knew I had to go inside.

What if it's a trap? We already knew we were in a rat's maze, this was all part of it. I'd longed to step inside the ziggurat since I'd started recording my dreams, to understand their true nature. I couldn't refuse this enticing offer, no matter how much potential danger lurked ahead. I had to go in.

As I stepped forward, Maggie's hand grabbed my arm and I turned to face her.

"We should be careful," she said, her eyes pleading. "Remember we've not got much time before night fall."

I took another few cautious steps before turning back and motioned for the others to follow.

"We'd better take this with us," Charlie said grabbing the disc from the open doorway as he stepped inside. There was a groan and then a thunderclap, I swivelled in my padded boots, just in time to see the stones rolling back into place. We were plunged into darkness.

"Oh great," Tom said. "So, we're trapped in here now too?"

"We don't even have any supplies," Craig commented. "Nice going Charlie."

"We'd best keep moving," I said, ignoring their argument. Before I took a second step I froze and shouted, "*Stop*!" I heard loud hissing against my suit and when I cast my torch around, I noticed grains of dirt blowing at us from all directions. The noise grew, drowning out the elevated voices of the others over the radio. It was like a hundred snakes ready to attack. I shuddered. When the noise died away it left me feeling dizzy in the head.

A click echoed all around, and then flaming torches exploded into life down the length of the passage, lighting up into the infinite distance. I noticed Craig was cowering by the sudden appearance of flames.

"This shouldn't be possible," Maggie said. "You need oxygen for fire."

I tried to move and then I understood.

"We've just gained a more Earth-like gravity," I said, moving my arm to demonstrate. Tom shook his head, unable to understand.

Maggie attempted to move and almost tumbled over. She let out a laugh. "Oxygen and gravity," she said. "But even so I doubt we have a safe and breathable atmosphere. We'd better remain on internal air."

"Agreed," I said.

"They *really* knew we were coming," Charlie smiled.

All our training hadn't prepared us for this sudden, unexpected change. It felt like learning to walk all over again, and it took a few moments to adjust.

It took a bit of time to master the art of walking normally now that the full weight of my suit bore down on me, but once I'd adjusted, I led the team deeper into the heart of the ziggurat.

CHAPTER 15

Intricate carvings and designs covered the walls. I could make out two distinct styles of text scrawled along the corridor, some I recognised, similar to the scriptures, cuneiform perhaps. The other type of text was pictorial, conveying a hidden message. I didn't need to see Charlie's childlike and delirious grin with beaming eyes, to know he was euphoric.

My eyes scanned the walls, it had been over two-and-a-half million years since anybody last understood the secret messages. It brought back memories of awe, staring at the writings in the Rora Habab Temple, knowing they were by my ancestor's hand. The same power was contained within them.

Seeing my ancestors in my dreams, I'd expected to find traces of a more advanced civilisation than our own, but it was clear from the scrawls across the walls that I'd been wrong to make such an assumption. Not once had I seen the humans creating technology, and I think I now understood why. Technology was not of our ancestors' design. It painted a different cultural picture to our own people. The citizens of the moon were inferior, their curiosity stunted – nobody asked about the meaning of life, although Magi Eritrea was starting to.

Maybe that had made the passage to Earth easier for them. I'd presumed that it'd be like stepping into the dark-ages – I struggled to think of a world without mobile communications, or the internet available on the go – but now I saw my thinking was incorrect.

Our ancestors were never intelligent in that way, their lack of hostility towards one another was not because they were civil people but because of a lack of knowledge and the desire to learn. Knowledge equates to power, and power equates to destruction.

These were qualities we now had in plentiful supply.

"I think I understand something," I said facing the others. For a moment Charlie seemed annoyed, as if he thought I was about to steal his thunder and decipher the messages plastered across the interior of the ziggurat. "Our ancestors were docile, living in harmony with the world. Magi Eritrea was troubled towards the end, and she started to see the world for what it was. She started to believe in a dystopia, a dysfunctional perfection. In my dreams she told Russia about her desire to break free. It must have been this anti-utopian thinking that caused the destruction of this colony." I allowed myself a moment to breathe. "The aliens that created our ancestors bred them with a lack of knowledge and understanding of the world around them. If they didn't know that they *could* question their surroundings and their purpose, then they never *would*."

"Then why did we survive?" Maggie asked a pertinent question I hadn't considered and I had no answer. I shook my head. "You said the scriptures contained a warning, a prophecy that our alien creators would return to destroy us," she looked at Charlie. "But why wait?"

"Maybe they were testing us, like they're testing us now."

Charlie's words were slow and precise. "Maybe they wanted to see what people we'd become on our own." That made sense, but why would they want to know what became of us? Charlie must have seen the uncertainty in my eyes as he began to scramble to piece together further explanations, his mouth flapping but his words did not follow.

"What do these say?" Maggie focused our attention back to the texts splayed across the corridor of the sacred lunar ziggurat. "Can they help us?"

"I already know what they say, for the most part," Charlie said without even glancing upon the writings again. "They're written in the same pre-Sumerian cuneiform." He reached out, touching one of the carved characters. "They're intricately carved into the mudbrick, unlike the scriptures painted in the Temple. Then there are these." He pointed to the other sections of the wall with painted pictographic symbols. "They interrupt the flow of the text, they are so elaborate in detail, they look like Egyptian hieroglyphs."

"Is it possible there were two languages?" Tom asked. "The language of the people and the language of the Gods?"

"Anything is possible," Charlie said.

"So…you can understand them?" I asked.

"That's not what I said." Charlie shook his head. "It took me years to decode the scriptures, and it would take longer to understand this. I recognise only a handful of the glyphs, there are almost eight hundred known Egyptian glyphs. It's not a simple case of understanding what the text says, I have to understand what the glyphs mean first."

"It's a good job we brought a linguist with us," Craig spoke with more than a hint of sarcasm.

"Shut the fuck up or I'll do it for you," Tom growled, looming over him. I didn't fancy my chances if I were up against him.

"Don't think for a minute we'd stop him," I said studying

his face through the glass of our helmets. I could see the sudden change in his eyes, the realisation he was outnumbered. His mouth twitched and any trace of a smile disappeared.

Charlie pulled out a camera stashed inside a pouch at the front of his suit and began work, photographing the glyphs, cataloguing our discoveries. The sharp flashing light blinded me for a second and I stumbled back. When my eyes focused, I moved away from the rest of the group to look at some of the designs up ahead, carefully considering their size and possible meanings. As I moved farther down the narrow corridor I noted there was a distinct end to the writings. The cuneiform and glyphs both stopped, making way for simple cave paintings, much like the ones I'd seen in the caves leading to the scriptures back at the Rora Habab site. One of the pictures caught my eyes. It was a small blue outline of a man, holding a rocket. It was just like the one on the disc I'd found and identical to the SARA logo.

Who was the man in blue and why did he keeping appearing?

2

"Have a look at this," Tom's voice was distant, I found him a little farther ahead. I followed the sound, heading deeper beneath the ziggurat complex. The passage seemed to narrow, the ceiling dropping with rapid ease. "Do you see that?" I followed his pointing finger.

"Yeah," I said. "But what is it?" I looked at the ancient pictures. The first painting was of a small woman painted in white with rays emanating in all directions, a crowd of others bowed before her. The second image was of a red man holding a white sceptre above his head which pointed to the ground, white rays emanating from it in all directions. Red flames leapt up where they touched the ground. The third and final picture we all recognised. A blue man, standing alone, holding a rocket in one hand and his other reached up to the heavens – it was the SARA logo again.

As I looked at the images, a wave of emotions built deep within me, Russia was crying out to be heard. I closed my eyes and listened to this quiet inner voice.

“I think I know what this is,” I said pointing at the first image, repeated what Russia had told to me. “The white woman, she represents the humble servant to the alien race. She ruled the colony, allowing it to grow and prosper. This depiction is Magi Eritrea.”

“What is she holding?” Charlie asked peering in at the picture.

“The rock of power,” I said. “J-Power.” There was a hint of green, mostly worn away with age and most likely exposure to bacteria.

“Everything with you men is always about power,” Maggie said, shaking her head as she joined us. “You never know when to quit.”

“Who is this then?” Tom asked pointing at the red man. “Is that Magi Eritrea? What did she do?”

“No,” I said. I felt an angry fire burning in my stomach, rising quickly. “This is another man, I don’t know his name, but I have seen him in my dreams. I think he wanted the power of the creators for himself. I think it was his greed that destroyed the colony.”

“Then who is that?” Maggie pointed to the final picture.

Russia couldn’t shed any light on the subject.

“This is their history,” Charlie said. “Their past.”

“Of course,” I said pointing to the first image. “This was their beginning, then this.” I pointed to the second image. “This is the present which they lived in, before their world was destroyed. That makes the last one their future." I pointed to the blue image and frowned. "This was left for us."

"Why?" Maggie asked. "What does it tell us?"

"If this is their future, who is that man?" Serge asked, having remained quiet. I turned to him, a creased look upon his face showing his confusion. "I've never noticed that before – he's holding something in his raised hand." Serge leant forwards, blocking my view for a moment, when he stepped back, his frown deepened. He looked uncomfortable. "This wasn't left here for us," he said slowly. "This was left here for you. Look, he's holding a grey disc."

The new information took me off guard and I slumped back against the chamber. It was a long while before it fixed into my brain and when it did, I shuddered. What did it mean? Did the third picture – the future – the man in blue represent Russia, my ancestor? Nobody could know I'd be the one to see this image. A cold shiver ran across my arms and I shook. This was too weird and creepy.

The more I thought about it, the less sense it seemed to make. Russia had been the one to lead humanity to its future, he'd set us free from the alien creators' grip. So why was it a blue man and not a boy? And most important than that, why a rocket? It seemed to imply that Russia wasn't the one to lead the new colony to their future. Maybe it was me...

The thought was inconceivable. There was no colony left to lead and how could anybody know of me? And what about the disc, what did that have to do with anything. The metallic disc already in my possession was more important than just a simple key, else why would it be in the image. No, it had to be something far greater.

And then it struck me. What if the disc represented knowledge? Knowledge and freedom were intrinsically linked, so that made sense, but how would could it represent knowledge?

Could it be a key to the future of our civilisation, a future predicted millions of years ago? It was impossible and incomprehensible.

“I want to get out of here,” Tom said. He’d obviously forgotten that we were now trapped inside the base of the ziggurat structure, either that or he was too scared to remember.

“The portal is our only route home,” I responded. I didn’t hold out much hope that we could understand the alien technology blocking our escape, and that meant *Altair* would remain on the surface of the moon whatever.

Without further argument, we pressed on.

3

Serge tensed as he turned, catching a glimpse of a different glyph on the opposite wall. He froze, mid-turn, his heart pounding in his chest, the distinct feeling of liquid rising up his body, ready to wash over him. His breath echoed in his helmet.

Terrified, Serge faced the demon hidden inside the glyph. It remained static, staring back at him. As his eyes closed over he heard a voice in his head and his tongue caught at the back of his throat.

Anubikhanisis, it said to him before the blinding green light engulfed him.

The power pulsing through Serge felt like nothing he’d experienced before, it was a rush to his system, his heart thumped, his eyes rolled helpless to the back of his head, the green light surrounding him inside his mind.

All the while he heard the whispering voice,

Anubikhanisis.

He felt the pain of a civilisation dying, flames springing up all around, destroying the world, eradicating all traces of the people that had once lived there. A lightning bolt of pure green shot out across the land, scorched destruction lay in its wake. It was a scene his ancestor recognised.

There were tears in his eyes as he turned away. He was not alone, there were others fleeing, running towards the sacred ziggurat, a little boy leading them. This was Russia he knew, he'd seen this much in other dreams, these were the final moments of their dying home.

As he followed Russia, he felt the anger of his ancestor. For the first time in his life, Serge put a name to that man; his name was Antigua. This, he knew, was his ancient name, and as he fled to safety, he screamed inside of the injustice as the power of Anubikhanisis' fury raged on, enveloping everything he knew and held dear.

When Serge's eyes finally opened, he found himself staring at the same hieroglyph. His ancient memory of Antigua read it to him, *Anubikhanisis sees all*, and he shuddered. The life-force had a name.

In the distance he heard footfalls padding away from him, he was suddenly aware he was alone, lost in the depths of an ancient ziggurat. Serge shuddered, then he burst after the others.

4

With each footstep, a thousand minuscule shuffles echoed rhythmically around me, the solid walls magnifying our noise, refracting and reverberating. I found myself breathing heavily, my heart pounding.

"Are you sure we're going the right way?" Maggie asked

from behind.

"Just keep moving," Charlie said from the back of the line.

As if to reinforce my own claustrophobic feelings, a bead of sweat dripped from my forehead and ran along my cheek.

It was strenuous work trying to crouch and walk at the same time, the ceiling closing in on us with every step. I had to hunch over to continue. Among the shuffling noises of our feet I heard something else, something mechanical and I stopped, the group rearing into me.

Tom swore, sandwiched in between Maggie and Craig.

Craig hissed, "What're you doing?"

"Shhh!" I said, straining to hear. My eyes closed and trained my ears. The noise was too distant to determine, or maybe I'd imagined it. Whatever, I couldn't hear anything now.

"Come on!" Charlie sounded irritated. "I'm sweating like a pig back here. Whatever you heard, I don't hear it."

I stood upright and whacked my helmet on the low ceiling. I yowled, "*Shit*!"

"Keep going." I felt the weight of Maggie's hand on the back of my suit. "We don't have all day." We had all the time in the world, but I didn't argue.

"Okay, okay!" I blinked back the last of the pain, hunched over once again and began crawling through the still narrowing corridor.

5

The narrow tunnel came to an abrupt end, opening out into a vacuous cavern. Burning torches flickered below, casting ghostly apparitions into the darkness above. I looked upwards into the vast expansion of space which sloped inwards as it climbed inside the various platforms of the ziggurat.

I stepped out onto the small ledge, peering down into the abyss. To one side dangling over the edge, I saw a set of crude wooden ladders, lashed together with a kind of cord. Even from a distance they looked weak.

Now, the mechanical noise was much louder, like the ticking gears of a running motor. It felt impossible, like everything here. How could anything continue functioning without maintenance for so long? In our modern world, parts were replaced every few years, which meant the technology behind this place was staggering, but again, I reminded myself, it was alien technology.

Maggie glanced over the side of the ledge and when she looked at me, I knew her thoughts. How could we climb down there in our ungainly suits? We didn't have enough free movement to go down.

"Do you hear that?" I asked, looking at Serge. "What does that sound like to you?" He tensed, a frown wrinkling his brow as he focused. To me it was a constant and steady clanking.

"It reminds me of old-fashioned mine shafts, a pulley system perhaps." He cocked his head. "It has the same kind of rhythm. Do you think there is a lift down?"

"That's exactly what I'm thinking," I said. "There must be some kind of activation mechanism around here. It could be another disc shaped hole." Serge was already looking, Charlie was staring down at the platform below, Maggie almost clasped onto him, either protecting him or seeking his reassurance, while Tom gazed up at the smooth surface of the mudbrick roof. I glanced over my shoulder to see Craig perched in the opening to the corridor we'd come from.

A smug smile filled his face. "Is this what you're looking for?"

I followed his hand, seeing the glint of the silvery-blue lever under his fingers. Before I had chance to say a word, the lever moved under his control.

A loud crack burst out, a puff of sand blew across my suit. Then the cranking of a gear engaged, chains clanking through brackets. Slowly we began to float down as the platform swallowed us.

Maggie grabbed a sharp hold of Charlie, Serge jumping backwards, knocking Tom over in the process.

I didn't panic, as if I'd expected a smooth and gentle descent. Russia had used this to lead our ancestors to Earth.

Still, I couldn't stop myself swinging for Craig. I belted his helmet, rattling his head inside. I yelled, "You're a fucking prick!"

"We're okay," Charlie said, taking hold of my swinging arm as it recoiled ready for another attempt. "Don't give him the satisfaction." The sharp metallic taste of blood-lust filled my mouth. "Look, we're almost down."

The ledge came to a gentle rest and I stepped onto the solid ground of the platform. The ground sprawled out with two large set doors. On one of them there was the same symbol which seemed to be following me around, the blue outline of a man carrying a rocket. My attention was hooked, I felt drawn to it.

Either side of the doorway were two, winged gargoyles protruding the entrance; their eyes piercing hot, their bodies strong. They looked terrifying.

"Wow," Charlie let out. "They're almost Assyrian, like the winged goddesses guarding the entrance to a sacred vault. This *has* to be the gateway." His hands rested on them. "Look at their eyes, they're burning." He was right, red gem stones were fixed, gazing at anyone who dared to enter. For a moment I thought I saw a flicker of a flame dancing behind them.

My gloved hand stroked the character engraved in the

stone door, but I couldn't feel anything through the thick protective padding.

In a sheer moment of madness, I reached for the release valve, letting my gloves fall free. They zipped to the floor with a hiss as my suit filled with the stale air. I gasped for breath, stumbling to the floor and then I began to drift into seizures.

"Hey!" I heard Charlie yelling, footsteps racing towards me. Soon, I saw blurring faces towering over me, powerless to help as I struggled to gulp down the alien air. My throat was hoarse, my body convulsing as I fought for life.

Finally, I drew a deep breath of air and the world faded to black.

CHAPTER 16

My body felt light, the world swimming around me. I tried to call for help, but I couldn't force any noise from my mouth. I looked down at the floor inside the sacred ziggurat, my fitting form writhing in the dust. I realised I was watching from outside my body.

"We need to keep his airways open," Tom said, working quickly to roll my empty body over. I floated down next to him and as he turned he seemed to look right at me, but he couldn't have known I was there, hauntingly close.

Pulsing green lights flashed behind my eyelids and I felt the power of the rocks life-force flowing within me. My eyes fixed on my shuddering body, burning deep into my corpse, willing it to rest.

The fitting stopped.

"Is he alive?" Maggie crouched next to my lifeless body. She reached for the green button on my suit and pushed it. Charlie helped her twist my helmet free, allowing them a closer look.

"I'm not getting a pulse." Tom's voice was eerily calm. I saw the screen on my arm which usually displayed my vitals. It was blank.

"What do we do?" Charlie had panic in his eyes, his breathing quick and shallow. He reached out and touched my dulling skin with his gloved hand. He jumped back with a yelp. "He's burning hot!" He shook his hand in an attempt to cool it. "It burnt through my glove."

I caught sight of his glove as he held it up to Maggie, there was no evidence of burning. Serge touched my body in the same way, and snatched it back, shaking it furiously in the air.

I wanted to scream, to make my presence known, but no sound escaped my gaping mouth. Not knowing what to do, I hung in the air without a body. It felt strange knowing nobody could see me. I shivered, yearning for warmth. As soon as I thought it, I felt my fingers tingling with heat. It quickly grew until a fire raged across my temple and seared through my veins.

With gritted teeth, I kicked hard to escape the heat, but I had nowhere to hide. Even as I floated in mid-air, I felt the current dragging me down, reeling me in closer and closer to my lifeless corpse, until I was right upon myself.

My eyes snapped open and I stared up at the world, a scorching heat sizzling through my body, I reached out and grabbed Maggie's arm.

She opened her mouth and a terrified scream echoed into the chamber.

"This is impossible," Tom wailed, his finger trembling, pointing at the small display on my suit which displayed my life-vitals. "You're *dead*." I shook my head feeling more alive than ever before. I followed his stunned gaze, watching the static screen. Tom was technically correct, according to my monitor, I was clinically dead – my pulse rate and blood pressure read zero, my brain wave frequencies non-existent.

I said, "There must be a fault in the equipment."

"I don't think so." Maggie's voice tense. "Is it me or does anybody else see that green glow in his eyes?" Charlie was peering over her shoulder, his eyes wide with fear. "We should contain him." I couldn't keep the smile from my face, Maggie had finally let go, disregarding protocol.

My eyes glazed over as I focused on my extinct vitals, the screen burst into action. In that instant my heart rate reported from zero to three-hundred-and-fifty beats per minute.

"This is insane," Tom let out. "Something isn't right. We should listen to Maggie, before anything else happens."

"*What is he*?" Charlie's words screeched from his vocal cords as I lurched towards him, my hands outstretched. Maggie took a cautious step backwards with Charlie in an attempt to keep away from me.

"I'm fine." As I spoke, I felt a sudden thud in my chest. My heart pounded. I glanced at the digital display at my wrist; it read sixty. I held it up for the others to see. Exhaustion set in and I dropped back to the floor, sinking to my knees. I shivered, now cold.

"What the hell happened?" My voice forced from my throat, weak.

"We should contain him until we're sure he poses no risk." Craig's suggestion had the backing of the others, their heads bobbing, their eyes still conveying their fear.

"Look, I'm breathing," I said demonstrating, taking three deep gulps of air.

It took a few moments for my strength to return and I hauled my body upright, the weight of my suit pulled me back. It was a constant battle of wills. I won. I looked to

Maggie, trying to see reason in her uncertain eyes, but she shook her head, edging backwards a further step.

"Maybe he's right." Serge broke ranks, taking a hesitant step towards me. It was a start. He looked into my eyes, and for a moment I saw a secret dancing in the flickering light of the torches, reflecting in his stare. I saw a change in him, some new information he'd yet to express. Before I had chance to question, he turned to the others. "He's alive and breathing, it must be safe."

Maggie's mistrust was all too obvious as she held onto Charlie, yanking him back as his weight shifted, his foot almost off the ground. He said nothing.

"But what about that *thing*?" Tom waved his hand towards me. "That wasn't Mark."

"We can't be sure of anything," Maggie said, studying me. "I'm not taking any chances and I don't believe any of you should either." She turned her back to me, facing the others. "Our suits are fully functional, I see no reason to divest, even if there is safe oxygen in the atmosphere."

But Serge was shaking his head with vigour. Before Maggie could talk him out of it, he was at my side, his finger resting on the button to unfasten his suit.

"*No!*" Maggie screeched, but it was all too late. Serge dropped to the floor, gasping and choking as the oxygen ejected from his suit. It took Serge a few moments to haul the alien air through his lungs and when he did, he rolled over coughing and hacking.

"I'm okay," he said, forcing himself into an upright position, clasping at his neck. "It's strange." His voice returning to normal. "I feel like I'm high on something, like the air is *alive* and it's filling my lungs with clean, powerful oxygen."

"Now do you believe me?" I turned to Charlie, knowing his views were always closely linked to my own. I saw a glimmer in his eyes, agreement perhaps.

"But what happened to you?" Tom demanded to know. "I'm not convinced."

"Maybe the fragments of life-force in your DNA connected to the particles in the air," Serge offered, shooting me a knowing look. It confirmed my suspicions, he knew more than he was letting on. "I think they attract each other, like opposite ends of a magnet. You drew in the life-force and it became you."

Charlie popped his helmet and was unaffected, he didn't even gasp. Craig was next, releasing his gloves first, sending them shooting to the floor. I smiled, watching him take a deep breath. Tom looked to Maggie for guidance but she had none. The fear in his eyes vanished and slowly he removed his suit. His helmet clattered to the floor as he inhaled, taking his first extra-terrestrial breath.

That just left Maggie. She scowled at me through her visor.

2

The others were moving around freely, unrestricted, but Maggie didn't believe there was any reason to do the same. She struggled to stomach the stupidity of her team, a bilious taste filling her throat.

She scowled at Mark, she could see he was expecting her to remove her suit like the others, to trust him. She let out a huff, pushing away the group, wanting to be alone.

Her head thumped.

Maggie perched in the shadows of the overhang above, which afforded her just a few quiet moments away from the prying eyes of her supposed crew for a second time on this fateful voyage.

I'm meant to be their leader, but they don't listen to me.

That didn't matter anymore, the standard protocols no longer applied. Mark was leading the team now for a simple reason, he knew the most about this place – he was after all the 'payload'. It was clear they'd come ill-prepared for the mission, except they hadn't. Mark was the only preparation they needed, and he was doing just fine.

Give him a chance, the voice of her ancestor, Paraguay, filled her mind. *Little Russia is doing his best, he's led you this far hasn't he?* Maggie couldn't deny that. Mark was doing everything he could and if this was some kind of test, as it appeared to be, he was completing it with ease. She had to admit, Mark was their best chance of survival and the only one who could help them home.

But Maggie resisted, shaking her head. She couldn't let go like the others, she didn't want to die.

Get a grip girl!

Her fists balled up. It was now or never.

Maggie's hand was trembling as she reached to undo her helmet, her heart pounding wildly in her chest. Her breath caught as the button depressed, releasing the valve with a loud hiss that filled her ears.

When the helmet toppled to the floor Maggie took a gulp of the foreign air and then she felt the euphoria the others had described. The air was *alive*, and now she felt it burning in her lungs, the fire of a thousand tiny daggers burrowing into her cells, tranquillising the pain as they went.

Now crouched in the shadow, her helmet discarded, she felt foolish for resisting. Her cheeks flushed with heat. When she felt ready, she re-joined the group. Beaming smiles filled their faces as they saw her.

And then there was Mark, she looked at him, compassion in his eyes. He said nothing. She returned a smile. He was their leader and he always had been, just as the cave paintings in the corridor at Rora Habab had predicted.

3

The sealed doorway loomed before me, even though they appeared weak from a distance, the wood was thick and there was no give when I attempted to shove it. It would take more than a shoulder barge to open it.

I stared at the emblem in the centre and traced the outline with my bare finger. The little blue man was smooth, not a single imperfection in the design. As my fingers ran across the emblem, I saw a needle point protruding from the centre. Before I had chance to stop the movement, my finger grazed past the point and I felt the sharp prick of the proud spike as it drew blood. I withdrew my finger, turning it over to see the bright stain gathering where it penetrated.

"I'm bleeding," I said, my voice distant. No one moved. The world swayed around me, bending and flexing and then my vision pixelated as it had before when I'd seen the obelisk.

The world flooded with harsh colour, the twisted vibrant images still contracting and expanding. When it stopped, I felt disorientated as I looked out at my new reality.

Magi Eritrea hung from the wall of her cell, a position I'd seen her in before, but nonetheless distressing, bound and broken by her harsh treatment, stripped of her robes and left battered with only a stained linen cloth around her waist to keep her warm. Angry dark welts filled with dried blood covered her body.

Across from her cell I heard Magi Eritrea's captors arguing over who should take their defiled Magi's clothes as their trophy. It was ruthless and cold-hearted, but these men didn't know any better. They were acting on the wishes of another man.

Even though Russia was a genetic memory inside of me, I felt his pain, witnessing his master's brutal torture, the glowing green fields of energy binding her to the wall.

I turned to see a tanned face sneering at me. I had seen him only in the shadows of my dreams before, but Russia recognised him instantly. He was responsible for our master's decline, he had warranted her arrest and my mind flooded with hatred.

Russia had known Indonesia for a long time, he too was a servant to Magi Eritrea, the eldest and therefore most trusted. In retrospect it was clear Indonesia had not only betrayed his master but everyone and everything that lived and breathed in their world, all for the sake of greed and power – not emotions Magi should possess.

"It was worth it, Magi." Indonesia's words came out callous and calculated. A moment later a cackle erupted from his throat. "You were worth it, to bring you to justice." His sneer stretched, twisting into a horrific mass of smug self-satisfaction. "Come," he commanded Russia, staking claim to *his* servant.

"Never!" Russia's voice escaped my throat. Indonesia shot back an angry sneer before storming off. Russia turned back to Magi Eritrea. "They are to kill you." His voice now gentle. "I know you have no guilt, but that will not stop them. They will still end your torment."

"I know." Magi Eritrea seemed to smile, her lips whispering a silent meaning. "You'd better leave now before Indonesia orders you to join me." Compassion in her ever-radiant eyes.

"I want to save you." Russia's pain transcended the ages, ripping my heart in two. I felt red-hot tears burning my eyes, staining my cheeks.

"No." Her voice remained calm and soothing. "You cannot save me, but you may save yourself. Indonesia has the key." She leaned closer, pushing her body away from the wall as far as she could, before letting out a shriek of pure pain and jerked backwards, the green chains of justice sparking her back against the wall. "You must do what I say. *They* will soon arrive to destroy us. I tell you this, because you have time to escape *their* justice. You must lead all those who will listen to safety."

"You look sick." Russia ignored the words of his master.

"You *must* take the key," she said, with a little more force. "Whoever remains here will be unmade like me, turned into the dust of the deserts. Take as many as you can assemble, use the key to activate the forbidden portal. Set the co-ordinates which I have given you." Russia didn't know what to make of this. Why would all the others die? Even though he didn't know, he trusted his master.

"Will the Gods not strike me down?" A shiver trickled through Russia, afraid.

"No, my child." Magi Eritrea laughed. "*They* will not. *They* will come for Indonesia and will destroy this world before he gains *their* power." Her arm moved slightly, crossing the green beam and she let out a second, weaker screech. "Do it for our people." I felt questions poised at the tip of Russia's tongue when the chamber door burst open and Indonesia stormed in. It was time.

As the world faded, I felt I understood the cave paintings a little more; Indonesia was the depicted 'present' – he had led the civilisation to its destruction. I still didn't know exactly what caused this and for now at least, Russia didn't give up those details.

My vision pixelated, and drained of its vibrancy as I returning to the dull colours of reality and then relative darkness of the ancient ziggurat.

"Did you hear me?" Maggie asked from behind, I turned to her, shaking the remaining fuzz from my mind. "You opened the door."

I turned back and peered into the hollow darkness.

"It recognised you," Serge said. "Your blood triggered the locking mechanism." I stared into the black, unable to pick out any detail.

4

Serge stood back from the others as they pushed through into the dark opening. There was a strange voice in his head, the same as before. *Sacrifice*, it said. The word floated around inside his mind, echoing and pulsing through his thoughts.

With every reverberation of the word, he felt a greater need to do something or see something until it became an excruciating pain bludgeoning him with its endless and relentless fury.

It overpowered Serge, forcing him to his knees, and as he bent over the noise vanished into the ether. He didn't know what was causing it, but he *knew* it lay ahead of him, lurking in the darkness of the next room.

5

The light of the torch in my hand flickered inside the chamber casting curious shadows, picking out unfathomable details. In the distance I saw a dance of light as the beam of Tom's torch flared across strange shapes.

I followed Tom deeper into the unknown, taking careful steps.

We came to a halt in front of a large sarcophagus shape on the far wall of the chamber. It was similar to the one I'd seen in my dreams, but looked flatter, malnourished. The flashing beam of the torch revealing more carved glyphs which covering a raised lid, more cuneiform.

"A cartouche," Charlie let out from behind me as the light steadied on the writing. "Look, the central glyph is Magi Eritrea, the woman of power surrounded by humble servants." He stepped closer, his body partially blocking the light. "They appear to use the same language system as the ones in the corridor."

"I don't think we need to understand them," I said, Russia speaking through me. "We need to get power into the system." I swept the torch across the walls close to the portal sarcophagus, searching for the small round hole to place the metallic disc. The light reflected off the stone work, catching the details of its construction. About half way up the side sarcophagus I stopped and focused. "I got it!"

I placed the metallic disc into the waiting hole, instantly it began to spin. Vibrant rainbow-coloured sparks illuminated the room as it reached its tremendous speed, letting out a high pitch squeal which rose in intensity.

"What's going on?" Maggie yelled over the din, raising panic in her voice. Her hands clapped over her ears, a look of sheer terror in her eyes. The squeal was ear splitting for a couple of seconds and then it tailed off, perhaps reaching frequencies I guessed were beyond our hearing range. Maggie once again latched onto Charlie and when they looked at each other, I saw shared compassion; the look of lovers.

The ground shook beneath us, bowling me over.

"Are you all okay?" I yelled, bringing myself upright. I caught sight of Craig and Tom cowering, now in the opened doorway, braced as if waiting for the impact of an impending earthquake. It didn't happen.

The sarcophagus groaned as it began to extend into the room and when it stopped, it looked more like the one I knew and recognised. A clunking noise told me it was now resting into place. A moment later there was a loud boom and the sarcophagus burst into life, white light occupied the air; the hypnotic music of the portal filled my ears. I felt my body give way beneath and I dropped to my knees, asking for mercy.

The bright light flooded the room, reaching towards Serge and engulfing him. As the light washed over him, he heard that same voice calling in his mind, its dark voice mesmerising.

Come to me, the voice beckoned, come to Anubikhanisis and be my sacrifice.

Serge grappled with his ears in an attempt to shield himself from the perverse thoughts, but there was no escape.

CHAPTER 17

"You wanted to see me?" Randall asked, peering around the pale-yellow curtain surrounding Thacker's bed. Thacker gave a limp wave; his gaunt cheeks and pasty complexion painted a bleak picture. He seemed a shadow of his former strength and military stature.

Randall had overheard Bates arguing with the doctors, they were alarmed at the speed of Thacker's decline, he was losing weight before their eyes, but Bates would not authorise a transfer out of the facility. His view was that this, whatever *this* was, had to be contained. The general public couldn't know the truth.

"Yes," Thacker's voice was as weak as he looked. He attempted to sit up, a pained expression sparking across his face. He let out a yelp before sinking back. "I know why we've lost communications."

"Oh?" Randall took a seat, intrigued. He ran his fingers through his hair, twiddling with a wisp. Thacker's face contorted into a smile.

"There's a transmitter on the lunar surface." Thacker

hacked, his body tensed. "I've seen it. I'm certain it was programmed to activate upon our team's arrival." Randall's eyes narrowed. "*They* left it there, waiting for our return."

"Why?" Randall wasn't sure, but he suspected they were talking about the big '*they*', the alien creators. He'd heard stories, but he'd never seen *them*. He'd seen *their* destructive force in his dreams, he'd seen the burning embers of his ancestor's home world, but still he did not believe what others told him. "What is the point of blocking our signals? If there is a transmitter like you say, maybe they are sending out a high-powered message of their own, interfering with our communications in the process."

"That's it!" Thacker's eyes lit up, and he let out a delighted cackle before moaning and writhing in pain. "You're on to something."

Thacker grabbed Randall's hand, pulling him closer. Randall smiled, pleased he'd come out on top. He loved people stroking his ego. Truth was, he knew how skilled he was, but he loved the validation from others.

"I want you to prove it," Thacker whispered.

"I'm not sure I can?" Randall scratched his head for a moment. "It depends how advanced the signal is. If it is within standard ranges then I can do a simple scan of the airwaves and discount known frequencies."

"No." Thacker dropped hold of Randall. "You will need to use *unconventional* techniques." A cold chill blew across Randall, the hairs on the back of his neck standing to attention.

"What are you saying?" Randall's eyes narrowed.

"Reinstate *Project Serenity*," Thacker whispered.

Randall raised his eyebrows as he drew in a deep breath. He left the medical wing knowing what he must do.

2

Randall unlocked the heavy vault, removing the prototype design from storage. The *Serenity* was experimental and its unstable nature made it volatile, its power destructive. He unfurled the plans, spreading them across his desk and began to think. He didn't need to read the project brief, knowing the details in full already – he'd written them after all.

By harnessing the power from nanoparticles of Jeometamorphic rock, the *Serenity* device could send long-wave radio transmissions into deep space in a fraction of a second, while the antenna was a wide-band receiver, able to pick-up a broad range of frequencies. At least that was the intention.

In effect, it created a mobile phone that could see and speak far into the universe.

Randall knew, as the project lead, *Serenity* unleashed an awesome power on the Earth. He remembered the devastation from the first test phase: *Serenity* caused a potent earthquake in the surrounding area. The media picked up on the story and called it a 'natural disaster', but Randall knew otherwise.

He shook his head as he poured over the designs. He'd made mistakes, relied on unsound assumptions. He hadn't understood J-Power enough to make it work and he blamed himself for that, too eager to be the first to develop the technology.

His mind turned to the second phase, which was more disastrous with the project paying the ultimate price. He'd made some major modifications to the designs, re-routing the J-Power through a different line of CPUs, transistors and circuitry, but even this hadn't been enough to tame its potency.

As he closed his eyes, he felt the rattling of the Earth beneath him as if it were only yesterday. When the test finished and the tremors stopped, the damage was all too obvious. The buildings above, just like the project, crumbled and collapsed. There was no discussion, the funding was removed with immediate effect.

Randall was sure Thacker didn't have authorisation to restart the project, but he knew it wasn't his place to question. Thacker was still a superior regardless of his condition. In the NASA days projects like this required signatures from the President himself. Even so, he felt ready to complete *Serenity* having been away from it for so long. His thinking had matured and technology advanced since the original prototype unit.

I can do this, he confirmed to himself as his eyes darted back and forth, his mind analysing and critiquing the blueprints. A pen rested in his hand, and after just a few seconds he began to scribble, re-routing circuits and adding additional components.

Randall let out a sigh, running his fingers through his hair and resting his hands in the nape of his neck. It would be a long afternoon. Sooner or later he knew he'd get caught in the fallout of Thacker's deceit, he just hoped he had enough time to get the thing off the ground and wouldn't be the one left to take the tumble.

A pot of coffee later, Randall stumbled across his first significant breakthrough. All the other changes were minor by comparison, simple cleansing of his overly-complicated system. This was a major flaw.

Randall had been studying J-Power for three years under Thacker's watchful eyes before the *Serenity* brief took shape. It was his first attempt to harness the rock's power, and as such he'd treated it as any other source of energy. Now, of course, he knew the rock was a living breathing force, it couldn't be contained like a docile electrical current. It flowed in a more organic way and needed to be treated with different care and assumptions.

An idea leapt into his mind as his attention focused on the central core unit of the *Serenity*.

If he could pulse the feedback through J-Power and interpolate that with a second outflow channel on the CPU, he may just be able to bypass the resonating pattern which was more than likely the culprit for the devastation. This also allowed the rock to function at free will, travelling tri-directional without losing functionality.

That just may work, he congratulated himself, allowing a smug smile to swamp his face.

He screwed up the scribbled jumble of paper on his desk and flung it against the wall. It dropped, beside the waste paper bin. As Randall started over, jotting out the equations he'd been working on with the J-laser system, he knew he was on to something. They hadn't allowed him to perfect the laser, but he'd said all along that his theory was sound – the mathematical equations were correct. Now he was certain they could fix *Serenity*.

Within an hour he'd drawn up the new schematics for the device – he'd not expected to get quite so far so fast, but the idea had permeated his mind like a shot of caffeine in the morning and jolted his brain into a frenzy. Satisfied, he locked up his office and left for the night.

3

I gazed into the shimmering light of the activated portal, Russia's tears filling my eyes. *Isn't she beautiful,* his voice echoed through my mind and I agreed, its enchanted music both magical and wondrous.

"It's stunning." Maggie looked entranced, her eyes wide and unblinking, taking in the glorious sight. Her hand reached out towards the light of the portal. "I have seen this before, I saw my ancestor, Paraguay, she was here..." Maggie sniffed as her voice trailed off.

I turned to face the rest of the crew, seeing the same captivated expressions. Tom's mouth was wide open; Charlie held his fingers across his mouth, speechless; Craig was mesmerised, his lips mouthing soundless words I couldn't make out, and then I saw Serge, sitting motionless on the floor, facing the wall.

"Serge?"

He didn't reply.

4

You know what you must do! The words hissed in Serge's mind, a dark unseen force that wouldn't be silenced.

He tried to look away, but his eyes were fixed, staring at the glyph carved on the wall before him, inside another cartouche. It was a name and while he couldn't understand what it said, his ancestor could.

A white-hot flash blinded him, and a tingling sensation shot across his body. Serge was unable to stop his eyes from snapping shut as the world turned bright green and his nostrils filled with the stench of death.

Anubikhanisis, the name came to him once again, along with the word *sacrifice.*

As his vision cleared, he saw a young boy, his body limp but his chest rose and fell in steady rhythm, he was alive. Three men held him in the air, carrying him out of the sacred ziggurat. The boy's head lolled to the side, blue paint staining his forehead, a beaded necklace of green crystals hanging from his neck.

When the men reached the shore of the backwards flowing river, they stopped. One spoke in a language Serge couldn't fathom, and then they threw the boy's body into the waters, dropping him face down. The boy did not fight. Serge wanted to scream out, but he realised he could do nothing.

The vision faded.

Serge opened his eyes to the real world, the word *sacrifice* pulsing in his mind, the dark voice beckoning from inside the moving images of the cartouche. Birds were soaring in the skies, plants, trees and wildlife he didn't recognise. They all lived because of the green life-force, because of Anubikhanisis.

And now Anubikhanisis was waiting for a sacrifice.

5

I tapped Serge on the shoulder, he didn't stir. His body was stiff, rigid in his daze. I followed his gaze to the hieroglyphic cartouche on the wall, but I didn't recognise the significance.

"I know what I must do," Serge whispered, without breaking his intense stare. "It's the only way." His voice partially lost to the swaying trance of the portal's music, but I heard him. He reached out and touched the glyph before getting to his feet.

Without a word, Serge stepped around me and disappeared through the doorway back to the platform.

"Hey!" I let out. "Hey, everyone!" My voice echoed through the chamber, breaking the serenity. Questioning looks were returned. "Something is wrong. Serge!" I pointed after him before rushing out.

"What are you doing?" I found Serge standing by a second door across the open cavern. "What's wrong?" He didn't turn and an uneasy feeling pressed upon my stomach. "What did you see?"

"We need to stay together," Maggie said, following me out onto the platform. Serge didn't acknowledge our presence, he barely even moved, staring at the sealed doorway, his hands flat at his side. "What's up with you?" She stopped short as a rumble shook the ground beneath us. "And what was that?"

"It's awake." Serge's spoke with robotic precision.

"What is?" I couldn't conceal my concern. Having been through the same kind of thing, I asked, "tell me, what do you see?"

Serge said nothing.

The ground shook once again, and I stumbled backwards. Serge didn't flinch. A moment later he reached out and touched the carving in the centre of the doorway, tracing the pattern with his finger – birds, trees and beasts, it was the same as the glyph he'd been studying in the cartouche.

"What's wrong with you?" Maggie nudged Serge on the shoulder. He turned around and glared at her, a scowl covering his deathly pale face, a burning green glaze in his eyes. Maggie jumped back.

Another small rumble shook the ground beneath us.

"Look at me," I said, taking hold of Serge. Slowly his head turned. I put my hand to his head. He was cold. "Tell me what you see?" I asked. "What is going on in that head of yours?"

"Anubikhanisis," he whispered.

"Anubi...what what?" Maggie asked.

Russia trembled inside of me and I shook. Through his eyes I saw a small boy motionless on an altar, his naked chest silent, his hands clasped together as if in prayer, a necklace of Jeometamorphic rock wrapped around them. As I watched, the green life-force began to flood the chamber until only the boy was left, floating on the surface of the altar. But the green torrent did not stop, it covered the boy and only stopped when it reached the ceiling of the chamber. When the liquid drained away, the altar empty, the boy gone; taken.

Sacrificed.

There was another low rumble.

"Anubikhanisis." The words fell from my tongue with a shudder. "You don't need to do this." I shook Serge by his shoulders. "This isn't your calling." But it was, I felt it. His eyes flashed green before glazing over once again.

"I know what I must do," he said. "I have been chosen."

"No," I said. "I won't let you do this."

"Do what?" Maggie was tugging at my arm, but I didn't respond. "Will someone please tell me what's going on?"

"And what is Anubi..." Craig trailed off.

"Anubi-khan-isis," I said splitting the word, stressing each part.

"It's the rock." Charlie's voice came from the darkness beyond the portal doorway. A moment later he appeared. "The Egyptians believed green was symbolic of resurrection and immortality and in fact Osiris was often depicted with green skin..." His eyes widened, a look of dawning realisation. His fingers rose into the air like a conductor ready to instruct his orchestra. "I've been totally blind. I can't believe I missed this."

"What?" I couldn't help frowning.

"In mythology, Osiris is the *dying* God of the afterlife."

"Wait," I said catching his eye. "When I first met you, in the Rora Habab caves, you showed me a painting of Anubis – a jackals head with human legs. You told me he was the God of the underworld?"

Charlie grinned as he spoke, "You remembered. The cult

of Osiris came about as the cult of Anubis fell from favour. Anubis is said to have stepped aside for Osiris; taking his place to judge the dead. As the story goes, Osiris was killed by his brother, Set, and the distraught queen, Isis, pieced together his body creating the first mummy and giving him the afterlife."

"And what does that have to do with anything?"

"Anubikhanisis *was* our God," Charlie said. "Not just God of the dead, but of everything. It's the name *they* gave to the life-force; the green rock."

"God?" Maggie was confused. "You're talking about religious rituals."

"Of sorts," Charlie confirmed, we were back in his realm. "The scriptures tell us that the rock – the life-force – was considered sacred, it was both worshipped and revered." He pointed at a glyph to the side of the door, the image depicted three men bowing before a glowing green rock. "Even the name runs across the cultures of Earth. Anubis, the underworld; Khan or Han, a military ruler across parts of central Asia and then there is Isis, the Goddess of fertility and motherhood. Isis is the sister and wife of Osiris. Don't you see? It's everything."

"And what does *it* want?" Maggie's voice conveyed calm, but her eyes spoke of her panic, darting from Charlie to me.

"Anubikhanisis wants sacrifice." The words fell from Serge's lips. "It wants me."

"You can't." Maggie took hold of Serge, but he brushed her hand away with ease. He continued to study the door. I only realised what he was doing when he placed his finger to the side and let out a groan. When he removed his finger, I saw the reddened needle point.

The floor shook as the door rolled open.

"Like I said, it's in the blood," Serge said, his voice flat. "I must go." Before anybody could stop him, he stepped into the chamber, light exploded around him and the door sealed shut.

"Get him out of there!" Maggie yelled at me, her hands balled into fists. I shook my head, there was nothing I could do. Serge had accepted what he believed to be his fate and there was no changing a man's mind in that state.

From inside, I heard a loud hissing as Anubikhanisis rose.

A green mist descended as time stood still. Out of the fog, I saw Serge, standing inside the chamber, his back to me. I felt his unspoken fear as he peered up at the altar.

I felt the power of the rock burning inside of me, and as the pain grew strong, the fine green spray cleared until I could see everything happening inside the chamber. It was as if I were in there with Serge. The same life-force that would take his life, gave me the power to see. After all, we were all connected; part of a bigger being.

"I am here." His words echoed in the empty chamber. "I am ready for you." He looked to the altar, taking his final steps towards it. A puddle of green formed at his feet as he pulled himself up and lay down.

Even as the hissing rang out all around him, Serge remained calm on the exterior, this was his destiny, there was no use fighting it. Sprawled across the altar I felt Anubikhanisis near, God of the rock.

The green liquid continued to rise, now half way up the stone legs of the altar. I was surprised when a smile flourished across Serge's lips, a serene look in his eyes. When the green liquid reached his body I shuddered, feeling a sudden numbness. I tried to cough, my throat dry. Serge just lay there as the green waters washed over him, now at his neck. I listened to his short rasping breaths, knowing that each one may be his last.

The tide rose on.

Anubikhanisis touched Serge's lips and his eyes snapped closed. I heard the thoughts running through his head as he took a final breath of the alien air, thinking of everything he'd achieved with his life and the images flashed before me; his former lovers; the first house he'd owned; the beautiful view from the top of the Cretan mountain he'd climbed; the friends he'd made at university, and those that he'd lost over the years. The final image – the Earth viewed from space and the dark light of the hidden skies above it – this was his true passion, and it stuck with me as the liquid poured through his open mouth. Tears fell from my eyes.

Serge let out a gurgle, I felt a flood of strength washing over him, the power of the rock joining him; becoming him. His last thought came to me, pure exhilaration and bliss. And then the life-force swallowed Serge.

The green mist returned, clouding my view.

"It's over." A deflated sigh escaped my parted lips, and I slumped to the floor.

6

The platform filled with an eerie, still, silence and it terrified me. Maggie looked horrified, one hand grasping her head, the other hung at her waist. Beads of sweat formed on her brow. She was lost for words.

I knew she didn't understand Serge's actions, he'd given his life for us, but it wasn't clear why he felt he had to. Was this all part of our trials too? If it was, it seemed harsh, but what was one life against an entire civilisation? For all we knew, Serge may have saved the entire human race. But we *didn't* know for sure and it was clear Maggie held me accountable. She scowled as I left.

A comforting hand touched my back, but I didn't feel like being comforted and brushed Charlie off. I stopped and peered at the glyphs Serge had studied so intently before his rash decision.

Inside the cartouche I found the same images which were carved onto the stone door Serge activated – the birds, the trees. To the side of this, a man knelt, his hands pressed together in prayer. Rays of light cast all around him, coming from what looked like a fountain. Behind him there were distinctly five others, also on their knees. I doubted that this was a coincidence, after everything we'd seen and understood. I just couldn't believe in chance.

Maybe Serge was right, he was meant to give up his life.

As I looked around the room, I found no clue, only other strange characters and glyphs.

"Why did you let him go?" Maggie demanded, thundering in, a storm gathering in her voice. When I turned to her, I saw the tears in her eyes. "You could've stopped him. He *listened* to you!" Venom igniting in the air, her eyes angry red. "You could've talked sense into him. You could've convinced him it wasn't necessary."

"No," I said, my voice flat and withdrawn. I shook my head, refusing to believe that Serge gave his life in vain as Maggie seemed to think. There had to be reason and I was determined to find it. "Look," I said, pointing at the picture. "There are six people in that picture. *Six*." Maggie shook her head, denying the obvious. "He handed himself over for us, he sacrificed himself to Anubikhanisis to save *you*."

"The scriptures don't mention anything about sacrifice." I scowled at Charlie, he wasn't helping.

"You told me the scriptures were incomplete records," I said. Charlie's legs jittered, his mouth twitching. "That is why we are here, right? To understand? Except we're not.

We know that now. For reasons beyond me, it was our destiny to be here. I am depicted as the future of mankind, you all saw that; Serge *believed* it. That was *my* fate." I shuddered, still unsure what that meant. "*This*. This was Serge's fate."

"*Fuck* the scriptures!" Maggie yelled. "And fuck you too!" Her tears were now a constant stream. Charlie tried to take her in his arms, but she pushed him away, her head in her hands.

Charlie froze, his gaze fixed on something new. "I think you should see this." The oppressive atmosphere was pierced by Charlie's voice, he seemed excited and it caught me off guard. I shot him a harsh look and he looked away embarrassed. "Sorry," he said.

"What have you found?" I followed Charlie's gaze. There at the bottom of the sarcophagus were a set of keypads, alien glyphs written on them. Russia's memory translated them into a numbering system; it was *theirs*.

"They weren't there before," I said, adding, "were they?"

"No."

I tried to catch Maggie's eyes, but she averted my gaze. Charlie let out a muffled groan and shook his head.

"This whole expedition has been nothing but a test," Tom spoke from behind. "Maybe we needed to prove we were worthy. Serge was willing to sacrifice everything for us."

He was a Magi in all but title. He had given his life for his people.

7

My eyes glazed over, detecting vivid golden colours and then my world collided with the past – my mind transported to the day of Magi Eritrea's death.

When my vision cleared, I stood in a room, staring through Russia's eyes.

"You called for me, master." Russia's voice escaped from my mouth as the memory replayed.

"You," Magi Eritrea said, stepping closer, but she was not talking to Russia. "There are visitors coming, make preparations." I turned to see Indonesia, he bowed to his master, but as he turned away, he caught Russia's eyes and scowled. As soon as the door closed, Magi Eritrea settled her hands upon Russia's shoulders. I felt her soft warmth upon my own shoulders and I smiled.

"I am so proud of you." Magi Eritrea spoke with the loving compassion of a mother. Russia never knew his, she'd died giving birth, but Magi Eritrea had told him much about her. "I have a favour to ask of you."

"Anything." Russia bowed. "You know I would." While Russia knew Magi Eritrea wasn't his mother, she'd treated him as such and in return he'd always respected her.

"I need you to keep a secret. I need you to hide it so deep that nobody can ever find it. Can you do that?" Russia nodded. "I am to be arrested tomorrow, on Indonesia's orders."

"No, no!" Russia shook his head. "I will not let him."

"You must," she said. "Your life depends upon it."

"Why do you say that?" I felt Russia's sorrow as he looked into the swirling compassion of Magi Eritrea's eyes. "Why would you say such things?"

"You may never be a Magi my child, but you will have your kingdom." I thought I knew what she meant, having the experiences that Russia could not, but I felt Russia's confusion. Maybe she knew she was not talking to Russia, but directly addressing me. "Our world is to be destroyed."

"How do you know?" Russia asked.

"Indonesia will take the throne and our alien protectors will come to destroy our world. You must not trust

Indonesia." I found my head bobbing with her. "He has spoken of using *their* power against *them*, this is something *they* will not accept."

"Why don't *they* take him?"

"This is bigger than one life," Magi Eritrea said, a sudden look of horror crossing her face wiping out her beauty. "The minds of our people have been infected with deceit and greed. The idea of *their* power has led to corruption of our values, and Indonesia is the leader of this movement. *They* will cleanse our world to wipe away the disease that spreads among us. *They* know this, but before they act, Indonesia must come to power to complete the cycle. I must lay down my life so that you may live."

"Let me die," Russia said. "You have been a good Magi and I am humble to you always."

"No," Magi Eritrea said. "I have a job for you. You must live. Take this." She handed Russia a small piece of parchment with red pigment scrawled upon it. Written, in the alien language Russia had seen many times, were a series of numbers. "These co-ordinates will link the sacred portal to our nearest star; an uninhabited planet." Russia repeated the numbers in his head, memorising them. "Use them when the time comes."

"I will." I'd already seen further debate about this in a previous vision. Russia didn't understand his master, but he wasn't meant to yet. Magi Eritrea continued to speak to me.

"You will become bigger and better than I ever could." Magi Eritrea looked into my eyes, a spark of intense white light flashed between us and the vision faded into the obscurity of my mind.

The dream moved on in time. Russia perched in the shade of a tree, watching the sun and Earth descending through the sky as it vanished below the horizon. The air was still warm. He'd just been to see Magi Eritrea in her cell and now the tears streamed from his eyes.

He wept for his master, he'd loved her as a son should love a mother.

Flustered chatting of the other servants filled the air, interrupting his mourning. Russia got to his feet, rushing to see what was happening. He was just in time to see three guards dressed in red and black robes, escorting a limp Magi Eritrea from her cell. She said nothing, didn't even attempt to rebel against her fate, embracing it as all Magi should. Russia's eyes dried that instant, remembering his master's words; he had to act fast.

As the guards led Magi Eritrea into the waiting crowd, Russia managed to catch her eyes, and shared a last moment of joy. It was time, he knew.

Russia chased through the crowd taking hold of the people he knew would listen to him.

"Please, we have to leave," he pleaded. "We are in danger. You must trust me."

Russia didn't understand why, but the eighteen people he gathered believed him without question. With hindsight I was disappointed more hadn't. Russia led them away from the crowds, explaining as they went. He instructed them to gather a few possessions, whatever they could carry.

He left them, rushing back to the packed courtyard. Magi Eritrea now stood on the podium awaiting her punishment, her only real crime was to have trusted Indonesia. The charges of corruption and misuse of her powers as Magi held no truth and no weight, yet the crowds bayed for her blood in her last moments. Indonesia had indeed rallied up support for her deposition and handover to the aliens. In that moment I caught a glimpse of the greed and envy that Magi Eritrea had spoken about; we had become infected as a people. There was no denying that the disease had spread.

Russia waited for his chance and when he saw it coming, he didn't waste time. He burst forth and snatched the metallic disc-like key from Indonesia's belt and slipped away into the crowd before Indonesia could do anything. Before he fled, he cast one last longing look across his shoulder. Magi Eritrea stared at him, her beaten body weak, but still she managed a prideful smile for her little Russia.

He caught a glimpse of the silvery-blue weapon glistening in the light as the executioner took aim at Indonesia's order. I recognised the object, I remembered seeing the same things hanging along the corridor of the SARA building. Now I understood their purpose. They definitely weren't art.

Russia fled, not wanting to see the weapon blast his master into dust. As he ran, a cheer leapt from the crowd and he knew the their Magi's ordeal was over. He could not believe they were rejoicing in their leader's death and then his thoughts turned to Indonesia. *How could he do this to our leader, my master! She had been nothing but a mother to us all.* Russia's rage burnt in my chest. *He will never survive the wrath of Anubikhanisis!* A tear slipped from his eyes, but still he pushed on and met up with the others he'd gathered. Without hesitating, Russia led the group into the sacred chamber beneath the ziggurat.

They arrived in the forbidden portal chamber, time an enemy. Russia worked quickly to activate the system, opening the gates to destiny. He set the co-ordinates Magi Eritrea had given and he had committed to memory; they were going to the bright blue globe with swirling white patches, clouds perhaps, which always appeared in their sky – today I knew this was Earth.

Indonesia's guards would soon arrive to arrest them. This fear spurred Russia on, hurrying the group through the portal and into the great unknown of their new home world.

Powerful light filled his eyes and the hypnotic music of the portal occupied the air.

The harsh reality of the real world swam into view.

Everything was starting to make sense, the pieces slotting together. While my visions hadn't happened in chronological order, I now understood what was going on. The visions were finally making sense.

Magi Eritrea was setup by Indonesia. She'd been handed over to the aliens, but there was more to it than that. She'd told me that she'd given her life so that I – Russia – might live. But I didn't believe that was exactly what she meant. Russia had led a group of people to Earth. Magi Eritrea had given her life for this to happen, and she'd known that we would survive. Had she known who we would become?

And then the thought struck me. Had Magi Eritrea reached a deal with the alien creators?

CHAPTER 18

"It's time to go home," I said, the light of the portal flickering on the edge of my periphery. As I looked around at the solemn but hopeful faces, I felt the gaping hole that Serge should have filled. We couldn't forget what he had done for us.

I turned to face the portal, only then realised I was leading the group, just as Russia had done. I was Russia, the saviour of humanity. A sense of satisfaction stole over me.

When I looked at the keypad below the sarcophagus, I no longer saw the alien numbers, only our modern equivalents. I bent down, punching in the digits as Magi Eritrea had instructed Russia.

There was no delay; the light of the portal grew in intensity, and a cool breeze rushed past my legs. The luminance extended outwards, filling the chamber, blinding me in the process until it had consumed everything.

The ghostly music of the portal was louder now, surrounding us. Its high-pitched humming inter-spliced with a deep thundering whoop, reminiscent of a bullroarer. Its song enchanted with the voice of our ancestors.

Slowly, the light faded, the shimmering mirrors of the connected portal swimming into vision. The room hummed in tune. It was everywhere and it was beautiful.

"How can we be sure this is the right way home?" Tom's voice was distant over the graceful rhythm of the portal. "How do you know this isn't just another test to trap us?" I knew he wouldn't like the answer and as I turned to look at him, I saw his face drop. I didn't need to say anything; my expression said it all.

2

"I'm picking up something!" Bates heard Beth yelling across the control room. He rushed to the railings and peered down. Khan raced over to Beth's workstation, grabbed her headset and pressed it against his ears. Khan tensed.

"What we got?" Bates wanted to know, making his way down the stairs and jogging across the control room, zeroing in on Beth's position towards the front and centre. "What is it?" Khan turned, his eyes wide, his lips parted and dry.

"I don't know," Khan said and then to Beth, "Bring it up. I want to know what frequency it's on and I want to track a location."

"In progress." Beth's finger tapped across her keyboard with speed. Within moments she had details on her screen, and fired them onto the large LED displays so that everyone could see the results. "I've got an unknown foreign modulation pattern...it's coming from the lunar surface, but its signature is definitely not from our equipment."

"Any ideas?" Bates looked between the two.

"No," Beth said with a quick shake of her head. "It's not in our standard broadcast frequencies, and it's an unstable pattern." The speakers around the room burst into life, filling the control centre with a deep harmonic hum, superimposed with a mesmerizing whooping – a distant helicopter beating the air.

The music played, and Bates eyes snapped shut against his will, white hot light exploding behind his eyelids. He felt the change, as if the room had skewed on an event horizon. His mind splintered, pulled in different directions, swirling in the appearing vortex of light.

When Bates opened his eyes, he felt the room moving, bobbing and rocking as if he were drifting in the ocean, bouncing with the waves. And still, the music thrummed, fuelling his imagination.

"What is that?" Bates grabbed hold of the desk to steady his swaying legs. Blank faces stared back. A moment later he darted from the room to find Thacker.

The music filled Thacker's ears as he woke, opening his eyes and seeing the world afresh. The tranquil tones of the music called to him, beating inside of him. The voice of Indonesia, his ancestor, filled his head with excited chanting; *oola-oola-oola*.

He still felt weak, but he was on his feet dressing quickly. In a hurry, he left the medical wing, breaking into a trot, bursting through the entrance of TICC control. The harmonic moaning sounds floated in the air, underneath this a resonant thunder shrieked its agony, enchanting everyone who was listening.

Thacker smiled, understanding. The *Constellation* crew were still alive and they had opened the portal.

3

"Maybe we should test it." Tom's voice was flat. His staring eyes bore through me. He didn't need to say anything, I already knew who he wanted to perform the trial run.

"You can't be sure this thing will work, can you?" Maggie said, rubbing at the red marks staining her cheeks.

"No." I shook my head. "I can't be certain of anything, but we got this far, I don't believe this was setup for us to fail at this final hurdle."

"Okay," Maggie said, a sudden sparkle in her eye. "And we don't know where it leads?" I said nothing. "Then as Commander of this mission, I can't let you attempt this." There was an ambitious look upon her face and I knew she wouldn't back down. Without another word, Maggie stepped towards the shimmering vortex that filled the sarcophagus. "I won't let anyone else die in vain under my command."

Without another word, Maggie stood before her uncertain future, staring into its sparkling abyss. She hesitated, unsure if she could trust the ancient technology, but then her hand reached out and touched the mirror surface, closely followed by the rest of her body as she stepped into the oblivion.

"Wait," I said, but the music of the portal grew louder in my ears drowning out my voice.

I watched as the last of her brown curls vanished into the brilliance of the portal, absorbing her. As soon as she'd gone, the mirror returned, bouncing back to its original state.

We stood, waiting, watching and wishing.

"Should it take this long?" Charlie finally asked, anxious. It had only been around a minute, but even I felt the time dragging.

"I don't know," I said. Russia had only ever seen someone go through the portal, as far as I knew he'd never seen someone emerging from it. We waited in silence for at least five more minutes.

"Where is she?" Craig asked his voice impatient. "I think something went wrong. She should be back by now." He turned to Charlie, then Tom before finally resting his gaze on me.

I shook my head. I had no answers.

"I'm going through." Craig stepped towards the portal and as he did so I noticed a flicker on the mirrored surface of sarcophagus and grabbed his arm.

"Wait!" I pointed to the white hump appearing in the light. Slowly the bulge took the shape of a woman and then Maggie burst through.

"Wow!" She let out as she fell forwards.

"Are you okay?" I jumped to her side, helping her up.

"Yes!" Her eyes wide, a huge grin plastered to her face. "I'm fine. It just knocked me for six. It's fantastic." She dusted herself off.

"What was it like?" Craig wanted to know.

"I felt myself being dragged in to a swirling wind, music humming all around me." Maggie said, unable to control the smile that danced across her lips. "It felt like I had no physical body and I was soaring in the breeze." Her eyes lit up, sparkling and I saw the moment replaying in her mind. "It was extraordinary."

"Was it easy to get back?" I asked.

"Yes," she gasped, still breathless. "I didn't know where I was, but I came out of one of these." She pointed at the sarcophagus. "I just came back through." I was pleased she'd made it back and smiled, her face full of life and joy, almost as if she'd forgotten our ordeal. Charlie took her in his arms, squeezing her tight, it was clear to me that their love was resurfacing. Maybe it had never gone away.

"Any idea where the other end might have been?" I asked.

"No," Maggie shook her head. "It was a dark room, very cold, air-conditioned perhaps." Her shoulders heaved. "The only source of light came from the portal itself, and I didn't want to scout around in the pitch-black."

"I think I might know." Charlie pulled back from Maggie, I saw the concern welling behind his eyes.

"You didn't?" Maggie's brow creased. "Tell me you didn't know about this all along?"

"What?" I stepped closer. "You knew?"

"It was Thacker," he said as he edged away from me.

"He knew about this too?" I felt the blood rushing to my face and my cheeks began to burn with anger. "You knew all along and you didn't think to mention it. You let Serge sacrifice himself?"

"I didn't know about that." Charlie spat, stepping back and stumbling over a fragment of rock. Tom and Craig joined me, glaring at him, sickened by the turn of events. "The scriptures say..."

"Fuck what the scriptures say!" Tom hissed. "Is that all there is to you? Is that everything you have, your precious fucking stones? Well fuck 'em and fuck you too!" He pushed away from the group towards the portal. "I've had enough of this shit. I'm going home." A flash of pain ignited across my forehead and temples. Something was wrong, I felt it.

"Don't," I said grabbing Tom's arm. "Let's hear his explanation. We owe it to Serge, don't forget what he did for us." When I felt sure his attention was held, I turned back to Charlie.

"I found the sarcophagus in the Rora Habab," he said. "I didn't know what it was, and I had plenty of other things occupying my interest that when Thacker ordered its removal, I didn't think it was a problem. I never had chance to examine them closely, but I swear I didn't know what it was." His voice pleaded, and I believed him. Thacker had a habit of keeping information to himself, so this was of no surprise, but if Thacker knew about the portal it changed everything. Why would Thacker keep this secret? Was his goal to activate the portal?

"You said there was something about this in the scriptures?" I prompted.

"I swear I didn't know." His voice pleaded again. "They mention that our ancestors travelled by the light, that's all." He looked to Maggie for support, a momentary flash of compassion filled her eyes, and then the steely eyed look of a leader replaced it. I rested a hand on his shoulder to reassure him.

"Charlie?" Maggie's voice calm and focused. "Where is the sarcophagus now?" Her jaw clenched.

"A secure room inside the SARA complex."

The pain flared across my temples once again and I buried my head in my hands, rubbing my forehead to ease the symptoms. I felt a deep unease about this new information, my body began to ache all over. I inhaled the alien air, filling my lungs and closing my eyes, trying to visualise what was happening, but I saw only the darkness behind my eyelids.

Maggie broke the silence, asking, "What do we do now?"

"I don't know. I really don't."

When I closed my eyes again, an image of Indonesia flashed in my mind, I saw only his face, a wry smile playing across his lips. He was grinning at me, just as he had grinned at Russia before he stepped into the portal. Why was he smiling? Russia spun around to face his demons, but all he saw was the flickering torch lights beyond the chamber.

Brilliant light filtered through my closed eyes and they snapped open. I was just in time to see Craig vanishing into the shimmering light of the portal.

"Stop!" I yelled, but he didn't hear, his head already gone, legs trailing behind.

4

Thacker stood in the doorway of the control centre, his hands gripping his forehead. A constant pain thumped, like rapid gunfire ricocheting inside his skull. It was getting worse.

A burst of static erupted inside the control room, interrupting the ghostly music, hissing and crackling in pulsing waves.

"What the hell is that?" Khan demanded to know. "Come on people, I need answers!"

"It's on *Altair*'s frequency." Josef pushed back from one terminal, swivelling around to face a second before bringing up more information. It was happening too fast, Thacker couldn't keep up, his brain could no longer process what was happening. The pounding grew in intensity, harder. He thought he knew the cause; someone was transiting the portal system.

The static stopped, casting the control room into stunned silence. Thacker's pain dulled, returning to a light tapping, an engine ticking over.

"Tell me what is happening." Khan demanded with what seemed like rising panic. "Where has it gone?"

"The transmission stopped," Josef reported. "I'm getting nothing on that frequency and nothing on the emergency broadcast system either. We're still picking up the previous background signal." The enchanting music resumed inside the control room, causing a haunting shiver of activity calming the momentary panic.

"Any ideas?" Khan asked, but he got no reply.

Thacker closed his eyes, feeling the music inside of him.

He saw Indonesia standing in the central plaza of the ancient civilisation, a crowd gathering. He held Magi Eritrea's sceptre, made of silvery-blue metal and raised it into the air. Thacker knew through the memories of his ancestor that this was how a Magi acquired his title – a passing ritual, like the inauguration of a president or the coronation of a monarch.

Magi Indonesia was still standing with the sceptre raised when he heard it in the distance, the unmistakable music of the alien spacecraft. It shot through the sky, halting above him.

A white light began to glow from the green Jeometamorphic rock mounted at the end of the sceptre. As the light grew, the ground shuddered and the people before him began to scream, scattering as the tremors shook their feet from underneath them. Thacker watched as burning hot rays of white shot out in all directions from the glowing rock. Where the white touched the ground, or people, flames leapt up. The world was engulfed within moments. Indonesia did not move, his eyes wide as he watched the horror of *his* world as the aliens destroyed it.

A beam of green descended from the spacecraft, engulfing Magi Indonesia. As he felt the beam dissecting him, he remembered that this was Magi Eritrea's work, Russia a useful ally. A moment later his body exploded into splinters of jade green, strewn in all directions.

Thacker opened his eyes, hearing Indonesia's last thoughts, rage burning inside him.

He looked at Khan with scorn and fled from the room, almost knocking a research assistant over. He paced to the end of the corridor, climbed into the elevator, flashed his badge to the reader and pressed the button for sub-basement.

As the lift descended, he felt a deep sickness wash over

him and a crippling pain in his head. He reached out. As he did so, his eyes flickered shut and a green image flashed.

He saw one of the alien creators, their unmistakable shining skin, scale-like. It was with Magi Eritrea and they were talking in private. Another image shot into his mind, Russia whispering to Magi Eritrea before she passed a small piece of parchment to the boy.

A final image leapt into his mind, Russia stepping through the portal.

The lift came to a halt and the doors opened, a realisation washed over him. Magi Eritrea had given up her life as a sacrifice so that Russia could live on. *Why did she do that?*

His heart suddenly filled with Indonesia's rage. Magi Eritrea had betrayed him, handing him over to the alien creators. In a final act, Magi Eritrea had given her own life, proving her worth. It had robbed Indonesia of his glory as Magi.

Thacker reached a conclusion; Russia was still plotting against him, trying to remove his life for a second time and Indonesia's memory raged inside of him, he could not allow Magi Eritrea's devious work to continue. Thacker knew what he must do.

He stepped out of the lift and went through the security systems. As the room opened, bright lights poured out, but he knew there were no windows down here. He shielded his eyes and stepped into the light and waited.

5

"I don't like what I'm seeing." Khan said standing over the technicians looking for an explanation. "Where did that signal come from?"

"I don't know." Josef was shaking his head.

Khan shook his head, none of this made any sense. He was uncomfortable in the knowledge that the crew of *Constellation* weren't responsible for this rogue transmission, yet they were the only ones up there, weren't they?

"Find Bates. And where did Thacker go?" Khan turned to instruct one of the administrative staff. They saluted before fleeing from the room.

The air in TICC control was dry and stale, filled with malodorous sweat which lingered in his nostrils, and Khan knew it would only get worse. The transmission screeched and he flipped his headset away from his ear a moment. As it played out, he began to scratch his chin.

"I'm getting a second signal overlaying the first," Beth said, listening carefully. "It's identical to the first, but it's delayed, like an echo." Khan rubbed his chin harder; he couldn't fit all the information in his head.

"And another," Josef said.

"Three transmissions?" Khan questioned. "All of them on the same frequency?"

"Yes sir," Josef said. "It's like a nuclear bomb just went off up there and we're picking up the blast waves."

6

I could do nothing to stop Charlie and Tom following Craig, slipping into the light of the portal without a care for my warning. When they had gone I turned to Maggie, she looked drained, the dancing light in her eyes replaced with distrust and fear.

"Shall we?" I motioned towards the portal.

"Wait," Maggie said. "We should take our radios, just in case." Maggie left the portal chamber and when she returned she handed me a headset from one of our discarded suits. "After you." I attached the headset and adjusted the ear piece. "Always, after you." I smiled back at her before stepping towards the light and as I approached, Magi Eritrea's voice filled my mind.

Take the disc, she said to me. You will find use for it again, someday.

I reached over and took the metallic disc.

Go now! The voice finally said.

I glanced at Maggie before I stepped into the shimmering mirror. Bright light filled my eyes and the haunting music of the portal poured into my ears as my body was sucked through space, transported to another world.

As the light faded and my eyes adjusted, I saw the bodies of Tom, Charlie and Craig scattered before me. My mouth fell open and I let out a whimper, and then I caught a glimpse of his wild smile

I looked up and saw the image of Indonesia.

"You!" I hissed. His smile remained.

"What was that?" Khan stood, training his ears. All the signals had gone, but he'd heard something else, someone speaking. He was sure of it. He adjusted his headset and turned up the volume.

A burst of static faded and died, and then he heard it again. A male voice.

"I got something," he shouted. "Listen, I got someone."

Beth tuned into the frequency and listened. Her mouth dropped open.

"That's Mark," she said. "And it's coming from this building." Her finger tracing the signal on her screen.

"That's impossible."

"Err, that signal is coming from inside *this* building." She repeated.

"I'm telling you, *that's* impossible,"

"I can confirm," Josef said. "They're here."

Out the corner of his eye, Khan spotted a flickering image on the central screen. He turned to see Linda's face pixelate and then stabilise.

"This is Linda, Co-pilot of the *Orion*, is there anybody out there?" Her voice ever hopeful, but devoid of life.

"Copy that Linda," Beth confirmed. "We're reading you. Can you confirm your position?"

"Oh, thank God!" Linda said with vigour. "Roger that. I remain in lunar orbit at the projected altitude. It's a pleasure to have you back!"

"I'm getting video feed from *Altair*." Josef reported, as a further image flashed up on his screen. It displayed the interior of the craft. "No signs of the crew."

And then Mark's harrowing voice filled the control room, spitting rage.

CHAPTER 19

"*You!*" I hissed, Russia's anger coursing through my veins, his searing pain pulsing across my temples. "How could you?"

"Put your hands behind your head," Thacker's menacing voice ordered. "I don't want any heroics from you." I looked down at his hands, a gun trained on my position. I shook my head as I placed my hands behind my head, bitter hatred pouring from my DNA. How had Indonesia survived. He'd died long ago with the lunar civilisation, there couldn't have been a genetic ancestor on Earth...and yet, here he was.

"You betrayed me," I growled. "*All of us.*"

"Don't talk to me about betrayal," Thacker's venom shot towards me. "You think you understand, but you don't. I am not the bad guy in all this. Magi Eritrea betrayed me, she is the one that brought our demise, and for what?" I scowled at him, distrustful of his words. There was no evidence to back up his accusations.

"How dare you bloody my master's name!" I boomed, Russia's hatred spilling out of me. "I know you. Your actions killed our master. How dare you even utter her name!"

"Enough!" Thacker yelled, his grip tightening on the weapon, taking better aim. "It all ends today!" His face full of wrath. My body tensed as his finger squeezed on the trigger. In the same moment I saw a flicker – almost confusion – pass across his face, but it was too late to stop the chain of events.

I watched in slow motion as the trigger snapped back before the pop of the cordite explosion, propelling the bullet spiralling through the air towards me. I tried to shout, to scream for help, but there was little use, my words too slow. I felt the rushing wind as the metal tip punched into me, throwing me backwards and knocking me off my feet.

I blinked. A red splatter filled my hands, the stains of my wound. I blinked again and as my eyes opened, everything turned green and I saw Indonesia standing before me, a wry smile crooked on his face.

It was only then that I *felt* something; searing heat bursting through my body. The last thing I could smell as the world faded was scorching flesh and searing heat. The taste of tin that filled my mouth.

Maggie was in transit, flying, soaring on the wind within the portal.

She felt herself being pulled from the portal, she'd reached her destination. As she looked into the glowing light before her, she thought she heard the echoing of gunshot, deep in water and then she saw red spurting into the shimmering air before her.

There was no doubt in her mind, it was blood.

Her body absorbed into the portal as she hurtled

through. She emerged into the massacre. A whimper leapt from her throat at the carnage. She saw Craig first and then Tom. Something caught her attention and as she glanced down, she saw Mark writhing on the floor, his hands clasping at his injury; in an instant she assessed the seriousness of the situation.

Please, not Charlie too, she thought. She daren't look. And there she saw him, limp, drained of his precious life. A fury burnt inside of her as she looked up at Thacker.

He looked startled by her arrival and hesitated.

2

"Put your hands behind your head." It was Thacker, his voice menacing.

Bates was standing in the corridor when the voices crackled over the intercom. He had an unsettling feeling in his gut and darted to his office to grab his wireless headset and then ran through the halls, tracing the signal to the sub-basement. He raced to the end of the corridor and called the lift.

"You betrayed me." He heard Mark's voice. "*All of us.*"

He tapped the closed lift door impatiently. "Come on!"

The lift opened with a ping and he rushed in. He didn't waste time, punching the button for sub-basement hard, the doors closed over.

"Enough!" Thacker's voice rang out in his ears. "It all ends today!"

Bates eyes widened, feeling the danger in Thacker's voice. And then the gunshot rang out, clear and unmistakeable. He gulped, picturing the bullet in his mind, hurtling through the air, striking Mark and throwing him backwards.

He'd read the files on Thacker, he knew of his impeccable aim.

Thacker seemed surprised by Maggie's sudden appearance, knocked off his stride, as if he'd not been expecting her. Rage burnt inside of her as she rebuilt the massacre in her mind and pictured Charlie being murdered at Thacker's hand. She saw red. Fury.

Maggie caught hold of the opportunity, hurling herself towards Thacker with the full force of her strength behind her. Before Thacker could take aim, Maggie's body slammed into him, sending him flying to the floor.

He struggled for a moment, managing to upright himself.

Maggie rolled across the basement, letting out a deep groan as her chest hit the ground with an uncomfortable thud. She looked up and saw Thacker's gun trained on her. She cursed herself for not doing more, she should've known it would take more than a mere knock to topple a military man like Thacker.

Maggie blinked, waiting for the inevitable, but as Thacker's finger squeezed on the trigger the door behind him burst open and she saw Bates standing there, his fists drawn. Luck was on her side. Bates didn't hesitate, diving on top of Thacker, pinning him to the floor, battering his hand until the weapon dropped free. He kicked it away. Maggie grabbed it.

"You bastard!" Maggie bellowed, targeting Thacker with his own weapon, but her hands trembled and she couldn't see straight, the rage eating away at her. "*You...*" Shock took hold and she collapsed to her knees, bitter tears dropped to her cheeks.

She'd lost Charlie, the only man she'd ever loved.

3

In the darkness I felt searing pain in my chest, burning with the heat of the sun, tearing through my flesh and blood. A bright orange scorched into the back of my eyes and fire began to spread through my veins.

I tried to moan, to let the pain out, but my mouth did not respond. My brain seemed severed from my body and I realised I was powerless to do anything.

In the distance I heard panicked voices and then I heard another voice from a different direction.

"Get up my child." It was Magi Eritrea. The orange in my eyes melted into green, but the penetrating pain remained. "Raise yourself my son." Her words were so clear, so powerful. I felt her presence near; my master was with me. "Wake up and walk with me."

Through the crippling pain, I bit down, fighting with all my effort, forcing myself from the darkness, hauling with the core of my being. As I grappled, a harrowing scream escaped my lips.

I felt movement, I knew I was getting close.

With one final swell, I sucked in a deep, haunting breath and stood up.

4

"Can you tell me your name?" The doctor's penlight flashed into my eyes as he examined them. I looked at him, blank.

"Are you able to tell me who you are?" I thought on his question – what a dumb thing to ask me.

"Yes," I said finally. "Mark. Mark Besant." I didn't blink, looking straight towards him as he switched to examining my right eye.

"Do you remember what happened to you?" He asked pressing a cold metal opti-scope into my ear before peering through the lens. After a moment he stepped around the bed and repeated on the other side.

I closed my eyes for a moment to think and an image flashed through the darkness.

"He tried to kill me," I said.

"Who did?" His voice was flat and I could tell he had all the information he wanted; he was testing me. As part of the medical examination, the doctor was testing my brain recall function, and my ability to think and process thoughts into words.

"Thacker," I said. *Indonesia*, I thought. "He tried to kill me. He murdered the others." I pictured the scattered bodies of the *Constellation* crew and shuddered as sadness swept over me. My extended family were gone. We'd returned from the most amazing place I'd ever been, but none of that mattered now. Their lives were wasted, their blood spilt.

"Maggie!" I yelled, jolting forwards. She was behind me when I stepped through the portal. "Please," I begged, "Tell me she's okay." My diaphragm leapt and I winced, my chest aching.

"She's alive," the doctor said, easing me back into bed. "I treated her myself. She's in shock, nothing more." I relaxed a little, allowing the doctor to rest my shoulders. I couldn't imagine what Maggie was going through, she'd been last through and must have seen everything. If she'd stepped through the portal before me, maybe it would have been a different story and I shuddered at the thought. I knew this was little consolation for the love she'd lost.

The doctor finished his examination and left the room. Through the glass, I saw Bates stop him. Deep fissures creased his brow.

"How are you feeling?" Bates had a smile pinned to his face as he stepped into the room. I didn't think I needed cheering up, so I assumed it was for his benefit, to keep his spirits up.

"I'm fine," I said. He set himself down in the chair to my side. "*Really* I feel fine."

"You've looked better."

"I just want to get out of here," I said. "Please, I hate all this."

"You will..." A frown replaced his smile, his mouth parted but he said nothing further. He began playing with the collar of his shirt. I didn't know what he was hiding, but his uncomfortable fidgeting irritated me. "Your mother called, she was worried when she hadn't heard anything in the news."

"Did she sound well?"

Bates mumbled something about it being a message passed to him by someone else in the office. I had made a point of not telling anybody about my mother's illness, it was a private matter and I knew she'd hate to weigh down others with her problems. I'd have to call her soon, I doubted she'd let on, even if she were on her deathbed.

My mind turned to other matters.

"Why didn't Thacker kill me?" I asked. His eyes widened with the sudden directional shift of the conversation. Bates stared back, blank. "He killed the others, why not finish the job? He had the chance, but I'm alive."

"Yes, you are." Bates took a deep breath. "We're grateful for that."

"I wish I could say the same."

Silence rose, Bates continued to snap his fingers back and forth over the collar of his shirt. He must've caught me staring, his strumming fingers stopped. I decided to press him on the point.

"Thacker has perfect aim," I said catching his eyes, hoping for a reaction. "He's a military man, a single bullet was all he needed. I know he didn't miss by accident. I saw a change in him in the moments before he pulled the trigger, confusion almost." There was only further silence to greet me as a response. "Why am I alive?"

Bates swallowed, edging forwards in his seat, leaning closer. "We thought you were dead."

I frowned.

"You didn't have a pulse, you'd lost a lot of blood," Bates said. Now I understood why he'd come across nervous. "We thought we were too late."

I remembered the voice.

"I heard Magi Eritrea," I said. "I remember darkness and I felt a burning pain in my chest." I reached out and touched my chest and howled, my fingers grazing over the healing wound. "Magi Eritrea spoke to me. She told me to get up."

"And you did. You scared the shit out of us too." He chuckled. "You sat up in the middle of us with your eyes closed and screamed. You weren't the only one. It gave the nurses a fright too."

"I was there, listening the whole time."

"And yet, you were clinically dead." I noticed his mouth twitch. There was more. I looked at him questioningly for a moment. He let out a stifled sniff, knowing I needed the truth and nothing but. "We found traces of the rock in your blood."

"Really?" I pretended like I didn't already know.

"It was one of the technicians that noticed it first. The congealed blood on the floor had formed into lumps of the green rock."

"Is it dangerous?"

"We don't know," he said. "Or at least we don't think so." I wasn't filled with confidence, but I saw he was being honest. "The doctors can't find anything wrong with you, no unusual symptoms other than the obvious trauma." But even I knew that didn't mean anything. Time was the only way to be sure.

"What happened to Linda?" I asked. "Is she still up there?"

"Yes." His tone irate. "Linda piloted the *Orion* back safely. It was a risk coming back on her own, but *we* were prepared for all eventualities." His emphasis on *'we'* made me think that perhaps Linda had disagreed with the approach. "You may not get to meet her again. I don't think she will be extending her contract."

"And Maggie?" I asked. "How is she?"

"She's taking it pretty hard," his voice softened. "She's taken leave, she blames herself for their deaths." I remembered seeing Charlie sprawled across the floor of the basement room and even though she'd never said as much, I knew she had still loved him. I could only pretend to imagine the difficult times ahead of her. Bates leaned closer. "We'd appreciate it if you gave her a call some time, a friendly face and all." Bates sank back into the chair.

"What about Thacker?" I wanted to know.

"He's been held in a secure location and will be court-martialled in due course." I shuddered. With Thacker harbouring Indonesia, was there such a place as a 'secure location'. "We found this in his office."

Bates reached into his pocket and pulling out a lump of green rock. I saw a flash of energy and felt it pulse within me. I longed to reach out and grab it, but Bates held it out of my reach. He knew about its purpose, I presumed.

All remnants of a smile faded from Bates's face, his words bitter. "We're still unclear of his motives, but he must have uncovered *something*..." I understood his hidden inference, his words carefully chosen.

I bit my lip and said, "I might be able to help you."

It was the reaction he'd wanted, a smile flourishing on his lips.

"Well, that's not for now." He stood. "I've already taken up too much of your rest time today." As he moved to the door, I got the feeling that had been the entire point of his visit, but I said nothing. Bates was a breath of fresh air compared to Thacker, and I wasn't about to question his motives too. "When you're fit and ready, I'll be placing this rock in your possession. I have a feeling it will be of more use to you than anybody else."

Bates dropped the rock back into his pocket and I noted he seemed unaffected by its power – perhaps his genetic memories were too weak. No wonder he rarely understood the motives of Thacker's obsession at getting to the truth no matter what the cost. I shuddered, thinking of my fallen crewmates, and I felt a pang of regret that I was still alive; I could have prevented their deaths, I was sure of it.

As he reached the doorway, he turned back. "I forgot to ask how the moon was."

He was the first to ask.

"I'd rather forget it," I said, my memories spoilt. Bates said nothing further and left.

5

Thacker stood in the dense jungle surrounding the sacred ziggurat, scouring the foliage through Indonesia's eyes. In the distance, he caught a glimpse of Magi Eritrea's colourful robes in among the greenery and fought his way to her side. Her olive skin was swathed in sunlight.

"You summoned me," Indonesia said, but Magi Eritrea did not look. Her hand was extended, holding seeds to the birds. A lapwing dropped from the sky and took the food from her hand.

"We all have secrets," Magi Eritrea spoke, her voice calm as she refilled her hand. Indonesia didn't understand, stepping closer, taking his master's hand and bringing her back to reality. Magi Eritrea slowly turned to face him. "I hear Siberia is with child."

"How..." Indonesia's words stumbled in his throat, a sudden burst of anger. "Who told you, master?"

"It is unimportant how I come to know the things that I do," Magi Eritrea said unimpressed. She gave a shake of her head and a flick of her wrist.

"I beg your pardon master." Indonesia spoke with remorse, his head bowed. "I did not think."

"Neither did I." Magi Eritrea shook her head. Indonesia looked up at her, frowning, unsure what to make of this. "I told you, everybody has secrets." Nature's silence returned to the jungle, birds glided through the sky, and a monkey screeched high above them.

Thacker felt Indonesia tense, waiting for the striking blow as he asked, "What do you propose to do about it?"

"I grow weary." Magi Eritrea settled on the stump of a fallen tree. "Our alien protectors demand more of our people, and when they return they are never the same as before - they will not speak to me about what happens. The Ambassador also won't tell me what *they* need our people for." Indonesia perched next to his master. "*They* say we are free, but we are not. When I attempt to stand up for our people *they* force me back down, as if I mean nothing to *them*, my title useless. We are blots on *their* existence."

"You do not want it to be this way?" Indonesia offered.

"No," Magi Eritrea said looking up as a flock of birds swooped low, their pattern shifting and changing direction with swift ease. "We are not alone, I know we are not the only ones."

"What do you mean?" Indonesia frowned, bewildered. Thacker shared his bemusement. "Do you ever question why *they* look after us?" She looked deep into the eyes of Indonesia, her stare piercing. Thacker felt them, as if directed at him. "We are not our own people, we are *their* people. *They* rear us, but *they* don't care for us. *They* descend on us and take away *my* people, I am sure *they* test us to see if we are ready."

"Ready?" Indonesia questioned. "Ready for what?"

"I do not know," Magi Eritrea said, waving her hand and dismissing the thought.

"Master," Indonesia placed his hand upon Magi Eritrea's shoulder. "You are speaking in riddles. Do you think *they* mean us harm?"

"I'm afraid that *they* may." Fear in her voice, something Indonesia had never heard before. "I do not know what *they* want with our kind, but I am sure *they* have designs for us, though *they* will not speak it to me"

"If this is true, then you must put a stop to it right away," Indonesia was concerned for his master.

"*They* don't listen." Magi Eritrea pulled away from Indonesia as she stood. She paced back and forth. Indonesia had never seen her in such a quandary before. "*They* say I am interfering with *them* and the Ambassador has already threatened to remove me as the Magi."

"We must stop *them!*" Indonesia growled through gritted teeth, suddenly incensed. "If *they* don't listen then we must take action." His foot pounded the ground in annoyance. Thacker felt his rage, and an image flashed into his mind; the bodies of the *Constellation* crew. "*They* have always respected sacrifice. Maybe if we could create a situation that requires great sacrifice, you could bargain with *them*."

"We have nothing to bargain with," Magi Eritrea said with a sigh. "We have nothing of such sacrificial value to please them."

Thacker heard the words before they left Indonesia's lips. "Your life," he said.

Indonesia felt his master's eyes studying him in the silence following their discussion. It was uncomfortable, even for Thacker as he watched through his dreams. Indonesia looked away, unable to face his master, what he'd suggested was deeply disturbing and also devious manipulation.

After years of searching, Thacker finally felt like he was getting somewhere. The answers he wanted played out in the darkness of his sleeping mind.

"I am sorry master," Indonesia finally spoke. "It was wrong of me..."

"Yes," Magi Eritrea said, thoughtful, stroking her chin. She ran her other hand through her flowing hair, catching the sunlight as she did so, creating the effect of a cascading waterfall. "It was wrong of you, but sometimes I feel rules are there to be broken, don't you?" Thacker saw the playful look in Magi Eritrea's face. "I doubt that a single sacrifice to Anubikhanisis will be enough to please the Ambassador. It must be many." *Anubikhanisis*, Thacker thought, Indonesia's memory filled the missing pieces with the green life-force that lived among them all.

"What are you suggesting master?"

"Are you prepared to make the ultimate sacrifice?" Magi Eritrea's face stiffened, her look stern. "A Magi should always be prepared to forfeit life in favour of another. Are you willing to take the journey with me?"

"Yes master." The words fell from Indonesia's lips without a thought in his head.

"Then it will be done," Magi Eritrea said. "I will summon the Ambassador and tell him of a plot against me and I will sow the seeds of distrust throughout my servants. And you too must sow seeds of distrust so that when I fall you have the ears of everyone else. I will do my best to make provisions for *our* children, we shall live on through them."

"Master, what if they do not accept our terms?"

"Do not doubt me." Magi Eritrea stood firm. "I am your Magi. If they do not accept then our deceit will grow stronger until we have the power to stand against them in combat."

As the light of the jungle faded around him, Thacker found himself restless inside his mind, unsettled by his new understanding. As he drifted off into a dreamless sleep, he knew he'd have to face up to the consequences of his actions. He'd killed innocent people because of a misinterpretation of the facts. He was a military man, but stoicism couldn't get him through this. He'd have to deal with his guilt.

6

A few days into my bed rest, I found myself longing to escape the boredom of the medical facility and take a look at our world through fresh eyes. The only saving grace was the constant attention from both the doctor and nurse that occupied my time, providing medication and extracting further blood samples for examination.

But even this did little to interrupt the movie reel playing in my mind, sickening me with its images – the reality of the situation still overpowering. Of course, I knew there was nothing I could've done. All three of them – Craig, Tom and Charlie – ignored my warning but I felt this was a rather harsh price to pay. It was the cost that I now bore.

Things could've happened differently if only I'd been the one to step through the portal first. Maybe I'd have stopped Thacker's murderous rampage, or died trying. I considered that might've been a better outcome for us all, at least I wouldn't have to put up with this infernal guilt and the tears that came with it.

The nights were cold and restless, the situation re-enacted in my mind like video footage on constant loop keeping me awake. Even when I did manage to close my eyes and drift off, it was short lived. I had no dreams, only the nightmares of the past. I longed to see the tranquil landscape dominated by the ancient, yet familiar ziggurat, but I felt like it had deserted me in my time of need.

I sat up in bed, watching the television, with one eye on the nurse at the other end of the hall. She busied herself arranging my next batch of medication. I guessed it must be lonely work for her too, spending most of her time travelling to and from the local hospital where she worked, except on occasions like this.

A knock came at the door and I looked over as Bates stepped in followed by a short stocky man. I recognised him from the television, the SARA press conference, but couldn't recall his name.

They joined me at my bedside.

"This is Charles Humber," Bates said. "The SARA administration met last night in light of recent events and appointed Humber as my direct replacement. I have assumed Thacker's position."

"Hello," I said, shuffling forwards and offering my hand. Humber took it and gave a firm shake.

"I've heard so much about you," Humber said. "How are you feeling?"

"I'm fine." My voice whined, no attempt to hide my frustration. "As I keep telling the doctor, I'm *fine.* I want to get out of here!"

"About that," Bates said, putting his finger to his chin. To me it looked like an unconscious gesture, he was uncomfortable in his knowledge. "We also discussed your appointment with SARA and have decided you are free to leave, if you wish."

"Your contract is void." Humber assumed control, it seemed to be a reoccurring theme for Bates. "Thacker broke all trust and for that we are deeply sorry. Of course, you will be paid for your services to SARA, over and above our original contractual obligations."

"You are no longer assigned to SARA, and once you have delivered a full written report you are free to leave our facilities..." Bates trailed off, still visibly uncomfortable. I felt a wave of relief, knowing my ordeal was over and I couldn't hide the smile from my face as I digested the news. I was a free man. All I wanted to do was go home and see my mum and everyone else...

It caught me unaware, and when I finally realised, the smile dropped from my face. I didn't want to go back to my empty house with a meaningless life. Here, with SARA, I had a purpose. There was nothing left for me in the outside world now, I'd seen too much.

As I blinked, an image flickered before me, the cave painting on the wall of the ziggurat. It showed the future of our ancestors, a man holding a disc in his hands; it depicted me.

"The disc," I said. "What happened to the disc?"

"We kept it safe *for you*," Bates said, a smile pressed to his lips. "What are your feelings on redrafting a new contract?"

I smiled, feeling a powerful surge in my body as a wave of endorphins took over.

"What do you have in mind?" I asked.

"You told us that the disc was left on the lunar surface for you to find," he said. "We thought you'd want to know what it contains and why. Our journey is not over yet, our knowledge is incomplete."

I was hooked, and seeing this seemed to bring the conversation to a close. "When you are ready, drop by my office and we can negotiate terms." Humber returned my smile. I knew we'd get along nicely.

"There is just something I have to do first," I said gazing across at the window. It was another cloudless day, the autumnal sun still warm enough to take the chill out of the air. Already I could feel it.

I stood in the silence of the courtyard, my arms outstretched, breathing the fresh air of the Dartmoor countryside.

It was the first time I'd felt real wind bustling past me since I arrived back to Earth and it was magnificent, a far cry from the deserted moon ziggurat. The yard was full of life; birds nesting in the trees, chirping away and bees humming their merry tune as they searched for a new home to see them through winter. Then I saw a line of ants trooping past my feet, carrying fragments of leaves and food, collecting their last stores before the frosts descended, destroying much of their supply chain.

The scent of freshly baked bread wafted from the kitchens. I started to salivate, it smelt divine. I smiled, remembering the magical world in which we lived. I never thought it possible, but I'd missed it.

The warm air brushed across my naked arm, stirring the hairs and tickling. It was blissful and surprisingly peaceful in my cocooned fantasy.

"Is that you?" I heard a voice calling from behind and

when I turned I found Beth staring back at me, her face beaming with joy. I waved to her, motioning her over. "You're looking well." I realised, like the rest of life, she looked great too. I took a seat on the bench, making room for Beth and tapping it lightly. Beth sat. "Sorry I didn't come to see you sooner."

"Not to worry."

"It's been crazy the last few weeks." She shook her head, looking down at her feet for a moment. "So, what was it like?"

"The moon?" I asked. "Disappointing." My voice deflated. "It was so sad. I've seen that place over in my dreams, but it was nothing compared the reality. It was empty and dulled by millennia of silence."

"Really?" Beth said with disbelief, putting her hand to her chest. "I thought..." Her words trailed off for a moment. "I figured you'd be pleased, your dreams finally realised."

"Yeah," I said, distant. "So did I."

"I guess Thacker put paid to that," Beth snorted. "It's been no piece of pie back here either." She looked into my eyes. "I thought I'd lost you for good."

"I just wish I understood better." I ignored her comment. "Even if Thacker was under Indonesia's control, he didn't gain anything by killing the others. And then there was me. If he believed Russia had conspired with Magi Eritrea, why am I still alive? He hesitated." I huffed through my nose into the beautiful air. "It just makes no sense."

There was only one way I could solve the problem, I needed to ask the questions and for that I had to gain access to Thacker.

"I'm sorry it wasn't as good as you expected."

"Look," I said squeezing her hands. "I could've been killed, but I wasn't. I'm here and now, more than ever, I believe there is a reason for that."

"Well I hope you're right," she said. "People died and I'd

like to think there was a higher purpose."

I gave Beth a quick hug before she departed.

As I watched her leave, I was glad to have an old friend back, the love I had felt for her now replaced with affection. Neither of us were the same people, I felt like a stranger in my own body, the old me transformed.

THACKER & SERENITY

CHAPTER 20

I lay awake, restless in the icy grip of insomnia's hold. After five arduous hours, I gave up and flicked the bedside lamp on, filling the room with the warm glow of its ambient light.

It took a moment for my eyes to adjust; the world swam into focus and I looked up through Russia's view. The smell of ancient dry air filled my nostrils. He was curious, as often boys are, and that's why he hid in the shadows, watching his master.

I knew this had to be a few days before Magi Eritrea's arrest; Russia's memories were coming out-of-order. As I watched, Magi Eritrea prepared herself for her daily duties.

Magi Eritrea held a red felt pouch, roughly the size of a purse. She dropped it onto her bed before lifting the feathered mattress. From underneath, she pulled out a second pouch. She looked up, startled, as if someone had crept up on her. She glanced around.

I froze, along with Russia, as Magi Eritrea's eyes crossed the shadows where we hid. She gave a nod, as if she knew, but said nothing and turned back to the task in hand. She emptied the second pouch, revealing the metallic disc which bounced onto the bed. It was like watching a grazing animal, Magi Eritrea looked up again, and then she hurried from the room.

Silence fell.

Russia blew out a breath and I realised he'd been holding it. He strained to hear. There were voices below in the courtyard, but no one in close proximity to see him. Russia crept out of hiding towards his master's bed and picked up the pouch, running the velvety material through his fingers. He placed it back onto the bed, taking the disc.

He recognised it. During rituals, Magi Eritrea would use it to open the sacred chamber within the base of the ziggurat, but she never let it out of her sight. Russia had the overwhelming feeling Magi Eritrea wanted him to have it, but this thought was broken by footsteps padding towards the room.

Russia panicked, shoving the disc back into the pouch and without care left it where it fell on his master's bed before sliding into the shadows beyond his master's chamber, just as Magi Eritrea ushered the alien Ambassador inside.

That's odd, Russia thought. It was the Ambassador's second visit in a week. Something was wrong.

The door closed behind. As Russia strained to hear in the silence, he saw Indonesia edging forwards. He stopped at the door, peering through the cracks and tensed. It seemed they both had the concerns about their master's erratic behaviour.

The dream world swirled away into the dazzling light of my room.

I blinked, stretching as the images faded in my mind, but one thing caught my attention, the disc. Magi Eritrea had intended for me to see it; it was important.

Maybe it had a second use.

2

Thacker opened his eyes inside Indonesia's mind and looked out at the world. Again, he found himself in the dense jungle beyond the ziggurat, wading through the spiky fronds and slapping branches. He stepped into the clearing and found Magi Eritrea waiting.

Magi Eritrea's eyes were full of sorrow when she turned to face Indonesia - Thacker looked into the darkness lurking there. He saw the storm clouds gathering and shivered, just as Indonesia did.

"Master?" Indonesia's concern obvious. "What news do you bring?"

"The seeds of our deceit have been sown." Magi Eritrea shook her head, letting her hair drift across her face. "But as you feared, *they* do not accept our terms."

"Master, we must not let that stop us."

Magi Eritrea let out a rapturous cackle. "We will not stop at *their* saying." Her anger echoed in the jungle, unsettling a bird which took flight, setting off the irate chatter of the macaque monkeys overhead.

Indonesia shuddered, shocked by the strength of his master's outburst.

"They are to destroy our sacred world and our people." Magi Eritrea's voice calmed. "I've made provisions for just eighteen to start a new world of their own." She looked into Indonesia's eyes. "As my most trusted, I am sending Russia to continue my work, be sure that Siberia finds her journey safe."

"What about the others?" Indonesia thought of the sacrifice his mother made bringing him into the world. She had given her life so that he might live, just as Russia's had. What would she think of him now, making his own sacrifice for his unborn son? "We cannot leave them. They will be obliterated if they remain here."

"It is a sacrifice we must make," Magi Eritrea said, sorrow filling her eyes once again. "This is *our* chance. We will give our children a new world, independent from the Ambassador and the shackles of his protection."

"What will become of our children?"

"They will become much more than we ever could. I have seen these people in my dreams, they are happy in their freedom. They do not give sacrifice nor hand their people over to the Ambassador."

"And what of us?"

"At your bidding, I shall be arrested; the charge, my only sin." She shot Indonesia a knowing look. "Spread the word, tell everyone of my deceit. My people must not know the charges are false, they must not know the truth." Indonesia agreed with this. "The Ambassador knows you covet the destructive force of Anubikhanisis and you shall use it against *them*. It shall begin the moment you take the Magi title. The rest is up to our children."

"Do we have assurance of their safety?"

"The Ambassador will remain close-by for protection, but for this compromise they shall not live in our luxury. One day they will become people like us, it is through our children that we continue to live, I have seen this too in my dreams."

"How do you mean, master?" Thacker was intrigued; it seemed Magi Eritrea had inner-sight, perhaps the gift of the rock. Was it even possible that generations – even future generations – were linked through its mystical power?

"We have until our rebirth," Magi Eritrea said. "And then the harvest shall begin again."

The haunting warning was still in Thacker's mind when he woke and sat up inside his cell. His heart pounded wildly in his chest.

It was light outside and in the morning glow he was sure he saw the ghost of Magi Eritrea, waiting in the shadowy darkness.

"How long do we have?" he asked into the silence of his four walls.

There was no response.

3

Bates escorted me – even I didn't trust myself to be alone with Thacker once he'd answered the questions riddling my mind. I wanted to see Thacker punished, but first I needed to understand.

The interview room was dilapidated with the festering stench of years of decay, mixed with the taste of stale sweat.

"You came! I knew you would, sooner or later." Thacker welcomed through the glass, as if he'd forgotten his current location and was inviting us in for a nice chat over a freshly brewed pot of tea.

"I want to know why you did it," I said, the lifeless bodies of Tom, Charlie and Craig floating across my view; my murdered family. I shuddered, knowing I almost joined them. "After everything we saw and learnt. Why did you do it?"

"I didn't understand," Thacker muttered as he shook his head. "I thought I understood, I was consumed by Indonesia's rage and I snapped. I see things clearly now. In my dreams I watched Russia and Magi Eritrea. Indonesia was sure they conspired against him and I unleashed his fury."

I bit my lip, feeling my rage burning in my chest.

"I am Russia," I said slamming my fist onto the shelf in front of me. "Why didn't you kill me?"

"I couldn't control Indonesia, his memory too strong, his anger so overpowering I could not fight it." His face stiffened. "Our dreams can be dangerous. I shouldn't have trusted my memories and now the ultimate price has been paid for my failure. Indonesia's hatred and bitterness consumed me. He forgot why he *had* to die." I frowned, remembering my visions. I'd seen Indonesia waiting to become Magi, bringing about the destruction of the colony in doing so. "I should have known."

I leant forward in my seat, "What are you talking about?"

"Magi Eritrea saw it," Thacker said. "I see it now. She gave up her life for us. She wanted *you* to live."

"Let me get this straight." My voice firm. "*You* want *me* to believe that Magi Eritrea sacrificed herself willingly?" My fingers and toes curled with anger. "Why do you lie? Magi Eritrea told me that Indonesia shouldn't be trusted? Why did you betray *our* master?"

"I feel your anger," Thacker said, his head cocked. "You came here for answers to condemn my actions, but everything you hold true is a lie. Russia *had* to believe the deceit. The aliens were watching, it was too risky for Russia to know the truth." His eyes filled with sadness. "I swear I never knew. I just wish Charlie could be here to understand with me. The answers were with us all the time, locked in mythology. We didn't see them in time."

"How do you mean?" I felt my anger dissipating as we talked.

"It's not exactly a picnic in here. It gives a man plenty of time for his thoughts. I followed Charlie's work for years, but one of his papers spoke to me and I never knew why. Now I see."

Thacker's voice filled with Charlie's enthusiasm as he spoke, "In Egyptian mythology, Osiris was a popular ruler well respected by his subjects. His brother, Set, was consumed with jealousy and plotted against Osiris – much like you thought Indonesia plotted against Magi Eritrea. Set finally tricked his brother and had him sealed inside a casket. Isis, his wife, breathed new life into Osiris, earning him the title of the king of the underworld."

I knew part of the story, Charlie had told me some of this. And now I remembered what Charlie had said about Serge – he sacrificed his life. "Where do you fit into it all?" I allowed Thacker to take me along with his new thinking. "I mean Indonesia."

"It is difficult to separate the two, I know." Thacker had a wry smile on his face. "Magi Eritrea told the alien Ambassador that Indonesia was plotting to use the power of the Jeometamorphic rock against *them* and offered her own life as a sacrifice to show them her loyalty. In doing so she also signed Indonesia's death warrant."

"Surely they knew Russia had escaped with seventeen others?" I asked, trying to slot all of the pieces together, building a complete picture.

"Magi Eritrea pleaded with the alien Ambassador for your safe passage, along with the others. The Ambassador believed it was a great opportunity to continue their work while ridding our kind of evil, starting again from scratch. A chance to purify."

"But what about you?" I said. "Why do you have the memory of Indonesia? He was destroyed, along with the rest of the moon civilisation."

"Siberia," he said. "She was pregnant with Indonesia's child. It is through her genetics that Indonesia was reborn. Magi Eritrea also had a secret child that travelled to Earth and she too will be reborn one day."

"So, after all that sacrifice, why are we not free now? Was all that blood shed for nothing?" I asked, thinking of all the lost lives. "Why do the scriptures say we will be destroyed? That's what all this was about right, gaining our freedom?"

"You said yourself, it bought us time. Our plan," Thacker

said. "We have developed differently to our ancestors. We advanced technologically. You saw the temple and the scriptures, you know we've changed."

"How long do we have?" I asked. "Do you know?"

"Mythologically speaking, until Magi Eritrea is reborn," he said. "And then the aliens will harvest us, like the others." He looked anxious at this, and I felt like he knew more than he was letting on.

"And how long is that, exactly?" Bates sat forwards, breaking his silence.

"I don't know." A wry smile flourished across Thacker's lips. "There is proof out there, if you are willing to listen." His face pressed against the glass. "Ask Randall if *Project Serenity* is operational."

"*Serenity!*" Bates snapped. "What have you done?"

4

"Where is Randall?" Bates demanded. Even I shuddered.

"I don't know." One of the technicians answered as he ferried a trolley of equipment from storage. "I haven't seen him all day."

"He's been in and out," a second technician said from behind his workstation, a jungle of test tubes racked along his desk, surrounding him. "If you find him, tell him we're starting work on CLIO-768."

"I will," Bates said, with a dismissive wave. I guessed Randall would never get that message. "If you see him, tell him to report to me immediately."

"I saw him heading to the sub-basement earlier," a voice spoke from behind. It was Beth. She stood in the doorway carrying a stack of yellowing folders, old fashioned files. She dropped them onto the first desk. "Is something wrong?"

"I've got to go," I said, darting after Bates who was making good headway towards the lift already.

"Was it something I said?" she hollered after me.

Bates was already getting into the lift as I turned the corner. I grabbed hold of the fire escape door and bolted down the stairs.

I didn't know what *Serenity* was, or why it had Bates fuming. I didn't get chance to question Thacker, our interview terminated as soon as Bates rushed from the room.

My legs almost fell out from under me as I reached the bottom of the stairwell, but I didn't stop, pushing through into the secured area. In the distance I heard the clatter of equipment.

Bates stormed out of the lift to my side, unlocked the final security door and yanked it open.

Randall looked up at us, startled, the colour draining from his face.

I felt him tense as the truth caught up with him.

"What the hell is going on?" Bates demanded. His eyes bulged as if they were about to explode and I heard Randall gulp. I remained silent, staying out of the crossfire.

"I..." he couldn't find his words. "Thacker..."

"That man no longer works for SARA," Bates hissed. "I am the Administrator and I asked everyone to clarify what they were working on. You failed to tell me you had reactivated *Project Serenity*. You had no authorisation." He glared at Randall. "I thought you, of all people, knew the dangers of this initiative."

"Is *Project Serenity* operational?" I leapt in. Bates turned to me, his eyes glaring, his dismay obvious. He looked like his fuse might explode at any moment.

"Yes." Randall hesitated. "I think it is."

"I need to know what *Serenity* does. Can you show me?" I

stepped closer to Randall, blocking Bates from finishing his fiery speech.

"Who do you think you are?" Bates pushed me aside. "Neither of you have clearance for this. I should have you both…"

"Listen to me," I said, looking at Randall but addressing them both. "Thacker told us that *Project Serenity* could help us track our alien creators." I felt conflicted. After everything Thacker had done, it was hard to believe anything he said, or his motives. "After everything I've been through, after everything I've seen, please let me show you."

It was an uncomfortable silence.

"You better hope this works, for all our sakes," Bates said, deflated. "We're not in the desert now; these are real lives at stake." He slumped into a chair. The volcano had vented, there would be no eruption today.

CHAPTER 21

"The *Serenity* device," Randall began, "is capable of intercepting and transmitting communications – encrypted or otherwise – deep into the universe. Thacker believed he could prove there was an alien transmitter on the lunar surface blocking our own communications."

"Yes," I said. "There was, I've seen it."

"Then Thacker was right to restart the programme." Randall took a snipe at Bates, but he didn't bite. "This is *Serenity*." He pointed to the trolley of jumbled circuit boards and trailing wires. A glistening lump of Jeometamorphic rock sat on top alongside a small silver satellite antenna. It didn't look like much.

"That's it?" I cringed at the strength of my own surprise.

"And you're sure it's problem free?" There was pleading in Bates's voice.

"Everybody take your positions, the performance is about to begin," Randall said, ignoring the question and tapped out the necessary start-up string on his screen, his finger wavering before finalising the command.

The room filled with a green glowing light as the prototype booted up. Bates looked anxious, studying Randall's precise movements. The terminal went black and then a message appeared.

Ready

"So far so good," Randall said as his fingers worked to set the next module going. After a moment the screen began to fill with numbers, line after line, spewing out.

The room began to rumble.

The terminal screen went blank and another message appeared.

Scanning all known frequencies...

The room continued to rumble and the small antenna on top of the *Serenity* began to rotate in slow ascending arcs. The green light grew in intensity and I stepped backwards, shielding my eyes.

"It's working!" Randall shouted, elated. The second monitor in front of Randall displayed live readings from seismologists and observation stations across the globe, although I didn't understand the read-outs, there didn't appear to be any fluctuations. "They're all normal." His fingers followed a number of lines across the screen. "We're operational, good to go."

He looked to Bates, seeking his approval, but nothing was forthcoming.

2

"It's been over an hour now," Bates said as he paced back and forth. "Something must be wrong with your designs." It was a small room, filled with terminals and cabling. Every time Bates passed me, stepping over my feet, I felt the icy fingers of impatience flaring across my vision.

"Still nothing yet." Randall didn't sound concerned. He glanced up from his terminal. "I set it to ignore known frequencies which I programmed into the data-bank. It may need some adjustments, but I think *Serenity* is at optimal operation. The scan is still in progress and I've limited CPU usage to avoid draining SARA of its other operations."

The words barely left his mouth when the computer gave a piercing shriek which turned into a steady beep. At first Randall didn't respond, he appeared to be considering, perhaps tweaks he'd need to make in the configuration files.

He jerked his head up and then turned to the terminal behind him, the shrill noise finally broken through the barriers of his thoughts.

"We're picking up a signal of unknown structure."

"Can you get a location on that?" Bates leapt across the room, but the look of puzzlement on his face suggested the data on the screens meant nothing. "Can we pinpoint it?"

"Of course," Randall snapped. "I'm working on it." His fingers bunny-hopped across his terminal. It took him a few minutes to run the right commands and decode the data stream from the *Serenity*. When it stopped a new screen appeared showing a simple picture of space. "You're not going to believe this, Thacker was right."

"Well I'll be damned," Bates said, tapping the screen. "It's coming from the moon." Randall worked quickly to zoom in on the area.

"It's a few metres away from the projected mission landing site."

"I was right too," I said joining them at the screen. "That's right where we found the rubble, the remains of an obelisk."

"And that's what you think blocked our signals?" Bates perched on the edge of the desk, shaking the terminals. "Thacker saw this 'device' too?"

Randall smiled. He didn't need to say anything.

"We've been so stupid," I said slapping my forehead. "Serge was right, it was in my blood." I looked up at their questioning faces. "It was rigged to recognise my blood. That's why it activated when I went up into space."

"From the research I've conducted with J-Power I'm pretty sure it's as close to an unlimited energy supply that we'll ever see. I can imagine it being capable of juicing up an antenna for millennia..." his voice trailed off, alive with his passion.

"And what is the signal?" Bates wanted to know. "Is it a message to us? Can we find out what it's meant to say?"

"Ah," Randall said ominously. "*Serenity* can't interpret the data format of the transmission, at least not yet." His voice deflated. "And the only one who could read their language is no longer with us."

I thought of Charlie's wealth of knowledge and then it came to me. "But maybe there is a way, through Russia."

"It's worth a shot," Bates said turning to Randall. That was an order, Randall didn't need telling twice. His fingers were already at work.

Whatever was said next was drowned out by a deep pulse throbbing in my ears.

3

Thacker sat in his cell, his eyes fixed on the wall.

He felt something stirring deep inside of him, calling his name. His eyes flickered closed, filtering out the dull light. A pulse of pure green light flooded the darkness, transporting him away from reality. His body felt light, as if he were floating, high above the world.

Out of the glow a rhythmic beating undulated all around

him, the air electric with its pulse. It grew louder in his ears and he felt his heart pounding in his chest, dancing the same tune. It developed in strength until it was all he could hear and feel; alive. The drum of the alien life-force called out to him, the signature tune of the alien creators. He almost felt *them* breathing.

He saw the face of Mark swimming in the sea of green, the structure of the life-force flowing through his cells connecting him to all living creatures that came from the sacred rock.

And there he heard the alien message.

4

"*They* are coming," I shouted above the rhythmic beating of the message flooding my senses. The puzzled looks from both Bates and Randall told me that neither heard nor understood the pulsing energy that occupied the airwaves. "*They* know we are almost complete."

"Who?"

"Our alien creators." My voice flat. "*They* are coming back to reclaim our race."

The drum beat stopped, but my ears continued to ring. I shook my head, but it didn't clear. Slowly my vision clouded with millions of fluttering specks of darkness, fading my world to black, but I knew I hadn't passed out. I could feel my body lurching forwards. I felt my way to a seat and slumped into it, allowing my body to recover.

Once my strength and vision returned, I met Bates's concern.

"You don't look so hot."

"I heard *their* message," I said, ignoring him. "I felt it running through me. It was in *their* language, and I could understand it." I shuddered. The furrow in his brow deepened. "Didn't either of you hear it?"

"What did it sound like?" Randall looked perplexed.

"A very low, deep beat," I said, shaking my head. "It was the drum of *their* life."

"You said *they* were coming for us?" Bates stood up now. "Is there anything we can do?" My hands reached for my face, rubbing my cheeks before coming together before my chin, as if in prayer.

"That disc was left for *me,*" I said. "I need to understand its significance."

"Is it like a DVD?" Randall asked. It was a simple question but the consequences were massive as the first explosion tore through the barriers in my mind.

I'd been blind, looking for answers when they were right in front of me all along.

"You're a fucking genius," I said grabbing his hand.

Both Bates and Randall were once again stunned, waited for an explanation.

5

A surge of power, like electricity, flowed through my fingers and along my arteries as I took the metallic object from its storage container. It was a strange, cold feeling, as if I'd been holding onto a block of ice for too long. Frostbite took hold, its icy grip around my chest and squeezing the air out of my lungs.

I forced a cough, clearing my airway and allowing in a deep breath.

"You've seen the processed pictures Craig took from inside the ziggurat." I caught Bates's eyes. "There was a cave painting depicting three men; the past, present and future.

Serge noticed the future man carried this." I held up the disc. "*I* am *that* man."

I sniffed as my throat filled up, remembering my fellow *Constellation* crew. I fixed Randall's gaze. "It's a disc, just like you said."

"But if it's alien technology, how do we access whatever information might be on there?" Bates shook his head.

"That's where Randall comes in," I said.

Randall remained silent, his fingers running across his face, his eyes closed. His hands fell still as he opened his mouth and said, "Maybe, just maybe..." His fingers wagging in the air.

"It spins," I interrupted, picturing the disc whizzing round before opening the entrance to the sacred chamber and then the portal sarcophagus. "If that's any help to you."

"Here's the problem." He got to his feet, pacing in front of me. I grabbed his arm, stilling him before he could get too far. "I'm making a lot of assumptions, but if it works along the same principles as our technology *and* it contains data in a structured, logical fashion *and* can be read with lasers *and* we can find the correct spin speed, *and* we don't melt the disc in the process, then we may just be able to get something useful from it."

"Can you do it?" Bates wanted to know, cutting the crap. Randall looked to me.

"Yes... maybe... yes," he said finally.

"I need a timescale on this." Bates's eyes narrowed.

"A wing and a prayer," Randall said. "And maybe we'll be on the move by Christmas."

As I placed the disc back into the storage cabinet, the image of the blue man flashed into my mind. I didn't understand why, but Russia had led his people to the dawn of mankind, and now I felt I was following in his footsteps.

6

"Can't you people ever let me eat in peace?" I growled at Humber as he perched in the seat opposite me. I'd barely even touched my breakfast, and given my sleepless night, I was in no mood for morning chatter.

"I don't want to push anything upon you," Humber sounded concerned. "But I've been discussing your situation with Bates and we both feel you are of critical benefit to us." I said nothing, glaring at him. "We need you. That's why we want you to sign *the* contract with us – but only if you feel ready to take on the work?"

"What work?" I asked, already knowing his answer.

"I understand there may be some kind of message or information stored on the alien disc." I returned his knowing smile. "If this is the case, it is crucial that we understand what it is as soon as possible. We feel you are best placed to lead *Project Renaissance* given your close association to our ancestors." Humber had clearly been touching up on his history. "It's your call, but make no mistake, this could be our only chance to understand not only the true threats of our alien visitors, but also give us what we need to prepare for *their* onslaught." He was making assumptions about the contents of the disc, just like the rest of us.

"I expected that," I said. I didn't need to think about my answer, it was already upon my lips. "You can count on me. I feel it's my duty to overcome." Humber left me to finish what was left of my breakfast.

When I was done, I went to find Randall to tell him the news. He was sitting at his desk, pouring over some schematic designs.

"So, what are you thinking?" I asked. Randall looked up,

coming out of his daze, it was clear he hadn't heard me come in.

"I don't see why the same kind of technology can't be applied to this disc," he said pointing at the blueprints in front of him. I peered down at them, they meant nothing to me. "The trouble is I need to understand how the data was originally stored on the material. If it was man-made, maybe I'd know where to start."

"I can't help you there," I said holding my hands up in surrender. I felt a sharp throbbing at the back of my head; the beginnings of a headache. "I don't know anything about that."

"My major concern is that we only have one copy of the disc." His concern obvious as he spoke. "My J-Powered lens technology is far too temperamental, I've ruined thousands of DVD's during my tests, which is fine, but we can't afford that to happen with this."

I sat on the edge of his desk, swinging my legs back and forth in thought. An image flashed in my mind, Magi Eritrea putting the metallic disc in the pouch and at the same time, the image zoomed in on her clothes. There was an identical pouch hanging from the rope tied at her waist, holding his garments in place.

"There was a second disc," I said. "If I could get hold of it, you'd feel a lot more comfortable right?"

"Sure," he said. "But how?"

"Leave that to me," I said rushing from the room.

I found Humber standing in the corridor outside Bates's office, talking into his mobile phone; when he saw me coming, he quickly ended the call. I took him into Bates's office and explained everything.

"I understand what you are saying," Humber said, exchanging glances with Bates. "But I'm afraid the risks are too great." I frowned. There were no risks, as far as I knew. Thacker was out of the picture.

"We need to try," I pleaded.

"Do you know there is definitely a second disc?"

"I'm sure."

"And you know where it is?"

I remained silent. It was all they needed to hear to make their decision.

7

Bates came into the office and closed the door.

"I've discussed your idea with both the Russian and US governments. The transmission is of grave concern to them," he said, a deep ravine running across his brow. "This is the greatest threat to our national security since the Cold War. It *must* be our highest priority to understand the danger posed to our civilizations, in order that we can protect ourselves against it." I wasn't sure where his point was going. "It is recognised that your work will be of great importance and SARA have been given access to virtually unlimited funding to deal with this project. Tomorrow I am meeting the British Prime Minister and his aides. In preparation, the Prime Minister and the UK Space Agency have authorised us free range of their research facilities."

"What does that mean?" Randall wanted to know.

"As of this moment, I am transferring all of you, including your technicians to the UK Space Agency facilities. Your assignment as part of *Project Renaissance* is to understand the threats posed against humanity." I shuddered at his war cry. "Gentleman, the governments of Earth will not tolerate the destruction our ancestors were subjected to. We want to be in a position to fight back if we so need."

"Why the UK Space Agency?" I wanted to know.

"As you are aware, the British government captured an alien spacecraft which they hold at their facility. All parties agreed it best for you to conduct your research into the alien technology alongside the craft." He turned to Randall. "All your equipment will be transferred today, along with your technicians."

I didn't need to look at Randall to see his excitement, I could feel it.

"There will be a car waiting in thirty minutes," Bates said. "Humber will be joining you."

I didn't need telling twice. I went to my room and packed everything I thought I would need. It only took a moment, so I decided to give my mother a quick call and update her. She sounded weaker every time we spoke and I felt a pang of regret for not visiting since my return to Earth, but she told me everything was okay and to enjoy myself while I could because life often has its cruel moments.

I promised to call her again in a few days and maybe even visit if I could get the time away – surely they would understand, but time was not a friend on either side of this dilemma.

Randall was already loitering in the reception area when I arrived.

The car turned up a few minutes later.

8

I relaxed in the comfort of the leather seat in the large foyer of the UK Space Agency building, waiting for caffeine to strike my system, an empty mug of coffee in my hands. The arduous traffic of the rush hour had left me drained.

A short rotund man pushed through a set of double doors to the left. He took Humber's hand as he approached. I was slow to stand, last to shake hands and didn't catch his name.

"Follow me." He had a deep resonant voice which appeared out of place to me, and I stifled a laugh. He led us into through the old wing of the building which housed a public museum and through into a secured section at the back.

It felt like we were inside a maze, wandered through large never-ending corridors, turning many corners – all of which were painted in the same opaque blue making it incredibly difficult to distinguish one place from another. Every so often there were doors leading off into various sections, but we continued, until we reached a large metallic door.

The small round fellow swiped his security pass and handed it to Humber as he stepped inside.

"You are entering a sterile environment. There are enviro-suits inside for you all." He held open the door. "You are required to shower and change into them. Once you have done so, please wait at the door at the far end."

"I could use a shower." Still feeling sluggish, feeling the heat under my armpits.

I stepped into the shower and let the water do its magic, the temperature just right. By the time I joined everyone else at the far end of the room, I was refreshed. I found the clinical white suits amusing and couldn't stop laughing at the others until I caught a glimpse of myself.

The smile faded as the door released in a hiss of escaping gas.

"Please stand on the white lines below you." A voice said. "We're just going to disinfect the outside of your suits."

The door hissed closed behind and a white cloud descended upon us.

I coughed, although the fog didn't penetrate my suit, but my visor misted as I blew out a breath. It was like someone had turned up the heat inside my suit.

A blast of cold air dissipated the cloud of gas, blowing it into the exhaust.

The door in front opened, revealing a wide set of stairs leading down into the depths of the facility. By the time we reached the bottom, I felt sweat running along my arms.

We met a final wall of glass. Inside, a swarm of gleaming white suited people busied themselves, they didn't look up. The air inside my own protective suit smelt sterile and tasted of disinfectant.

The doors parted and we stepped in.

9

An older man stood waiting for us at the front of the room. He had a large white tuft of hair in the centre of his head, which made him look eccentric, but I guessed the combination of being a scientist and working underground for any length of time would do that to you.

"This is Professor Cernan," Humber said and the professor extended his hand.

"Huh," I said. "Any relation to Eugene?" I shook his hand.

"Yes... how did you know?"

"A lucky guess." I said. Randall peered at me questioningly, but I didn't expand.

Cernan led us to a large stainless-steel door. He stopped, entered a code on the pin pad to the side and the door released.

"You should find everything as requested inside," he said. "Your shipments are arriving as we speak and will be brought down very soon once they have been decontaminated." He looked at Humber. "Enjoy and let me know if you need anything more."

“I need you to prepare the craft for us.” I looked at Randall, but he said nothing. Humber was staring straight at Cernan, their eyes interlocked in a battle of wills.

“You have clearance?” Cernan seemed astonished. “Nobody has been allowed in there since…”

“We have the necessary authorisation,” Humber interrupted. “I’m granting you permission.” Cernan gaped at him, it was clear he didn’t know how to react. *Was Humber his superior?*

After a long pause he said, “I’ll make the necessary preparations for you, but it will take some time to bring the temperature up, it’s been in deep freeze for a long time now. It will be ready by morning.” Cernan looked worried, but said nothing further and left.

“Who is Eugene?” Randall asked.

“The last man on the moon,” Humber said. “The commander of Apollo 17.”

“Wow.”

When our equipment arrived, we unpacked crates of electronic gizmos, most of which I couldn’t even identify. It was clear from the amount of stuff, it hadn’t been a snap decision to relocate us. Maybe it had always been Bates’s intention.

“Why was Cernan so reluctant?” I asked when Humber had left the room. “He seemed nervous, almost afraid.”

“Maybe he knows something we don’t.” Randall raised his eyebrows.

“He’s just being protective, I think. Maybe he is worried we will find something that he couldn’t.”

“I’m sure we’ll find out in the morning.” A childish grin filled his face, a new toy to play with.

PROJECT RENAISSANCE

CHAPTER 22

Humber joined us at breakfast.

"There are a few things I have to explain." His eyes narrowed. "I understand Thacker told you about your father's involvement in UFO investigations for the British government."

"You mean he was a UFO chaser?" Randall sat forwards, his mouth gaping, his eyes wide darting between the two of us.

"Yes," Humber said. "He spent many years tracking our alien visitors and investigating sightings."

"So was my grandfather, Joseph." I confirmed. "It runs in our blood."

"Both your father and grandfather kept catalogues of each of the different craft they encountered and from that we were able to track activity and it has helped us predict future visitations and locations." Randall was like an excited kid, I almost expected to see him foaming at the mouth. "Did Thacker tell you how Joseph captured the craft in 1947, Roswell?"

"Is *that* what's here?" Randall gasped.

"Joseph never had chance to study the craft for himself. At the time there was great demand for his services. Visitations were on the increase and the government poured a lot of funding into his undisclosed department. Eventually the team expanded, splitting into two separate divisions; an alien research team and advanced alien tracking. While Joseph worked on AAT, later Leon joined ART. Their findings have been closely guarded secrets until now, but it's down to your family that we know what we know." He patted my shoulder.

I suddenly felt proud of my family. I'd always felt my father's short life was in vain, but since joining SARA I'd come to understand the hidden depths. His work meant little while he was alive, but now had renewed importance. My father was a pioneer – way ahead of his time – just as my grandfather had been before him.

I saw an image of my father playing the part of Spaceman, a tin-foil hat strapped to his head and I smiled. Many fathers wanted their children to follow in their footsteps, but for me, it was inevitable; my father had known that. I was sure of it.

The sense of pride dissipated as I remembered the fractious relationship with my mother after dad died. She was the only blood-relative left, now her life was reaching its end and I shuddered. Family was important, now more than ever. An image of my dead crewmates flashed through my mind. *Fuck!*

Humber didn't seem to notice the storm surging behind my eyelids, and he continued to talk, "A quarter of all reported sightings have official evidence thanks to your family's work." I blinked back the tears, and tried to smile – a sober pride. "Your grandfather's formula still works, enabling us to track visitations, even predicting the length and frequency." I watched as Humber took a large wad of bound pages from beneath the table and handed it to me. "I thought you should have this."

"What is it?" I asked taking the folder from his outstretched hand.

"I found it in Thacker's effects," he said. "It belonged to your father and to his." I saw satisfaction in Humber's smile. "While the craft in this facility is the only one we have intact, every one witnessed was catalogued. I thought it might be of some assistance to you."

"Thank you," I said, unable to hold back the tears this time. I felt my father close and as I blinked, I saw his smiling face. The sparkle of light reflecting from the tin-foil hat filled the void behind my eyelids.

2

I opened the docket to the first page. The once pristine bleached pages were darkened from years of oxidisation.

There was a blurred photo of a rather large grey disc with a couple of lights dotted here and there. It looked like the UFOs used in television shows back in the 60's and 70's.

A label at the top named this type *Saucer*.

I looked at the image and pictured my father sitting with the catalogue in his lap. I felt a sense of satisfaction and imagined my father had enjoyed the job a great deal.

As I flicked through the pages, my hand froze mid-air. The beating of the alien life-force surrounded me, pulsing within me. I'd seen this craft in my dreams, and I knew it was close. It was in the building.

"This is the one!" I pointed at the picture. "This is the one my grandfather captured." Humber looked surprised. I found his reaction intriguing, as if he'd somehow doubted the alien knowledge I'd gained through Russia's memories.

I examined the photo.

Although the colour of the image had faced into hushed tones of black and white, it appeared in vivid colour in my mind, remembered from my visions. A glint of sunlight sparkled, reflected off the metallic surface.

I scanned the list of dates underneath, the last entry struck me as odd; 21st July 1969 – 02:56:15 (UTC).

"Doesn't that strike you as intriguing?" I pointed at the date. Bates's expression remained blank, oblivious to my point. "Apollo 11. It's the day Armstrong took his first step onto the lunar surface. I bet if you check the timecode, it would be an exact match."

"Oh, so it is," he chuckled, his hand moving to his chin. "What does that mean?"

"I don't know." I shook my head, I had no theory. Why would this craft never have visited again since while many other had?

My eyes scanned the picture of the craft. It looked like a stingray, which I presumed was why my grandfather had labelled it so. I studied the picture and saw the tail waving behind it, a slight green glow at its rear.

"It uses J-Power." My finger traced the source of the light. Humber peered at the picture, but he seemed puzzled. I knew he couldn't see it. It was a tiny white speck which was difficult to distinguish from the grainy faults of the printed image, but I knew what I was looking at.

My mind started spinning.

Thacker told me my grandfather had taken a lump of Jeometamorphic rock from the crash site at Roswell and that my father had later passed it on to him. I understood it to be the power source of the craft, and now I had the distinct feeling my father had known this too. It raised questions. Why had he given it to Thacker?

Even though he wasn't there to answer, I felt my dad's spirit near. It seemed both my grandfather and father knew more about the aliens than they'd let on. Maybe they'd had some of Russia's incomplete inner-sight. My father was always scared of his dreams and it could easily have provoked him to keep the rock as far away from the craft as possible.

"The British never got their hands on J-Power," Humber said, seemingly reading my mind.

"Wait, what? You're telling me they've had this craft for over seventy years," Randall began. "And they've never had its power source?" Randall's bemused voice now animate. "Precisely what have they been studying all this time?"

"A very good question." A wry smile flourished across his lips. "You can ask them that yourself."

"Take me to see *Stingray*," I said.

3

"Do you want me to show you around?" There was still a note of caution in Cernan's voice. I knew it was a rhetorical question, Humber said nothing. Cernan placed his ungloved hand on the palm-pad to the side of the door.

The door opened with a beep and we moved to enter.

"You must understand." Cernan blocked our way. "Very few people have been close to her since..."

"We have the highest authority possible." Humber waved his hand dismissively.

"Who?" Cernan enquired.

"Both the President of the USA and *your* Prime Minister." Humber had a wry smile. Cernan stepped out of our way.

"Why haven't many people seen it?" I asked breaking the uncomfortable silence. "Did something happen?"

"Yes," Cernan said, looking at Humber, but even Humber seemed puzzled. "Just before the project closed, the team haemorrhaged, taken onto other projects. Sometimes we'd only have one person on the craft for a whole month." His voice trailed off. "That's when the accident happened."

"An accident?" I prompted.

"It was the first time the craft responded to human presence." Cernan explained. "The investigator was trying to open one of the hatches with a crowbar and somehow this caused the craft to roll, crushing both his arms and legs underneath the tail of the craft. It was lucky he wasn't paralysed."

An image of my father flashed into my mind.

"Why was the project shut down?" Humber wanted to know.

"It was a drain on resources," Cernan said. "The accident was the catalyst."

The image of my father came to me again, his arms and legs in plaster, blue bruises across his chest. He'd told me he'd tripped down a flight of stairs, but now I questioned this. Maybe he'd activated the craft with the J-Power and something had gone wrong. That would've been enough to frighten him. If that was true, I knew what we must do.

We stopped at the end of the corridor, the door opened with a whoosh and a cold blast of air rushed towards me. I looked inside into the clouds of dry ice that filled the vast hangar. The ventilation system purred into action, but it was slow to disperse. Through the dying vapour I caught a glimpse of the shiny metallic shell.

I felt a surge of energy inside of me, the power of the rock growing, responding to the situation. As the moving fog dissipated further, I stepped down into the room and saw the craft clear in my mind, even though my eyes only recorded the outline in the distance.

The remaining vapours cloaked me as I rushed towards it.

I felt dizzy running the last of the way, stopping short as the craft swam into full view. I stood side on, able to see the full extent; its tail reached back a good ten metres; the flat, slender wings appeared paper thin and fragile. A giant husk of a dormant stingray.

"Wait! It's not safe." Cernan's voice called after me.

The craft was magnificent.

A spark of electricity shot from my fingers as I ran them along the body of the craft. The overpowering drum of life pulsed in my ears. My eyes snapped closed and as they did so, I took a long cooling breath of the chilled hangar air.

The spacecraft was there in my mind, resting on the lunar landscape, many millions of years ago. *Is this the same craft?* I asked into the hollow of my inner psyche. It was of the same variety, I knew, because there it was, right in front of Russia and me.

He reached out, running his hand along the metallic husk, feeling the material breathing beneath his fingers. I felt what he felt, seeing it as he saw it.

In his mind he watched a man he didn't recognise touching the craft. To Russia, the guy was dressed in strange attire, but to me it seemed normal and I recognised him; my father.

My hand dropped away from the craft, the connection terminated and I swayed unsteadily on my feet, feeling physically drained. I turned back to see the others appearing through the last of the smoke.

"This is *Stingray*." Cernan had a proud grin. "Isn't she something?" He noticed how close I was to the craft, "Don't touch it."

"She's breathtaking," I said, ignoring his concerns. I felt light-headed and breathless.

"Unimaginable," Randall's voice distant, his face filled with childish glee.

"You can leave us to it," Humber said, turning to Cernan.

"Call if you need anything." While Cernan sounded civil enough, he was scowling, almost disappointed. I watched the door close behind him as he left and then turned back to the craft. Randall was reaching out to touch the craft and I dived to his side.

"Don't!" But it was too late, his hand was already on the wing, almost the same place my own had been. Nothing appeared to happen.

"What's the matter?" Randall shook his head. "It's perfectly fine."

"I'm not so sure." The memory of my father's injuries flashed in my mind.

"It looks perfectly safe to me," Humber added.

"I think it's reacting to me," I said. They both looked at me with questioning eyes. "I don't understand how that's possible, but I saw my father. Then I remembered what my mum had said to me: *your father was right, it is a gift and it's your gift. You gave it to him.*

The silence remained for a good minute.

"We've been talking about Leon a lot recently," Humber offered, but I shook my head. It had nothing to do with our conversations. Russia saw my father, millions of years before his conception. It was incomprehensible.

"My father broke both his arms and legs in a work accident," I said. "Somehow he managed to activate the craft with the rock, maybe his enquiring mind got the better of him."

"Why'd he conceal it?" Randall was puzzled. Humber was looking at the floor, his head cocked to the side as he listened. He was deep in thought. "It makes no sense. Why did he activate *Stingray* and then give the rock away?"

"It wasn't for him," Humber said, looking to me. His eyes narrowed, boring straight into me. "Like everything else, it all comes back to you. He was waiting for you."

Not long after, Humber left us to examine the craft. Randall couldn't contain his excitement and started circling *Stingray*, exploring its shell, his hands tracing its body just as I had, but he seemed unaffected by visions and flashing images.

I sat to one side watching, allowing myself time to soak in the vast alien craft, sniffing the air. It smelt fresh yet I could taste a coppery energy at the back of my throat. The *Stingray* sat motionless, held by a harness and a heavy framework of stilts. The beauty of the craft partially lost, covered by the restraints keeping it safe and stable. It seemed impossible that my father could have sustained such injuries from such a heavily fortified vehicle.

As my eyes closed, I imagined it flying free, its wings gently rippling to keep it in place and I felt a sense of tranquillity I'd only felt before in my dreams. I allowed my body to relax and drifted into a lucid dream watching the mesmerising and gentle motion of *Stingray*.

4

I stood on the brow of a hill, looking down on the familiar world I now knew once thrived on our own moon. From my vantage point I saw everything, busy people in the village streets, the temple atop the ziggurat bursting from dense jungle and there in the floor of the valley, I saw the *Stingray* craft, glittering in the light, hovering. Its wings gently rippling, keeping her steady, the tail poking straight behind.

As I watched, Magi Eritrea approached the foot of the craft, her arms outstretched, but not to me. They were pointing towards the alien head that appeared at the entrance, glinting in the bright evening sun.

Daylight faded, replaced by the flickering of flaming torches. When my eyes adjusted I found myself, as Russia, sitting on Magi Eritrea's lap looking up at her.

A memory sprang forth from the dark recesses of my mind, this was story time, and Russia's favourite story was of a traveller and the creation of a world. I now understood the story, it was the beginning of time for the moon civilisation.

"This is what you are looking for." Magi Eritrea's voice was gentle as she unrolled the parchment.

The memory vaporised from my sight, and I found myself once again staring from the summit of the hill. The *Stingray* craft was hovering, its wings fluttering in the breeze. Magi Eritrea had gone.

As my dream vanished into darkness, I opened my eyes.

A niggling question clawed my attention, what was the importance of the *Stingray* craft and why had it reacted to my presence? I couldn't believe in coincidences any longer, I'd seen enough to know there was a purpose to everything.

It's waiting for you, Magi Eritrea's calm tones floated through my mind.

5

Randall burst into the hangar making me jump.

"I think you should see this," he panted, standing still only long enough to catch a breath. "Come on..." He was already out the door. I darted after him, following him to his workstation.

His screen was full of applications, the desk cluttered with half drunken coffee cups and snack wrappers. It wasn't obvious what he wanted and I asked, "What am I looking at?"

"Remember the modified laser I showed you back at SARA?" He looked up, but didn't wait for my response. "Some good news, the alien material seems to withstand the laser's beam. No damage whatsoever." I remembered his demonstration, the stench of the frying DVD disc fresh in my nostrils. His hands tapped in rapid bursts on the virtual keyboard at the bottom of the terminal display. "But something is happening to it. It's changing."

Frowning I said, "I'm not sure I understand. What do you mean it's changing?"

"The material is *changing*!"

"How?"

"You've got me." Randall scratched his head. "It becomes more unstable at faster spin speeds."

"What speeds are we talking about?"

"DVDs vary up to around six thousand revolutions per minute, but using a coating we've created from J-Power I'm using seven thousand," Randall sniffed. "But in theory I could take it up to forty-five thousand." He took the disc from the desk. "I didn't want to risk it though. I don't want to be *that* guy, bringing down every project I work on."

"Do it!" My eyes locked onto his. I saw the uncertainty swimming there as he tensed. "Trust me. You won't screw this one up."

"I've a bad feeling." He sounded uncomfortable and shook his head, his eyes breaking away from mine. "Don't you think we should…you know…speak to Humber?"

I grabbed his arm and his eyes crossed mine once again.

"It will be okay, trust me." My voice sedate. He seemed to relax a little, his arm loosened up and I let go. "Crank her up."

Randall placed the disc into the rigged contraption, locking the reinforced glass casket surrounding it, keeping us on the side of safety. His fingers rapped the desk before dangling over the screen.

"Here goes." He hesitated, before confirming his commands.

The motor whirred into action and the disc began

spinning.

"Faster," I said. "More speed."

Even though I studied the rotating disc, I saw Randall clearly in my mind, biting down on his lip, still nervous. I heard the slow padding of his fingers on the terminal as the disc picked up speed.

I felt it happening inside me first, something stirring, dark chambers opening, bright green light pouring out and flooding my body. As it did so, I felt myself rising, higher and higher. The unmistakable sizzling taste of the Jeometamorphic rock's power stole over me, recognisable from the dream where I drank the river water.

A dazzling light covered my vision as the green liquid flooded.

And in the brightness, I saw the gleaming surface of the disc, shining in its fervent beauty. Except the disc was no longer spinning to me, replaced by a bright orb of light hovering around it.

"It's working!" I shouted above the furious roar of the liquid in my ears.

"What is?" I heard Randall, distant and gurgling in the brightness. I saw in my mind his concern, even though his voice was emotionless. It was clear he couldn't see; his human eyes didn't recognise the beauty that came literally from within.

"The disc isn't unstable," I yelled. "It's opening up!" I watched the floating orb of green light, waiting. "Faster," I thundered. "It must go faster."

The orb began to drain of colour, turning dark and cloudy.

And then it came.

I saw the alien message playing in the orb of light.

The orb displayed the image of a new world, barren and foreboding, just like the one I'd seen once in my dreams. I recognised the shape of the landscape. This was the beginning of time for the lunar civilisation, the first footprints of life to etch themselves onto the surface of the dusty terrain, but I guessed I was about to see the same story through different eyes.

Nearby stars sparkled around the crisp rocky lunar surface, casting shadowy aspersions throughout the universe.

It was beautiful to see the moon as a planet – even though I understood technically that this wasn't so – pure uncorrupted nature, pitted by stardust falling from the heavens. It was startling just how accurately the picture reflected our moon as we knew it. As the film played on, the occasional meteorite struck the terrain, blemishing it further, molten magma rivers retreating as time passed.

In the brightness of just one day, a craft identical to *Stingray*, fell from the sky in a cloud of green smoke. The rippling wings tore open as it ripped another crater into the barren land. White smoke billowed from the dying craft's wounds, and I caught a glimpse of five creatures inside; the alien race that Russia knew.

It was clear to me they were stranded, their vessel irreparable.

A lightning bolt shot to the ground, and in that moment, I felt their fear. A piercing cry rang out, the *Stingray*'s distress call, screaming into the emptiness of the universe.

The orb changed feeds, like a video reel. The view was now from inside the cockpit of the devastated craft. Green fog clung in the air, seeping out of instruments. The aliens screeched at one another, unable to escape the dying craft. Silence fell, and as the mist cleared, I saw them crowded around a lifeless corpse, their limbs upraised. Pure green tears seeped from their eyelets.

The silence was shattered when the four other aliens began chanting incomprehensible but musical words, their raised limbs beating the air as their bodies swayed in rhythm.

It was obvious this was their leader – their master – but I wondered if all of their kind got the same treatment. It seemed almost human in ritual.

As they wept, their tears fell to the lifeless husk of their ruler.

The orb zoomed in, following the droplets of green on their voyage as they fell from their swaying faces. The tears continued on their journey, rolling through the wreckage below, gaining momentum before reaching the dusty terrain.

One tear touched the dead embers of the once green glowing rock that had powered the craft, it began to flash. As days descended to night and nights turned into days, the alien creatures began to wither and fade, chanting and swaying together in their harmonious melody.

The video sped up, and I saw this continued for thirteen days.

On the fourteenth day, the emptiness of space took hold and the craft fell silent as the weak creatures passed from life into death.

I shivered seeing the haunting images of the dying aliens, gaunt and ill, looking like my father had when his cancer had finally overruled his life.

As the days passed, the glowing of the rock grew stronger and stronger, until on one particularly dark night, jade-green light blasted into the atmosphere creating a halo around the world. As it descended from the sky, the world exploded into flames of green and a new world was born.

For a moment I had opportunity to reflect and I thought I understood the mythology of this story presented to me. Everything came from the power of the rock which had mixed with dormant genetic material contained in the craters of the planet. Where the two converged, flames of life leapt forth. This continued for seven years and seven months, burning carbon from the rocky terrain, superheated atoms fused to create heavier atoms, emitting oxygen and carbon dioxide in the process.

When the fires burnt out, the atmosphere was rich with everything needed for life and the newly formed planet was cast into a misty fog. As the temperature cooled, the mist cleared and the dust settled, plants and trees took root and claimed the world as their own. The genetic material evolved using the power of the rock, changing itself, until animals were born and roamed the world. A green river swelled through the centre of the planet, feeding the animals and plants, flowing within them and bearing yet more life.

As time passed more and more animals evolved until human like creatures emerged. On that very same day, another alien craft arrived, answering the distress call of the long-since-reclaimed *Stingray*, twelve years on. They saw the world and the diversity of life and sought to protect it from other travellers, the foragers of the universe.

The light in the orb began to fade. I watched the last image of alien and man, standing hand in hand, shoulder to shoulder with one another. The world was at peace. As the light vanished from the orb, I saw the destruction of the moon world – my own memory from the *Constellation* mission. It was a far cry from the beauty and harmony that the images of the orb had shown, returned to the dust before time began.

The light diminished until I returned to reality.

I knew what I had seen was just a story, baked in myth – Charlie's pursuit of truth had rubbed off on me. The mythology I'd been presented with gave me an understanding of how we came to be – one of life's ultimate questions – and now I knew something more about our relationship with the aliens. While we were not the same species, we evolved from them and their life-force. I now understood why the aliens policed our world. It was an act of love, in memory for their fallen leader and her crew. It also explained something that had puzzled me right from the beginning, why had the aliens gone to the trouble of supporting life on an inhospitable place such as our lunar satellite when there was a habitable planet within reach.

I felt a throbbing in my head and I dropped to my knees, my eyes firmly shut.

I let out a shriek as pain pulsed through me, a distant beating filled my ears until it reached a crescendo, a voice screaming. I heard what it had to say.

It is time. It said to me. It is time for us to return.

It was the shrill harrowing cry of an alien, unmistakable.

As the wave of pain faded, I shook with anger, knowing I'd fallen for their trap. I'd fallen in love with the beautiful imagery *they'd* shown me, but it was a lie to hook my attention and nothing more.

The final test was complete; *their* return was imminent.

6

The door rocked in its frame as Humber stormed in, letting it slam behind.

"What's going on?" Humber's angry voice demanded. "The power's out across half the region and the trail of blown fuses leads down here!"

Randall's mouth continued to gape. He turned to me in stunned silence. I too, said nothing.

"Is somebody going to tell me what the hell you've done?" He followed my gaze to the disc, now at a gentle spin – and still slowing – inside the safety chamber. His face shot back to mine and I saw the spark ignite as he pieced things together. "What have you done?"

"I spun the disc up to maximum speed..." Randall stammered.

"I thought you said that was unsafe," Humber questioned.

"I told him to do it," I said. Humber shook his head, no wiser. "Randall thought the disc was unstable, but it wasn't. The molecular structure shifted at high speeds. It opened up, and revealed its secrets."

"What are you talking about?" Humber turned to Randall. "Did you see too?"

"No." Randall seemed confused.

"What did you learn?"

"I'd seen the birth of the moon civilisation before, but I understood that was just a story, a tale recounted throughout the ages and retold to us in the scriptures." I thought of Charlie, missing his influence and passion for the Rora Habab Temple and its deciphered meaning. My eyes misted up. "This was that same mythology, but as recalled by the aliens themselves."

As I recounted the tale of creation, I felt a deep sense of dissatisfaction. Like the scriptures, what I'd seen could not be trusted. It too was a biased message, a corruption of the truth, passed from generation to generation. It was too convenient, too coincidental.

In the silence of the room, I shifted uneasily in my seat.

Again, we were left without direction. Our avenues were closing off, leaving us nowhere to turn.

A thought pushed its way into my mind; both the disc

and the craft were important to us. I remembered Magi Eritrea had left the disc on the bed for Russia to see. There had to be more on the disc than just the alien message, she'd made sure Russia had seen it. I felt like Magi Eritrea was trying to pass me messages through Russia's memories; a trail of breadcrumbs.

Then there was *Stingray*. I'd seen Magi Eritrea there too, and pictured the view from the top of the hill looking down the valley and onto the craft. This too seemed significant.

This is what you are looking for, I heard the voice in my head once again, the alien craft hovering in my mind.

The message on the disc was not from Magi Eritrea, but perhaps she'd left something further for me. Whatever its purpose, the disc seemed inextricably linked to my memories of *Stingray*.

"We don't have time to sit around," I said, standing. "We need to prepare for the return of our alien creators."

CHAPTER 23

My mind swam with questions as I lay on the bed, I couldn't switch off; sleep now a distant hope. I didn't want to admit defeat, but the realisation took hold and I gave up. I flicked the bedside lamp on and stared blankly at the ceiling. My eyes traced the pattern of a cobweb to one corner.

I felt the distant, longing cry of *Stingray*, asking for my help, wanting to live again. I couldn't ignore it and dressed, leaving my room, heading straight towards the chilled hangar. As the door opened and the cool burst of air brushed past my enviro-suit, I shivered. It was peaceful.

Stingray waited, motionless, poised.

As I drew closer, I felt the beating of the life-force within, the connection alive. My eyes snapped shut as I reached out. A sigh of satisfaction slipped from my lips as my fingers ran along the numb surface of the metallic giant. A spark of energy transferred between us, forcing me to suck in a deeper breath than I'd anticipated.

A voice whispered my name and when my eyes opened, I saw the sands of the world I'd once inhabited as Russia. I looked around, there was no one in sight. To one side I saw the temple at the peak of the sacred ziggurat and I instantly knew my orientation, pin-pointing my exact position.

I heard my name whispered softly on the breeze and my eyes flickered until I stood in the dullness of the sparse chamber, *Stingray* still beneath my fingers. My hand dropped away and I took a step backwards. The beating seemed louder in my ears now and I felt a buzzing in my chest as if my heart was racing. It grew stronger with each breath I took.

And then I heard it, loud and clear. My own voice echoing in the chamber, but I hadn't spoken. I stumbled, tripping over my own feet, my eyes darting around the room, checking.

"What do you want?" I called, but there was no reply. "Tell me what I need to do?" I tried again. It felt like I was conducting a séance, trying to bring the spirits forth from the other side – wherever that may be.

I stood in the silence, shivering in the cold emptiness, feeling scared and alone. I knew I could've left the room, but for some reason I felt the overriding urge to stay. And then I saw a figure lurking in the shadows, watching me.

"Who are you?" I asked, staring straight at the shadow to my right. There was no answer. "I'm not afraid of you, show yourself." I commanded, barely managing to conceal my fright. The figure watched, saying nothing.

I shot to my left and blinked, startled by the image of Magi Eritrea coming my way. She was escorted by one of the alien creatures, its skin shimmering, dancing as it passed under the strip lighting.

I stared, dazed for a moment until I realised my dream-world had collided with reality. From the safety of the facility, I was watching an event that took place on the moon's surface many years ago. The merged reality played out in front of me.

Magi Eritrea said nothing to me as she passed, but then I remembered it would have been impossible for her to know I was there. She stepped into the opening of the craft and moved out of sight. I studied the metallic ramp leading to the gaping entrance of the craft and as my gaze moved up I caught the craft moving, breathing. It was alive.

I heard the hiss of a door opening behind me and spun round. Cernan stood in the entrance, studying me from above. I turned back to the craft, the entrance gone, the shadows vaporised, the breathing stopped.

Cernan's footfalls echoed as he clanked down the metal steps.

"I often come down to see her when I'm struggling to sleep," he said, looking at me with a knowing smile. "I know I shouldn't, but I've never been able to keep myself away. It's our secret." I smiled back, wanting to ask him how that was possible if the hangar had been in deep freeze before our arrival, but I knew these scientists always had ways around life's tricky problems. My questions went unasked, as I assumed many did around here given there was nobody keeping tabs.

We sat together in front of the *Stingray* in silence for a while, just staring at the static craft.

"I don't know how," I said to Cernan, "but I believe this is the same craft that visited our ancestors over two-and-a-half million years ago. I'm sure of it. How else could Russia have seen my father?" Cernan remained silent, watching the craft. "Isn't that incredible? Who'd have believed a spaceship could live for so long." I realised I'd referred to it as living, which Cernan didn't seem to question. Except in reality it was dormant, but alive. That was a very different matter altogether.

"That would be something if it were true." Cernan seemed almost dismissive. "Even if we could get a response, I don't see how – mechanically speaking – it would even work after all this time. Except for the incident, it's never shown any sign of life."

"This isn't the kind of metallic contraption conceived by human minds," I said. "It's a breathing creature in its own right, and it's been starved of its life-force since it arrived on our planet. Without its power source it's remained dormant, waiting."

"Waiting for what?" he asked.

"For me." I smiled. "My father, Leon, he knew it too."

"I couldn't be sure at first, but your passion makes it obvious," Cernan said with a shake of his head. "You sound just like him, before his accident." He looked concerned. "Be careful."

"It's not a matter of being cautious." I fixed his gaze, dismissing his worries. "Whatever mistakes my father made, I'm not going to follow in his footsteps. Anyhow, it *knows* I'm here, and I'm sure it will take care of me."

I thanked Cernan and left to get some rest, knowing tomorrow would be a long day. I needed all the strength I could muster. Lying in bed before my eyes closed, I felt excitement building.

2

The instant Randall placed the sealed container into my bare hands, I felt the shift of power surging through me, the box vibrating, beating like a drum, desiring to be set free. I'd broken protocol removing my enviro-suit. I didn't see the point, no human hand could damage this craft, no single stray hair would block its engines. Now my fingers worked freely without restriction, unlatching the case and revealing the rock inside; entrusted to me just as Bates had said. It glistened under the strip lighting, shining like a polished gem.

I let the case clatter to the floor as I gripped the stone. It was warmer to the touch than I expected and when I looked down into my cupped hands, I saw a pulsing green luminescence, the rest of the hangar seemed to drain of its dull grey colours.

"It's time to set you free." I took a step towards the dormant *Stingray* vessel.

In the coolness of the air-conditioned breeze, I heard a whisper, too quiet to comprehend.

"Did you say something?" I asked, turning to Randall. He shook his head. I looked back at the metallic giant, edging forwards.

I heard it again, crisper in my ear and I realised these were not words, but the longing cry of the *Stingray*, calling out to its power source. It knew it was close, I felt it. The beating of the life-force pulsed in the depths of my genetics, and I felt *Stingray*'s pain...yes, pain, it cried out in anguish, aroused by the urge to be alive once more.

I looked down at the rock, now a bright steady glow. It continued to heat up in my hands, and then I realised the Jeometamorphic rock was vibrating. As I drifted towards the craft, reality dimmed further.

Tracing the form of the *Stingray*'s metallic body, I stepped towards the tail of the craft, where I'd seen the glow in the pictures my father had taken and also from my visions. I'd seen the British reports, their so-called experts had labelled the hole as the 'exhaust' because of its precise size and small round protrusion – exactly like a car exhaust. It was underneath the rear body of the craft, conveniently placed to divert the attention of all but the keenest of eyes.

As I began my approach and moved along the underbelly of the craft, it struck me how easy it would be to get trapped underneath if the craft staggered or swayed – the tail was stiff and restrained while lifeless, but when it became fluid it would fall directly down, there was insufficient structure in place to stop this. I recognised that this must be how my father sustained his injuries, the craft simply dropped onto him; not a mistake I intended to make.

As I inched towards the power pipe, a tide of happiness washed over me. It was not my own, but *Stingray*'s playing through me. Did spacecraft have souls, and was it possible for them to feel anything? The pain and anguish I'd been experiencing, and now the sheer joy, made me think that they did.

My hands were sweating in the heat, the rock now searing into the top layers of my palms. I held the rock towards the small opening, and the heat rose in a rapid burst and I let out a howl as the rock scorched the fingertips gripping hold of it; still I held on. My fingers squeezed tighter in a chain reaction, determined to maintain my grasp. As the pain torched through me I bit down on my lip, tearing a gash.

With a screech, I let go.

I was too busy waving my hands in the air and dancing around to notice it first, it was only when I followed Randall's astonished gaze that I realised. The rock hadn't hit the ground as defined by Newton's laws of gravity or the many other laws that physics was built upon. Instead it hovered in the air, spinning on its upended axis.

Humber grabbed my arm, ripping me from underneath the craft to a safe distance, a luxury my father hadn't had. When I turned to thank him, I found his eyes wide and his mouth gaping. It was an expression of pure disbelief.

The glowing green rock spun faster and faster, brilliant white and green sparks flew from it as its intensity grew and I shielded my eyes. Magical music played in my ears, the same harmonic tune as the portal. I could imagine the craft speaking to each other, communicating through their hypnotic song.

I ducked away, a blinding flash ripping through the hangar.

"It's gone." I heard Cernan's voice through the speakers, observing from the glass panelled room towering above the chamber. "This is utterly astounding; the craft took it!"

The ground beneath us shook and I grabbed Humber, steadying both myself and him as the room burst into an orchestra. The whole place was alive with music and it grew louder as the craft reanimated, coming to life before our eyes. As I anticipated the tail dropped first.

Two lights flickered below *Stingray*, and as they did the craft began to roll, the restraints holding it in place creaking and groaning. I realised it was hovering freely in the air, the craft's tail gently wafting, the wings fluttering and rippling as it held its position.

With a metallic shriek, the restraints snapped, one by one. I sucked in a sharp breath as a piece of sheared metal buckle whizzed past my ear. The scaffolding underneath the craft sighed in relief, but did not move.

The noises died, the shaking stopped, but I still felt the joy of the craft inside me, alive and ready for action.

"I hope you're getting all this," Humber said, looking up towards Cernan.

"It's all recorded," Cernan said in a singsong voice, full of glee, and I wasn't surprised. We were witnessing something beyond the wildest imaginings of most. I could envisage Cernan dancing around and waving his hands. He'd been around *Stingray* for a long time, it had to be good to see it active after all that time.

And I was proud too. We'd achieved more in a week than the British government had in the years they'd observed the craft. I knew my father would be proud too, this was his moment.

"Thank you so much," Cernan's voice echoed, "I honestly didn't believe in you and I'm *so* sorry for that." That didn't matter to me now.

Thacker dozed in his cell, a dreamless sleep filling his mind with emptiness. He felt a sudden acceleration, the take-off of a jet perhaps. He was thrust into a rainbow of colour, a drum beating all around him, thumping deep within his chest.

He sat bolt upright, bringing himself out of sleep in an instant, ready to cry out for medical attention fearing another heart attack. When he heard the clear calling in his mind, a green filter flickered across his eyes and his chest pounded louder and louder.

The music of the portal filled his mind, but this was different. He felt something else, a living creature coming into existence and as he looked deeper into the green he saw the *Stingray* craft, hovering, its wings gentle and majestic as they stirred the air.

Stingray was alive.

3

A round entrance beckoned from under the closest wing, glistening silvery-blue steps hovering in mid-air inviting us inside. As I walked under the fluttering wing, my fingers rolled along its smooth shell, hard and metallic but now warm. Mesmerising ripples purred across the craft's skin in peristalsis; organic in nature.

I stepped closer to the entrance, but found myself snagged. Humber had a firm grip on my arm and a cautious look in his eyes.

"We should take care," he said. "We don't know what's inside." I returned him a polite smile, but said nothing. Our aliens – friend or foe – were unlikely to rig up traps to catch us. True, they had setup a series of tests to check on our progress, but they weren't pirates of the sky, there would be no booby-traps.

Humber loosened his grip.

I could see inside from the third step up. There were strange lights glowing and pulsing, casting long shadows that moved with the hovering craft. They seemed to come from every direction, the ground, the ceiling and the walls. They appeared to react to my presence, dimming slightly, as if it recognised my naked eyes needed shielding from the glare.

I peered at the bizarre grey interior – almost metallic, almost biological – rippled with vessels which ran beneath the skin of the corridor. As I watched, I felt the craft's movements, contracting and expanding as it breathed. The vein-like network pulsed, and perhaps this was down to the power of the rock being drawn from the engines, feeding various parts of the ship.

The corridor split in two directions, one heading towards the tail, the other the head and wings. Humber appeared behind me and I heard Cernan muttering something in his excited voice.

"Thacker told me the craft crashed," I said. Humber's eyes crossed mine, he knew where I was going, but that didn't stop me from voicing my concern. "If it crashed, why is it intact? And what happened to the bodies?"

"There were none," Cernan answered quickly. "The craft was in perfect condition."

"I was afraid you might say that." I shuddered, glancing to Humber, feeling a deep uneasiness in the pit of my stomach. "What brought it down?"

"We don't know." Cernan now latched onto the collective unease. "You don't think anything survived, do you?"

I choose not to answer.

We stayed close to one another as we edged towards the head of the craft. With every nervous step, moving deeper into the core of the vessel, I knew the exit was that little bit further away.

I shuddered, thinking about what could lie ahead of us. While it was impossible to believe any of the aliens could have survived, I knew it was probable we'd encounter some other form of life. On more than one occasion, we'd witnessed the awesome power of Jeometamorphic rock. It had reanimated an entire spacecraft, wasn't it plausible that it could reincarnate other forms of life too.

A clatter echoed behind us and I jumped, spinning round.

I heard Randall cursing in the distance and I took a deep breath, wiping my brow with the back of my hand in relief.

"Do you want to go on?" Humber checked.

"I'm fine," I said with a large puff of air.

We pushed on.

The corridor continued, the bright lights emanating from all directions, like hundreds or even thousands of tiny eyes staring at us, spying on our movements. I shuddered at the thought.

Up ahead I caught a glimpse of something, a door perhaps. As we moved closer, my steps became less sure as I realised what I thought was a door seemed to be hovering liquid, a force-field of some kind.

"What is that?" Cernan reared up from behind.

I stopped in front of it, staring at the liquid wall which shimmered in the strange glow coming from more eyelets of light beyond. It reminded me of the activated portal system, the shimmering mirror, but I doubted this was a portal and there was no light pouring out of it from behind. It was dark in contrast to the walls. With great caution, my trembling hand reached out. My fingers did not penetrate it, its surface cool to the touch.

"I think it's a door of some kind."

"How do we get inside?" Humber wanted to know.

"Just give me a minute," I said, searching the nearby walls. "Everything in the sacred chamber was activated by blood. It is possible..." I trailed off. "Yes!" I let out, finding the small needle to one side. I pricked my finger, ignoring the sting of pain.

In a flash, the silver liquid parted, allowing us to pass.

Even from the outside I had recognised this part of the craft would be the cockpit, and therefore the hive of alien activity when occupied. But standing inside the room there appeared to be no physical remains, no skeletons piled up, no bones of any kind. It was empty.

"Look," I said, pointing to a small pile of glittery ash to one corner. As I peered closer, I recognised the gleaming fragments of Jeometamorphic rock. "I think that was one of *them*. *They* must decay, breaking down into their component parts." If that was true, they didn't have much to them.

I turned my attention to the front of the craft, looking out into the hangar beyond and reached up to touch the window. It was silky smooth, seamless. Just like the molecules on the metallic disc, it seemed the properties of the craft had changed too, allowing us to see out, while on the outside it had remained the same, like one-way glass.

It was astounding.

Below this was a line of orb like controls, commands written in more alien hieroglyphs like the ones I'd seen in the portal chamber of the moon ziggurat. I remembered Charlie hadn't deciphered their meaning. To one side, I saw a small round space and I realised it was the same as the disc-shaped holes we'd founded on the lunar surface. Again, the round space was exactly the right size to fit the metallic disc.

"That's it!" I turned to Cernan, excited. "I've found it! Get Randall quick; tell him to bring the disc."

Cernan was panting when he returned, the alien disc clutched in his hand. A few moments later Randall exploded into the cockpit area. He looked concerned, but it didn't last long, replaced with his excited grin.

"What's happening," he asked, looking around the cockpit.

I said nothing, taking the disc from Cernan and placed it into the embedded area. It fit snugly and without delay began spinning, whirring round and round. I heard a click and then the disc blurred as it reached terminal speed.

The window in front of us flashed into life, a small black screen filling the bottom left-hand corner. A small white flashing cursor appeared, ready and waiting for a command.

All eyes turned to me.

4

The craft contracted and expanded all around as I sat cross legged on the floor of the cockpit, my head in my hands, while the incessant clicking of Cernan's camera grated. I ground my teeth with every flash as he recorded the craft's interior in minute detail. I understood Cernan's scientific eagerness – it reminded me of Charlie – having studied the vessel for years without a breakthrough, but his enthusiasm crowded me. All I wanted was the space to think in silence.

I heard a gentle voice but I missed what it was saying. "What did you say?" I turned to Cernan.

"I didn't say anything." Cernan shook his head before

snapping another area of the controls.

I said nothing more, burying my head once again into my hands in an attempt to drown out the world. The voice came to me once again, louder, but still distant. It was the familiar calm tones of Magi Eritrea and she was calling me.

Slowly, I moved towards her, drifting into the darkness, the click of every photograph fading into the distance. A little way into the blackness of my eyelids, I saw a splinter of white light and I floated towards it. It grew, doubling in intensity until it expelled the darkness.

Stand my child, I heard her voice.

As I stood, my eyes sprang open.

I almost jumped, Magi Eritrea was standing at Cernan's side, her startling olive skin as real as the day Russia had last seen her. She reached out to the controls, crossing right through Cernan's snapping camera and pressed a sequence of buttons on the control panel.

Magi Eritrea turned to me, extending her hands. I got the feeling she wanted me to do the same. I reached out towards the control panel, but before I had chance to touch anything, Cernan snatched my hand.

Reality smeared and I realised Magi Eritrea had gone.

"I haven't finished cataloguing this area," Cernan scolded.

"I know what I'm doing." Before he had chance to respond, I placed my hand on the screen and pressed the sequence of orbs as Magi Eritrea had shown me. I didn't need to look at Cernan to know his eyes bore down on me, his anger as if I was somehow betraying him.

The control panel seemed to be heating up beneath my fingers and I snatched my hand away from the screen. The characters on the controls began to change, morphing before my eyes, the unrecognisable symbols span themselves into whirls of white, and as they slowed and steadied, they became recognisable black characters.

I could read them.

Every orb reconfigured itself in this fashion, the hieroglyphs changing into ones I recognised, cuneiform, written in the language of the moon people. Through the genetically reconstructed memory of Russia and the power of the rock surging in my veins, I was able to read the information.

"Look what you did!" Cernan's voice shrill. "I'll have to start all over again and you'll have to document what you did…oh this is getting messy. We can't work in such an unscientific way."

I ignored him, as Magi Eritrea appeared to my side once again, and as I reached out to her, my hand punched straight through her holographic projection and onto the other side. Cernan seemed surprised by my movement and watched me with caution.

"I know this message will reach you well my little Russia." Magi Eritrea's voice sounded as real now as it had in my dreams. It was chilling and a sudden wave of sadness washed over me. "I realise I have put you through a lot, but in time you will come to understand."

"Oh, master," I whispered.

"I have downloaded information onto this disc," she said. "It will tell you everything you need to know about our alien creators." And then Magi Eritrea turned to where Cernan stood, Randall now behind him. "*They* are coming." I shuddered, her eerie voice sending a tingling chill down my spine. Cernan looked horrified, stumbling backwards into Randall and I realised that they both saw her too. Magi Eritrea turned back to me. "By now *they* know it is almost time and *they* will come."

"When?" I asked. "How long do we have?" I felt stupid asking a hologram, knowing it couldn't possibly answer, but Magi Eritrea seemed to register my questions.

"The disc contains everything you need," she said

repeating. "I know you will understand what to do with it."

"Tell me about the creation of your world?" I asked. "What is the truth?"

"As you have seen my child, there are always different truths to be told," she responded. "I wish there'd been a better way, but I did what I felt was right for us all. Farewell my little Russia, I am sure we will meet again, one day."

As the projection of Magi Eritrea disappeared, I shuddered. *What did she mean we'd meet again?* Was she referring to her genetic memory, lurking inside, unbeknownst to that person? Thacker had told me about that, but I didn't understand the significance. *Why would* we *be meeting again?*

I felt there was a lot to learn and I still didn't know how long we had.

5

Sitting in front of the hovering craft, I relaxed, allowing the hysteria of the day to fall, drifting into the silence of the hypnotic motion of the *Stingray* craft. Everyone else busied themselves around me, carrying equipment and taking measurements.

In the blissful hush, I found my eyelids heavy and before long they closed.

As one world passed out of focus, another swam into vision.

I stood in the doorway of a room I recognised; my father's study as it had been before his death. The walls were stacked high with row upon row of shelves, all of them full to bursting point with books from all decades.

I blinked. This couldn't be real, the room had changed drastically after my father passed away and then of course my mother had sold the property, unable to suffer living alone in the family home. Now my mother was in the final days of life, acting as if nothing was happening and making sure I did not fuss over her. This time it would be me dealing with her affairs when she passed.

No, this was a chamber inside my mind, recalled for a purpose.

I reached out and took hold of the first book I saw – drawn to it – and pulled it from the shelf. The title written along the spine, in well-fashioned ink characters said, '*In the beginning…*' I flipped the book in my hand, feeling its weight and then turned to the front cover. It was a history book, the story of creation, or so it claimed.

I did not recall seeing a book like this before in my father's study, but then this wasn't really that room. As I thumbed through one of the shelves, it dawned on me that this wasn't just a memory of my father's study, the books were all different. Nor was this the memory of Russia, this was something different. These were tales of our ancestors – not unlike some of my father's books. This was the information Magi Eritrea had encoded on the disc, and it seemed to be playing to me through *Stingray*, as if it had access to my unconsciousness. Was this the soul of the craft?

A light sparked in the distance of my mind. The book in my hands had to be the *real* story of the moon world's creation; the unadulterated truth.

My father's chair waited in the corner of the room, and I let out a sigh as I dropped into the seat. All these books, they were waiting for someone to pick them up and read them – waiting for someone to uncover all their information. That someone was me.

The book fell open in my lap.

On the seventh day a routine scouting mission came across a developing world with a large moon. As life already existed on the planet, they remained passive observers, abiding by their own codes for peaceful co-existence. This did not apply to the lunar object as it was uninhabitable in its current form, so they scanned it for mineral content. There was no value in the materials there, however, they encountered a dormant form of life in the geological composition.

The craft landed to take samples of the quiescent life form.

While on the ground one of the crew, the leader, suffered from an unknown illness and the others made the decision to remain there until he'd made a full recovery. However, the illness' grip was too tight and he succumbed, passing away into the next world; his name, Anubikhanisis. So far from home, the aliens buried him in a ceremony of his life before leaving.

Unbeknownst to them, as their leader's body decayed, breaking into its original components, and leaching into the surrounding rock, to mix with the dormant organisms on the moon surface. The power of the green rock that lived inside Anubikhanisis activated the dormant genetics, accelerating their growth until they burst from the ground. From the death of one, an entire world formed.

On the twenty-first day, another scouter came across the same planet, and they reported a single fissure in the ground where their buried leader rested, bubbling green light danced from the crack. Not long after, more scouters came to witness the wonders of the new world forming from their fallen comrade.

Having seen the birth of worlds before, the alien creatures generated a protection field around the lunar satellite and gave it a habitable atmosphere. Over time, the planet filled with life of all kinds. Birds took to the skies, beasts occupied the land and a green river erupted from the opening fissure, welling up like a spring. Immediately the scouters recognised this. It was the same as their own rivers back home. Somehow, Anubikhanisis lived on through this new world, integrated into all the thriving life.

When the reports reached the scouter's home planet, the General High Council decreed that this planet was in dedication to their now reincarnated leader Anubikhanisis. It was through his death that new life appeared.

The last act of the General High Council that semester was to assign the world 'colony' status which afforded protection to everything that lived on the planet. They assigned an Ambassador to tend to the young world's needs.

As the planet grew and changed over millennia, mankind was born, naked and pure. Born out of their loss, the aliens sought only to defend the sanctuary dedicated to Anubikhanisis. Their intentions were peaceful; they were not savages.

But as time went on, the men joined force with the aliens and the memory of Anubikhanisis became corrupted and fragmented. Soon the real reason why generations of alien Ambassadors protected the colony was lost and new reasons assigned; a lie took its place, and the aliens observed the men with envious eyes.

Anubikhanisis was no longer their dead leader, he was a leader waiting to take his rightful place, a hybrid alien. First, he needed the right flesh and that was a matter of breeding.

More worlds were born, created by the alien Ambassador to speed up the never-ending search. Only the purest of souls could come close.

I closed the book, lightning flashes of knowledge triggering in my mind in a cacophonous cascade as the jigsaw took shape and the whole image swam into focus. These books were living records of our creation, and now I understood; our alien creators were looking to restore *their* leader, Anubikhanisis. For that *they* needed the perfect vessel, the perfect body with a pure and uncorrupted mind. That was why *they* used Magi, respecting the sacrifices they made, but *their* search had been in vain. If *they'd* found what *they'd* so sought, we'd already be free, but the hunt continued. *They* visited us, taking our people and testing them to this day. It all made sense, *they* needed us in order to bring back their fallen leader.

Now I understood why Magi Eritrea wanted freedom and why she'd placed all her faith in Russia. Through him, Magi Eritrea had given me access to the knowledge and wisdom I needed to lead our people into a new era. I'd done it once before as Russia, and now it fell to me to do it all over again.

A new war had begun, and I was leading the battle. We had an advantage too, we were no longer the same people, humanoid creatures obeying alien rules and doing *their* bidding. No, we'd become bitter, our minds full of fury and destruction. We could bring *them* to *their* knees, everything humanity needed was at my fingertips, and that made me the most powerful man in the world.

We also had one of *their* craft, and that had to count for something didn't it? Somewhere in the midst of all the books, I knew I'd find one that told me how to fly the craft, and then we'd master the skies for ourselves.

I traced the spines of the collection with my fingers, searching for the instructions, and when I stopped, I found my hand grasped around one particular book entitled 'Phase Two'. I looked at it, confused, that wasn't right.

Intrigued, I pulled the book from the shelf, but before I had chance to open it my eyes slammed shut with the weight of my eyelids as if in aversion to the information that book contained. I fought against it, not ready to leave the study, prising my eyes wide. When they opened, I stared out from my father's seat disorientated by the sudden change.

I shook my head in confusion. Maybe there was a time-lock on the information in that book, although I didn't know how such a thing could exist in my own mind. Nevertheless, I resumed my search of the books, allowing my hands to roam aimlessly, touching each of them in turn. It did not settle, moving to the next shelf until my busy fingers stumbled and stopped.

I blinked at the empty space, the book missing.

I stood on my tiptoes, peering into the darkness of the void, puzzled by the loss. This was my mind, my study, and nobody else had access to it.

The study light began to fade and as reality swam into view, and I found myself sitting before the *Stingray* craft, alone, the hustle and bustle of the day almost over. As I left the hangar, my mind remained baffled by the misplaced book. It had to be somewhere, and I felt it was vital I find it.

6

The blurt of my ringing mobile phone cried like a siren, piercing through my dreamless sleep. I rubbed my eyes in the darkness, glaring at the eerie blue numbers of the clock. It was a little after four in the morning.

I slid open my phone, it was my mum's home number.

"What's up," I answered the call. A sharp stabbing sensation shot across my right shoulder distracting me for a second. I flexed my arms, biting through the pain, I must have slept on it. "Mum, it's early." I paused, I thought I heard a faint sniffle. "Mum?"

The line remained silent. I pushed the phone hard against my ear and heard a pained whisper, a struggled breath perhaps. I came to my senses and sat bolt upright, my back rigid.

"No ambulance," the strained rasp of my mother's voice.

"Oh mum, wait for me." My voice warbled, tears filling my eyes. "I'm on my way, just you wait for me." I shot out of bed, stumbling in the dark and brought the bedside lamp crashing to my foot. "Talk to me..." the line went dead. "Shit!"

I pulled on some clothes before darting from my room.

The night sky was crisp as I flew outside, my footfalls crunching in the ice. My car was parked underneath one of the nearest trees, and I was glad to see the frost had skipped over it, leaving only a light dusting; I didn't have time to waste.

I blinked back a tear, trying not to think as I revved the engine and tore out of the compound, heading straight to my mother's house. The sky had brightened by the time I arrived, but I felt the cold chill of my mother's passing close at hand. The car screeched to a halt and I jumped out.

As I ran to the door, I fumbled with my mother's front door key, I'd never given it her back. Now I knew why.

A wintry silence greeted me beyond the doorway. "Mum!" I yelled. "I'm here, just you hold on!" I raced up the stairs, taking them two at a time. As I neared the top, I saw my mother's bedroom door ajar, light drifting out into the hallway.

I stopped, transported in time, a forgotten memory stole over me bringing back the overwhelming starchy smell of boiling potatoes as if they were cooking now. My mouth dropped open as I remembered. Just thirteen years old, I stood at the bottom of the stairs ready to shout up to my bedridden father to announce dinner was almost ready, but my words caught as an overpowering sense of change washed over me. I was just a boy, creeping up the stairs, my knees trembling, already knowing the truth behind my fear. The bedroom door was open, the light filtering out.

Standing on the stairs, it all flooded back to me, and I felt like that thirteen-year-old kid all over again, not wanting to face the truth but knowing I had to.

The fists of fear pounded in my chest, forcing my stomach into my throat, but I was determined to beat it this time; I would not retreat. I hadn't had the courage to witness my father's last moments, and mother had taken the brunt of my pent-up anger, but it was time to face death's cold glare.

I surged forwards, pushing through my mother's door and staring at the gaunt figure lying uneasy on the bed. Her deteriorating health seemed rapid to me, but in truth I knew she had hidden behind our phone calls, not wanting to panic me, never giving into the fear but knowing her life was almost over all the same. Again, I felt regret, I should have taken time away from SARA as soon as I'd been set free.

But there was no use regretting these things, it wouldn't change anything.

"I'm here," I soothed, taking hold of her hands. "There is nothing to be afraid of anymore."

The only sign of life was the weak rasping that escaped my mother's lips and the faint squeeze of my hands. Her eyes bulged, offering only the occasional flutter. I'd arrived in time, I'd been given a chance for redemption from my own torturous mind.

I'd always imagined death was painful and drawn out, but sitting by my mother's side, watching and feeling her body failing by the minute, I knew I'd been wrong. Even as her life drained away, there was a smile pinned to her pale lips.

My mother's passing was both peaceful and quick. One

moment I was certain she was alive, the next I wasn't so sure until her hand twitched or her eyes rolled beneath her paper-thin eyelids.

There were many things I wanted to say, before it was too late, but as I travelled her final voyage with her, I realised there was no need to say anything. I was there, I hadn't fussed over her during her illness, respecting her wishes as she'd wanted. It was clear my mother had held on for me, surely knowing that this would be her last act of kindness, a gift from mother to son.

I only realised I was holding my breath when my lungs forced me to take a gulp of air, and in that same moment I understood my mother had gone. Her throat silent, her chest still.

I fought back my tears as I searched her neck for a pulse, almost frantic to know if her suffering was over. When I found none, I kissed her lukewarm forehead, wishing the best for her, she was free of her ailing body – and if there was such a thing as an afterlife, she could find my father who had cruelly been taken away from us.

It was hard to let go of her hands, knowing that I'd never have the sheer pleasure to do so again. And then it struck me, the final farewell concluded. I got to my feet, holding my free hand across my mouth. It was over. I hadn't prepared myself for this and the feeling of sorrow was overwhelming. What now?

The old-fashioned Bakelite telephone handset dangled by the bedside. I dropped it back to its cradle and that's when I noticed my name scrawled at the top of a note beside it.

Mark, you have always been a good son to me, no matter what you believe. From birth, I always adored your cheerful face and your inquisitive nature. You were always up to something, it was one of your father's traits too, one I dearly loved and sorely missed.

I realise now I shouldn't have attempted to separate you and your dreams. How could a mother get it so wrong? Few things could make me prouder than I was seeing you blast into space and reading about your heroics in the papers – you got that from your father too.

Always remember the good times we had together, never forget them.

I wish you all the love in my heart, my dearest son.

It was signed and dated three weeks ago, it may have been the last time she'd picked up a pen with her own hands. As I glanced over the note again, it was clear she'd known this day was rapidly approaching, it was written on headed stationary, Uppercroft Undertakers. I picked up the phone and dialled.

"My mother..." I said. "The name is Besant."

"Margaret?" The director asked, his voice solemn.

"Yes," I confirmed. "She's been in contact with you..."

"I'm afraid so," he said. "Your mother took care of all the arrangements, paid in full. But I assume this wasn't a courtesy call?"

"No."

"I am sorry for your loss, Mr Besant." His voice full of sympathy. "We'll be over right away. Have you spoken to your mother's doctor?" I shook my head, but he seemed to interpret the silence. "Not to worry, your mother gave me those details, I'll arrange a visit for you, it's a formality you understand." I said my thanks and hung up.

The doctor arrived within fifteen minutes, it seemed everybody had expected my mother's imminent death except me. I sat in silence, staring blankly out of the bedroom window, as the doctor certified my mother's death.

Soon after the funeral director arrived. It was the same man I'd spoken to on the phone, I recognised his voice. He was a portly guy, dressed in a jet black suit and well-polished shoes. I stayed out of his way as he took care of my mother's body, before removing her from the house – his younger colleague helped, but spent much of his time standing around watching.

"Your mother gave me a list of people to contact, it isn't very long; do you want me to inform them?" The funeral director asked, but I was in no mood to answer and he saw this. "No problem, I will make the final arrangements and give you a call in the morning to discuss dates."

When I was finally alone, in the emptiness of my mother's house, my strength broke and I crashed onto the sofa. My eyes were sore and heavy with sorrow, and it wasn't long before they closed altogether. Sleep was quick to follow.

7

"Son," I heard a whisper in the darkness. I opened my eyes, sat up on the sofa and my mother's living room swam into view. There was no one there. "Is that you son?" The voice came again.

I saw my father sitting in the corner of the room. I squinted, rubbed my eyes and then focused once again. My father stared back, and now I saw the rows of books behind him, fading in. I couldn't stop myself from blinking, trying to refresh reality, still numb with sleep.

"Don't be afraid," he said and I realised I was frowning, my arms trembling. "Come here son; let me see what you've done." I felt drawn to his voice and I stumbled to my feet.

"Dad," I whispered. "Is that really you?"

And then I saw a boy moving across my field of vision, stopping next to my father. I recognised myself from pictures of my childhood. I was carrying a sheet of paper, and I remembered the moment. This was the day I'd drawn my dream for the first time – the very picture my mother had given back to me before I joined SARA.

"That's very good." His voice beamed with pride. He stared at the picture for a long time and I saw the subtlety of his expression, a secret smile I previously never understood. "We shall hang that up on your wall."

"No," the boy said shaking his head. "Mummy says it will make my nightmares worse."

"Does she now?" My father's voice full of parental intrigue. "Well I think you should hang it up *somewhere.*" He pushed himself out of the chair and to his feet. "Let's see what space we can find." I watched as he set the book he'd been reading into the chair behind him, placing his reading glasses on top of it. As he left, he faded out of view.

I looked into the empty corner of the study, my eyes focusing on the book.

"That's it," I said, slapping my forehead as the vision retreated. "That's the book I want!" I turned back to see my ruffled blanket on the sofa. In my mind I pictured the book, *Flying a Kite* it was called. On the cover was a colourful photograph of a kite which had a UFO printed on its large flat sail.

Had my mother kept my dad's old books?

I looked back to where I'd seen my father. For a fleeting moment I thought I saw my mum holding my dad's hand.

My mind focused back to the question in hand, my father's books. If mum had kept them, they were probably up in the attic. That's where she'd stored most of his things.

I made myself a coffee, needing a hit of caffeine to keep me awake, and then climbed up into the loft.

Everything was covered in dust and cobwebs stretched from rafter to rafter. It had been a while since anyone had been up. I tried to ignore the spiders, moving carefully around them, swinging the torch light in an arch to search out the boxes.

I settled into my search, kneeling on a precariously balanced piece of boarding as I rustled through each box. In the last one, I found the book I was looking for and took it into the light of the hallway.

As I flicked through the book a tatty sheet of paper, brown at the edges, fell to the floor. I stooped down to pick it up and as I unfolded it I couldn't stop myself from grinning. I'd found the instructions I was looking for.

"Thanks mum," I whispered with the book and paper clutched in hand. "Love you." I stopped at the front door. For just a moment I felt my mother was with me and imagined her smiling face. The words '*love you too*' drifted through my mind.

8

It was almost midday when I arrived, and I wasted no time, bursting into Humber's office, holding up the book and paper.

"Where have you been?"

"I've found it!" I said triumphant, ignoring, Humber's question, putting the problem of my mother out of mind for now – there would be a time for grief later. He peered at the notes clutched in my hand. "This is what we need to make *Stingray* fly."

"Are those instructions?" Humber eyed them suspiciously. "Where did you get them?"

"I told you, Russia and my father saw each other through *Stingray*, somehow it connected them and knowledge transferred between them, downloading into my father's mind." For a moment Humber looked puzzled. "He wrote them down and kept them with this book." I showed him the front cover of the kite. “He left it for me.”

I couldn’t stop myself beaming with pride.

“Do you think you could fly it?” Humber wanted to know.

“I’m sure of it.”

CHAPTER 24

"Charlie would've *loved* this." A familiar voice spoke from behind, breaking my gaze from the alien control panel.

"He would," I said, turning to see Maggie, I was surprised to find a smile stretched across her lips. "What brings you here? I thought you'd dropped out of SARA for good."

"I took some time out to get my head straight." Her voice bouncy, but her eyes dull. "Everyone keeps asking me how I'm coping and I'm getting tired of saying how fine I am." I opened my mouth to say I thought she still looked tired, but Maggie continued. "Honestly I'm good." It was clear it was just an act. Maggie was hiding her true emotions from me, maybe even from herself, but I didn't want to pry further. We'd all got varying degrees of grief to contend with, and it wasn't up to me to suggest that she was doing it wrong. I'd found purpose, and maybe in time she would too.

"I'm glad to hear it," I said, feeling a little uncomfortable.

"I heard about you." Maggie was quick to change the subject. She came to my side. "I heard you were here and what you'd done, and I wanted to be with you, like the team we were." There was a glint in her eye, the remembrance of our amazing experience. "Is there anything I can help with?" I understood Maggie's desire to recapture the innocence of space travel, to skate over the sour times. Who was I to stand in her way? I felt Maggie's urge to get out of Earth's atmosphere, the inference of her question obvious to me. Who wouldn't want to flush away the dark memories of our ill-fated mission?

"Are you sure you're up to this?" The glint in her eye evaporated and the smile faded.

"Like I said, I'm okay. I just needed time to work through things." She waved her arm, dismissing my thoughts, but for a little moment there was pain and anguish lurking beneath her exterior. "I'm sorry!" But it was too late. A tear rolled down her cheek.

I took her in my arms. "It's okay." I soothed. The warm tear struck my shoulder, darkening my t-shirt. When my eyes closed, I saw the bodies of the *Constellation* crew, heaped before me. I shuddered, the thought of my mother's frail body swept the image aside and for a moment, I felt my anguish rising. I took a deep breath – for now I needed to keep my mind focused.

"I'm so sorry," I said as she backed out of my arms, looking down at the wet patch on my t-shirt. She attempted to compose herself, forcing a smile, her streaked cheeks pulling back.

"We did what we had to do," She said.

"I tell you what, if you feel up to it, we still have to find a co-pilot to fly this thing with me." Her smile extended, a real one this time. "I'm sure you'd be perfect for the job."

Maggie dropped into the second seat to my left. It was almost time to get *Stingray* back into the skies.

2

I unfolded the instructions, placing them into my lap and took time to study the controls once again. I looked to Maggie, sitting silently and watchful, her eyes full of hope. With a deep breath, I closed my eyes and visualised the controls, I felt ready to test my knowledge.

"Buckle up," I said into my radio headset. "I'm taking her out of here."

I placed my hand onto the panel in front and rotated the first orb a quarter turn to the left and then pressed the orb underneath. My hand released.

A deep rumble filled my ears and the craft began to vibrate. *Stay calm,* I told myself, *you can do this.* I took another deep breath, watching as the orbs on my armrests began to glow, according to my father's doodled notes, this was the steering mechanism.

"How do we look down there?" I asked. I could see the equipment trembling in the hangar, the room shaking from the engine vibration. Papers shifted on a desk, fluttering in the current from the beating wings. It looked amazing from inside, and I could feel the joy of those watching us from the other side of the glass.

"You're good to go," Humber reported. "The weather is dry and as always with your country, there is a mass of cloud covering. The conditions are perfect to keep this under wraps." I heard Cernan saying something about the beauty before Humber's voice interrupted. "We're tracking two uncorroborated reports of alien activity in Havana. Be careful out there."

"I'm always careful." I sounded more insulted than I'd intended. I turned to Maggie. "Are you ready for this?"

"Let's do it!" She let out, her eyes filled with reignited

passion.

"This is for you," I whispered thinking of my mother and father holding hands once again. I felt their pride radiating inside my mind, warming my heart for a moment.

Gently, I rolled my hand forward on the orb, the craft responded as we hovered higher, gently wafting towards the opening in the ceiling. I pushed down harder, stroking the orb further and the craft burst out of the hangar and into the night sky.

As the ground hurtled away and we rose into the sky, I noted how relaxed I felt with the power of an alien craft at my fingertips. It was a different experience to going up in the *Orion* module; there was no shaking, no noise. It was soft, and all the while I felt the *Stingray* craft breathing, the beating of its life-force filling me.

"Yee-haw!" I yelled out with joy, as we drifted through the atmosphere in double quick time.

I'm ready for you, I thought. *Just you try me*.

3

I felt crazy, sitting there with my hands directing the alien craft, taking it this way and that, reacting to the slightest twitch of my fingers. The beautiful tune of the craft hummed beneath us, playing in my ears and I smiled.

I saw Russia standing by Magi Eritrea in my mind, they were beaming at me, knowing and seeing what I'd done.

"This is so smooth," I remarked into the radio, as I took the craft into a low orbital pattern. "I bet SARA wish they could build something like this! Ha!" Even I was surprised by the speed of the craft and the technology behind it. We'd travelled in the blink of an eye – how was that even possible?

"I could live out here," Maggie's voice was distant, and when I turned to her, I felt her pain. I saw the yearning look in her eyes, I knew she was remembering, recaptured the innocence of space, moving to a time before the doomed *Constellation* mission.

We both needed closure. It was time to let go, we needed to see the moon once more.

I directed the *Stingray* into a low lunar orbit. As we drifted through space, I saw images of myself staring out the window of *Orion*, and I felt the joy and tranquillity all over again, seeing the moon close up, admiring its beauty. It was overwhelming.

My mind turned to those we'd already lost, the moon people, Charlie, Craig, Serge, Tom. A sigh escaped my lips. *Goodbye old friends,* I thought, *you won't be forgotten.* And then we were there.

I took the craft down, performing a fly-by over the lifeless outlines of the ziggurat. It was a harsh landscape with a dramatic history and we were only beginning to reveal it. There was so much to learn about the untold, forgotten history of our people. So much left for us to see.

The only thing I knew for sure was that our alien creators were drawing closer, *their* net closing in. We had to do everything in our power to gain our freedom, releasing us from their powerful grip. I had the knowledge and the power to bring the battle to an end. Humanity's destiny loomed heavy above me, as it always strangely had.

"I've got a call for you." Randall burst into the observation room and Humber jumped. "It's urgent. They wouldn't give details, just said it was imperative they spoke to you immediately; they used an official code word."

"Humber here," he said picking the phone up and placing it to his ear. He listened for a moment. "What?" He dropped the pen from his hands and pushed his seat back, jumping to his feet. The phone clattered to his desk, he didn't even bother to terminate the call. Humber darted from the room.

"Don't just stand there," Humber yelled over his shoulder as he ran. Randall chased after him, following him into the hangar. Cernan was replaying video footage of the *Stingray* take-off. "Get your coat, we're going back to the SARA facility."

"What's going on?" Randall panted.

"It's begun."

4

"It's happening all over the world," Bates said. I frowned, trying to understand. "We've got sightings from England to Japan, day or night, rain or shine. There are thousands of them, across the globe, unidentified spacecraft in our skies."

"What are *they* doing?" I asked, peering at the photographs of the alien spacecraft Humber brought up on his screen. There were a number of different types of craft, one of which I recognised as the 'wasp' from my father's notes. It was clear where it got the name, its body in two parts and a small tip at the back which looked like a sting.

"*They* don't land." Bates shook his head. "We've only got reports of lights in the sky, no abductions. I've spoken to both the US and Russian presidents, they are fully aware of the situation and have called an emergency meeting of the United Nations, but that will take some time. Our media team have been working on keeping these stories out the press, but sooner or later one will get through and then the deluge begins."

"Why are *they* just hanging in the sky?" Randall wanted to know.

"*They're* searching," I said. "Thacker said that *they* would come back one day to destroy us, but he also told me that Magi Eritrea had a secret child that travelled to Earth. Thacker believed *they* were waiting for Magi Eritrea to be reborn."

"And who is Magi Eritrea exactly?" Bates wanted to know.

"I don't know." I thought on this for a moment. "But we'd better get to her before *they* do. If we can keep her identity hidden, we'll control the timings of everything. Did Thacker ever mention anybody else? Was he stalking others in the same way as me?"

Bates's cheeks flushed hot red. "No."

"If I know Thacker, he's already identified the memory of Magi Eritrea and somehow planted the seeds to bring her to our door." I knew of course by that token it could be anybody in the room with me, but I dismissed the thought. It would be dangerous to expose that person too early, but that wouldn't have stopped Thacker ushering them in the general direction. No, it couldn't be any of us in the room.

"We'd better hope that's true." Humber seemed troubled, as if this was all too much for him. "But what do we do in the meantime."

"Let me send out a message," I said. "We can project it, using *Serenity*. Let's send it as far and wide as possible."

"Will *they* hear us?" Bates wanted to know.

"And would *they* understand?" Randall asked.

"I think so," I said, all eyes focused their attention, puzzled by my reasoning. "*They* have been here with us from day one, watching us develop, right?" Nodding heads concurred across the table. "Then I am sure *they* know the languages of our people. English is an international language, one of the most widely spoken so it's safe to assume the aliens have some kind of understanding of it. Besides, if we construct the transmission carefully, it doesn't matter if *they* understand what I actually say."

"How do you mean?" Humber leant forward, hooked.

"If we start with images from our ancestor's past, images from the moon and inside the ziggurat, the temple and the scriptures, maybe even a star chart representing our position in the sky – I presume that is possible?" Randall's head bobbed. "We can show *them* that we became fighters if we finish with images from *our* wars, maybe some video footage of detonating bombs and the destruction left in its wake. It'll act as a warning to *them*. What about a simulation of potential future conflicts…?"

"I like that." A sly smile swept across Humber's lips. "Hopefully they won't see it as a declaration of war, but it should make *them* squirm."

"How soon?" Randall asked.

"I'm ready now," I said feeling the burning desire of fury bursting inside.

"Shouldn't we get approval?" Bates seemed unsure, his eyes almost pleading for us to reconsider. "We don't want to antagonise *them*, we don't know what they are capable of."

"No," Humber said, taking the lead. "It's time for action."

5

I sat behind the desk, ready to go for another take. We'd been rehearsing all morning and the recordings seemed to do the trick, but even with the most recent take I didn't feel happy. There was something inauthentic about not doing a live broadcast, but it wasn't this that was niggling at the back of my mind. The question appeared, as if from nowhere. *What if I'm wrong? What if I'm leading humanity to the brink of war with my actions?*

It wasn't an unreasonable thought. After everything I had learnt and seen, it was possible I'd misinterpreted the information. Thacker had done just that, and so had little Russia. The truth was, even with only part of a story, the human mind constructs something that feels complete – we need that kind of closure, we hate unanswered questions and inconvenient gaps.

I'd learnt the truth behind the creation of our ancestors' world, and I'd seen how the story had been corrupted by both our alien 'masters'...I stopped myself, I no longer believed this was the right way to view them. Towards the end they may have become masters, but they were our guardians, the guardians of their fallen leader's legacy.

With that cleared up in my mind, I turned back to my original question; was I choosing the right course of action? A further question pushed to the fore. *What would Magi Eritrea do?*

The question was an intriguing one. She had sought to protect our ancestors and had reached a deal with the aliens. She made sure that the old world crumbled, so that a new world could take its place. Her hope was that we could be rid of our negative emotions like rage, greed and our lust for power. All of these emotions remained and in fact they were greater now than they had been during our time on the moon colony – the harmony of the lunar world was gone. I doubted we could ever live in that kind of tranquillity again. Humanity was not necessarily unkind, we had our many moments, but we also had others that were less inclined to the way of life our ancestors had lived by.

Getting back to the point, I considered Magi Eritrea once

again. She could not have known the true creation story. She'd referred to our people being harvested for an unknown purpose, and that's why she was fearful. No, she was not in possession of the full facts. But a thought passed through my mind: she'd had faith that one day we would have the full facts and that we would understand what to do with them. She'd passed that torch onto me, the leader of our kind; a Magi in all but name. But Magi Eritrea had a secret child, and someday soon I knew I needed to pass the torch back to her.

"Wait," I said, louder than I was expecting. Maggie, Randall, Humber and the camera operator all stopped what they were doing and turned to face me. I saw from Humber's eyes and his creased brow, he was concerned. "What if we're doing this wrong?"

"I know how to work the technology and I..." Randall began, but I waved a hand dismissing his thoughts. I wasn't challenging the technological aspects of the plan.

"What do you mean?" Humber stepped into the fray.

"We're standing on a cliff edge, facing into the abyss," I said. "What if we're meant to be looking up rather than down?" The questioning faces told me I was being cryptic. They did not understand me. "What I mean is that misdirection is key to any illusion. A good magician tricks people by telling them to look here and to ignore what might be happening over there."

"Okay, I get the principle," Humber said, "but what's your point?"

"Throughout this whole experience, we've been fixated on reacting to the information that we think we know, right?" It was a rhetorical question and I left only a momentary pause before continuing. "Right now, we know how our lunar ancestors came into being – you've read my report on that. But these creatures don't know that we know this. We're one step ahead of them."

"Are we?" Humber pondered. "We don't know that for sure."

"No, but we have evolved," Maggie said, channelling Charlie's thoughts. As if sensing that she knew this, she added, "Charlie talked about us evolving into different people."

"Exactly," I said. "They don't know who we are anymore, and if the story of our creation and their fallen leader was corrupted already, we can assume we're probably featuring as villains having defiled the life that we'd been given by their fallen leader. What if we're wrong to act with aggression?"

"But your report referred to *them* coming back to harvest us," Humber said.

"Yes, that's what Magi Eritrea believed, and the wisdom that she passed on to Indonesia," I said. "But she came to that conclusion from the half-truths she had at her disposal. She reached the deal with *them* on the basis that we'd become free from them – and so we have."

"I don't want to be too direct," Humber said, frustration in his voice. "But can you come to the point, quickly."

"If we're going to send *them* a war cry, shouldn't we stop to think how *they* might react?" I said, taking a pause to let that sink in. "What if they call our bluff and retaliate in kind?"

"We'd be screwed," Maggie said.

"You do make an interesting point," Humber said.

"It's a choice," I said. "Do we follow the same path that led us to destruction – rage, greed and a thirst for power – or do we learn from the mistakes and show them our new-found wisdom? We're human. We try diplomacy first."

"You have a point," Humber said. "But..."

"How did I know that was coming," I said.

"But, that's not a chance that we can take. Besides, you said yourself that they're waiting for Magi Eritrea to be reborn. We have time yet. We may antagonise them, or they may learn to respect us. Either way, it's time to show we mean business."

I shook my head. I wasn't sure that a military minded reaction was the right course to take. I knew it had been my idea, but I'd been swept away in the moment and I'd had time to change my mind. I opened my mouth to speak, but Humber cut me off.

"There is no use in trying to argue with me," Humber said. "This conversation is over. Randall, bring up the cameras."

6

"We're ready to transmit." Randall called from behind his screen. We huddled around his monitor and watched.

The video played, images flashing up every 2 seconds, a star chart pointing out our location as seen from the moon, the deserted ziggurat from the *Mistral* probe, the photographs Charlie had taken of the glyphs and finally the portal glowing.

I appeared on-screen sitting behind a desk, my face stern, my cheeks red glowing with fury.

"We know who you are." My voice full of bitterness. "I am the genetic reincarnation of Russia, servant to Magi Eritrea, and I know what you want with the people of Earth. Magi Eritrea spoke to me of *your* designs and I know of the *others.* I speak for all the people of *our* kind when I say this; we will *not* stand by while you take away our freedom, we will *not* go quietly into the night and we *will* defend ourselves against any attempt to reclaim our people. We are no longer the silent, dutiful people you once knew – we've learned to defend ourselves." I leant forward, bringing my face closer to the camera to appear more threatening.

"You have twenty-four hours to withdraw *all* your spacecraft from the vicinity of our world before we declare war. Do not underestimate our ability, we will blast *your* craft from the skies and use every resource that we have at our disposal." I pulled my lips into a furious grimace and thumped my fists on the desk, rattling the frame. "Message out!" A deep rumbling growl came from my throat and in one swift motion I shoved the camera away in anger, the chair behind me clattering to the floor, knocked over in my swift movement.

The video of the room faded out, followed by a series of old archive footage of war, Soviet troops marching nuclear warheads through the streets, Nazi marches, napalm strikes from Iraq. To finish, Randall had constructed a simulated nuclear strike against our alien invaders, blasting *their* spacecraft from the sky and turning them into flaming balls of debris.

"I think our message is clear." Humber said, a smile pressed upon his lips.

I felt a pang of regret, my intuition told me we'd sent the wrong message – we could've had the opportunity to send an intelligent message but instead we'd issued a challenge, and foolishly revealed everything we knew.

My thoughts were cut short when Humber said, "And it's working."

"Look, *they're* already dissipating," Randall said, staring at the radar screen tracking the numerous alien craft in various sections of airspace – there had been numerous sightings in recent weeks, and it was getting harder to deny the media reports.

I watched the stream of red dots drifting away from the centre of the screen. Randall's screen displayed the output from *Serenity* and it showed that craft were retreating and their signals vanishing.

"Is that it?" Randall asked. "No fight?"

"Looks like we made the right choice," Humber said.

"Only time will tell," I said. With a shake of my head I left them to their deluded self-congratulations.

With the day done, I stepped outside into the courtyard and into the driving ice-cold rain. The drumming of the water washed over me as my emotions began to stir. I stopped part way across to my car, the pain in my chest growing. I dropped to the bench just as my heart broke, and I let out all the tears I'd been holding back.

I wept for the loss of my mother and my crew-mates.

EPILOGUE

In the darkness of my dreams, I opened my eyes.

I stood at the foot of an ancient and once forgotten ziggurat, the staircase to which was brimming with light. For a moment I basked in the glow before passing through and stepping into another familiar place, my father's study.

Dropping to my knees I sighed, relaxing into the peace and tranquillity of the world inside my mind. Rows of books filled the space, stacked to the ceiling. Knowledge and power surrounded me, my own secure area that nobody else could access. It was far safer than any encryption on digital files.

Everything I needed to know about our ancient civilisation, our ancestors, stared back at me and I thought of my father, knowing how proud he'd been of his study. Seeing it now, restored to its former glory, I couldn't contain my smile, allowing it to flourish.

A book called to me from the shelf, and when I pulled it out, it was titled 'Magi, past and present.' The book fell open, turning to the centre page displaying its contents – a list of names and dates. The last name at the bottom of the page written in cuneiform was the name Magi Eritrea. I smiled once again, placing the book onto the chair in the corner of the room and turning to the window.

I looked out, seeing the whole world. A crowd gathered, waiting with bated breath for their leader to take them to a new future. I was their leader, and I was already guiding them into a new age. I'd seen off our alien creators for now, but knew they'd be back.

I was ready for the fight, it was my destiny. And I had to succeed.

AUTHOR'S NOTE

Untold History is the result of a long process, beginning in 2002, involving countless hours of dedication; tears of joy, sadness and frustration; and most powerful of all, the help of those closest to us that pull us through to the end of the journey and reassure us that we're on the right track.

The premise for the novel evolved from the conspiracy theory that the Apollo moon landings were faked (we'll not go into this as such conspiracy theories don't warrant attention and are born out of our need to interpret complex data). This led me to the idea that there could be a different understanding of humanity's evolutionary path to the one we know. In this book, I've attempted to draw out that alternative, while remaining generally faithful to current anthropological knowledge. Needless to say, any mistakes or deviations from actual anthropological or archaeological data are mine alone and invented for the purposes of entertainment.

In writing this book, I've taken a great deal of inspiration from the storytelling approach of many authors (Stel

Pavlou and Eric Brown to name a couple), but primarily from Michael Crichton; a master of the craft and sadly missed. His expert ability to turn complex ideas into accessible and exciting narratives, spurred me to write speculative fiction. Although read after my first draft of Untold, there are two pertinent points raised in Crichton's introduction to his 2002 novel, *Prey*, that helped me develop subsequent drafts of Untold for which I'm very grateful: '*The notion that the world around us is continuously evolving is a platitude; we rarely grasp its full implications,*' and '*If we were to grasp the true nature of nature – if we could comprehend the real meaning of evolution – then we would envision a world in which every living plant, insect, and animal species is changing at every instant, in response to every other living plant, insect and animal.*'

You wouldn't be reading this, had it not been for my partner and husband, Bruce. Together we have built a wonderful space to allow our creative minds to grow. Without his useful criticisms and insights in the early years, and then his continued support, this wouldn't have been possible. My deepest love and gratitude always go to him.

The final draft was prepared with the eagle eyes of another special person in my life, upcoming author, E.J. Coates. Not only has his assistance prevented many unwelcome errors making it to this final version, but his reassurance has spurred me on. My love and thanks, and I hope I am able to repay the favour.

Others have helped refine this story and my writing style through the years; John Jarrold (a fantastic editor), Geoff Nelder, Leigh Barlow, Mark Iles, Sharon Odams, Adrian Faulkner, and Terry Jackman.

The final mention is to my dear step-dad, Charlie, who sadly passed away in 2006. Although we didn't always see eye to eye, he had a great influence on my life and I was honoured to be there with him at the end. Gone, but never forgotten, and forever in our hearts.

Chris Rimell
May 2019

Printed in Great Britain
by Amazon